be•liev•a•rex•ic

For Sam—

We all have monsters.
May yours be a friendly, loyal luck dragon
who will fly you in the direction of your dreams.

Ω

Published by
PEACHTREE PUBLISHERS
1700 Chattahoochee Avenue
Atlanta, Georgia 30318-2112
www.peachtree-online.com

First trade paperback edition published in 2017

Design and composition by Nicola Simmonds Carmack

Printed in June 2017 in the United States of America by LSC Communications in Harrisonburg, Virginia
10 9 8 7 6 5 4 3 2 1 (hardcover)
10 9 8 7 6 5 4 3 2 1 (trade paperback)

Library of Congress Cataloging-in-Publication Data

Johnson, J. J., 1973-
  Believarexic / JJ Johnson.
     pages cm
  ISBN 978-1-56145-771-7 (hardcover) / 978-1-68263-007-5 (trade paperback)
  Summary: An autobiographical novel in which fifteen-year-old Jennifer Johnson convinces her parents to commit her to the Eating Disorders Unit of an upstate New York psychiatric hospital in 1988, where the treatment for her bulimia and anorexia is not what she expects.
  [1. Psychiatric hospitals—Fiction. 2. Anorexia nervosa—Fiction. 3. Bulimia—Fiction. 4. Depression, Mental—Fiction. 5. Family problems—Fiction. 6. New York (State)—History—20th century—Fiction.] I. Title.
  PZ7.J63213Bel 2015
  [Fic]—dc23
                                                    2015002404

be•liev•a•rex•ic

J.J. Johnson

PEACHTREE
ATLANTA

— Before —

Thursday, November 17, 1988

It's 2:04 a.m.
Your eyes are dry and big.
You are in your bed,
burrowed under blankets and quilt.
Spike is curled in a sleeping curve at your feet,
barking quietly, a bad dream.
You stroke his ears until he relaxes, soothed.

You are not soothed.
You are the opposite of soothed.
You are wretchedly hungry.
But you won't eat
because you are too tired
to make yourself throw up again.

Somehow, for no good reason—
or at least no reason you can figure out—
you have a monster inside you.
It is hunting you from within.
It waits around corners; it stalks.

Before

A horrible beast—
greedy, disgusting, toxic.

The monster tells you,
You are not what you are supposed to be.
You are not good
unless you are sick.

Be the broken one,
it tells you.
Pare yourself down,
do everything just so,
empty your stomach,
scrape lines in your flesh,
throw yourself down stairs,
drop to your bare knees on gravel.

You want it gone, the monster.
There is no safety or comfort while it lives.
You yearn for it to be slain.
You want it dead.

And yet: you need it.
It is what makes you
special.
It sets you apart.
It helps you.

It focuses your whirling vortexes of thoughts
and your frenzied typhoons of feelings
into the exact precision of
hunger.
The meticulous control of
losing weight.
The sparkly glamour, the pride,
of being the
skinniest
person
in
the
room.

But you are sick.
Sick, as in unwell:
shaking, dazed, light-headed.
And you are
sick, as in tired:
sick of wondering why you are so sad,
sick of feeling alone at a crowded party,
sick of thinking happiness is simply
not meant for you.
You are sick of being sick.

There must be a way.
A questing hero finds a weapon
and slays the dragon.

You are no hero.
But you have looked everywhere for
a monster-slaying sword.
Where is it?
Not inside a shrunken stomach,
or on the scale,
or in the tang of bile, vomit.
Not in the pop-fizz of diet soda,
or the melted, muddy pools at the bottom
of a pint of Ben & Jerry's.
Not in the glinting edge of a razor blade.
Not in the bitter swill of stale beer,
or letting boys inside you.

Not even in the right things:
confiding in your friend,
or trying to tell your mom,
or your guidance counselor,
or your dog, with his sweet brown eyes.

No sword.
No exit.

♥ ♥ ♥

There's one thing you haven't tried.
One last thing.

Maybe a hospital.
A place for you to heal,
with clean white sheets and
smiling nurses and doctors
and vases filled with flowers
on the table by your bed.

Last week
you saw a TV commercial
for a place like that.

The commercial showed bare feet
stepping on a scale,
but instead of pounds,
the dial on the scale showed a phone number
to call
for information.
Or help.

Specialists
who may know the way out
of this labyrinth
and
how to fight the monster
until you kill it.

Or else maybe it will kill you.

Before

At least then it would be over.
One way or the other,
you're getting too tired to care.

But then again
of course you care.
You care so much it hurts.
You want
you want
you want
more than anything
for someone
to understand you,
for someone
who will
reach in
and
pull
you
out
of
this
maze
and away from the monster.

The monster howls with laughter.
You are not skinny enough for a hospital.
You are not sick enough.
If you lose twenty more pounds,
then maybe.
Thirty would be better.

But.
There must be something more than this.
There has to be light
somewhere.

And so tonight, you
throw back the quilt and
make your way to your parents' room.
Spike follows you,
his toenails clicking on the wood floor.

Your mom and dad
are asleep and snoring.
You feel around for the phone.
You tug the cord gently so it will stretch to the bed
and, with shaking voice,
whisper, *Mom?*
Mom?

Before

With
volume rising in increments,
you make a whisper ladder,
until your words
break through and
your
mom
finally
hears
you.

— Admission, Part One —
Screening Interview

Friday, November 18, 1988

This is it.
The phone dialed,
the appointment scheduled:
an admission screening interview
with the director of the
Eating Disorders Unit,
Samuel Tuke Center,
Syracuse, New York.

Mom had been so groggy when Jennifer
woke her last night.
Grunting, she pushed the phone away,
led Jennifer downstairs.
She snapped on the lights, and,
blinking, both rubbing their eyes,
they sat down.

Admission

Petting Spike's soft ears,
Jennifer begged her mother
to pick up the phone,
punch the buttons,
make the call.

Mom didn't
—doesn't—
really believe that Jennifer has a problem.
But she does love her daughter.
And so she called
and made the appointment.

Jennifer knows what Mom thinks
the specialist will say:
Your daughter does not need a hospital.
Your daughter is not sick.
You are a good mother, but for some reason,
your daughter is an attention seeker.
Counseling might be a good idea, but no,
she does not have an eating disorder.
And that will be that.

♥ ♥ ♥

They have made the drive,
an hour and a half.
Jennifer reads the directions
through downtown Syracuse,
past the War Memorial,

a left turn, a couple of blocks,
and here it is, on the right,
the Samuel Tuke Center.

The building is not fancy,
like Jennifer had pictured it.
One half looks like a shabby two-floor motel.
The other half is newer,
plain, tan brick, like a high school.
The two buildings are oddly conjoined
by a long corridor in the middle.

Mom tips the blinker, turning their car
into a small parking area,
just a few diagonal spaces
next to the older building.
There is a squalid convenience store
with iron bars on its windows
separated from this parking lot
by a chain-link fence.

Mom shifts the car into park, turns off the engine.
Jennifer reaches for the door handle.
"Better lock it," Mom says.
Jennifer pushes the lock,
checks the latch after she shuts it.
They never lock things at home.

Mom opens the door of the building
and they step into
a glass vestibule.

Admission

Jennifer yanks the interior door,
but it does not give.
They are in a transparent trap.
They are on display,
like an exhibit in a zoo:
human daughter, fifteen years old, scared;
human mother, forty years old, annoyed.

A box on the glass is labeled *Press to speak.*
An arrow points to a red button.
Press to speak.
Jennifer feels like Alice,
cascaded down the rabbit hole,
on the fringes of Wonderland,
the little bottle that said *Drink me.*
Will this button shrink Jennifer,
like the potion shrunk Alice?
Or will it be more like the cake,
the one with currants?
Will she expand like Alice did,
so huge she can't fit through doorways?

Mom presses the button.
A voice squawks,
"You have an appointment?"
They can see the receptionist,
her mouth moving,
but her voice comes through the speaker,
disembodied.

"Yes, with"—Mom flips through a small notepad—
"Dr. Wexler."
"Name?"
"Dr. Wexler," Mom repeats.
"No. Patient's name," the receptionist says.
Mom's face whitens,
as if she is stunned.
Patient's name.
Patient is both
a noun
and
an adjective.

"Jennifer Johnson," Mom says.

A loud buzz fills the space.
An automatic latch thunks.
Mom opens the door.

"Follow me," the receptionist says.
She unlocks another door with one key
from a massive keychain.
They climb a flight of stairs.
Light blue carpeting,
buzzing fluorescents,
walls painted to match the carpet.

At the top of the stairs is another locked door.
More key jangling.

Jennifer studies the grimy fingerprints
along the handrail.

This is too foreign a place.
There are too many locks.
Too many strange noises.
Maybe Jennifer has changed her mind.

While the receptionist looks for the right key,
the door swings open from the other side,
held by a man who says,
"Jennifer and Juanita?"
Mom nods.
"I am Dr. Wexler," he says. "Please, come this way.
Thank you," he tells the receptionist.
"I'll call you when we're done."

Dr. Wexler shakes their hands,
says, "Nice to meet you."
He is tall, with gray hair, gray beard, glasses,
and flabby stomach.
He notices Jennifer peering down the hall
and says, "The EDU begins a few doors down."

The EDU.
Eating Disorders Unit.

Where are the patients?
How skinny are they?

"Come in, Jennifer."

She follows Mom.
His office is dim,
lit with lamps,
slatted blinds drawn.
The furniture smells of mold and cigarettes.
Framed diplomas cover the wall.
Bookshelves sag under the weight of heavy books.

Mom settles onto the small couch.
Jennifer sits, slumping away from her.

Dr. Wexler sits in a big leather desk chair
and crosses one knee over the other.
"Well. Let's get started."
He opens a manila file folder,
rests it on his lap,
straightens papers inside the file,
and the questions begin.

"Can you tell me why you're here today?"
He directs the question at Mom.
Jennifer's skin prickles;
her stomach rises into her throat.
Finally this is going to happen.

"Jennifer says she has an eating disorder,"
Mom tells Dr. Wexler.

Jennifer says.
Not: Jennifer has an eating disorder.

Jennifer did her research.
She watched the movies
and the "very special episodes,"
she read all the library books.
This is not the way it's supposed to happen.

♥ ♥ ♥

What Is Supposed to Happen

Jennifer's parents see she is sick. They are worried about her, bordering on panic. They rush her to the hospital. Nurses lay her on a gurney, fly her through halls.

The doctors stabilize Jennifer. She settles into her sunlit hospital room. Her whole family cries at her bedside, asking for her forgiveness, pleading with Jennifer to please, please, our baby girl, please get better.

Of course, at first Jennifer is stubborn; she resists treatment. But then another patient in the hospital dies—probably, but not necessarily, her roommate—and Jennifer has an epiphany. She becomes open to recovery. She covers her walls with magazine collages and vision boards. Slowly she gets better, with the help of sympathetic nurses and a near-retirement doctor who is gruff but obviously loves her very, very much (more than any other patient, although he would never say so).

After a few weeks Jennifer emerges from the hospital, walking between her parents' arms, holding a bouquet of balloons leftover from her room. She is still skinny, but she will be okay.

She makes a triumphant return to school, most likely at her prom. Her best friend Kelly is named prom queen, but Kelly sets the crown on Jennifer's head instead, in front of everyone. Kelly makes an impromptu speech about how Jennifer deserves it more, because of how brave Jennifer has been, and how proud she is—how proud they all are—of Jennifer's courage. The whole school cheers.

Fade to black, roll credits.

"Her father and I...," Mom says,
"we don't think...
well, er...she's not failing school,
she's not collapsing."

Unfortunately true.
But not for lack of effort.
She's not collapsing.
She's not failing school.
She's failing this.
(But also: success.
She is so good at hiding her obsession
and pain,
her compulsions, her vomiting,
her hidden bottles of wine and boxes of diet pills,
that Mom and Dad do not have a clue.)

Still, the biggest strike against Jennifer
is that she wants to be here in this room.
Because if you ask for help with your problem,
then, by definition,
you do not have much of a problem.

Dr. Wexler writes notes in the file.
He looks at Jennifer.
"Do you ever feel dizzy or light-headed?"
Jennifer nods.

She picks at the hem of her pants,
her favorite pair of ankle-zip Guess jeans.

Dr. Wexler asks, "When?"
"When I stand up," she says.

"Do you get leg cramps?"
"Yes, my calves, in bed at night."

"What did you eat yesterday?"
"One slice of toast and a glass of
orange juice for breakfast,
skim milk for lunch,
mashed potatoes and green beans at dinner,
a bowl of cereal later."

"Do you purge by making yourself throw up?"
"Um..."
Mom is here. What will she think?
Will Mom even believe her?
"Um, yes," Jennifer says.

"How often?"
"Er, it depends. One or two or three times a day."

"And did you purge yesterday?"
Again, Jennifer nods.

"When, yesterday? At what time?"
So many secrets spilling out in front of Mom.
"Last night," Jennifers says quietly.
"After the cereal."

"Do you take laxatives, diet pills, or diuretics?"
"Yes, laxatives. Yes, diet pills. Diuretics, no."

"How many? How often?"
"Not many. A diet pill every day,
laxatives every day, but just one or two.
I'm not physically addicted,
like when you have to take hundreds."

"How much do you exercise?"
"Not enough."

"And what does that mean?"
"I take dance classes three times a week.
I do aerobics the other days.
And sit-ups.
Sometimes I jog."

"How often do you weigh yourself?"
"Four times a day."

"How long would you say you've had
disordered eating?"
"I don't know." She hesitates again.
"I started dieting and throwing up
in eighth grade."

"So that was..."
"Two years ago."

"Do you consume alcohol or illegal drugs?"
Jennifer can feel Mom's eyes
lasering into her neck.
"Um. I drink. I've smoked pot a couple times,
but nothing big."

Mom makes a clicking sound in her throat.
The questions are merciless.
Answering them in front of Mom is agony.

Dr. Wexler continues,
"How often do you drink?"
"Um. Every weekend that I can.
Friday and Saturday nights."

"When was the most recent time
you drank alcohol?"
"Saturday night. This past weekend."
She stares at her hands.

"When was the first time you became inebriated?"
"Inebriated?"
"Drunk," Mom interjects, coldly.
"Oh," Jennifer says. Her face burns.
"Uh, not this past summer,
but the one before.
When I had just turned fourteen."

"When was your last menstrual period?"
Safer territory. "Not sure.
Maybe two, three months ago?"

"Have you ever attempted suicide?"
"Um. Kind of."
Mom takes in a quick, loud breath.

"How?"
"I...cut my wrists a few times. But not deep."

"Were you ever in serious danger?"
"No. My parents didn't even know."
Mom sighs. Regretful? Irritated? Worried?

"Have you ever been hospitalized
for your eating disorder, or from self-harm?"
"Sort of."
Mom's head whips toward her,
but Jennifer still can't meet her eyes.

"Sort of? Can you explain?"
"Uh, well, at summer camp, I wasn't eating,
so I got dizzy and semi-passed out
and kind of also...threw myself down the stairs
because I wanted to go home
and my parents wouldn't come get me.
The camp sent me to a hospital for X-rays
and kept me overnight.
So it was related to the fact
that I wasn't eating. Kind of."

22

Jennifer doesn't want Mom here.
She's hidden this so long,
protecting Mom,
and
protecting herself
from Mom knowing.
Years of secrets
are unraveling with every answer
to every question.
Because they are the right questions this time.

Dr. Wexler asks, "Does your heart race?"
"Sometimes."

"Have you ever fainted fully,
to the point of lost consciousness?"
"I don't think so."

"How is your sleep?"
"Not so good.
It's hard to fall asleep.
And I wake up a lot during the night."

"Do you ever dream about food?"
"Oh God. Yes. All the time.
How did you know that?"

"And what about school? How are your grades?"
"Straight As."

"Are you missing school
because of your eating disorder?"
"Sometimes I don't feel good enough to go.
But my parents usually force me to."

"Do you participate in extracurricular activities?"
"Dance, like I said.
Piano lessons.
Student government, honor society.
I have an after-school job
teaching art to little kids.
And babysitting, if that counts."

Mom straightens up and says,
"I called her counselor, and he said that
obviously she's doing well in school,
and in all her activities. Which indicates that
she does not need to be hospitalized."

Dr. Wexler raises his eyebrows, high,
above the frames of his glasses.
"On the contrary," he says.
"Most of our patients are straight-A students.
Eating disordered girls will do
almost anything
to keep their grades up."

Almost anything. *Yes.*
Yes. Almost anything.
Yes, Dr. Wexler, yes, thank you, yes.

"Oh." Mom deflates slowly,
like a punctured tire.
Dr. Wexler asks,
"Does this come as a surprise?
You scheduled this appointment,
didn't you?"

"I called because Jennifer asked me to.
Her father and I can see she hasn't been happy,
but she has a history of needing attention—"
And here it comes.

Jennifer interrupts.
"Don't you remember?
Don't you remember when I came home wasted,
drunk out of my mind,
puking all over the place last year?
And I told you I don't eat
and I purge all the time,
and I want to die?"

"Yes, I remember," Mom snaps.
"That's why we took you to counseling."
Her mother looks at Dr. Wexler and continues,
"That is the counselor I mentioned. He said
hospitalization isn't necessary."
Turning back to Jennifer, Mom says,
"He sounded as though
this eating disorder business
was news to him."

25

"Because I was hiding it, Mom!"
Jennifer is on the verge of hysteria.
"Okay. Fine," she says. "Then what about the time
I took all those caffeine pills in eighth grade?
I confessed to the nurse
I'd been throwing up and dieting!"

Mom purses her lips and says to Dr. Wexler,
very calmly,
"The school nurse
and Jennifer's guidance counselor—
both of them told us quite clearly
that the dieting was just a phase."

The air is heavy, thick, and quiet
except for Jennifer's sniffing,
because she is crying now.

Dr. Wexler looks from one to the other of them,
mother to daughter,
daughter to mother,
like this is quite interesting,
professionally, clinically interesting.

Mom clears her throat and asks,
"Do you think—
does it seem like—
she should be hospitalized?"

Jennifer's ears burn.
This is the moment.
Here is the expert.
What will
Dr. Wexler
say?

Time
slows.

Time

almost

stops.

"Based
on
your
daughter's
responses,
yes.
She
belongs
in
a
hospital."

Dully,
from
far away,
he continues,
"If she's dizzy and
light-headed, it would suggest
her blood pressure is a concern
and her electrolytes may be imbalanced.
Leg cramps indicate a potassium deficiency.
And her weight is, obviously, quite low."

Blood crashes inside Jennifer's ears.
She can't look at Mom.
Jennifer is not as relieved
as she thought she'd be,
or vindicated,
like she'd hoped.
She is terrified.

Dr. Wexler continues,
"As to your question on the phone,
Jennifer is clearly very bright—
and yes, she could be answering my questions
based on research instead of personal experience.
This could, indeed, be attention-seeking behavior.
But we must proceed in the interest of safety."
He flips the folder shut and says,
"At any rate,
time will tell
if this eating disorder
is legitimate."

Mom begins to cry.
And how the hell
should Jennifer feel?
If this eating disorder is legitimate?

Dr. Wexler looks at his desk calendar.
"Weekdays are best for admissions.
Let's schedule it for Monday.
I'll ask our admission coordinator
to call you at home later today.
They will talk you through
the insurance filing process.
You will receive full orientation on Monday,
but for now, in brief,
our philosophy at Samuel Tuke is that,
in order to recover from their eating disorders,
patients must do three things simultaneously."

He holds up his index finger.
"First, they must return to safe health."
He looks at Mom. "We will monitor Jennifer's
physical condition to make sure she does so."

"Second," Dr. Wexler says, adding a second finger,
like a peace sign, or a V for victory,
"Patients must separate
from unhealthy enmeshment with their families."

He sticks out his thumb. "And third,
patients must relinquish all control
over food and eating.

This includes access to toilets.
Bathrooms are locked and monitored.
Our staff assumes complete responsibility
for patients' dietary decisions
and maintenance-weight range.
We keep that control until patients earn
privileges back, one step at a time,
as they learn to make healthy choices."

Icy dread
claws up Jennifer's spine.
"Will I have to gain weight?"

His eyebrows again.
"Most likely."

"But how much?"

He sighs, like the question is tiresome,
and intones, as if he has to repeat it often,
"Your weight will be a range appropriate to your
height and age. While you are here,
until about a week before your discharge,
you will be weighed with your back to the scale."

Dr. Wexler looks at Mom and says,
"A person with an eating disorder,
her whole day can be ruined
by the number on a scale."

Mom inhales slowly.
This is news to her.
This
is news
to her.
Does she not hear the rattling
of the bathroom scale
every morning?
And afternoon?
And night?
The expensive new scale
that Dad bought in preparation for
his latest round of dieting.
A very loud scale, which clanks and bangs
no matter how delicately Jennifer tiptoes.

It's like they haven't been living
in the same house,
or planet,
or universe.

Jennifer takes a deep breath and asks,
"How long will I have to be here?"

Dr. Wexler shrugs and lifts his hands, palms up.
"That mostly depends on you.
Your length of stay will be determined by
how long it takes to reach
your maintenance weight,
and by how hard you work the program."

"Work the program?" That sounds
very different from Jennifer's image
of resting and recuperating
in a sunny hospital room.

Dr. Wexler nods. He turns to Mom,
as if she had asked the question.
"While Jennifer is here,
she will attend daily group therapy
and classes for wellness, nutrition, body image,
that sort of thing.
I will see her for individual therapy, and
she'll have weekly sessions
with a psychiatrist.
We will also ask you
and your husband and your..."
He looks at the folder in his lap.
"Your son..."

"Richard," Mom says.
This answer she is sure of.

"Richard. Thank you."
Dr. Wexler writes in the folder.
"We will ask all of you to come in
for family therapy
every so often."

"What about school?" Mom asks.
She is now taking her own notes
in a little notepad.

Dr. Wexler says, "Jennifer will be transferred
to the Syracuse City School District,
which is required to provide tutors for
hospitalized students."
He closes the folder and sets his pen on the desk.
It feels like a cue for dismissal.
"Any other questions?"

I have a question, Jennifer thinks,
but does not say.
Will you get the monster out
before you kill it,
or will you murder it
while it's still in me?
Will I walk around,
always,
with a monster carcass rattling inside?

— Admission, Part Two —
Intake

Monday, November 21, 1988

Jennifer is riding in the backseat,
behind Mom. Dad is driving.
He took the day off work.
Both are ominously quiet.
Jennifer would give anything
to know their thoughts,
but she won't, can't, couldn't possibly, ask.
She would shatter on impact.

Richard is in school, like a normal Monday.
Will anyone there wonder
why she's not around?
Probably not until the absences pile up.
Does anyone besides her brother and Kelly
know where she is headed?
What about her teachers?
Did Mom and Dad notify the school?

She is wearing headphones,
listening to The Smiths,
The Queen Is Dead.
Cassette wheels turn in her Walkman.
Morrissey sings his dread of sunny days.

The weekend was terrible.
Her parents were suspicious, watchful.
She was grounded.
There was a family meeting.
Richard's eyes had gone wide with surprise,
then back to blank. Just another annoyance
from his kid sister.

The minutes had dragged,
as if she had to carry them,
slung over her shoulder,
lumbering up a mountain of Saturday,
over the other side of Sunday.
Jennifer endured them quietly,
with empty stomach,
and The Smiths and James Taylor.
She and Spike staked out a fort in her closet,
like when she was little,
except instead of thermoses of apple juice,
she drank wine from bottles hidden in ski boots.

Admission

The seat belt presses against her hip bones.
She runs her finger along the window,
moisture condensing
from the difference in temperature,
cold outside, warm inside.

The sky is a dark ceiling of clouds.
Brown grass blurs past,
broken cornstalks, sad late-November farmland.
Deer look up from their browsing, watch her pass.

They come to a big highway
encircling Syracuse.
Dad merges into traffic.
A highway exit, down the ramp,
through stoplighted intersections,
into flat downtown.
And now, they are here.

"Turn." Mom points, and
Dad steers into the little lot.
Jennifer pulls her headphones
down around her neck
and clips her Walkman to her belt.
They park,
get out of the car,
lock the doors.

Pillow in one hand,
Jennifer slings her backpack onto her shoulder.

It is stuffed with every book and notebook
from her locker at school.
She pulls her heavy suitcase out of the trunk,
and it slams against her legs.

"I'll take that," Dad says.
"I've got it," Jennifer snaps.
She is unable to speak to Dad with any kindness,
even if she wanted to.
Everything he says is infuriating.

Inside the glass vestibule,
Dad tugs at the locked door.
People in the waiting area turn to look.
He pulls again, aggravated.
He wasn't here Friday.
He doesn't know.
"You have to be let in," Mom says.
She presses the red intercom button.

"Can I help you?"
"Jennifer Johnson," Mom says.

"Patient admission?"
Mom waits a heartbeat.
"Yes."

The buzzer sounds.
Jennifer's stomach plummets.

This is a psychiatric hospital.
What was she thinking?
How is she here?
How is this her life?

They sit. They wait.
Time slows until it's a slug,
creeping,
leaving a slime trail.

"Jennifer?"
She had been waiting,
but her bones startle when she
hears her name.

A short woman with a file folder
stands before her.
Sweater dress, padded shoulders,
heels *Flashdance* high,
the sort of shoes Jennifer had thought,
when she was nine or ten,
that she'd wear when she was in high school,
but of course she doesn't.
The woman has huge poufy hair,
like an immense wad of cotton candy,
except it's dull black instead of bubblegum pink.
She has medium-brown skin,
the color *Seventeen* and *YM* obliquely call "olive."

Mom and Dad stand.
Jennifer stands.

"Hello," the woman says.
"I am Dr. Prakash, and I am a psychiatrist.
All patient intakes must be conducted
by a physician, such as myself,
in addition to the unit director.
I'll see Jennifer alone first, please."
She has a thick Indian accent:
Ah'll see Jenny-fah fahst, please.

Dr. Prakash leads her into a small room
with a sign on the door that says *Admissions.*
She plops down in the chair behind the desk,
and motions for Jennifer to sit.

She opens the folder
and asks Jennifer questions:
"How long have you had an eating disorder?
When was your last period?"
A lot of the same things Dr. Wexler asked.
Her *th*'s sound like *t*'s,
and her accent is so thick that
Jennifer's ears struggle
to decipher the words.
"Was yoah gar-ham-muttah tin?"

Was...what?
Jennifer doesn't want to be rude.
This lady may become her psychiatrist;
Jennifer wants, maybe even needs,
Dr. Prakash to like her.
But she can't make sense of the last word.

"My grandmother?" Jennifer asks. "Was...
was she what?"

Looking at the paperwork,
Dr. Prakash repeats, "*Tin*."

Jennifer still doesn't get it.
"I'm sorry. Was my grandmother..."

Dr. Prakash looks up,
presses her tongue to her teeth,
stares at Jennifer, and makes a very,
very exaggerated *th* sound.
"*THHHHHHHHHHH-in*."

Jennifer's cheeks blaze.
The psychiatrist thinks she's racist.
What a terrific start this is.

"Oh. Um, not really," Jennifer says,
trying to sound casual, and
casually nonracist.
"Um, she was just regular."

"*Bote gar-ham-muttahs?*" Dr. Prakash asks.
Jennifer nods. "Um, yeah. About the same."
"*And yoah gar-ham-fatttahs?*"
"I'm not sure. They both died before I was born."
The process of asking seems like more trouble
than this information can be worth.

40

The door opens
and Dr. Wexler appears
with Jennifer's parents in tow.
Dr. Prakash's part is apparently over;
she signs some of the papers,
gives Jennifer a small smile,
and totters out,
high heels stabbing the carpet.

More questions.
Excruciating
with Mom and Dad here.
One or both of them borrowed
Dying to Be Thin from the library this weekend.
(She saw the bright yellow cover
on the kitchen counter,
the library's only copy, its pages worn from
her own previous, secret readings.)
And yet they are still utterly clueless
about their daughter's eating disorder.

Talking about it in front of them
makes Jennifer squirm.
It is so embarrassing.
She is ashamed.
And angry.

"Okay, folks. Voluntary or involuntary
admission?" Dr. Wexler asks.

Jennifer's feet are freezing.
Her thin red socks are bunched up
where her jeans taper at the ankles.
They certainly aren't doing a good job
of keeping her feet warm.
She studies her shoes,
her favorites:
black patent-leather loafers
with multicolored buttons decorating the top.
Mom calls these her "Jenny shoes,"
because she thinks they personify her daughter:
colorful, creative, unique.
Maybe those words described Jennifer
when she was little.
But now? Who is she?
She is the girl with the eating disorder.
What should that girl's shoes look like?

She can feel her parents looking at each other.
"What's the difference?" Dad asks.

"Well, since Jennifer is fifteen,
voluntary admission
means much the same thing
as involuntary.
Both of you must sign her in,
along with Dr. Prakash and myself.
In order for Jennifer to be released,
both of you must sign her out.

Legal minors under the age of eighteen
cannot sign themselves in or out.
And if you want her to be released
before we feel she is ready for discharge,
both of you must request it in writing.
Even then, there is a mandated
three-day waiting period."
Dr. Wexler taps a pen against the papers.
"Written requests to leave against
treatment recommendations
are referred to as a '72-hour letter.'
They are, needless to say, highly discouraged."

Jennifer starts crying.
She wipes her cheeks with her sweater.
"Involuntary," Jennifer says,
voice choked,
because
she didn't choose to have an eating disorder
or feel so hopeless
and also right now
involuntary
is how
this
hospitalization
feels.

"It's your decision," Dr. Wexler tells her parents,
not even looking at Jennifer.
"But I suggest voluntary,
since again, it's much the same thing."

Dad nods.
"Voluntary will look better."

Yes.
Voluntary will look better.
Because what if she wants
to be the president some day?
Or an astronaut?
You can't be the president or an astronaut
if you've been involuntarily committed
to a psychiatric hospital.
But...can you be the president or an astronaut
if you're admitted voluntarily?

Will this moment,
this exact moment,
annihilate Jennifer's chance at a future?
Which future?
The presidency? Walking on the moon?
Or going a full day without
vomiting dry toast?

Dr. Wexler picks a different pen
out of the plastic desk organizer.
He hands it to Dad
and slides the papers toward him.

No.
"Wait. I don't want to do this," Jennifer sobs.
"I changed my mind."

Their attention focuses into intense beams.

Dr. Wexler clears his throat.
"Do you really have an eating disorder, Jennifer?"

"YES!"
It comes out before she can think.
Why?
Because screw them, that's why.
How dare they question her pain?

And so
it is admitted.
The fact of the eating disorder.
And then,
so is Jennifer:
admitted.

Samuel Tuke Center
Eating Disorders Unit

Rules and Therapeutic Expectations
Treatment Stages

Stage One: The dual focuses of stage one are (1) medical safety of patient, and (2) patient acceptance that he/she has an eating disorder requiring treatment. Stage one includes:

- regular monitoring of vital signs and medical concerns
- no unsupervised showers or tub baths until medically cleared by physician
- no off-campus trips, passes, or excursions unless approved by physician
- one-to-one staff-to-patient ratio, with ten-minute checks. At staff discretion, a stage one patient may be allowed in bedroom without staff; staff will check on patient at a minimum of once every ten minutes during waking hours.

Stage Two: Patient may request and start earning privileges as approved by treatment-planning team. Stage two privileges can include:

- off-campus meetings and activities supervised by staff
- up to three off-campus passes per week, totaling ten hours per week, with approved chaperone or accompaniment. (Chaperone MUST be patient's legal guardian if patient is under 18.) Destination must be preapproved.
- morning walks (7:00 a.m.) at indoor track, Syracuse University (outdoor if weather permitting). Patients with morning walk privileges must drink one 8 oz. juice in addition to meal-plan exchanges before leaving for walks and must remain in staff view at all times.

- supervised "shop walk" to stores downtown when offered by staff
- art room access with supervision
- outdoor smoking courtyard access

Stage Three: Patients underweight at time of admission must reach maintenance weight to be considered for most stage three privileges. Stage three privileges include:

- 7:00 a.m. walks, jog-walks, or jogs as approved by treatment team (8 oz. juice and eyes-on supervision as in stage two)
- breakfast in downstairs dining room
- lunch in downstairs dining room
- regular trays
- unsupervised bathrooms
- meal planning
- one weekend day pass with lunch out, with approved accompaniment or chaperone
- snack out with staff
- meal out with staff
- knowledge of weight
- discharge date
- discharge plan

All rules are subject to change without notice by staff.

— Stage One —

Monday, November 21, 1988

Paperwork signed,
fate sealed,
they follow Dr. Wexler
up the blue carpeted stairs.
He leads them down the hall of the second floor,
the EDU hall.
Past his office,
past a larger room with couches and tables.
A couple of doors further,
to a room on the right.

Inside the room is a closed door,
which Jennifer hopes is a private bathroom.
Two twin beds,
two nightstands and bedside lamps,
two chairs, like the ones in the waiting room.
Two dressers, one closet with sliding doors.
Thin beige carpet.
Windows with ugly curtains of multicolored matchsticks
prancing on a putrid orange background.

This is where she will live.
This is not a bright, sunny hospital room,
with white sheets and flower bouquets.
This is an old motel room,
mildewed and airless, with sour
odors from other people's bodies.
The first bed is messy,
pillow bunched in a corner, sheets jumbled.
A digital clock sits on the nightstand,
next to a book that looks like a diary.

Dr. Wexler motions to the bed near the window.
It is a bare mattress and box springs on a metal frame,
with a stack of folded sheets and blanket, waiting.
"This will be your room, Jennifer," he says.
"Your roommate's name is Heather."

Numbly Jennifer lets her backpack slump to the floor.
She places her pillow at the head of the bed.
Mom hefts her suitcase onto the mattress.
The bed jiggles under the weight of her belongings.
Belonging.
This is her bed now,
and for how long?

"Your parents need to go," Dr. Wexler says.
"Don't draw out your good-bye.
It will be harder if you wait.
I'll see you at group tomorrow morning.
Don't unpack yet.
A nurse will be right in."

Tears glisten on Mom's cheeks, and in Dad's eyes.
Jennifer is crying, too.
Attention-seeking behavior?
She got their attention,
but now they are leaving her.
She hugs Dad,
and then Mom,
holding on for dear life.

They go.
Mom looks back,
taking Jennifer's
heart away with her.

This is a mistake.
This is by far the biggest mistake
of Jennifer's life.
Her heart is galloping.
She can't think.
It's too much—
there is too much
cortisol,
or adrenaline,
or whatever it is that circulates fear,
throbbing through her body,
flooding her brain.
This is a mistake.
She lurches toward the door.

A woman walks in,
stopping her.

Middle-aged, stout, with pale skin and short, curly hair.
She isn't wearing a nurse's uniform.
She's wearing regular clothes:
pastel floral mock turtleneck,
navy blue stirrup pants,
white low-top Reeboks.
Her bosom is enormous, like
a big shelf has been installed on the front of her body.

Nurse Bosom (not her real name—
does she even say her name?
Jennifer can't remember)
is holding a round wicker basket the size of a hubcap.
She sets the basket on the dresser and says,
"We need to check for contraband.
We'll start with this."
The nurse lifts Jennifer's backpack onto the bed
and opens it without asking.

Nurse Bosom pulls everything from the backpack
and sets the stuff on the mattress,
books and notebooks sliding into an array,
like a deck of cards fanned out for a magic trick.
Blue-spined *French for Mastery: Salut, les amis!*
with happy teenagers on the cover.
Heavy biology textbook, covered in the thick brown paper
of a folded grocery bag, as required by her teacher,
who is also her next-door neighbor,
and the father of the first boy she kissed,
because Norwich is a small town.

A dense trigonometry book,
the boring *The World: Past and Present* for social studies,
her English textbook, and some small books,
all stamped "Property of Norwich High School."
The Old Man and the Sea, *The Elements of Style*,
Romeo and Juliet, *The Great Gatsby*,
The Poems of Edgar Allen Poe.

Next are Jennifer's own books, her nonschool books,
their pages bent from multiple readings.
Big, floppy paperback collections of
Bloom County and *Calvin and Hobbes.*
Her mother's copies of Richard Bach's books,
Illusions and *The Bridge Across Forever.*
Also *A Wrinkle in Time*,
and *The Prophet*, old, with a rip in the cover.
Nurse Bosom fans through pages
and shakes each book upside down.
When she's done,
Jennifer stacks them gently on the dresser,
feeling sorry for her books,
treated so ingloriously, like they are criminals.

As Nurse Bosom inspects Jennifer's stationery,
she says, "Oh, about that dresser.
The top drawer turns into a desk. See?
Pull it out all the way, and the sides fold down.
You can use it if you meet your tutors here on the unit
before you're medically cleared.
But usually you'll meet downstairs
in the main dining room."

Nurse Bosom lifts her backpack again,
like she is determining whether it feels empty,
then unzips its small front pocket.
She withdraws the four rolls of quarters Mom packed
for pay phones and laundry machines.
Nurse Bosom presses each roll carefully,
perhaps checking that they contain quarters only,
then tosses them onto the dresser,
where they bump to a stop against her books.
Last in the backpack is a line of postage stamps,
folded on perforated edges like a tiny accordion.

"Suitcase next," Nurse Bosom says.
Jennifer takes a breath, chews her lip.
Why do they have to do all this?
She's not trying to sneak anything in.
And also, does Nurse Bosom have to be so…
what is the word? Crotchety? Peevish? Impersonal?
Would it kill her to be nice
while she rifles through Jennifer's things?
Maybe now that she knows Jennifer wasn't
smuggling anything in her backpack,
Nurse Bosom won't have to press and feel and shake
every single thing in her suitcase?

This time Jennifer does the unzipping.
She takes her things out,
making small piles on the bed.
As she unpacks, Jennifer tries
not to look too closely at the mattress.
If it has stains, she doesn't want to know.

Surely the sheets they gave her will be clean.
Or maybe she should have packed her own sheets
along with her pillow and quilt.

Nurse Bosom plucks a black leather belt off the bed.
"Do you have a belt on?" she asks.
"You need to give it to me."

"Right now?" Jennifer asks.
"Right now," Nurse Bosom says.
Jennifer unbuckles her belt and slides it out of her belt loops.
The waist of her pants is loose without it.
Nurse Bosom coils the two belts into the wicker basket.

Jennifer continues unpacking.
Nurse Bosom confiscates three framed pictures:
the Olan Mills family portrait that
Mom forced them to get for the church directory;
the picture of Jennifer as a kid, holding tiny puppy Spike;
and her favorite picture of her and Kelly
from the summer they turned nine,
when Kelly's dad took them to Darien Lake.

Nurse Bosom says, "Take your pictures out of these.
We'll keep the frames in your suitcase,
which goes into storage until your discharge date."
With shaking fingers,
Jennifer unlatches the back of her picture frames,
pulls the photos out, sets them on the nightstand.
What else will they take from her?

Jennifer's heart continues its hard thumping
as she watches Nurse Bosom grab
her can of Pazazz hair mousse,
her Daisy razor,
her tweezers,
her small case of dental floss,
her triangular bottle of Liz Claiborne perfume.
They all go into the basket with her belts.
Nurse Bosom writes on an index card.
"I'm listing your items," she says.
"Double-check and initial here.
This basket stays in the nurses' station.
You can sign it out when you need something.
Make sure everything's accounted for
when you sign it back in."

Don't they trust her?
Jennifer *wanted* treatment.
Doesn't that give her the benefit of the doubt?
Jennifer tells herself to breathe, be rational.
Maybe it makes sense for them to take her razor,
except how could anyone get the blade out of its plastic shell?
And why take her picture frames? Is it because of the glass?
Tweezers? Because they're sharp?
Hair spray? Perfume? Because they could be poisonous?
Her belts? Is it because she uses them to measure her waist?
But dental floss?
What is the point of taking that?

Nurse Bosom has produced a sheet of stickers
and a black Sharpie marker.

She writes "Johnson, EDU" on three stickers,
peels them off their waxed backing,
and, again without asking, sticks them on Jennifer's
small boom box, digital clock, and purple blow-dryer.
"Electronics get sent down to Facilities," Nurse Bosom says.
"Safety inspection.
You'll get them back in a week, maybe two.
When you get your hair dryer back,
it will be kept in your basket at the nurses' station.
You can listen to music quietly
on your tape player here in your room, but
no headphones allowed, so these"
—she picks up Jennifer's headphones and Walkman—
"will stay in storage."
The sharp scent of Sharpie hangs in the air.
No headphones?
Maybe they want to know what music she's listening to,
if it's too sad or violent,
the reason her brother hates The Smiths.

Someone appears in the doorway.
Pale blue sweater, red hair, fat.
She looks sixteen or seventeen.
Scowling, the girl looks at Jennifer,
gaze traveling up and down, scrutinizing.
She leaves without speaking.

"That's Heather, your roommate," Nurse Bosom says.
"She'll warm up to you."

Her roommate?
Why is Heather fat?

Jennifer thought everyone would be pin thin,
had agonized over whether she was skinny enough
to belong here.

Nurse Bosom pats the length of Jennifer's pillow.
Feeling the lump that is Bearibubs, she takes him out
and frisks her poor teddy bear, like he's a felon.
She shakes out Jennifer's quilt,
and then her clothes,
everything,
one at a time:
jeans, shirts, sweaters, socks, underwear, bras.
Then she hands them to Jennifer
to refold and put in the dresser drawers.
"Nope, no sweatpants," Nurse Bosom says,
stuffing them back in the suitcase.

"But I wear them for pajamas," Jennifer says.

Nurse Bosom puts her hands on her hips
and tilts her head, smiling, like she's amused.
"Nice try, Jennifer. We know all your tricks.
You won't be sweating out your weight here.
Not on my watch."

But…that's not one of Jennifer's tricks.
Hot tears fill her eyes.
She doesn't want to cry,
but she was telling the truth:
sweatpants mean snuggly comfort,
not a nighttime sauna.

The burn of being falsely accused
and prejudged,
along with everything else that is happening
makes her want to scream.
And crying is what she always does
instead of screaming.

Nurse Bosom twists the cap off Jennifer's shampoo,
puts the rosy pink bottle to her nose,
inhales, screws the lid back on.
She pops the top off Jennifer's deodorant,
sniffs, puts the top back.
Then the pot of Vaseline
for Jennifer's persistently chapped lips,
and the blue jar of Noxzema,
wincing at the waft of potent menthol.
She twists open the plastic jar of Stridex pads,
the box of Tampax,
and Jennifer's soap container,
checking under the fresh white bar of Ivory.
Next, each of Jennifer's cassette tapes,
clicking each case open and shut,
checking between cassette and folded-paper album lining.

Jennifer is learning all sorts of places to stash things.
They are places she hadn't thought of.
Hidden spaces,
inside, underneath, in-between.
The dark corners of the soul.

"Here are the rules."
Nurse Bosom hands Jennifer a thick set of papers,
stapled in one corner.

"That copy's yours. You need to read those.
Circle any questions you have,
and we'll go over them later."
Jennifer looks at the papers,
then sets them on the nightstand.
Nurse Bosom chuckles, "What are you waiting for?
A maid to do it for you?"

"Um," Jennifer says. She has never had a maid.
Where does this nurse think Jennifer comes from?
"Do you want...," Jennifer says, "I mean,
am I supposed to read them out loud?"

Nurse Bosom barks a laugh.
"Not out loud. I already know them.
You sit right there and read them to yourself,
and I'll sit right here and do my notes."

Jennifer looks at the first page.
Her brain is so muddled and distressed
that the words look like hieroglyphics for a while.
Eventually they morph into English.
Her tears splat onto the pages.

♥ ♥ ♥

A different girl, not fat, but certainly not skinny,
knocks on the frame of Jennifer's open door.
She, too, has pale skin,
with freckles big enough to see from across the room,
and permed, shoulder-length brown hair with frosted tips,
the kind you get from a home kit.

She is wearing the sort of practical, comfortable clothes—
oversized sweater, nondescript pants, sensible shoes—
that a second-grade teacher would wear,
except she looks young for a teacher.
Maybe she's twenty or twenty-one.
She is cute, but not pretty. Not beautiful.

"Come in, come in," says Nurse Bosom,
who is still writing notes.
"Monica, this is our new admission, Jennifer.
Why don't you take her into the lounge
and introduce her to the rest of the girls?"

Jennifer follows the patient—
Monica, Monica, she must remember Monica—
to the lounge.

It's a bigger space, double-wide,
as though someone knocked down a wall
between two of the bedrooms.
The air is hazy with cigarette smoke.

Heads turn.
The other patients.
Teenagers, women.
Different sizes, different ages.
Two are African-American.
Jennifer didn't think African-American people
got eating disorders,
and wonders if it was racist of her to think they wouldn't.
There are five…six…seven patients in the lounge,
sitting cross-legged on tatty couches,

60

fidgeting on upholstered rocking chairs,
seated around a small table, playing cards.

Monica introduces them, listing names
Jennifer knows she will not remember.
All of them look at her,
sizing up the new girl,
eyeing her neck and legs.

In front of the couches,
a thick coffee table is covered with familiar magazines,
the bibles of the thin and the aspiring-to-be-thin:
Vogue, Elle, Glamour, Seventeen, YM.
Aluminum foil ashtrays pepper the tables.
They are the kind you see
in the smoking section of McDonald's.
Tiny, filthy pie tins.

A television is on, the volume low.
Downtown Julie Brown is reading the MTV news.
And then Adam Curry—Jennifer's least favorite VJ—
with hair like a haystack helmet, comes on.
Somewhere, life continues,
because the *Dial MTV* votes have been counted,
and here are today's top videos, starting with Bon Jovi.

In the far corner someone sits on a folding chair,
talking on a pay phone.
The figure is made of bones, teeth, hair.
It is as if someone put a wig on a skeleton.
Jennifer shudders.

This is the anorexia she expected to see here.
This is what she had strived to become.
But the figure on the phone
is not the shiny beauty and glamour
Jennifer had envisioned.
It is more relic than human.

The skeleton slides coins into the phone
in jerky, furtive movements.
Jennifer wants to run to the phone,
shove the skeleton aside
(it wouldn't be hard),
and call Mom to come get her out of here.
Right now.

How many more hours until she can pick up that handset,
feed her coins into the slot,
punch the number pad,
talk to someone who knows her, loves her?
She looks at the clock on the wall.
It is almost 5:00.
Her admission was at 2:00.
She has been here three hours.
Forty-five more.
Forty-five hours until she can make her first phone call.
She can't do it.
She won't survive the wait.

"Jennifer, you're bulimarexic, right?" Monica asks.
Eyes stinging with tears, willing them not to fall,
Jennifer nods.
Monica says, "The diagnosis they'll give you
will be bulimia. Sorry, sweets.

If you binge, ever, you're bulimic.
Bulimia, anorexia nervosa, or compulsive overeating
are the only official diagnoses listed in the *DSM-III*.
But in here, we know
bulimarexia is a real thing.
Right, ladies?"

The patients who are listening nod,
and so does Jennifer, even though
her stomach is a maelstrom of disappointment.
She had prayed that Samuel Tuke
would be on the cutting edge, and use the term
from the newest book at the library: *Bulimarexia*.
Clearly all the patients know it. It means something.
But bulimia?
God.
A diagnosis of bulimia?
It dismisses years of Jennifer's hard work.
It negates all her hunger,
her painstaking dieting, her weight loss.
None of them matter in a diagnosis of bulimia,
only the bingeing and purging.
No. She has bulimarexia. *That* is her real diagnosis.
The "rexia" is what you work hard for.

Still, Jennifer is stunned by how casually
her deepest, most secret self—
the name of her monster—
has been spoken.
Just after her name.
Jennifer. Bulimarexic.

A wheeled cart is pushed through the doorway,
and the patients stir.
It's time for dinner.
Jennifer finds herself at a table, sitting next to Monica,
other patients seated nearby.

A sectioned plastic tray is placed in front of her.
Three slices of turkey, like thin, dehydrated sponges.
A tiny salad: wilted iceberg lettuce, a floppy cucumber slice,
a tomato wedge with leathery skin and pink crystalline flesh.
One carton of skim milk, the kind they have at school.
Plastic fork, spoon, and knife wrapped in a paper napkin.

Rustling, clattering,
the other patients organize their trays and plastic utensils,
smoothing paper napkins onto laps.
The skinnier girls' trays are laden with food: chocolate milk,
gravy-swamped mounds of mashed potatoes and turkey,
a square of frosted yellow cake.
The greasy sheen of icing makes Jennifer's mouth water.

As she chews her dry turkey—
her first meat in sixteen months—
sipping skim milk to help it go down,
she is aware of the others talking.
Voices whose names and faces swim in her brain,
the way the turkey and salad and milk swim in her stomach
and her eyes swim in sockets puddled with tears.

Jennifer tries to eat slowly,
one tiny bite at a time,
like an anorexic would.

She wants to make a good impression on the other patients.
But now that the burdens of choice and responsibility
have been lifted,
now that the first bites are down,
now that she *must* eat,
she is famished.
Unappetizing as her food is, she devours it.
Afterwards, she is surprised
not by the fact that a nurse checks her tray,
lifting the napkin, looking inside the empty milk carton.
No. She is surprised
by what is missing:
guilt.
Guilt about how hungry she was,
about what she ate,
and how fast.

Guilt has been the biggest part of her meals,
bigger than NutraSweet
and food-moving and calorie counting,
and tonight, it is missing.

After dinner, time is not linear,
nor is the hallway,
and Jennifer gets lost
on the way from the lounge to her room.
She must ask a nurse for directions.

The nurse she finds is around the same age as Nurse Bosom,
but this nurse is crookedly thin,
with a grayish-white complexion,
a pointy beak for a nose,

and short, straight hair the color of sand.
The nurse eyes Jennifer with suspicion,
like she thinks there is no way
anyone could be so disoriented.
"Jennifer," she says. "It's three doors in a row.
Lounge, nurses' station, your room."
She makes karate chop motions
to indicate the doors she's naming.
"Do I need to note this behavior in your file?
Your room is right there."

There is a man in Jennifer's hometown
who walks the old slate sidewalks in fancy dresses,
pillbox hats with lace veils,
white gloves and shiny pocketbooks,
his hips swaying as he talks loudly to himself.
The first time she saw him, Jennifer asked her mother why.
Why would a man dress like a woman?
Why does he talk to himself like that?
Mom had answered, gently, "It's shell shock.
From Vietnam.
He does that because he's hurting, and because
it's the furthest he can get from being a soldier.
He doesn't know how else to be.
The shock of war made him a little crazy."

That is what Jennifer feels:
a little crazy.
Shocked by being here, and watching her parents leave,
and knowing she cannot sign herself out,
cannot call them for 48 hours,
cannot see them for seven days,

cannot go anywhere but this hall,
cannot open windows,
cannot breathe fresh air.
She is locked in,
like prison.

Inside her, a war has been raging
and no, there haven't been machine guns or napalm,
and yes, this prison has soft beds and a television,
but still, somehow,
she is a prisoner of war.
Shell-shocked.

♥ ♥ ♥

Before bedtime, Jennifer changes into her nightshirt,
quickly. She doesn't want Heather,
who still hasn't said more than two words to her,
to assess her body.

Jennifer slithers into the bed she made
in the nebulous hours between dinner and snack,
which was yogurt. Jennifer had never eaten yogurt before.
The container looked as big as a bucket,
and Jennifer shoveled load after load
of the tangy, sour, runny stuff into her mouth,
as tears dripped down her cheeks.
Now Jennifer opens her *Calvin and Hobbes* book, but
her eyes slide along the panels,
reading the same comic over and over,
until Heather grunts that it's time for lights-out.

Jennifer lies in the semidark
(hall lights on, door open at least five inches)
and squeezes Bearibubs to her chest.
She cries silently.

Soon Heather's breath becomes heavy,
dragging into ragged snores.

Jennifer shifts to find a patch of pillow
that isn't damp with tears.
When will her tears run out?
She hopes maybe tomorrow.

She listens to the sounds of older patients,
with later bedtimes,
talking, moving from lounge to bedrooms.
Eventually the unit quiets.

All night, at regular intervals, a nurse comes into her room.
Jennifer can't see Heather's clock,
but she guesses the visits must be hourly.
The nurse is quiet, but Jennifer is either awake
or dozing so lightly,
antennas alert,
that the soft shuffling rouses her.

The nurse moves in the same pattern every time.
She opens the closet's two sliding doors,
then closes them quietly.
She touches the things on Heather's dresser,
then Jennifer's, hands patting and deliberate,
like they are feeling for something specific.

The nurse goes to Jennifer's bed
and stops, listening.
Jennifer keeps her eyes closed, pretends she is asleep.
Playing possum, Mom called this when Jennifer was little.
She would curl up onto Mom's lap and close her eyes,
pretending to sleep through everything, even tickles.
What is this nurse listening for? Breathing?
Is she making sure Jennifer is still alive?

After listening to Jennifer, the nurse continues her routine.
She feels the nightstands between the beds,
touches the two lamps attached to the wall
above their headboards.
The nurse listens at Heather's bed,
and Jennifer listens to the nurse,
until her soft footsteps trail out the door.

Every time Heather moves, her bedsprings squeak.
So, not every EDU patient is a skinny white teenager.
And the rooms aren't bright, and the nurses aren't friendly.
What other assumptions will turn out to be wrong?

♥ ♥ ♥

Jennifer snaps to attention,
awakened not by the quiet nurse
but by the sound of screaming.

It's a woman's voice, wailing, shrieking, manic,
coming from down the hall:
"I AM JESUS CHRIST!
JESUS! I AM JESUS!

WATER INTO WINE!
I AM JESUS!"

Another voice speaks from the hall, over a loudspeaker.
A calm but firm male voice intones,
"Code Blue. Code Blue. Adult Unit.
All available nursing staff to Adult Unit.
Code Blue. Adult Unit."

A door bangs.
The footsteps of more than one person
run down the hall,
past Jennifer's room, around the corner.

"I AM JESUS!
WATER INTO WINE!
I AM—
NO!
GET AWAY!
NO NO NO NO NO NOOO!"

And the sounds of physical struggle.
The soft crashes and *oofs*
of people wrestling.
Hurting each other.

"NO NO!
PLEASE NO!
Please no!
Nooooo,
noooooooooooooooooo."
The screams slip into wretched moans.

Oh, God. What have they done to the woman?
Is she pinned under nurses' knees and hands?
Are they forcing her into restraints?
Are they stabbing her with a hypodermic needle
loaded with tranquilizers?

The moaning fades
and stops.
There are more sounds of movement,
like someone being dragged—
that's what Jennifer is picturing—
and the loudspeaker clicks.
"All clear. All clear.
Code Blue is neutral.
All clear."

Footsteps pass her room,
one or two nurses,
and the door at the top of the stairs unlocks,
locks again.

Heather is still snoring.
She slept through it all.
How is that possible?

Jennifer thinks of Kelly,
who snores, but would never have slept through this.
Her best friend since the first day of kindergarten.
When had their sleepovers started? That year? Or first grade?
Whispers and giggles in the dark,
bridging bed to sleeping bag.

Back when Jennifer knew how to laugh,
when happiness came easily.

They still have sleepovers,
they do all the things best friends do,
but it's been years since Jennifer felt like her laugh
has been anything but false, hollow.

When did it change?
When did she stop being happy?

She thinks back.
Second grade, her worry got overwhelming.
She cried every morning,
certain her mother would die,
or an earthquake would split the world,
or guerrillas would attack while she was in school.
Third grade, fourth, fifth: the anxieties changed,
but the distress was constant.
Worry colonized one-third of her brain,
and she needed another third to fight it,
or appease it with routines and rituals,
all while appearing well-adjusted.
It was exhausting.
And over those years,
sadness seeped into that last third of her mind,
so slowly it was hard to notice,
like the old story of how to cook a frog.
If you throw a frog straight into boiling water,
it will jump right out,
but if you put it in cool water,
and turn up the heat slowly,

the frog doesn't notice
until it's too late.

♥ ♥ ♥

Jennifer rolls onto her back, blinking at the ugly ceiling.
The TV specials and anorexia memoirs had, of course,
prepared her for the occasional dramatic moments
in a hospital:
an anorexic freaking out about gaining weight,
a bulimic getting caught vomiting.
The familiar turmoil of eating disorders.

This is different.
So completely different.
This is primal.
This is Code Blue,
and physical struggle,
restraints.
This is delusion and danger.

How many of the patients here are dangerous?
How dangerous are they?
Is there any protection from them?
Jennifer's bedroom door doesn't even latch.

And also—
what did they do to that woman?
How did they subdue her?
What can they do to patients in this place?

Terror shimmers through Jennifer's body.
What fate could await her if she does something wrong?

What if she temporarily loses it, goes crazy?
What would they do to her?
Straitjacket?
Handcuffs?
Tranquilizers?
Strapped to a bed?
Sedated?

Holy God.

Jennifer waits, waits, waits,
for her heart to slow to normal.
They won't do that to her.
She isn't delusional.
She just has an eating disorder.
She is a good girl with an eating disorder.
She will follow the rules.
She will get better.
Nothing like that will happen to her.

She should sleep.
But now her bladder won't let her get comfortable.
She has to pee,
she always has to pee in the middle of the night,
but it's different here; her bathroom is locked.
She turns onto her side,
tries to forget about her bladder,
closes her eyes,
waits for sleep.

It's no use.
She is wide awake
and her bladder aches.

She can't wait any longer.
She gets out of bed,
tiptoes to the door,
peers up and down the brightly lit hallway.
She's on the lookout for crazy people.
When she's sure the coast is clear,
she pads in bare feet to the nurses' station.

A woman sits at the desk.
She is the first person Jennifer has seen
who is dressed like a nurse.
Royal blue scrubs, white cardigan, white clogs.
This nurse is making notes, humming to herself.

"Excuse me?" Jennifer whispers,
but the nurse doesn't look up.
Jennifer clears her throat to try again.
The nurse jumps,
brings a hand to her chest.
"Oh, sweetie. You startled me."
"Sorry," Jennifer says,
but she's thinking, *I startled you?*
Shouldn't you always be on high alert for Code Blue?

"You must be Jennifer," the nurse says.
"I'm Beverly, the night nurse."

"Hi," Jennifer says, lifting her hand in a feeble wave.
Standing in her nightshirt, no sweatpants,
Jennifer feels small and child-young.
And isn't that what she wanted all along?

Wasn't an unreachably low target weight
her attempt at being small, child-young,
like a baby bird needing gentle care?
But this small and child-young is different:
it feels exposed and vulnerable.

"You okay, hon?" Nurse Beverly asks.
Not accusatory, like the day nurses.
Just concerned.

Jennifer nods, shrugs.
"I guess so?"

Nurse Beverly tilts her head.
"Did that little incident wake you?
Oh dear. What a welcome.
Rest assured that doesn't happen every night.
Did you need something?"

"I have to pee," Jennifer says.

"Sure thing, sweetie."
Nurse Beverly takes a large ring of keys from the desk.
She unlocks Jennifer's bathroom and says,
"Since it's so late, you can use the bathroom unsupervised.
Just be sure to close the door all the way when you're done.
It will lock automatically."

Alone in a closed room for the first time since she arrived,
she watches her tears drip onto the tile floor while she pees.

Tuesday, November 22, 1988

The light pops on,
a cold hand clutches her wrist.
Jennifer sits up.
"No. Don't move. Stay down."
It's not a friendly voice.
It's not Nurse Beverly.
The icy fingers dig between tendons to find a pulse.
Jennifer stays down,
rubs her eyes with her free hand, squints.
The light from her bedside lamp is glaring.
The nurse makes a *tsk*ing noise.
She sounds irritated.

Jennifer feels herself start to worry.
Did she do something wrong?
Why is the nurse mad?
She runs through possibilities, but she thinks
she did everything she was supposed to yesterday:
ate, followed all the rules, turned her light out on time,
and after using the bathroom last night,
she went straight back to bed,
shutting the bathroom door.
She even checked that it was locked.
It was okay to flush, wasn't it?

The nurse hasn't even said "Good morning,"
doesn't seem to be trying to be quiet,
even though, judging by her snoring,
Heather is still asleep.

There is a blood pressure machine on wheels
next to Jennifer's bed.
It has two coiled tubes:
one leads to an adult pressure cuff,
the other, pediatric.
The loud rip of Velcro,
the rough texture of a cuff sliding up her arm.
The nurse is using the pediatric size.
Jennifer is proud of this.

This cuff is a boa constrictor,
squeezing tighter and tighter until
click, the air hisses out and the pressure slackens.
"What are my numbers?" Jennifer asks.
Her pressure is always low.

The nurse snaps, "You know I can't tell you that."
Actually, Jennifer didn't know.
But she should have guessed.

"Sit," the nurse directs.
"Legs over the edge of the bed."

Outside of her blankets, the room is cold,
and Jennifer shivers.
From this angle, Jennifer can see Heather's digital clock.
It's 6:38.
It's her first morning at Samuel Tuke.

The cuff tightens again.
Jennifer watches goose bumps rise on her forearms,
her knees.
The cuff releases.

The nurse makes a note on a clipboard. "Stand."
Jennifer stands. Black dots prickle her vision,
edging out the beige of Heather's bedspread.
Jennifer wobbles.
The nurse grabs her elbow, hands like claws.
She steadies Jennifer. "Don't pass out."

Jennifer sneaks glimpses of the nurse.
She's the youngest nurse so far,
auburn hair in a chin-length bob.
White, like all the other nurses she's seen.
She's wearing decent clothes: Outback Red shirt
tucked into paper-bag waisted jeans, size eight or ten.

When the cuff releases, Jennifer plops back down,
bundling under the covers. She's shivering now.
Shivering burns calories.

Nurse Trendy—who still hasn't introduced herself,
let alone said, "Good morning"
or "How was your first night?"
or "Did you sleep well?"—
finishes her notes.
She sets a folded paper gown on the foot of Jennifer's bed.
"Put this on and come to the nurses' station for weigh-in."

In the other bed, Heather moans and turns over.
Nurse Trendy wheels the blood pressure machine
toward the door,
stopping to rattle a keychain
and unlock the bathroom before she leaves.

Jennifer sits up.
The bathroom is free.

"Do not take a shower," Nurse Trendy says, returning.
"I'm putting a urine hat and jug in the bathroom.
Use the hat to collect your urine for the next 24 hours,
and pour it into the jug.
Tomorrow morning, bring your jug to the nurses' station."

Jennifer's stomach contorts.
This place was supposed to make her feel safe,
help her get better.
But it is foreign and alienating and scary
and it makes her feel alone and hopeless.

She has felt this before.
But those times, all those times,
she had her eating disorder
for protection, distraction, company.

Jennifer takes the paper gown into the bathroom.
She closes and locks the door,
lifts her nightshirt,
scrutinizes herself in the mirror behind the sink.
She looks the same as yesterday.
Her stomach feels reassuringly empty.

Turning sideways, measuring her waist
by the width of her arm,
she decides that she hasn't gotten bigger yet.

She sees the same thing every time she looks in the mirror:
two images, stacked, one on top of the other,
like the clear plastic overlays
of the human anatomy pages in the encyclopedia.
But instead of layering musculature on bones,
or veins and arteries on organs,
Jennifer's transparencies are her whole self, fat and thin.
In one, she's ribs, hip bones, tiny breasts.
A very skinny, but not skeletal, fifteen-year-old girl.

In the other, she's double chin,
curving tummy,
cellulite butt,
thighs touching.
A grotesquely fat human hippopotamus.

She drops her nightshirt back down.
Under the sink, on the brown floor tiles,
sit two plastic urine collectors.
They look like old-timey nurses' hats,
but with a spout for pouring.
One says "Johnson" in black marker,
the other "Moore," which must be Heather's last name.
There are also two empty plastic two-gallon jugs,
one marked for Johnson, one for Moore.

Jennifer fits the urine hat onto the toilet rim,
sets the seat down over it.

Her pee is noisy hitting the plastic.
It is splashy and stinky.

She pours her urine into the jug,
and a little spills on the floor.
She wipes it up with toilet paper.
She wonders about pooping.
She wants to get it over with
while she can close the bathroom door,
wipe in privacy, flush the toilet herself.
But maybe she should wait until after she gets weighed.
She wants every ounce to count.
Is that cheating, though?
And if it isn't...
what about drinking water from the tap?
Not a lot. Just a cup or two.

She looks in the mirror again.
Surely she can get better without gaining weight.
And anyway, she can't function in real life
without her eating disorder,
because who would she even *be* without it?
Who is the girl with the eating disorder,
if she doesn't have an eating disorder?
Nothing.
No one.
A nonentity.

She squeezes her eyes shut,
tries to ignore the monster.
She wanted to come here, didn't she?

Because she knows
there must be a better life for her than this.
She needs to fight.

She takes off her nightshirt,
puts on the paper gown,
and goes to the nurses' station.

Someone is already being weighed.
The rest of the patients have to wait in the hall.
About half of the EDU patients are here.
The skinny ones.
Tired, quiet,
they've all just rolled out of bed.
The walking skeleton is chewing her fingernail.
Another girl is pacing, twitchy,
like a caged animal.
Jennifer can't remember their names.

She waits in line.
It's freezing.
When her name is called by the thin, beak-nosed nurse,
the one she asked directions from yesterday,
Jennifer steps into the room.
The nurse pats Jennifer down
like she's checking a criminal for guns.

"Put your back to the scale."
Jennifer turns and steps up, backwards.
It's an awkward motion,
and when the foot plate wiggles, it's hard to balance.
The nurse clanks the sliders on the scale.

"I know you girls count the noises
so you can figure out your numbers."

"Huh," Jennifer says.
That wasn't in any of the books or specials.
That's a level above any of the tricks she knows.

The nurse continues, "We move the weights all around,
to throw you off track.
So don't even bother to try to guess your weight."
The nurse seems so bitter and unpleasant.
She reminds Jennifer of the nurse
in *One Flew Over the Cuckoo's Nest*.
What was her name?

"Hm," the nurse says, frowning.
"Step down and then back on."
Jennifer does.

The nurse's frown deepens as she clanks the sliders.
She riffles through the pages in Jennifer's folder,
looking for something.
"Jennifer, I'm going to ask you a question,
and you need to be honest with me."

Jennifer's stomach tightens.
What now?
"Okay," she says softly.

"Did you tank this morning?" the nurse asks.

"Tank?" Jennifer says.
She doesn't know that term.

The nurse sighs heavily.
"Did you drink water this morning before weigh-in?"

Jennifer shivers; it feels like an arctic wind is blowing.
She can sense eyeballs and ears at the crack in the door.
"No." Jennifer shakes her head. "No, I didn't."
Should she admit that she thought about it?
Or would that make her look guilty?

"You weigh a lot more than you look like you should."
It sounds like an accusation, but Jennifer relaxes.
"Oh, that's what you mean." Jennifer keeps her voice low.
She doesn't want the other patients to hear.
"Yeah, I always win at amusement parks,
you know, those booths where the guy
tries to guess your weight?"

The nurse doesn't respond to this.
She taps Jennifer's file.
"According to the self-report on your admission interview,
yesterday you weighed less than you do right now."

"Well, that's okay, isn't it?" Jennifer asks.
"I'm probably supposed to gain some weight?"
She feels nervous again.

"Not by cheating," the nurse snaps.

"I didn't cheat," Jennifer says
through the lump forming in her throat.

The nurse flips through the pages of Jennifer's file.
"And where is your admission weight?
Didn't they weigh you as soon as you came to the unit?"

Jennifer shakes her head.
"Not that I remember."

"Not that you remember!" the nurse snorts.
"Don't you sound like quite the young politician."

"No," Jennifer says. "I just don't remember because…
yesterday feels like a blur.
But I don't remember being weighed, no."

"Well!" the nurse says.
"That is a huge mistake someone made.
Patients should always be weighed, first thing."
Eyeing Jennifer again, she says,
"Just looking at you I can tell something is off.
You'd better tell me, right now."

Nurse Ratched.
The name pops to Jennifer's mind.
That was the name of the nurse in *Cuckoo's Nest*.
Evil, power-mad, contemptuous.
Yes. That is the perfect name for this woman.
"I didn't…there's nothing to tell you," Jennifer says.
Panic is creeping into her voice.

Nurse Ratched says, "Jennifer.
I am going to give you one more chance to be honest.
Did you, or did you not, tank this morning?"

86

"No," Jennifer says, tears spilling.
"I didn't. I swear."

"Do you have weights on your body?"

"No!"

"You will need to take off your gown."

Unwrapping her paper robe, Jennifer thinks
maybe there is nothing worse than being falsely accused.
Except being falsely accused
and being forced to stand naked in front of your accuser.
She lets her paper gown fall to the floor.
It rests against her calves in stiff peaks.

"Is there anything in your underwear?" Nurse Ratched asks.
"I'm going to have to look."
She stretches the waistband of Jennifer's underwear
and peers in, front and back.

Jennifer has never imagined humiliation like this.

"All right," Nurse Ratched says. "Nothing there.
And your stomach doesn't look too distended.
You can put your gown back on."

The paper rustles
as Jennifer puts her arms through the gown,
wraps it around herself,
holds it closed with crossed arms.
She wipes her cheeks and running nose
with the back of her hand.

Ratched is writing in the file.
"We can't prove tanking, but you can bet
Dr. Wexler and the rest of your treatment-planning team
will be hearing about this."

"But I"—Jennifer can barely speak,
she's hiccupping sobs—"I didn't do anything wrong."

Nurse Ratched says, "Your tears don't work on me,
and they won't work on Dr. Wexler.
I'd say you're not off to a very good start here."

What should she do? What can she do?
"Can I go now?" Jennifer mumbles.

"Can you go? I'm not stopping you!" Nurse Ratched says.
"Jennifer, you need to learn
that everything you do here is your choice.
If you want recovery,
you need to choose to work this program."

Quietly Jennifer says, "I want recovery."

Ratched says, "We'll see about that.
We'll just see about that."

Back in her room, in the bathroom,
Jennifer splashes cold water on her face,
rinses out her red eyes,
takes deep breaths to try to stop crying.

What will happen to her now?
How can she make them believe her?

She rubs Noxzema on her cheeks.
Washes her armpits with a washcloth.
Gets her clothes from the dresser
and puts them on in the bathroom.
Heather is still asleep.

Stiffly, Jennifer makes her way to the lounge.
The Today Show is on.
Bryant Gumbel is saying that it is
the 25th anniversary of JFK's assassination.
They'll be interviewing Kennedy historians
for the next three days.

Monica is on the couch, smoking.
She motions for Jennifer to come sit.

"Sad," Jennifer says,
nodding toward the TV,
trying to make conversation.

"Yeah, it is sad," Monica agrees.
She glances over at Nurse Trendy,
then lowers her voice. "So, did you tank?"

Jennifer shakes her head,
mouths, *No.*

"Really?" Monica whispers.
"You can tell me."

"I didn't," Jennifer says.
"But the nurse didn't believe me."

"Nurse Sheryl." Monica nods.
"We call her Nurse Ratch—"

"Ratched!" Jennifer choruses,
immediately covering her mouth because she said it too loud,
and Nurse Trendy definitely heard.

"Jinx," Monica says.
"You owe me a Diet Coke."

"I thought we can't have diet soda," Jennifer says.

"When we get out of this hellhole…" Monica blows smoke,
waving her hand to move it away from Jennifer.

"Oh. Okay," Jennifer says, wondering:
will she really be able to go back to Diet Coke,
or would that break the rules of recovery?

"How often do we have to get weighed?"

"Every day, except weekends."

"Ugh." Jennifer pinches the bridge of her nose.
She has such a headache already.

"But it won't always be Nurse Ratched," Monica says.
"And once you hit maintenance, it's only twice a week."

"And blood pressure?" Jennifer asks.
"Is that every day?"

Monica nods, reaching for a tin ashtray from the coffee table.
She presses the butt of her cigarette onto it.
"Vitals every morning, including weekends,
until you're medically cleared. Five days a week after that,
until you hit maintenance. Then twice a week,
same days as weigh-ins."

"How long will it take for me
to get medically cleared?" Jennifer asks.

Monica wrinkles her nose. "It depends on—"

"You don't want to know," a girl interrupts,
leaping over the arm of the couch
and onto the seat next to Monica.
It's one of the African-American girls.
She looks college age, eighteen or nineteen,
and she's wearing a Syracuse sweatshirt,
dark blue with orange letters.
She's as beautiful as Denise Huxtable,
with the same flawless skin,
bright eye shadow. Curly hair in a small Afro
held back from her face with a scarf for a headband.
"It would just depress you," the girl says,
setting a pack of cigarettes on the arm of the couch.

"Oh. Are you?" Jennifer asks.
"Medically cleared?"

The girl nods. "Yeah, all of us are except, let's see…
Amanda." She points to a thin, very young-looking girl
with frizzy hair who is standing near the doorway.

"And obviously also Thriller over there." She nods
to indicate the skeletal girl who sits almost motionless,
looking at her hands.

"Thriller," Jennifer whispers. "Like the video?"
"Yeah. Not her real name obviously," Denise Huxtable says,
"but it's fitting, don't you think?"

"No, Bronwyn," Monica says. "You're right about Thriller,
but not about Amanda. She got medically cleared."
Bronwyn Bronwyn Bronwyn, Jennifer thinks.
She's never heard this name before,
and she doesn't want to get it wrong.
Bron-wyn. Remember:
Denise Huxtable's real name is Bronwyn.

"Are you at your maintenance weight yet?"
Jennifer asks Bronwyn,
hoping the answer will be yes,
because Bronwyn looks
on the thin side of the dreaded healthy,
instead of the puffy, bloated side of healthy,
like Monica and some of the others.

"Nope," Bronwyn says, eyeballing Jennifer.
"And they're going to need to fatten you up, too."

"Like lambs to slaughter," Jennifer says.
Bronwyn throws her head back and laughs.
"Ha, exactly! I like this one," she tells Monica.

Monica smiles. "I know.
Our little Jennifer here is a keeper."

It is such a relief that these two are being nice to her.

"How long did it take you to reach maintenance?"
Jennifer asks them both.

Monica says, "It took me thirteen weeks.
I've been here four months."

Bronwyn rolls her eyes. "Yes, Miss Anorexia.
We know you had a lot more to gain than us lowly bulimics.
I'm four weeks and counting," she adds.
"It's going to take you a while, Jennifer."

Jennifer's heart sinks,
even though she's proud they think she's underweight.
Four months. Monica's been here four months.
That is one third of an entire year.

"How long do you think it will take?" Jennifer asks.
"How much weight will I have to gain?"

Bronwyn narrows her eyes at Jennifer.
"Let me see your neck?"

Jennifer pulls her turtleneck away from her throat.

"I'd say a good fifteen or twenty pounds,"
Bronwyn announces.
"You think, Monica?"

"Seems about right," Monica agrees.

"That much!" Jennifer says.
It comes out in a terrified squeak.
"I'll look like the Kool-Aid Man."
This makes Monica and Bronwyn laugh,
but Jennifer isn't trying to be funny.
Fifteen pounds? Twenty pounds?
She'll be barrel shaped.

"So…spill it," Bronwyn whispers.
"Did you tank?"

Jennifer shakes her head.
Fifteen pounds.
Twenty pounds?

Bronwyn gives a small shrug,
like, *Okay, I believe you.*

"You get any sleep?" Bronwyn asks,
stretching her arms over her head.

"A little," Jennifer says.

"First night's always rough," Monica says.
"And last night was a doozy.
Jesus Lady really went to town, didn't she? Poor thing."

"What did they do to her?" Jennifer asks.

"Took her to the 'I see you,' probably," Bronwyn says.
She picks up her pack of cigarettes and walks away.

Did Jennifer say something wrong?
Why did Bronwyn leave?

Bronwyn stands in front of Nurse Trendy,
pulls a cigarette out of her pack,
and brings it to her lips.
Trendy flicks the lighter
and holds the flame to Bronwyn's cigarette.
Bronwyn puffs, then returns to the couch.

"What's the 'I see you'?" Jennifer asks.
"An observation room?"

Monica chuckles.
"She thinks it's *I see you*," she tells Bronwyn.

Bronwyn smiles. "Good one.
But no. It's not *I see you*, like *Peek-a-boo! I see you*.
It's the letters, ICU.
Intensive Care Unit."

Jennifer feels stupid.
She should have figured that out.
"What's the ICU like?" she asks.

Monica shrugs. "Not sure. It's not a medical ICU.
They use University Hospital for medical emergencies.
Thriller came from there—"

"And had to go back her first week," Bronwyn interrupts.
"We thought she was a goner."

"Oh," Jennifer says.
For Thriller, it probably was like in the movies:
rushing gurneys, emergency rooms.
"Sorry I'm asking so many questions," she adds.
She doesn't want to annoy these girls.
She needs friends.

"Don't worry about it, newbie," Bronwyn says.
They are quiet a moment.
Monica goes to Trendy for a light, comes back.

Jennifer watches them smoke.
Smoking seems to pass the time.
Maybe it's a way to punctuate hours.
If only Mom and Dad had signed the permission form
to let her smoke.
Then again, it's probably good that they didn't.
She'd end up with a two-pack-a-day habit.

"Is she—are the people like her—dangerous?" Jennifer asks.
"The lady from last night."
She doesn't want to disturb the quiet companionship,
but she needs to know.

Bronwyn shrugs. "She's never bothered us here on the EDU,
if that's what you mean."

Monica says, "She's more of a danger to herself
than anyone else."

"The nurse came in my room all night?"
Jennifer finds herself saying,
before she realizes she's asking a question.

96

"Yeah." Bronwyn taps her cigarette ash.
"They make rounds every hour when we sleep.
Every thirty minutes for newbies like you."

"Thirty minutes?" Jennifer asks.
"It felt like longer."

"Time flies when you're having fun," Bronwyn said.
"This place is the opposite of that."

"It seemed like she was feeling around for something,"
Jennifer says.

"Checking your lightbulbs," Monica says.
"To make sure you haven't broken one."

Puzzled, Jennifer asks, "Why would I—"

"To use the glass to cut yourself," Bronwyn says.

"Oh." Wow.
So much she doesn't know here.
It is uncharted territory.
She is grateful for these two guides.

♥ ♥ ♥

Samuel Tuke Center
Eating Disorders Unit

Rules and Therapeutic Expectations
Meals and Food

Newly admitted patients shall begin meal plan of 1200 calories per day for first week (seven days) following admission.

- If weight gain is required, caloric intake shall increase weekly: 1200, 1800, 2500, 3000 until patient reaches maintenance weight.
- If necessary, additional calories and supplements will be given to patients on 3000-calorie meal plan.
- If weight gain is not required, patient will continue at 1800-calorie plan, or other necessary for weight stabilization, as determined by treatment team.
- If weight loss is necessary, patient will continue at 1200-calorie meal plan.
- All meal plans are subject to change without notice as deemed necessary by treatment team.

Patients are REQUIRED TO EAT ALL FOOD EXCHANGES AS SERVED, with the exception of three dislikes.

Patients shall not be late for meals.
- Breakfast is served at 8:00 a.m.
- Lunch is served at 12:00 p.m.
- Dinner is served at 5:00 p.m.
- Snack is served at approximately 8:30 p.m.

Breakfast, lunch, and dinner shall be eaten while seated at dining tables in the lounge (except for stage three patients with breakfast and/or lunch dining-room privileges).

Patients must finish eating all food on tray within one hour from time meal is served.

Patients must remain seated at table for thirty minutes after finishing meal.

Patients must remain in the EDU lounge for an additional thirty minutes, totaling one hour of after-meal supervision.

Patients may not use bathroom for one full hour after meal is finished.

Patients may select up to two condiments per meal from the condiment tray.

Patients who are served salad dressing may make a 1:1 trade for a different flavor salad dressing from the condiment tray.

Garnishes and gristle do not have to be eaten. In the event of disagreement as to what constitutes "garnish" or "gristle," staff retains sole determination. Staff directives must be followed.

- Garnish examples: parsley sprig served with chicken, lemon wedge served with fish
- Garnishes are NOT: skin on chicken or turkey. This is not a garnish and must be eaten.
- Gristle examples: a distinct section of fat on the edge of meat
- Gristle is NOT: small lines of fat within meat. This is part of the meat and must be eaten.

Snack may be eaten anywhere in the lounge.

Snack must be finished within thirty minutes of serving, and patient must remain in lounge for thirty minutes after finishing snack.

DISLIKES: Each patient is allowed three "dislikes," for which they may make a 1:1 trade. Staff will provide patient with appropriate substitution.

- Dislikes must be specific (i.e., "red meat" cannot be a dislike; patient must choose "veal" or "roast beef" or "hamburger patty").
- Dislikes must be eaten once (or more) before they can be declared.
- Once a dislike is declared, it cannot be changed for any reason.

OPTIONALS: Patients are allowed, but are not required, to consume up to two "optional" liquids per day between meals. Optionals are subject to staff discretion.

- Choices include: 8 oz. apple, cranberry, or orange juice; one cup herbal tea; one packet decaffeinated instant coffee ("Sanka"); one packet instant hot chocolate; or one 12 oz. noncaffeinated, regular soda from the soda machine.
- Patients are responsible for paying for soda from the vending machine.
- No caffeinated drinks, artificial sweeteners, or diet beverages are allowed at any time.
- Patients may drink water, but should avoid tanking or binge behavior.

All rules are subject to change without notice by staff.

Breakfast arrives, trays slotted into the wheeled cart,
pushed into the lounge by Nurse Ratched.
She scowls when her gaze collides with Jennifer's.
Patients groan, complain,
crush out their cigarettes,
and assemble slowly around the tables.

Jennifer sits next to Monica.
Bronwyn sits across from them.
The four-seater table is rounded out
by the young, frizzy-haired Amanda.

The trays smell of food,
but they don't smell good.
It smells like cafeteria food: overcooked, indistinct.
Each tray has a yellow Post-it Note
indicating the last name of the patient it is for.

Heather enters the lounge.
"Nice of you to join us," Nurse Ratched says.
Heather grunts in response.

Nurse Ratched sets Jennifer's uncovered tray in front of her.
Jennifer looks at it.
A Red Delicious apple that is red, but doesn't look delicious.
A carton of skim milk.
In the middle of her tray is a yellow washcloth:
a scrambled egg.
She's never eaten plain, cooked eggs before.

Nurses Trendy, Ratched, and Bosom
continue placing trays in front of patients.

101

"No rituals, girls," Trendy announces.
"No tiny pieces, no eating things in a certain order.
Mix it up! Eat like normal people."

Normal people.
Normal people means everyone except
the patients on this unit.
Normal people means the three nurses on breakfast duty.
Three normal people watching abnormal people eat.

"You're so lucky, Jennifer," Amanda says in a quiet voice
as she opens her carton of chocolate milk.
"I'd give anything to be on twelve hundreds again.
Three thousands are impossible."
She says this with a hint of pride.

"Is three thousand the highest?" Jennifer asks.
She can't remember from the rule book,
and she wants to talk instead of eat.

Bronwyn shakes her head.
"Thirty-five hundred is the most."

"Thirty-five hundred is a three-thousand tray," Monica says,
"plus two cans of Ensure between meals.
I had to do it. It was awful."

"What are you on now?" Jennifer asks.
Monica's tray has eggs and fruit, like Jennifer's,
but two percent milk instead of skim, plus a sausage link,
and one of those individual serving-size boxes
of Shredded Wheat.

"Eighteen hundreds," Monica says.
"That's what most of us get, for maintenance."
She skewers her sausage with a fork.
The white plastic tines sink into the meat.
She slices it with her plastic knife.
"Heather's on twelve hundreds. They're trying to reduce her."

"Shut up!" snaps Heather from the other table.

"Sorry," Monica calls in Heather's direction.
"Just giving Jennifer some factual information."

"None of her business," grumbles Heather.

Monica raises her eyebrows at Jennifer,
like maybe she sympathizes with anyone
who has to share a room with Heather.

It gets quiet. Everyone is concentrating
on their food.

Jennifer looks at her tray.
The yellow washcloth.
Her throat is thick.
She can't eat this.
Not because she wants to break the rules,
but because it's disgusting.
What if it makes her gag,
and she accidentally throws up?
That has happened to her before
when she's had to eat something gross.
Like the time Kelly's mom served
Cream of Wheat for breakfast.

Jennifer barfed it up all over their table.
Doing that here wouldn't just be mortifying,
like it was at Kelly's.
Here, it would open a huge can of worms.

Ugh, worms. Don't think about that.
She pokes at the egg with her fork,
not ready to tackle it yet.

What does she know about the other patients so far?
Bronwyn is nineteen. Bulimarexic, gaining weight.
Monica is twenty-one. Anorexic, maintenance weight.
She's been here more than four months. Four months.
Amanda looks very young, maybe thirteen or fourteen.
Anorexic, obviously still gaining.
Thriller looks old,
but that might just be because she's a skeleton.
She's anorexic, and not medically cleared.
Heather looks like she might be Jennifer's age,
or slightly older.
She's an overweight bulimic or compulsive overeater.
Not sure which. But they have her on a diet.
The other patients, Jennifer doesn't know a thing about,
except whether they were in line to be weighed this morning.

Okay. If she doesn't get started eating,
Nurse Ratched will probably write it down in her file.
If she hasn't already.

Jennifer puts a bite of egg in her mouth.
She gags.
It's revolting.

She opens her milk carton quickly,
takes a swig of milk to wash the egg down.
With trepidation she takes another bite of egg,
gags,
drinks some milk,
starts to cry.

"You have to get it down, sweets," Monica says.
"Otherwise it follows you to your room,
and staff will give you grief,
and you have to sit there until you eat it."

"I know, I'm trying," Jennifer sniffs.

"Eggs are better with ketchup," Bronwyn suggests.

"Can't I put eggs on my dislike list?" Jennifer asks.
Tears drip onto her tray.

Amanda looks like she feels sorry for Jennifer.
"You can, but it's not a good idea."

"Definitely don't put eggs as a dislike," Bronwyn says.
"It's not specific enough. You'd have to say 'scrambled eggs,'
and then they'd give you powdered eggs every day,
which are even worse."

Tears. Tight throat.
"What if I say 'scrambled and powdered eggs'?"
Jennifer asks.

Monica shakes her head.
"Then they'll give you hard-boiled or fried.
You know, the kind with runny yolks."

The words "runny yolks" make Jennifer gag again.
She takes a packet of ketchup from the condiment basket.
Her hands are shaking; it's hard to rip the foil.
She squirts ketchup onto her tray.
The tines of her plastic fork bend
as she cuts a triangle of washcloth.
She stabs it with her fork, slides it through ketchup,
puts it in her mouth.
Oh, God.
It's worse with ketchup.

"Is it the texture?" Bronwyn asks.

Jennifer nods, wiping her nose with her napkin.

"What if you tried sugar?" Bronwyn asks.
Monica and Amanda look at Bronwyn
like she just asked, *What if you were a trapeze artist,
and your mother lived in an igloo?*

Bronwyn shrugs at them.
The shrug says, *She's bulimarexic, not anorexic.*
Meaning: the calories in a packet of sugar
don't mean the same to Jennifer as
they do to anorexic Monica and Amanda.
Jennifer has tried, and failed,
at pure, restriction-only anorexia.
Bulimarexia was the best she could do.

Anorexia is flawlessness.
Anorexics are iron-clad in their willpower,
untainted by overeating, ever.
They are, have always been, the highest,
most accomplished,
most emulated,
most envied people in the eating disorder hierarchy.
Jennifer may be a stranger in this foreign land,
but she has been studying its culture for years.
She speaks the language.
Even when the language is unspoken.

Monica says, "Well…I suppose…
If you care more about getting it down
than you do about the extra calories…"

Which Jennifer does.
She doesn't care about the calories right now.
Normally that should sink her to the bottom of the ranks.
But she's underweight. The "rexic" in bulimarexic.
It gives her higher status
than "normal" weight bulimics,
who outrank overweight bulimics,
who outrank compulsive overeaters.

Anything to get through this.
The entire universe has telescoped down
to one yellow washcloth.
This is the most important thing Jennifer has ever done,
eating this egg, greasy and limp in its plastic tray.
Jennifer selects a packet of sugar
from the condiment basket

and pours it on the other side of the terrycloth,
the side away from the ketchup.
She dips a bite of egg into the sugar.
Slowly the eggs go down.

She will eat eggs with sugar
every time she's faced with them.
And only much, much later
will it occur to Jennifer to wonder
whether Bronwyn was simply being kind,
just trying to help...
or whether she was delineating—cementing in—
Jennifer's place on the EDU's
anorexia/bulimarexia/bulimia/compulsive overeater
hierarchy of eating disorders.
Or both.

♥ ♥ ♥

Samuel Tuke Center
Eating Disorders Unit

Rules and Therapeutic Expectations
Therapy and Therapeutic Activities

Patients are expected to participate in all groups and therapeutic activities as directed by staff.

Patients shall comply with psychological and physical testing as directed by treatment team.

Patients shall comply with medical and therapeutic guidelines, including the taking of prescribed medication.

Patients will write a Personal Eating Disorder History and read it aloud to EDU patients and staff when assigned by treatment team.

All EDU patients shall attend:

- EDU group therapy (daily, Monday–Friday, 10:00 a.m., lounge)
- family therapy (time and location TBD, with assigned social worker)
- individual therapy with director of EDU (weekly, office of director, time TBD)
- individual therapy with assigned psychiatrist (weekly, office of psychiatrist, time TBD)
- Overeater's Anonymous when held in-house (weekly or twice weekly, lounge, time TBD)
- EDU Community Meeting (weekly, lounge, time TBD)
- Assertiveness Training (weekly, Monday 7:00 p.m., large 2nd floor lounge)

- Wellness and Nutrition (weekly, Monday 1:30 p.m., activities room 1)
- Meditation (weekly, Tuesday 1:30 p.m., activities room 1)
- Journaling (weekly, Wednesday 1:30 p.m., activities room 1)
- Art Therapy (weekly, Thursday, 1:30 p.m., activities room 1)
- Body Image Workshop (twice monthly, large 2nd floor lounge, time TBD)
- Sexual Assault & Abuse Survivor's Group, Alcoholics Anonymous, Narcotics Anonymous, Chemical Dependency Education, Al-Anon, Depression Workshop, etc., as prescribed by treatment team (various times, locations)
- Arts and Crafts (if not in prescribed therapy group, Tuesdays and Thursdays 11:00 a.m., activity room 2)

In addition, all medically cleared patients will attend:

- Off-campus Overeaters Anonymous and/or National Association of Anorexia Nervosa and Associated Disorders (ANAD) groups (TBD)
- Movement Therapy (1:30 p.m., Fridays alternating with Aerobics, movement studio)
- Aerobics (1:30 p.m., alternating Fridays, movement studio)

All rules are subject to change without notice by staff.

At 10:00, it's time for group therapy.
Dr. Wexler ambles into the lounge,
nodding at patients.
As if he has gravitational pull,
everyone gathers,
settling on couches, rockers, chairs,
forming a big circle.
Dr. Wexler sits on a folding chair
and crosses his legs at the knee.

Jennifer sits on the couch between Bronwyn and Monica,
and although it's good to be near two nice people,
she is scared and lonely and miserable.

Converging for group happens wordlessly.
It's surreal how many things transpire without words here:
sitting down for group and meals, getting a cigarette lit,
waiting for weigh-in.

Dr. Wexler clasps his hands around his knees, leans forward.
Does this mean the start of group?
Nothing.
Silence.
Patients pick at their cuticles, or fidget,
smoke cigarettes that were lit by nurses before group.
The discomfort builds.

Jennifer waits.
Shouldn't there be talking?
She'd expected Dr. Wexler to give them a topic,
or otherwise get the ball rolling,
like a teacher leading a classroom discussion.

Instead, it feels like the entire room is in a contest of wills
to see who will break down
and speak first.

After what feels like forever,
a girl with long, dark hair clears her throat.
"I have something to talk about.
I think there are a lot of people on this floor
who are showing major avoidant behavior."
Avoidant behavior. What does that mean?

A ripple of something—fear? anger?—
passes through the lounge.
"Could you be more specific, Eleanor?" Dr. Wexler asks.

"Yes, I can," Eleanor says.
"I specifically think Monica and Bronwyn
are being avoidant."

A moment of stunned stillness,
followed by a surge of voices,
words gushing out of mouths,
accusing, defending; angry, crying.

Monica and Bronwyn tense themselves into
tight bundles of angry energy.
Words pop like bubbles:
"denial" and "bathrooms"
and "milk trick" and "tanking"
and Jennifer's name.
But she is totally lost.

Jennifer looks from one person to another,
searching for clues,
desperate to figure out what is going on.
It seems like everyone is mad at someone.
The best that Jennifer can discern is that
Eleanor and a few other patients
are mad at Bronwyn and Monica for doing something,
something that is "avoidant behavior,"
but she doesn't know precisely what that means,
or exactly what they did.

As soon as Jennifer thinks she knows what's going on,
the topic shifts to something else someone did.
Jennifer hasn't spoken, nor have Heather
or Thriller or Amanda.
During a lull, Dr. Wexler asks each of them
if they have anything to say.
Heather and Thriller shake their heads.
Amanda says, "I believe Bronwyn and Monica."
Jennifer says the only thing she can think of to say:
"I didn't tank."

The air is still thick with acrimony
when Dr. Wexler says, "That's our time for today.
It seems this unit has a lot to talk about.
Perhaps we can continue this discussion tomorrow."

Jennifer stares at Dr. Wexler.
Nothing's been resolved.
How can he end the session, when everyone is still so upset?
That can't be good. Not for anyone.
Now they'll all walk around resentful
and angry at each other?

She scratches her forearm.
Her skin feels tight.
She can't stand when people are angry.
She hates confrontation.
It makes her want to disappear, fade into oblivion.

At school, there are girls who enjoy squabbling,
who regularly have big, ugly battles with each other.
Not Jennifer. She fractures into a million pieces
if anyone outside her family—
anyone, from closest friend to most passing acquaintance—
expresses even the tiniest hint of anger at her.
Anything remotely negative sends her into paroxysms
of panic, worry, doubt.

No, this can't drag on.
Jennifer is already hanging on by her fingernails here.
She at least needs the patients to be nice to each other.

But now Monica and Bronwyn jump up from the couch,
without a word or a glance at Jennifer,
and form a huddle with Amanda.
The three of them whisper and shoot dirty looks at Eleanor.
They leave the lounge in a tight knot of three.

Jennifer doesn't want to be alone.
She feels left out.
It reminds her of everything that's bad about school,
and life in general.
Always wondering if people like you,
always wondering if you're missing something,
if you weren't invited to a party,

114

if people are talking about you;
never sure of your level of social standing.
Jennifer wants to follow the girls out of the lounge,
find out what's going on, be privy to their whispers.
But she's afraid she would be annoying:
a puppy nipping at their heels.
The way her brother hates it when she wants to
tag along with him and his friends
on BMX tracks and ski slopes.
Keep up or ski alone. That was the Little Sister Rule.
So Jennifer learned to ignore her fear
and fly down those hills.

The rest of the patients linger in the lounge,
smoking newly lit cigarettes,
talking in low voices, not including Jennifer.
How can she learn what this is about?

Heather turns the TV on.
Bob Barker is chatting with a contestant
on *The Price is Right.*
Jennifer watches the contestant guess prices.
Watches the clock on the wall.
Starts to cry.
Tries to hold her tears in.
It's embarrassing, crying this much.

Eleven minutes and 42 seconds later
(not that she's counting),
Jennifer is jolted by the sound of her name.
Dr. Wexler has stuck his head into the lounge.
He says her name again,
motioning for her to come with him.

When they are seated in his office,
the same office as the intake interview,
but without Mom this time,
Dr. Wexler says, "So, Jennifer.
How's it going so far?"

Jennifer starts crying in earnest.

Dr. Wexler hands her a box of tissues.
"You seem sad, Jennifer."
You seem sad. How insightful.

Jennifer takes a tissue from the box.
"I miss my mom," she says. "It's hard here."

"The separation." Dr. Wexler nods.
"Is that what's distressing you most?"

Jennifer wipes her nose. "Not just that.
Overwhelmed."

"You're feeling overwhelmed?" he asks.
She nods.
"In what way?" he asks.

"In every way," she says.
Dr. Wexler doesn't respond. He waits.

"I wonder if I can even survive here," Jennifer says.
"It doesn't feel like I can survive."

"Can you say more about that?" he asks.

"I feel like I'm going to die.
As if I'm so sad, I'm going to just…stop living."

"Are you thinking of hurting yourself?" he asks.

Jennifer shakes her head. "No. It's just, I can't stop crying,
and if I do stop crying, it's only for a minute or two,
and then it starts again."

Dr. Wexler makes a note in her file.
"Is this new or unusual for you?"

"I don't know.
For a long time I've felt sad, and…alone.
At home, a lot of times, I feel like crying,
but I can't. I'm numb.
No, I've never cried this much.
I feel like something's been knocked loose inside me."

"Well, I think it's quite normal," Dr. Wexler says,
"for a girl who is as enmeshed with her mother as you are.
Of course you would feel pain on separating."

"Enmeshed," Jennifer says.
"What does that mean, exactly?"

"It means that you don't know where one of you ends
and the other begins."

Jennifer chews her lip, thinking.
"Isn't it okay to be close with your mom?" she asks.

"Normal teenagers rebel against their mothers,"
Dr. Wexler says.
"It's part of the process of individuation.
That's how you find out who you are."

Jennifer protests, "You're making it sound like
I'm a goody two-shoes.
I'm rebellious. I rebel."

"I suspect you rebel by turning it inward.
By turning against yourself.
Eating disorders are an unhealthy means of rebellion,
an unhealthy attempt at individuation."

"I guess," Jennifer says.

Dr. Wexler says, "And perhaps you have been waiting
to be in a safe environment
before you could allow yourself to experience this pain."

"Maybe." Jennifer sighs.
"I wonder which came first, the pain, or—"
She's about to say, "the pain, or my eating disorder,"
but the phone on Dr. Wexler's desk rings,
so she stops.

Dr. Wexler holds up one finger,
and swivels to pick up the handset.
"Dr. Wexler. Uh huh. Yes. No, that's not right…"

Jennifer can't believe it.
He picks up his phone in the middle of a session?
Without so much as an *Excuse me*?

Isn't that super incredibly rude?
Yes, it is. Unless…
Unless he thinks his time with her is not important.
She watches the minutes on the digital clock.
One minute. Two. Three.

Dr. Wexler deposits the heavy handset on its cradle,
makes a note on his desk calendar,
and turns back to Jennifer.
He doesn't say anything, or give any sort of sign,
no expression that says, *Sorry about that interruption.*
He just looks at Jennifer like he's waiting
for her to continue.

She folds and smooths her tissue over her knee.
Fold, crease, smooth.
Fold, crease, smooth.
The silence draws out,
increasingly uncomfortable.

Finally Dr. Wexler says, "I have a note here that you created
a commotion at weigh-in this morning."

"What?" Jennifer's head snaps up.

"You didn't create a commotion?"

"No." Jennifer shakes her head.
"The nurse thought I drank water,
but I didn't. And she wouldn't believe me."

Dr. Wexler leans forward, elbows on knees,
like he's thinking, *Now we're getting somewhere.*
"*Should* she have believed you?"

"Yes!" Jennifer's cheeks flush.

"Hm," says Dr. Wexler. "You seem angry, Jennifer.
Are you angry?"

Again with the *You seem such-and-such, Jennifer.*
"I'm frustrated!" Jennifer says.
"It's hard when no one believes you."

"How do you mean?" he asks.

"It's the nurse's word against mine,
just like it's my parents' word against mine.
The nurse thinks I have an eating disorder that's so bad
I would tank,
while my parents don't think I have one at all."
She starts sobbing. "I can't win.
No one believes anything I say.
Even you, even you didn't believe
that I have an eating disorder."
She can't meet his eyes, she's crying so hard.
"I have no way to convince anyone I'm telling the truth."

"Why do you feel like you have to convince anyone?"

Jennifer is practically choking on all the snot she's producing.
"Because," she says, "if I can't convince people
that I have an eating disorder, and that I want to get better,
and that I'm telling the truth,

I'm never going to get privileges.
And if I don't get privileges,
I'll never get out of here."
She tries to get her breath under control.
"Plus, it sucks…it sucks going around
trying to do the right thing.
I mean, what's the point if no one believes you?
I tell my mom I need help, I ask to come to the hospital,
I make an intentional decision *not* to drink water
before weigh-in today,
and what do I get for any of it?"

"What, Jennifer?
What *do* you get?"

"I get total…just complete and utter shit.
From everyone." She takes a deep breath, exhales slowly,
breath shuddering. "It totally sucks."

Dr. Wexler sighs. "I'll bet it does,
in your words, 'suck.'
But Jennifer, the only way to earn people's trust
is to be honest—"

"I *am* being honest!" she insists.

He frowns. "To *continue* to be honest
if you *are* being honest,
and to be consistent. Honesty and consistency.
That is how you build trust."
He looks at the clock. "Well," he says,
"That's our time. I'll walk you back to the lounge."

So abrupt. Dismissed.
Jennifer stands,
puts her wadded tissues in the wastepaper basket.
She follows Dr. Wexler out of his office, down the hall.

"By the way," Dr. Wexler says as they walk,
"we've determined your treatment-planning team.
Dr. Prakash will be your psychiatrist."

"Okay," Jennifer says.
"That's the lady from yesterday? From admission?"

Dr. Wexler nods. "Yes, from yesterday.
And your treatment planning will be Wednesdays."

Should Jennifer be writing this information down?
It seems important.

"Your secondary will be Chuck," Dr. Wexler says.

"Chuck?" Jennifer asks.

"You haven't met him yet?" Dr. Wexler asks.
"No, no, I suppose you haven't,"
answering his own question.
"And the head of your nursing team,
your primary, will be Sheryl."

Sheryl? Which nurse is she?
Didn't Monica say something about a Sheryl?
Wait…
No. Not—

"Nurse Ratched?" Jennifer blurts.
Tears stream down her cheeks again,
plus, now she feels like she's going to throw up.

Dr. Wexler chuckles. "I think she prefers to be called Sheryl.
She's tough, yes, but that might be just what you need.
She's the director of our nursing staff."

Nurse Ratched is what she needs?
It doesn't feel that way.
But Jennifer probably shouldn't trust her feelings,
should she?
Where have they gotten her so far?
Sick, sad, enmeshed, hospitalized, that's where.
So, yes. Surely the doctors, the nurses,
they all must know better than she does.

♥ ♥ ♥

After lunch, Nurse Ratched sits down at the table
across from Jennifer.
Behind Ratched, Bronwyn crosses her eyes
and pokes out her tongue.
Jennifer tries not to giggle.
Nurse Ratched taps Jennifer's file against the table,
stacks and straightens the papers within,
and then lays it flat.
Her short fingernails *tap tap tap* on the file.
"Well, Jennifer," she says,
"I'd like for us both to move past
what happened this morning.
I'm willing to give you another chance.
A fresh start."

Jennifer nods. The false accusation is lodged in her heart,
as big as an anvil. But she has to try to move on.
This is her primary. The head of the nursing staff.
A strict disciplinarian is what she needs.
Jennifer must try not to hold a grudge.

Nurse Ratched sighs, like she's sorry for what's coming next:
"That said, we're canceling your unsupervised bathrooms
starting tomorrow morning before weigh-in,
so we can support you in being safe from yourself."
Her index finger is still tapping.

"I don't…," Jennifer says, "I don't understand. You mean…
I have to be watched in the morning, too?"
No chance to poop in private.
The door will be open five inches.
Someone will watch her poop and wipe.
And will then look in the toilet to make sure
everything looks right,
and then flush it for her.
Jennifer is mortified.

Nurse Ratched tilts her head. The pointy tip of her nose,
stippled with blackheads, shines under the fluorescent lights.
"We want to support you in
fighting your disease, Jennifer," she says.
"This way, we can be sure
you won't feel tempted to tank before weigh-in."
Tap. Tap. Tap.
"And if your weight tomorrow
doesn't seem to have decreased significantly,
well…then we'll consider it water under the—oh!" She chuckles.
"Water! Under the bridge. No pun intended."

124

Jennifer swallows her anger.
"Fine," she says.

Nurse Ratched tilts her head to the other side.
"Fine?" she says.

"Fine," Jennifer repeats.

"That sounds rather passive-aggressive.
Are you angry?"

Jennifer forces herself to sound agreeable.
"No. It's fine," she says. "I'm not doing anything wrong,
so it's fine to watch me. It's just unpleasant, is all."

Nurse Ratched smiles.
"Well, yes, it's all rather unpleasant, isn't it?
But our job here is to keep you safe,
and sometimes that means
a staff member has to be the bad guy.
I'm okay with that.
And I truly believe that you'll come to appreciate it."

Jennifer grits her teeth, nods.
It doesn't seem like something she will ever appreciate.

"Now." Nurse Ratched opens Jennifer's file.
"Your notes indicate you went over the rules
with staff last night.
Do you have any questions for me?
Anything new that's come up since yesterday?"

Yes.
Are you always such a bitch?
Does it hurt to have such a big stick up your ass?
"I don't think so," Jennifer says, then remembers. "Oh wait.
Dr. Wexler said my treatment planning will be Wednesdays?
So, that's tomorrow? Should I do anything for that?
Can I make requests?"

Nurse Ratched exhales sharply. She shakes her head.
"Not tomorrow, I don't think.
Since you are not medically cleared,
you can't request privileges or off-campus passes.
And that is quite apart from the fact that
you haven't begun to demonstrate
that you are willing to do the work
it takes to earn privileges."

Jennifer doesn't say anything.
She has the feeling that anything she says could
be turned around and held against her.
She thinks of police shows: *Miami Vice* or *21 Jump Street*,
Johnny Depp cuffing criminals,
You have the right to remain silent.
Anything you say can and will be used against you.
Maybe Heather and Thriller are smart not to talk much—
except staff can hold that against you, too.
It's a lose-lose situation.

"And besides," Nurse Ratched is saying—
and Jennifer swears it sounds like she's enjoying herself—
"you haven't been here a full week,
so you can't receive visitors.

Next week we will meet and talk through
what your requests should be.
Or, really, whether you should even
make any requests at all."

"But I was planning—"
Jennifer's stomach roils. "I mean, next week,
I want to go out on a pass with my family."

"Let's not get ahead of ourselves."
Nurse Ratched purses her lips.
"One day at a time, Jennifer.
One day at a time.
Now, I'll walk you to Meditation."

Jennifer nods.
One day at a time.
But she's pretty sure that it was Nurse Ratched
who brought up the future.

♥ ♥ ♥

Samuel Tuke Center
Eating Disorders Unit

Rules and Therapeutic Expectations
Toilets and Bathing

- All bathrooms on the EDU, including those in patient rooms, shall remain locked at all times, except between the hours of 6:00 and 8:00 a.m.
- All patients may close the bathroom door and flush their own toilet between the hours of 3:00 and 8:00 a.m.
- When a patient is using the bathroom, the door must remain open at least five inches (except between the hours of 3:00 and 8:00 a.m., and patients with bathroom privileges).
- Patients must not flush toilets. Staff must check and flush toilets (except between the hours of 3:00 and 8:00 a.m., and patients with bathroom privileges).
- Patients may only use toilets on the EDU. Patients are not to use toilets in any other area of the hospital.
- Patients needing to use the bathroom during off-campus meetings and excursions must be supervised by staff.
- Patients must be medically cleared before they can take a standing shower.
- On request, staff will provide supervision of tub bath and/or hair washing for patients not yet medically cleared.
- Patients are expected to maintain good hygiene, as determined by staff.

All rules are subject to change without notice by staff.

Bathroom privileges.
It's funny, and diabolical, and infuriating
that using the bathroom is called a privilege.
As if it's a privilege to do her business in private,
without someone standing at a door
that always must be open five inches,
listening, watching.
As if flushing her own toilet is not something
she's done since she was two years old.

It makes sense, in theory.
They are taking away Jennifer's control
so she doesn't have to fight with herself.
In theory, it's a relief.
In reality, it is humiliating.

Made worse by her shy bladder.
Jennifer has never been able to pee
if she thinks someone can hear
or if someone is waiting for the bathroom.
She can barely let out a trickle in a public restroom
if any other stall is occupied.
There are people who can squat and whizz in milliseconds,
talking to their friends the entire time.
Her brother's girlfriend is one of these people.
Mom is one of these people.
Jennifer is not one of these people.

And now, here she is in the bathroom in her room,
because that's where her urine-collecting hat and jug are.
Nurse Trendy is listening,
her ear in the space between door and frame.

129

Pee hitting the hat will be louder than a jackhammer.
But better to do it here than the lounge bathroom.
"Are you okay in there?" Nurse Trendy asks.

Argh.
Every time Nurse Trendy speaks,
Jennifer's pee backs up into her bladder.
Up to her armpits.
"Yes," Jennifer says.
And…restart.
Bladder, come on. Come on, bladder. You can do it.

Jennifer can see Nurse Trendy's shoes moving.
Her eyeball in the crack of the door again.
"You sure you're okay?"

Damn it.
She's not puking.
She's not hiding anything.
She's just trying to pee.
And, good Lord almighty,
how much more embarrassing will this be
when it's poop, not pee?
What about when her period returns?
Jennifer murmurs, "I'm okay."

She cannot wait,
cannot WAIT,
to get bathroom privileges.
But there's no chance of that until she hits maintenance.
And her primary nurse has to approve.
So who knows how long it will be.

When at last Jennifer is finished,
and has transferred the urine to her jug,
she washes her hands while Nurse Trendy checks
that there is nothing but tissue in the toilet bowl.
Nurse Trendy uses her foot to press the flusher.
She composes her face, like she's trying to be businesslike,
but a wrinkle in her nose betrays her disgust.
If Jennifer had to flush someone else's toilet,
she would probably use her foot, too.
Still, it's hard not to take it personally.
It's easy to imagine that Trendy and Ratched and Bosom
don't want to get anywhere near
something that touched or came out of Jennifer,
because she is gross.

Wednesday, November 23, 1988

Jennifer is awoken by the light of her bedside lamp
and Trendy's cold fingertips pressing her wrist.
Blood pressure and pulse: lying, sitting, standing.
Heather grunts and snores.
It's 6:04 a.m.

"Weigh-in, right now," Trendy says
as she writes numbers on her clipboard.
She tucks the blood pressure cuff
back into its place on the cart.
"Change into your paper gown."

"I don't have one," Jennifer says.

"Where's your gown from yesterday?" Trendy asks.

"I threw it out," Jennifer says.
"I didn't know I was supposed to keep it."

Nurse Trendy sighs. "Come with me, then.
Save this one. They don't grow on trees, you know."
But aren't trees exactly what paper grows from?

"I really need to pee," Jennifer says.
"Weigh-in first," Trendy says.

Jennifer follows Trendy to the nurses' station.
Ratched and Bosom are deep in conversation with Beverly.
Trendy parks the blood pressure cart in a corner
and tosses the clipboard onto a desk.
Everything is quiet; the other patients are sleeping.
It's just Jennifer and the nurses.
They're dealing with her before they wake anyone else.

"Where's your paper gown?" Ratched asks,
more to Trendy than Jennifer.

"She threw it out," Trendy says,
like, *Can you believe the cluelessness of this girl?*
Trendy takes a new gown from a tall stack on a shelf.
Jennifer reaches for it,
but Trendy tucks the gown under her own elbow
and says, "Back to your room."

In her dim bedroom, Jennifer wants to curl up in her bed
and never come out.
"Go ahead and change," Trendy says,
keeping her voice low.

"You're going to watch?" Jennifer asks.
It sounds like a soft yelp.

"Afraid so," Trendy says.

Jennifer unfolds the paper gown and lays it on her bed.
Turning her back to Trendy,
she lifts her nightshirt over her head,
throws it on the bed, and puts the paper gown on,
holding the back closed.

"Underwear, too," Trendy says.
"I need to see."

Jennifer wiggles out of her underwear,
picking it up and tossing it into her clothes hamper.
She opens the gown quickly,
flashing her naked butt so Trendy can see.

Back in the nurses' station, Beverly is buttoning her coat.
She dons her hat, slides her hands into mittens.
"Have a good day, Jennifer," she says.
"I'll see you tonight, unless you're already asleep."
When Beverly leaves, the warmth leaves with her,
as if she tucked it into her coat and spirited it away.
Jennifer's flesh is prickly with goose bumps.
She shivers from cold, and dread.

Ratched looks at Trendy.
"Did you check her?"
Trendy nods.
Ratched swoops toward Jennifer, patting her down anyway,
pinching her waist, first from the sides, then front to back.
"Okay," Ratched says in a discordantly cheerful voice.
"Turn around and step right up."
She takes Jennifer's elbow,
guiding her as she moves onto the scale platform.
Trendy clanks the weights.

Jennifer holds her breath.
Bosom is watching from across the room.
Ratched looks at the scale,
her notes,
the scale.
"Come off and step back on," Ratched says.
Jennifer does.
The clanking repeats.

Ratched looks at Trendy.
Trendy and Bosom look at Ratched.
They don't talk.
They all stare at the numbers on the scale, behind Jennifer.
Why is this taking so long?
Her bladder is threatening to burst.
"Jennifer," Ratched says.
"I need you to step off the scale and
jump up and down for me."

"Jump?" Jennifer asks, mystified.
"Up and down?"

"Yes."

"Is…is everything okay?" Jennifer squeaks.
She is scared.
This is starting to feel like yesterday.

Ratched tilts her head and asks, slowly,
"*Should* everything be okay, Jennifer?"

"Yes, I think so," Jennifer says,
but she doesn't sound convincing, even to herself.

"Hm," Ratched says.
"I'm not so sure."

"I don't understand," Jennifer says.
Does she weigh more than yesterday? Less? The same?
Jennifer doesn't even know what to hope for.
What would satisfy them?

"Come off the scale and jump up and down."

Jennifer steps down.
The tile is freezing.

"Jump."

Jennifer gives a little jump.

"Higher."

Jennifer's bladder is killing her;
she's afraid pee will come out if she jumps too high.
She jumps a little more.

"Why aren't you willing to jump?"

"I'm sorry, I just really have to pee," Jennifer says.
"What…what's going on?
Is there a problem?"

"Let me see her room inventory," Ratched says to Bosom.
Bosom hands Ratched a three-ring binder.
Ratched flips pages.

"Four rolls of quarters?" she asks.
Bosom nods solemnly.

Ratched looks at Jennifer.
"You need to show us those rolls of coins."

"The...why?" Jennifer asks.

"Now," Trendy says.
Bosom, Trendy, and Ratched follow Jennifer into her room.
One of them pops the overhead light on.
"What the hell!" Heather says.
"Go back to sleep," Bosom says.
Heather grumbles and turns over.

Jennifer checks her dresser.
No quarters.
"They were—they were right here."
She scrambles, moving her books.
"I had four rolls. They were right here."
She gets down on her hands and knees,
presses her face to the carpet to look under the dresser.
"They have to be here."

"Jennifer, where are your quarters?"
Trendy asks quietly.

Jennifer's panic is rising.
If she doesn't have money, she can't call home.
She's supposed to be able to call home today.
Two o'clock today.
She's been counting the hours.

She has to call.
Her parents don't know the pay phone number.
They can't call her.
And Monica said they don't let you do collect calls.
How will she call?
She'll die if she can't talk to Mom.

Jennifer opens her dresser drawers,
paws through her clothes,
slams each to go to the next.

"Could you be quiet!" Heather yells,
but it barely registers.

Jennifer looks under her bed,
through her clothes hamper,
on the nightstand.
She searches everywhere.
Finally, panting, she turns to the nurses.
"They were right here," she says,
tears streaming down her cheeks. "They were right here."

"Why don't we go back
to the nurses' station?" Trendy suggests.

"Yes. Leave," Heather says into her pillow.

Back at the nurses' station,
the stark light reflects off white tile floors.
Ratched says, "Jennifer. Your quarters are missing.
We think it's quite clear what you've done."

Jennifer weeps, "I need those quarters.
I need them to call—"

Ratched interrupts. "You've hidden rolls of coins
in your vagina."

Jennifer blinks.
She swipes at her cheeks. "What?"

Ratched clears her throat.
"We didn't give you the opportunity to tank this morning,
and since you can't produce your rolls of quarters,
I have no choice but to believe that, at some point overnight,
you tucked rolls of quarters into your vagina."

Jennifer looks from Ratched, to Trendy, to Bosom.
This is a joke, right?
This must be a joke.
She waits for one of them to crack a smile.
Trendy crosses her arms over her chest.
Bosom sits.
Ratched waits.

"That's gross," is what Jennifer says.
Because, of all the thoughts in her brain,
she keeps coming back to the fact
that coins are filthy with germs.
"That's so gross," Jennifer repeats.
"I wouldn't do that. That's disgusting."

"That's your disease," Trendy says,
with a hint of compassion.

"We need you to take out the quarters," Ratched says,
with no hint of compassion.

"God!" Jennifer says. "Four rolls?
How would they even fit?"
She begins to laugh.
Not happy laughter; deranged laughter.
How spacious do they think her vagina is?
She uses tampons labeled *Slender, for teens.*
Her vagina is not a saggy, stretched-out balloon.
It could not hold four rolls of quarters.
Or maybe they think she put some of them up her butt, too?
Jennifer has to stop laughing;
it surely makes her look guilty. Plus,
a drop of pee is trickling down her leg,
but she can't suppress her giggles.

"If you won't show us the quarters," Ratched says,
"we'll have to order a gynecological exam."

That does it. A flip switches.
"NO!" Jennifer screams.
Her first pelvic exam is not going to be in a mental hospital.
It's not going to be a forced body-cavity search.
"NO! NO! NO!" she yells.

"Jennifer, calm down—" Bosom says.

"I WILL NOT CALM DOWN!
I DIDN'T DO ANYTHING WRONG!
YOU CAN ALL GO TO HELL!
WRITE IT IN MY FILE, I DON'T CARE!

JENNIFER JOHNSON TELLS ALL STAFF
TO GO TO HELL!"

"Jennifer," Trendy says, "calm down,
or we'll need to give you something to help you calm down."

Jennifer crumples to the floor,
and something wet and warm soaks her legs.

"Oh my God," Trendy says, horrified.

Jennifer is wretched, and alone, and accused,
and now she has wet herself.
She cries, sitting in her own urine.
She hears Ratched say, "Call custodial."

Finally Trendy says, "Come on, Jennifer."
She helps Jennifer up, leads her to her room,
unlocks the bathroom, runs the tub water.
She waits while Jennifer takes off her wet paper gown
and shoves it in the garbage.
She watches as Jennifer sits on the edge of the tub,
puts her legs under the water, uses a washcloth to get clean.

Jennifer dries herself, silently,
hangs her towel up, leaves the bathroom,
puts on her nightshirt, gets back into bed,
hides under her quilt.
She holds Bearibubs close.
Heather snores.
Trendy leaves.
Jennifer cries.

Yesterday she thought it couldn't get worse.
But today is worse.
She has managed to find a new low.
Ashamed, embarrassed, angry, alone, terrified.

♥ ♥ ♥

Somehow, she'd always thought that she could do this.
Even at her most desperate,
with her monster at its most vicious,
a part of her thought she'd eventually find a way.
She believed that when she grew up, she'd be happy.
A grown woman, healthy, with a good life.
But now, the path from here to there is gone.
Obliterated.
There is only a chasm.
An expanse of nothingness.
No path, no labyrinth, no floor, no ceiling.
There is nothing.

It's over.

The end.

♥ ♥ ♥

And yet, scrunched under her quilt, she hopes.
Incongruously.
A tiny part of her. A still, small voice.
Maybe because there is nothing left.

Maybe this moment, right now,
is why her parents gave her her middle name:
Hope.
Jennifer Hope Johnson.
Maybe they gave it to her to get through this.

Is hope what you need, in order to take a leap of faith?
What is a leap of faith, anyway?
Does it mean flinging yourself into nothingness?
Does it mean you close your eyes and jump off the precipice,
and trust that you'll sprout wings,
or someone will catch you,
or both?

She has no wings.
There is no one to catch her.
No one here except herself.
And Jennifer can't do it.

This Jennifer can't do it.

Unless.
What if this Jennifer isn't the only Jennifer?
What about the future Jennifer?
The happy, healthy grown woman?
If that person exists, there must, necessarily, be
a thread from then to now.

Jennifer closes her eyes.
She makes herself a promise.
If I ever grow into that person,
grown-up me will come back here,
to this Jennifer, curled up, crying in bed,
humiliated, with no underwear on, and no money to call home.

Grown-up Jennifer will catch her, and set her down gently,
and hold her hand, and walk her through this.
Because there's no other way.
She is alone. But
she cannot do this alone.

♥ ♥ ♥

The mattress dips,
and a hand settles on Jennifer's back.
Someone is sitting on her bed.

Jennifer tenses, but does not come out from under the covers.
She has heard the sounds of Heather getting up
and breakfast being served in the lounge.

"Jennifer." *Jenny-fah.*
"Jennifer," the voice says. "It's Dr. Prakash.
Please come out so we can chat."

Jennifer's life has hit rock bottom,
lower than she thought possible,
and Dr. Prakash wants to *chat.*
Jennifer doesn't move.

"You do not want to come out of hiding?"
Dr. Prakash's voice is light, almost chuckling.
"I am sure my voice can carry through your blankets.
All I ask is that you listen to what I have to say.
Can you do that for me?"

Jennifer doesn't move.

"Are you alive in there?" Dr. Prakash asks.

Jennifer nods.

"Is that a yes or a no?" Dr. Prakash asks.
"It's difficult to tell from here."

"Yes," Jennifer mutters.
Her voice is hoarse, her throat sore from yelling,
probably as loud as Jesus Lady.
She is mad, and humiliated, and frightened.
What happens now?
Will Dr. Prakash make her submit to a vaginal exam?
Will her parents be called?
What consequences will be forced on her?
Restraints? Tranquilizers? The ICU?

"Very well," Dr. Prakash sighs.
"Sheryl and the other nurses have filled me in
on what happened—"

"I didn't do anything wrong!" Jennifer shouts.
"I hate it here!
No one believes me!

145

This is torture! Torture is illegal!
I didn't do anything!"

Dr. Prakash's hand is still on Jennifer's back,
which is now heaving.
"Jennifer, you will need to please calm down.
Please, just breathe for me. Can you do that?
Just take deep breaths and listen?"

Listen. Why should she listen?
Dr. Prakash will side with the nurses.
Jennifer clamps her hands over her ears.
She doesn't care that it's juvenile.
She hates this place and everyone in it.
And if the nurses tell anyone that she peed herself,
she will die of mortification.

Dr. Prakash's hand moves on Jennifer's back.
Jennifer tries to shrug her off,
but Dr. Prakash starts to rub gentle circles.

A psychiatrist giving a back rub.
Isn't that a breach of medical ethics?
What kind of doctor is she, anyway?
The back circles continue.
And continue.

Dr. Prakash is taking all this time for Jennifer.
Just sitting here on her bed,
rubbing her back,
like a mom or a grandmother would.
Despite herself, Jennifer is comforted.
She is still mad and scared.

But more important than her anger
is her need for an ally—
the promise of grown-up Jennifer notwithstanding—
she needs someone who is actually here,
who can actually help, who actually cares about her.
Eventually Jennifer loosens her hands from her ears.

"Do you feel like you can listen a little now?"
Dr. Prakash asks.

Jennifer nods.

"Is that a yes?" Dr. Prakash asks.

"Yes," Jennifer mumbles.

"Good. Thank you. First, deep breath in"—
Dr. Prakash takes a deep breath herself—
"and out." Dr. Prakash blows an exaggerated breath.
"Once more, Jennifer. In, and out. You keep doing that, yes?"
She continues rubbing Jennifer's back.
"I have been informed by staff of what transpired,
but I would like to hear it from your perspective,
when you are ready.
For now, just keep listening to my words.
Can you do that for me?"

Jennifer nods,
then remembers to say, "Yes."

Dr. Prakash's voice is calm and reassuring.
She has probably had extensive training
in pacifying patients.

147

"I want you to keep breathing,
but I would like to ask you something.
I need a yes or no answer. Can you manage that?"

Jennifer nods under the quilt, then says, "Yes."
Her voice sounds pitiful.

"Excellent," Dr. Prakash says.
"Please do not get upset with me, Jennifer.
I do not wish to accuse you.
But I need for you to tell me the truth.
Did you use rolls of quarters, or anything else,
as weights this morning?"

"No!"

"Again, I am not accusing you, Jennifer.
But I would not be a very good physician if I did not ask.
So, once again, are you sure you are telling me the truth?"

Such an important word: truth.
With Dr. Prakash's accent, it sounds like *troot*.

"I'm telling the truth," Jennifer says.

"All right," Dr. Prakash says.
Jennifer waits for more, but Dr. Prakash just says,
"I am relieved to hear it."

She…believes Jennifer?
Just like that?
Impossible. It can't be this easy.

148

Dr. Prakash doesn't say anything else for a while.
Her circles on Jennifer's back turn into small, maternal pats.
"And your quarters are still missing?"

A sob shakes loose from Jennifer
at the mention of her lost money.

Dr. Prakash says, "I think I might know
what happened to your quarters.
We will see if anything can be done about it."

Jennifer can't stop crying now.

"Goodness," Dr. Prakash says.
"The disappearance of your quarters is this troubling?"

"I need to call my mom!" Jennifer wails.
"Now I don't have money for the pay phone!
I was supposed to be able to use the phone at 2:00!
And now I can't! And Mom won't even know why!"
Jennifer hates how whiny and pathetic she sounds,
but she can't manage anything better.

"Ah," Dr. Prakash says.
"Calling home is important?"

Jennifer sniffs, "Yes!
I've been waiting and waiting!"

"Well," Dr. Prakash says, "then it makes a good deal of sense
for you to be distraught. I have an idea.

How about we make a plan for you to use the phone
in my office today at—
what time did you say? Two o'clock?"

"Two," Jennifer confirms. "Really?"
Cautious relief washes through her.

"It will be a temporary accommodation," Dr. Prakash says,
"until your money turns up,
or your family can send you some new quarters.
Or perhaps a calling card?
Those can be quite useful in this sort of situation.
You can have a secret PIN code. It is safer that way.
That is what I give my own daughters
when they are away from home."

"Okay," Jennifer sniffs. "Thank you."
Her voice is the peep of a hatching chick.

"You are quite welcome," Dr. Prakash says.
"Do you think you can come out
from under the covers now?"

Is this a trap?
But Dr. Prakash is…nice.
She is going to let Jennifer use her phone.
Slowly Jennifer pulls the quilt off her head.
She must look unimaginably disheveled, red-eyed, staticky.
She sits up, bunching her pillow onto her lap,
hugging Bearibubs.

Dr. Prakash smiles, pats Jennifer's foot.
"That is better," she says. "That is much better.

I can see that your first few days have been difficult."
Dr. Prakash gets the tissue box from Heather's dresser
and sets it within easy reach.
"But Jennifer, I need you to understand
something very important.
Can you listen carefully to me?"

Jennifer nods, pulling tissues from the box.

Dr. Prakash says, "It happens, sometimes,
that our nurses make honest mistakes.
They are only human."

Jennifer's heart whips with anger. "But it's not fair!"
It sounds stupid and childish, but it's also exactly true.

"You are right, Jennifer. It is not fair," Dr. Prakash agrees.
"But it is the human condition to make mistakes."

"She shouldn't be my primary," Jennifer snaps.
Then, slowly, she asks, "Can you change it?
Can you make someone else my primary?"

Dr. Prakash purses her lips and squints slightly,
like she's considering the request.
"Jennifer, if I were to change
your primary nursing assignment,
I have to wonder, what road would we find ourselves on?
What would then happen when I make a mistake?
Will you say that I should no longer be your psychiatrist?
Will you want to swap me for someone else?"

Jennifer shakes her head. "That's different.
Nurse Ratch—I mean Sheryl—she's horrible.
She hates me for no good reason.
She accuses me of doing things,
things I would never do,
and she doesn't believe one word I say."

"Sheryl is human and fallible," Dr. Prakash says.
"She is doing her best."

Jennifer takes a deep, shuddering breath.
"Her best is pretty crappy."

Dr. Prakash laughs. "You are one tough customer, Jennifer.
Are you as hard on yourself as you are on other people?"

This question hits Jennifer in the gut.
She wipes her nose and eyes.
These hospital tissues are rough as sandpaper;
they scrape her puffy, tender skin.

Dr. Prakash touches Jennifer's knee with three quick pats.
It feels like a signal that they are finishing up.

But Jennifer needs to know her fate.
She searches Dr. Prakash's face for answers.
"Sheryl said I'm going to have consequences?"

"I do not believe that
you have done anything that requires consequences."

"I had a tantrum," Jennifer says
before she can think better of it.

"You certainly did." Dr. Prakash raises her eyebrows.
"That is something I would like you to work on.
Communicating your needs, asserting yourself
in a reasonable manner, yes?"

Jennifer nods.

"Good," Dr. Prakash says.
"Now, scoot off quickly to breakfast.
And do not let this ruin your whole day."

"I'll try," Jennifer says.

"Do, or do not," Dr. Prakash says.
"There is no try."

Even if Jennifer hadn't been inclined
to like Dr. Prakash before,
she would now.
Her psychiatrist just quoted Yoda.

♥ ♥ ♥

Jennifer calls home at 2:00,
using the phone in Dr. Prakash's office,
bursting into tears the moment she hears Mom's voice.

It's too quiet here without you, Mom says.
Rich says, *Take care, nerd. Spike misses you.*
Dad says, *We're proud of you, JJ.*
They talk about what they will do for Thanksgiving.

They make plans to visit Jennifer Monday evening at 7:00,
which is five extra hours from one week exactly,
but it's the soonest her parents can manage.

Jennifer has parked herself in Dr. Prakash's chair,
swiveling as she talks,
while Dr. Prakash sits on the couch, writing notes in files.

Jennifer borrows Dr. Prakash's pen when Mom
gives her the numbers of an old calling card,
just a few minutes left on it,
but enough for tomorrow, at least.
Mom promises to send a fresh calling card,
which should arrive in the mail Friday,
Saturday at the latest.

When Jennifer says good-bye, and hangs up the phone,
she feels as if her ribcage
has been pried apart with a crowbar,
her ribs cracked and jagged.
The phone call makes her miss home even more.

Thursday, November 24, 1988

Thanksgiving.
Weigh-in is mercifully unremarkable.
But the unit feels like a ghost town.
Everyone leaves after breakfast (powdered eggs),
comes back for lunch (spongy turkey slices),
and hightails it out again as soon as they can.

In the empty lounge, bereft of Bronwyn and Monica,
Jennifer stays at the lunch table with Nurse Chuck.
He is one of two male nurses on the EDU.
The other is older, middle-aged, and completely bald.
Jennifer likes Nurse Chuck better than Nurse Baldy.

Chuck is younger than most of the other nurses,
about the same age as Trendy,
twenty-five or twenty-six maybe.
He's tall, with a slight potbelly.
He dresses in that nondescript way most guys do:
T-shirts, Levi's, high-top Nikes.
He reminds Jennifer of a more likeable version of
Cameron from *Ferris Bueller's Day Off*.
Slightly dweeby. But he plays guitar in a band,
and his eyes have a lighthearted twinkle,
and he laughs a lot.

Chuck is similar to Dr. Prakash
in that they both treat her like she's human.
And, like Dr. Prakash, Chuck seems
happy to give Jennifer a chance.
He acts like he wants to get to know her before he decides
whether to believe Ratched's view
that Jennifer is a horrible, conniving little snot.

Last night, after she met him,
Jennifer attempted to describe Chuck in a letter to Kelly,
but it sounded all wrong.
She is afraid Kelly will think she has a crush on Chuck.
She tried to write that she has no romantic feelings for him,
because (1) she is not into boys right now—
here in the hospital,
her focus on survival is all-encompassing—
and (2) Chuck is way too old, and professional, and married.
And (3) even without the first two reasons,
nothing could kill a crush faster than the massive indignity
of unsupervised bathrooms.
Yes, male nurses flush female patients' toilets.

She had tried to explain to Kelly that Chuck is like an uncle,
or a big brother—except a *nice* big brother.
He doesn't make the bathroom situation worse
than it already is,
doesn't make her feel like a jerk,
seems to actually enjoy hanging out with her,
despite the fact that he has to because it's his job.

Jennifer had written all this,
and then she tore up the letter into tiny pieces
and sprinkled them into the garbage.

It sounded like she was trying too hard to convince Kelly,
which would make Kelly suspicious.
Even though it's all true.

Jennifer is Chuck's first secondary.
He's never had a patient specifically assigned to him before.
Nurses have to work on the EDU a while
before they get specific patient assignments.
If they do well as a secondary,
they can get promoted to being someone's primary.

Chuck seems proud to be a secondary,
which makes Jennifer feel good.
It's not a one-way transaction. She's helping Chuck.
Maybe if she does well, so will he.

Not that Ratched would believe Jennifer wants to do well.
Ratched, Jennifer's primary. What a joke.
As if she could ever be Jennifer's confidante or advocate.
But Ratched's got today off,
and maybe she'll fall off a bridge while she's gone,
so Jennifer never has to see her again.

Thank merciful heaven Chuck is better than Ratched.
Thank merciful heaven Ratched has other primaries
to divert her attention.
Not Chuck. Sure, he has to keep an eye on things,
but he has one, and only one, specifically assigned patient.
He is Jennifer's own private friend. Uncle. Nurse.

She has been crying all morning.
Of course she has been crying all morning.
Everyone else is out with their families.

"Feeling sorry for yourself isn't going to help," Chuck says,
but there is empathy in his voice.
He opens drawers in the cabinet behind him,
digging out construction paper and markers.
"Here," he says.

She wipes her eyes and nose with her sleeve,
shifts her slippered feet.
"What's this for?" she asks.

"Make a card or something. It's Thanksgiving.
List the things you're thankful for."

Jennifer considers rolling her eyes,
but it would take more energy
than she can muster.

"All right, I'll start," Chuck says. He uncaps a marker
and spreads his left hand over a sheet of blue paper.
He traces around his thumb, up and over his index finger,
roller-coastering up and down fingers
until he gets to the outside of his pinkie,
back to his wrist.

"What are you doing?" Jennifer asks, as if she doesn't know.

"Duh. I'm making a turkey."

"Duh. I'm not in kindergarten," she says.

"Come on. It'll make you feel good."
He says this in a singsong voice,

like they're in an ABC Afterschool Special
about peer pressure.
He slides the construction paper and markers toward her.

"Fine," Jennifer sighs. She selects a pink piece of paper.
She refuses to trace her hand.
Instead she draws a cartoon turkey.
And then adds platform shoes for its turkey feet.
"Do we have glitter? And glue?" she asks.

"Do bears poop in the woods?" Chuck asks.
He digs in the cabinet, then
hands Jennifer a bottle of Elmer's glue
and three small plastic pots of glitter.

She squishes glue into a circle, shakes glitter onto it.

"Whaaat it is?" asks Chuck.

"Duh. It's a disco ball." She smiles.

"You're grateful for disco?" Chuck asks.
"That's going to be a problem for me."

"No, not disco specifically," Jennifer says.
"I'm grateful for dancing.
School dances, dance classes.
At home there's a dance every Friday night at the Y."

"You set your calendar around that?" he asks.

"I do," Jennifer says.

159

"You feel good when you're dancing?" Chuck asks.
It's starting to sound like a counseling session,
but Chuck is still working on his turkey,
keeping his focus on his construction paper,
which helps it seem more conversational, less therapeutic.

"I think dancing is the only time I feel good," Jennifer says.
"Except when I'm drunk."

Her turkey is done, but she doesn't feel any better.
"Is my after-lunch hour up?" she asks.

He looks at the clock. "Yup."

"I want to go to my room, okay?"

"Sure. Allow me to escort you."

She curls onto her bed.
Chuck doesn't leave; he sits in the chair by Heather's dresser.
"Who is that?" He lifts his chin to indicate her teddy bear.

"Bearibubs."

"He looks like he's seen a fair amount of combat time."

She hugs her bear. "Don't you dare insult him."

"Take a chill pill. I would never insult
a patient's stuffed animal.
That's PNA lesson number one."

"PNA?"

"Psychiatric Nursing Assistant."

"Oh," Jennifer says. "Do you like your job?"

"I sure do." He stands and wanders around her room.
"Why do you have all this stuff?" he asks.

Her eyes are closed. They're sore from crying.
"What stuff."

"All these books.
None of the other patients have so many books."

"Maybe none of the other patients read enough.
Knowledge is power," Jennifer says.

He chuckles. "Aha. Yes."
She opens one eye.
He's looking at her plastic case full of cassettes.
"May I?" he asks.

"Can I stop you?"

"Probably not."
He takes the cassette bin to Heather's bed,
then takes the first tape out.
"Prince, *Sign of the Times*."
He sets it on Heather's nightstand.
"U2, *The Joshua Tree*."
He stacks it on top of Prince.
"Let's see…" He picks out some others.
"Sting, *Nothing Like the Sun*.

161

James Taylor, *Never Die Young*.
James Taylor, *Greatest Hits*.
Points deducted
for a greatest hits album, but still. JT is classic."
He stacks James Taylor and Sting on top of U2 and Prince.
"Paul Simon, *Graceland*, yes.
The Traveling Wilburys, good.
Eurythmics, okay.
Talking Heads, good.
These"—he runs his finger down the stack he's made—
"these are acceptable."

"Thank you for your validation," Jennifer says.
Her voice drips with sarcasm.
But she is deeply pleased he approves.

"You're welcome," Chuck says.
"But these?" He holds up a tape.
"The Smiths? No, too depressing, kid. Not good for you."
He starts a new pile.
"And The Violent Femmes?
Probably not the best choice, either."

Jennifer says, "You sound like my brother."

"Your brother must be a smart man. Let's see."
He pulls another tape out of the box.
"The Cure. That's not *too* bad." He adds it to the first stack.
"Crowded House, eh." He adds it to the disapproval pile.

"What are you doing?" Jennifer says. "That tape's
not depressing."

"No, it's just not good." Chuck smiles.

"You're judging my musical taste?"

"Of course," he says mildly.
"Oh, I see you have INXS, too. Going Australian, are we?
Hm. Terence Trent D'Arby?"
He sets it on top of Crowded House and INXS.

"Wait!" Jennifer says. "That's a great album.
So good for dancing."

"Dancing, maybe. Listening, I don't think so.
I have to say, this second stack, these are worrisome."

"I'm not supposed to care what you think," Jennifer says.
"I do not seek outside approval.
I'm supposed to work on my self-esteem."

Chuck laughs. "True. You're learning quickly.
Wait. Oh my God, is this Enya?"
With his fingertips, like the tape case is contaminated,
he holds it up. "You know what? This is not okay."
He sets it far apart from the first two piles.

"What! It's soothing."
Jennifer's face cracks into a happy, unforced smile,
which she quickly changes into a dramatic fake pout.
"I'm feeling very judged right now."

Chuck says, "That's because you *are* being judged.
Oh dear bearded Lord in heaven.
Tell me my eyes are playing tricks on me."

Jennifer says, "Oh, come on! That's on the *Billboard* charts.
He's a good singer."

"No," Chuck says. "No, I wouldn't be a good secondary
if I didn't confront you about this.
I think we need to call a meeting. An intervention.
At the very least, I'm going to have to
confiscate this to your basket.
You should have to sign this out.
I'm making it a treatment-planning goal:
Patient will listen to good music.
And that most definitely does not include Rick Astley."

It's nice to laugh, Jennifer thinks,
before she starts crying again.

Friday, November 25, 1988

Jennifer finishes tying her shoes.
It feels like a momentous occasion.
Like there should be a trumpet fanfare.
At 11:10 a.m., Jennifer Johnson laced up her sneakers
instead of wearing slippers all day.

Not that she can leave the unit.
She's not medically cleared.
Still, changing slippers for real shoes
seems like a metaphor for the fact that she's powering on.
A decision that she will continue to *live* while she's here.
That the EDU is not an alternate reality
or a parallel dimension.
This is actually her life right now.
And she's going to be here a while.
A fact that still flips her stomach and makes her chest ache.

She can't stand the idea of staying here.
Every hour, she wants to run away.
Except she can't. The doors are locked.
She's confined to the unit:
her bedroom, with hostile roommate,
or the lounge, toxic with cigarette smoke and sick patients.
Jennifer wants to scream.

But screaming
would provide a wonderful chance for Ratched—
or any other nurse, really—to write her up,
and ruin her already slim chance for passes next weekend.

Telling staff you want to get out of here
because you're not crazy
would only guarantee they'd keep you here longer,
because it would make them think you're crazy.
Isn't that the definition of a Catch-22?

There is a knock at her half-open door.
Eleanor stands in the doorway,
pulling her fingers through her long, dark hair.
"Can I come in?" she asks.

Jennifer hesitates a moment before she says, "Sure."
Monica and Bronwyn are still upset with Eleanor
because of her accusation in group,
the thing about avoidant behavior.
Jennifer doesn't want them to think she's a traitor.
But Eleanor's done nothing bad to Jennifer.
Actually, Jennifer doesn't see her that much;
Eleanor is on stage three,
so she eats breakfast and lunch downstairs
in the main dining room,
and she's out on passes a lot.

Eleanor stands near the foot of Heather's bed.
"Where's your roommate?" she asks.

"In individual, I think," Jennifer says.

"I feel sorry for you, having to live with her.
She's so…diseased." Eleanor looks around.
"And messy."

"You should see our bathroom after she uses it."

"No thank you. Anyway. I just wanted to say
that I found out my discharge date. It's next Friday."

"Congratulations," Jennifer says,
swallowing the lump in her throat.

"Oh, thanks," Eleanor says.
"But that's not why I'm telling you."

"Okay," Jennifer says.

Eleanor looks exasperated.
"Jennifer, I wanted to tell you because
I've heard other girls saying
you'll have to be here three or four or five months, like them.
But you don't. You don't have to be like them.
I'll be in and out of here in less than two months.
That's why I'm telling you."

Jennifer nods. It is, indeed, hopeful information.

"Fifty-one days, Jennifer. That'll be it for me.
And I can see you're really homesick, so I just wanted
to give you hope. If you work the program,
you can get out of here fast. Like me."

Jennifer asks, "Did you have to gain weight, though?"

Eleanor frowns. "No, I didn't. And you probably do,
so that might mean you'll be here a little longer than me."

Jennifer's stomach sinks with disappointment,
but of course she's perversely proud
that Eleanor thinks she needs to gain weight.

"People like you and me, who
work the program from day one,
we get out of here quicker than these other trifling losers."
Eleanor waggles her thumb toward the hall.

Jennifer is confused. "You think I'm working the program?
But Nurse Ratched accused me of—"

"That lady is one sick puppy,"
Eleanor says matter-of-factly.
"Everyone knows it." She seems to reconsider.
"Well, not everyone yet, but it's just a matter of time."
Eleanor comes closer, lowering her voice.
"Look. I know you didn't tank.
And I know you didn't shove quarters up your coochie.
I can tell by how you eat your meals, and
how you talk to people.
And I'll tell you something else."
Eleanor plops down next to Jennifer on her bed.
"I wanted to come here, just like you."

"You did? Really?" Jennifer's heart gives a little lurch.
because this would mean she's not the only one.

Everyone else says they were dragged here,
kicking and screaming, like in the specials.
Fighting treatment is a point of pride for every patient,
including Monica, Bronwyn, and Amanda.
"You wanted treatment?" Jennifer asks,
almost unbelieving.

"Sure did," Eleanor said. "After my esophagus went kaput,
I told myself I would do anything to get better."

"Your esophagus?" Jennifer's eyes go wide.

Eleanor nods, fingers in her hair, inspecting it for split ends.

"Did it rupture?" Jennifer asks. "Like in *Kate's Secret?*"

"Yeah," Eleanor says.

"Oh," Jennifer says. "So...did blood come out of your chest?"

"Use your brain.
Do you think if your esophagus ruptures,
the blood magically passes through your ribs and skin
and comes pouring out your chest?"

"That did seem weird." Jennifer feels dumb.

"They just did that to look dramatic on TV," Eleanor says.

"Right." Jennifer nods, like she knew this.
"Right. Well, um. What happened with you?"

Eleanor shrugs. "I started seeing blood when I purged,
and it hurt really bad. I mean, purging never feels good,
but this hurt really, really bad."

"Whoa," Jennifer says.

Eleanor sighs. "I had to have surgery. And a transfusion,
because I lost a lot of blood. Which of course
made my parents worry because of Ryan White."

Jennifer recognizes the name, but can't quite place it.

Eleanor studies Jennifer's face. "Elton John's friend?
The kid who got AIDS from a blood transfusion?"

"Oh, yeah," Jennifer says. "He was on the cover of *People*."
Then she stiffens, terrified. Does Eleanor have AIDS?
They say you can't get it from touching someone,
or from sitting on public toilet seats,
but what if they're wrong? What if—

"I don't have AIDS," Eleanor snaps,
"if that's what you're worried about."

"I wasn't," Jennifer says.
Uncomfortable silence.

Jennifer takes a deep breath, blows it out.
"So…wow. Your esophagus. Oh, wait, is that why
you have to take that medicine?"
The nurses make a big deal out of it at dinner and snack.

"Yeah. It's an acid blocker. The doctors say I have to take it
every time I eat, probably for the rest of my life.
And if I start purging again,
it would be really bad. I could bleed out, or something.
Internal bleeding," she clarifies.
"Not *Kate's Secret* chest bleeding."

A surge of pity rushes through Jennifer, but, as usual,
there is also a more sordid feeling at the core.
She's envious.
Jennifer is jealous that Eleanor
had an emergency room drama.
"That's horrible," Jennifer makes herself say.

Eleanor pushes her hair off her shoulders.
"No one to blame but myself.
I just really didn't think I'd done that much damage."

"It must have been pretty scary," Jennifer says.

"It made me want to stop purging, that's for sure.
I came here straight from the hospital.
The medical hospital."

"How much did you purge?" Jennifer asks.
"Like, how often?"

Eleanor shrugs, "Couple times a day.
No more than other people here.
But listen, Jennifer. I want to tell you something else.
I want to tell you not to get caught up in
these other girls' dramas.

Call them on their crap if you need to,
like I did the other day,
but really, work the program for yourself.
You are here for your own recovery, not theirs.
You know what I mean?"

"I think so."
But Jennifer can't imagine confronting other patients,
not if it meant they would be angry with her.
The only people she lets herself be confrontational with
are Mom and Dad and Rich, because they are her family,
so they are obligated to love her.
Every other relationship is too tenuous.
People can drop right out of your life if you're not careful.

"All right. Cool," Eleanor says. "Hug."
She opens her arms.
Jennifer leans in.
She tells herself not to worry about AIDS.

Eleanor is strong.
Her hug is strong, her arms are strong,
her words are strong, and her voice is strong.
There is no ambivalence about her.
Did Eleanor have a monster inside?
Did it rupture along with her esophagus?
Is that how she killed it?

♥ ♥ ♥

After lunch, Jennifer has an individual session.
Dr. Prakash sits in her big leather chair
and takes off her high heels.

They tip over without feet in them.
She lights a cigarette
and crosses her legs at the knees,
wrapping one calf around the other
like a snake twining itself up a tree.

Instead of the expected questions about
the dramas with Ratched,
Dr. Prakash says, "Jennifer. I would like you
to tell me about your drinking behavior."

Jennifer blinks, struggling to readjust.
"My drinking behavior?"

Dr. Prakash inhales smoke, nods. "Yes.
Your screening and admission interviews indicate that
you consume alcohol on a regular basis. Is this correct?"

Jennifer frowns. "Not totally regularly."

"Tell me, then," Dr. Prakash says.
"How often do you drink?"

"Most weekends. At night."

"Both nights?" Dr. Prakash asks.
"Friday and Saturday nights?"

"Sometimes not on Fridays, because I go to the Y—
it's a dance at the YMCA—
and you get expelled for life if you drink.
But most Saturday nights, I go to a party and yeah, I drink.
And over the summer, I drank almost every night."

Dr. Prakash exhales smoke.
"And when you drink, you become intoxicated?"

Jennifer nods.

"Always?" Dr. Prakash asks.
"Is it safe to say that you drink to get drunk?"

"Yes," Jennifer says, incredulous at the question.
Why does anyone drink?
Why else would she consume all those calories?

"And how does intoxication feel to you?"

Jennifer pulls her shoulders to her ears again,
lets them drop, heavy.
"Sometimes bad, but mostly good.
It makes me feel...happy."

"Ah. You feel happy when you are intoxicated?"

"Yeah."

"Be honest now, Jennifer. Think. Is it a sense of happiness,
or is it a sense of looseness? Of freedom?
Loss of inhibition, if you will?"

Jennifer's gut answers for her: "Yes.
That's exactly what I feel."

"And do you feel this loose and free and uninhibited
at any other time, besides when you are drinking?"

Jennifer shakes her head slowly, as she begins
to understand. "Even dancing isn't as good.
Drinking is the only time I can just...be."

"Just be what?" Dr. Prakash asks.

"Just be myself," Jennifer whispers.
Tears drop from her eyes.
"And not worry all the time."

"Worry? What do you worry about?"

"Everything. Constantly. I worry about
what people think of me.
And whether I'm acting the way I'm supposed to.
And I worry about why I always worry.
Why can't I ever just enjoy myself?
Why can't I ever enjoy anything?
And of course I worry whether I'm thin enough."

Dr. Prakash stubs out her cigarette
and hands Jennifer tissues.
"Can you tell me more about
not being able to enjoy yourself?"

"I can't describe it," Jennifer says.

"Just do your best. Please."

"I've tried to explain it before,
but no one understands.
It just makes me feel worse."

Dr. Prakash says, "Tell me about a time
you've tried to explain it
and it made you feel worse."

Jennifer doesn't have to search her memory;
there is already an image in her mind.
"A few months ago,
I was at the tennis courts with my friend, Megan.
We were hitting balls to each other,
waiting for some boys she said were going to meet us."
Jennifer picks at her jeans.
"I'm not a very good tennis player."

"Continue, please," Dr. Prakash says.

Jennifer hadn't realized she'd stopped.
She had been back at the tennis courts.
"Sorry. Megan was laughing, and I was smiling,
you know, because she was laughing,
so I knew I was supposed to smile."

"It wasn't a genuine smile?"

Jennifer shakes her head. "It's more like, my eyes observed
Megan smiling and laughing,
and the observation traveled to my brain,
and my brain said, *Jennifer,*
your friend is smiling, so you should smile, too.
So I used my face muscles to form a smile.
Like molding clay."

Dr. Prakash nods. "You said you tried to explain it?"

"Yeah. So Megan's laughing, and she's happy
and having fun, and she said to me,
See, Jennifer? This is fun. Stop being depressed.
You should just do more things like this. Lighten up.
Like if I just went out and played tennis more,
everything would be better.
But it didn't make anything better, and it doesn't.
I told her, *If I could feel better just by playing tennis,*
don't you think I would play tennis all the time?
It's like she thought I wanted to be depressed.
That I was choosing it."

Dr. Prakash nods. "So this friend of yours, this Megan,
she knew you were experiencing depression?"

"Yeah," Jennifer says. "She knew
I had cut my wrists a few times,
and that I wanted to die."

"And what did Megan say about that?"

Jennifer shrugs. "She tried to cheer me up,
like that time. But after a while, she quit."

"She quit being friends with you?"

"No, no. She quit trying to make me feel better.
She said she couldn't do anything but wait
until one of my attempts was successful.
Suicide attempts, I mean."

Dr. Prakash raises her eyebrows. "Let me get this straight. Your friend said that the only thing she could do for you was wait until one of your suicide attempts was successful?"

"Yup," Jennifer says.

"How did that make you feel?" Dr. Prakash asks.

Jennifer says, "It didn't make me feel good, but I can understand it."

"Understand it! My goodness. I cannot understand it."

"She was tired of my depression."
Jennifer goes quiet, thinking.

Dr. Prakash waits.

"I just keep wondering if I could have explained it better.
To make people understand." Jennifer sighs.
"It's like…it's like Megan and my other friends, they think happiness is a bouquet of helium balloons.
Picture everyone in the world,
each holding a bunch of balloons on strings.
Most people's balloons are plump and bouncy,
and they float really well.
Some people's balloons might be droopy
because they're sad, or sick, or something.
So my friends think my balloons are saggy,
and they try to help. They say, *Here, have some helium.
Let's get your balloons all floaty again.*"

"Because plump balloons would indicate
that you are happy," Dr. Prakash says.

"Right," says Jennifer. "But the problem is,
I'm not holding droopy balloons.
I'm not holding any balloons at all.
I'm standing there with strings that lead to nothing.
So even if my friends gave me helium—
tanks and tanks of helium—
there's nothing to put it in.
My balloons are just completely missing."
Jennifer wipes her nose. "I don't know.
Does that make sense?"

Dr. Prakash nods, slowly. "Not only is the depressed patient
sad and hopeless, she also experiences anhedonia.
Do you know what that means?"

Jennifer shakes her head.

"It comes from the Greek: *an* means not, or unable.
hedone, the root of the word hedonism, means pleasure.
Thus, anhedonia is an inability to feel pleasure.
Some patients experience anhedonia as
an inability to feel any emotion whatsoever.
So, yes, Jennifer. Not only does
your balloon metaphor make sense,
it is perhaps the best description of clinical depression
I have ever heard."

"Really?" Jennifer is pleased.
But, as usual, her pleasure is fleeting.
It floats away, like helium gas released into the air.

"May I use your description
with other patients?" Dr. Prakash asks.
"I think it would
help them understand depression in a new light."

"Sure," Jennifer says.

"Thank you," Dr. Prakash says. And then she waits,
as though she's giving Jennifer more time to think.
After a while, Dr. Prakash picks up her blue plastic lighter
and lights another cigarette. She inhales deeply.
"Tell me, Jennifer, how are you feeling right now?"

"Sad," Jennifer says. "Except, more tired and empty than sad.
Like I'm standing all alone, watching everyone else
play with their balloons."

Dr. Prakash balances her cigarette in the heavy glass ashtray
and looks through Jennifer's file.
She picks up a pen and says,
"I am writing an order for a blood panel.
We will look at whether you have a chemical imbalance
causing depression."

"A blood panel?" Jennifer asks, more curious than worried.

Dr. Prakash finishes writing. "A blood test. It might help us
zero in on a potentially helpful medication for you."

"An antidepressant, you mean?" Jennifer asks hopefully.

Dr. Prakash picks up her cigarette, takes a drag.
"Most likely an antidepressant.
Have you been on any sort of psychiatric medication before?"

"No."

"How would you feel about it?"

Jennifer hugs her arms tight around herself.
"I used to think it would be bad, like it would be cheating.
Or it would change me.
But now I don't care.
I'll try anything, if it could help."

"Yes. Maybe it would help you get your balloons back."

"That would be good."

"Indeed," Dr. Prakash says. "Jennifer,
I would like to tell you that I admire your openness.
We have covered a lot of ground today.
There are a few more questions I have for you.
Are you feeling brave enough to continue?"

Jennifer nods, hugs herself tighter.

"I would like to go back to alcohol for a moment and ask,
have you ever tried to cut back on your drinking?"

"Sure," Jennifer says. "Sometimes I think
it would be better if I didn't drink as much,
or as often. The calories, for one thing.

And sometimes I get myself into situations
that aren't so great."

"What do you mean, 'situations that are not so great'?"

"I mean, getting drunk
isn't always the best idea," Jennifer says.

"Have you ever been in danger? Or taken advantage of?"

"I don't know," Jennifer says softly. "Maybe a little."

"Can you please tell me about this?"

Jennifer takes a deep breath. "Well, there are times
I'm the only girl around—
because I have a lot of guy friends—
and the boys..." Jennifer trails off.
She figures it's pretty self-explanatory, what the boys do.

"Tell me, please," says Dr. Prakash. "The boys..."

Jennifer can't say it unless she just gets it all out in a rush:
"Once, when I was completely wasted,
boys took pictures of me.
I can't really remember.
I was pretty blacked out."

Dr. Prakash says, "If you were blacked out, as you say,
how do you know about these pictures?"

"Because I saw some of them. Polaroids.
The boys were passing them around at school,
you know, joking around about it. It looked like…
it looked like I was taking off my shirt.
You could see my tummy and my bra.
I don't know if there are other pictures,
or if I took off more clothes,
or if they did anything else."
Jennifer is crying again. "I do remember that
at some point, I was on a bed
and a boy was on top of me, kissing me.
But I don't think anything else happened."

"I see," Dr. Prakash says.
"Jennifer, I need to ask you,
did you have any bruises the next morning?
Or soreness? Please, think carefully."

Jennifer tries to remember. "No.
I was extremely hungover,
like alcohol poisoning hungover,
barfing and shaking like crazy.
But no bruises. Just the pictures."

"And was this the only time
something like this happened to you?
The only time you have been taken advantage of?"

Taken advantage of.
It sounds really bad when she says it like that.
"Um, it's not like
anything terrible has happened," Jennifer says.

"One time I had sex when I was really drunk,
but I kind of wanted to. And another time,
I was at my friend's house, a guy friend,
and all the boys said I should take a shower
to sober up, so I did, naked,
and they didn't let me close the shower curtain,
because they said I would be safer that way, and…
they, you know, took turns
coming into the bathroom to watch.
But they were my friends, so it wasn't that bad."

Dr. Prakash closes her eyes for a long time,
like she is angry, or annoyed, and trying to calm down.
She opens her eyes. "Jennifer,
have you ever heard the expression
'With friends like this, who needs enemies?'?"

Jennifer says, "I think so, but it's not—"

"Do you have any friends who look out for you?
Who protect you from being taken advantage of?"

"Kelly, probably," Jennifer says. "But she doesn't really drink,
so she doesn't always go to the same parties."

"I see. This is something that we will come back to."
She writes in Jennifer's file.
"I would like to continue my questions,
if that is okay with you."

"Okay," Jennifer says, even though she's surprised
to be talking so much about alcohol.
She's here for an eating disorder, not a drinking disorder.

Dr. Prakash says, "Have you ever felt annoyed
by someone telling you that you drink too much?"

Jennifer nods. "Kelly says I put myself in bad situations."

"This Kelly sounds like she is a good friend."

"She is. But it still annoyed me."

"Very well." Dr. Prakash makes another note.
"Have you ever felt guilty about drinking alcohol?"

"Well, yeah. Every time I drink.
Because I'm lying to my parents when I come home drunk,
and they don't know I've been drinking,
except for that one time when I barfed all over everything.
But I've been drunk in front of them tons.
And yeah, that makes me feel guilty.
Because they trust me."

"I see," Dr. Prakash says.
"And have you ever had an eye-opener?"

"An eye-opener?"

"Have you ever needed or wanted to
drink alcohol first thing in the morning?"

"Gross," Jennifer makes a face. "No way.
Why would I do that?"

Dr. Prakash shrugs. "Some alcoholics do this
to stave off withdrawal symptoms."

185

Friday, November 25, 1988

"I'm not an alcoholic."

Dr. Prakash raises her eyebrows.
She doesn't say anything.

"I don't…I'm not…," Jennifer says.
"I don't drink every day."

Dr. Prakash says, "Jennifer. These questions
I have been asking.
They are known as the CAGE Questionnaire.
They are a screening tool for alcoholism."

Jennifer shakes her head. "Alcoholism?
I mean…no. What are you talking about?"

"Do you feel tricked?" Dr. Prakash asks.
"I am sorry if you do.
But I could not very well tell you ahead of time
what I was asking, could I?
And so I am telling you now.
I would always like to be honest with you, Jennifer."

"I don't…" Jennifer's fingers are tingly.
Her heart is flickering. "I don't understand."

"CAGE is an acronym.
It stands for Cut back, Annoyed, Guilty, and Eye-opener.
It is a very simple but surprisingly effective screening tool.
Anyone who answers yes to two or more of the questions
has a 90 percent chance of being a problem drinker.
An alcoholic, Jennifer.

The last question, about an eye-opener,
is especially important
because it indicates withdrawal."

"But I said no to that one."

Dr. Prakash nods. "And you said yes to the other three."

Jennifer can't think of anything to say.

"We must deal with the fact that
you drink excessively, Jennifer.
You abuse alcohol. You are an alcoholic."

Jennifer swallows. She picks at a loose thread
on her sweatshirt wrist,
pulls both sleeves over her hands.

"Tell me, Jennifer. How does that make you feel?"

"Not good," Jennifer whispers.

"Not good, yes. What else."

"Scared." Jennifer grabs a tissue.
"Embarrassed. Like slime."

"Like slime? Why is this?"

"It's shameful. Alcoholics are bums.
My grandfather was an alcoholic
and my dad was terrified of him."

"Having a problem is not shameful if
you get help for it," Dr. Prakash says.
"Do you agree with my assessment?
That you are an alcoholic?"

Jennifer takes a deep breath. Slowly she nods.
"I guess. I'm not a homeless wino, but…
It's probably a problem."
Jennifer's chapped lips puff at the *p* sounds:
Probably. Problem.

"I think you will need to begin
attending Chemical Dependency group."
Dr. Prakash says. "It meets on the Adolescent Unit."

"The Adolescent Unit?" Jennifer squeaks.
Everyone says the kids on Adolescent are
scary goths and major drug addicts.
Adolescent is even more like a prison than the EDU.
It has insanely strict rules: no phone, no TV, no talking.

Dr. Prakash is nodding, writing in the file.
"And you will need to tell your family."

"Um. Can't you tell them?"

"No, Jennifer. It must be you who tells them.
But I want you to wait until a family therapy session."

"Oh," Jennifer says. Now that it's out there,
Jennifer doesn't think she can wait.
She needs to get it over with.
"When will that be?" she asks.

Dr. Prakash glances at a calendar.
"Next weekend, most likely.
Perhaps your parents can take you out on a pass afterwards."

Oh, sure. Great.
Confess to your parents that you're an alcoholic
and then just smile and go to the movies
like a normal, happy family.
But...wait. Dr. Prakash thinks she can have a pass?
"A pass? But I'm not medically cleared.
I'm not on stage two."

Dr. Prakash smiles. "I have noticed
you like to point out ways in which you do not feel
qualified for things. Do you notice that?"

Jennifer shakes her head. She hadn't noticed.

Dr. Prakash leans forward.
"Jennifer, you do not have to be medically cleared
to reach stage two.
I recommend that you request
a two-hour pass at treatment planning.
Or better yet, two two-hour passes,
one for Saturday, one for Sunday.
Fresh air would do you good.
If your parents can manage a visit."

"Really?" Jennifer says, a wide grin on her face.
"Does that mean I'm in stage two now?"

Dr. Prakash leans back in her chair,
crosses her arms over her chest.
"Jennifer, our stages are a continuum.
They are a journey you move through, if you will."

"Okay," Jennifer says. "But I'm moving
into the stage two journey?"

Dr. Prakash sighs. "Is it so important for you to have a label?
Must it be black-and-white?
Can there be no ambiguity?"

"I'm sorry.
It would just help me to know. I'm trying so hard.
I just want to know I'm making progress.
Ratch—Sheryl—told me not to bother requesting privileges."

"Jennifer, Jennifer," Dr. Prakash says.
"If it is this important, then I will tell you.
Yes. You are doing well.
You are in stage two."

Samuel Tuke Center
Eating Disorders Unit

Rules and Therapeutic Expectations
Treatment Planning

Treatment-planning meetings occur once a week for each patient (Monday, Wednesday, or Friday).

A patient's treatment-planning team shall consist of nursing staff (including patient's primary and/or secondary nurse), director of EDU, patient's psychiatrist, a nutrition team member, and relevant social workers/therapists (if applicable).

Each patient shall be made aware of his/her treatment-planning schedule within the first week of admission.

Patients must request passes or privileges IN WRITING TO THEIR PRIMARY OR SECONDARY NURSE, BEFORE 8:00 A.M. on the morning of their assigned treatment-planning day. It is the patient's responsibility to submit requests on time. Late requests for privileges will not be accepted for any reason.

Each patient shall be assigned a primary and a secondary nurse, who will inform the patient of treatment-planning goals, as determined by the treatment-planning team.

All rules are subject to change without notice by staff.

— Stage Two —

Saturday, November 26, 1988

Bronwyn's family brought a stack of magazines when they came for family therapy. I flipped through the November issue of *Seventeen*, which featured metallic party dresses with huge shoulder pads and drop-waist pouf skirts. One of those truly terrible Taylor Dayne videos came on MTV.

"You know how there are oldies stations on the radio?" I asked Bronwyn. "Music our parents grew up with? And how there are retro fashions, like cat-eye glasses and circle skirts—"

"And saddle shoes!" Bronwyn said. "Oh, man. I totally wish my mom kept her saddle shoes. I would wear them all the time."

"Me, too. But this?" I pointed to Taylor Dayne. "And this?" I held up the magazine. "I never want to see this current stuff ever again."

"For sure."

"Can you imagine a future where our kids wanted to dress up retro eighties? And radio stations played eighties music as oldies?"

"I can't imagine having kids," Bronwyn said.

"Okay, but if you did."

"Hm. Would our hypothetical kids think the eighties were cool?" Bronwyn tapped her finger on her chin. "Some of the music, maybe. Some of the movies. But none of the fashion."

"And none of the hair metal."

Taylor Dayne ended, and another video started: "Wishing Well," by Terence Trent D'Arby.

"This is a good song," Bronwyn said. "This should endure."

"I love this song!" I ran over and turned up the volume.

We sang along and copied Terence's moves, doing the choreography.

We giggled and sang and danced. For the first time since admission, I almost forgot where I was.

And then Ratched walked in. "Girls! Stop that this instant!"

We froze, mid–moon man stomp. Terence continued singing.

"You are exercising!" Ratched screeched.

"We're just singing along," Bronwyn said.

"You are engaged in unapproved physical activity!"

"But we're not trying to lose weight," I said. Surely one minute of dancing to MTV didn't count as banned exercise.

"I'm going to have to write this up," she said.

No dancing? Did recovery mean no dancing?

I felt another piece of my heart break.

♥ ♥ ♥

Later, Chuck's voice was soft when he asked, "You in here, Jennifer?"

"She's crying again," Heather said.

I had my quilt over my face. It was humiliating how much I cried. Monica said I'd float away. I was probably dehydrated from all the tears.

Chuck sat on my bed. "It's all right to cry…" He started singing the song from *Free to Be You and Me*. It made me cry harder.

193

"I'm leaving," Heather said. I heard her go.

"Come out for a second," Chuck said, tugging my quilt a little. "I want to show you something."

"No."

"Come on, just over to the window."

"Are you going to keep bugging me until I do?"

"Yes. Why yes, I am."

"Grr. Fine." I slunk out of my bed and joined him by the window.

He drew the curtains aside. Mobil mart, four-lane street with dribbles of traffic, a few pedestrians hurrying past old buildings that were in various states of decline. A dusting of snow on the ground.

"You see those people out there?"

I nodded.

"Well, I'm going to tell you a not-so-secret secret. Ready?"

I shrugged.

"The secret is: people are the same everywhere."

I waited for him to say more. He didn't.

"And?" I asked.

"And…everyone's got problems."

"This is a guilt trip. I knew it."

"No, no, not at all. Look at that dude right there." He pointed, tapping a thick finger on the metal mesh that "kept us safe" from our windows. "Homeboy's got problems. I'm going to say…his rent is due and he doesn't have the money. Now you try."

"Try?"

"Tell me what his problems are."

"How would I know?"

"Use your imagination."

"Chuck."

194

"Just humor me."

I sighed. I looked at the man outside. "All right. Maybe his dog died."

"Excellent. Dead dog. Heart wrenching."

The man waited for a car to pass and then trotted across the street.

Chuck said, "And the dog was a gift from his wife. Who is dying of cancer."

"Consumption would be better."

"Ooh, consumption *is* better. You're a natural. Okay. Now. That lady over there."

I looked. "I think she stepped on gum."

"But she's wearing her best pair of shoes, and she's sad because they're ruined?"

I nodded. "Crocodile leather."

"She got them in Australia when she was an exchange student," Chuck said. "And she can never go back to get another pair, even though her one true love lives there..."

"Because she's deathly allergic to kangaroos?"

He laughed. "There. See?"

"See what."

"Don't you feel better?"

"By imagining strangers' problems?"

"By putting things in perspective."

I thought about it. "Not really."

"You're just being stubborn. Look at me."

I did. His eyes were sincere. "The point is, everyone's got problems. Problems are part of what makes you human. You will get them figured out. You'll get through this."

"Ha."

"Don't *ha* me, kid. You put yourself in here. You stood up and told your parents you needed help."

195

"How do you know that?"

"How do I know that?" He smiled. "I'm your secondary, aren't I? And let me tell you, standing up for yourself, admitting you have a problem, reaching out for help? That's not easy. That's brave."

I couldn't help but smile. "You think I'm brave?"

"Yes. Very. Don't let it go to your head."

We stood there, looking out the window together, for a long time.

Brave. I didn't let it go to my head. I let it go to my heart.

Sunday, November 27, 1988

After dinner (dry pork chop), we had an in-house Overeaters Anonymous meeting. On the EDU, Overeaters Anonymous really meant All Eating Disorders Anonymous. And you couldn't attend OA unless you had an eating disorder, so it was just patients—no staff.

We circled up, like during group, except there was no Dr. Wexler.

"Who wants to lead?" Monica asked.

No one answered.

"All right, I'll do it. Welcome to Overeaters Anonymous." Monica smiled, looking around the circle. When her gaze snagged on Eleanor, she didn't hide her frown. Obviously they hadn't smoothed things over yet.

"I'm Monica, and I'm anorexic," Monica said.

"Hello, Monica," everyone said.

Was it bizarre for Monica to introduce herself as if we hadn't all been living on the same hall? As if we hadn't all just eaten together? Yeah. But no one else batted an eyelash.

Monica picked up a laminated page, which I recognized from the bulletin board in the nurses' station. "So. The Twelve Steps and Twelve Traditions." She looked at me. "Wait, is this your first OA meeting, Jennifer?"

I nodded.

"Okay. Well, the Twelve Steps and Twelve Traditions are from AA, Alcoholics Anonymous. Basically all Twelve Step programs—OA, NA, AA—are the same. OA and NA just say *food* or *drugs* instead of *alcohol*. OA says 'Admitted we were powerless over *food*,' like that. Anyway, I'll read the Twelve Steps and Twelve Traditions."

"You don't have to," I said. "I can look at them later."

"No, meetings always begin this way," Monica said.

She started reading. The longer it went on, the faster she went, like she was afraid people were getting bored.

When she was done, Monica looked at me again. "Also, it doesn't say this, but the rules for OA meetings are that we all go around and share, and you get one turn to share, and there's no cross talk."

Eleanor interjected, "Cross talk means you can't directly respond to something someone says."

"Like Eleanor just did," Monica said pointedly.

"Okay," I singsonged, trying to diffuse the tension between them. "Got it."

"Who wants to go first?" Monica said. She looked around.

"I guess I will," said Bronwyn. She sighed heavily. "Hi, I'm Bronwyn and I'm bulimarexic."

"Hi, Bronwyn," everyone said. Again, like we weren't all living together. So weird.

Bronwyn said, "My weekend was total crap. My parents and little sister came yesterday for family therapy, and it was such a shit show that they left right after, even though they were supposed to take me out on pass. And I had no say over the matter, and that just pisses me off."

I knew she'd had family therapy, but I didn't know it had gone so terribly. We had hung out all yesterday afternoon. Why hadn't she told me?

"And during my family therapy session, the social worker said I should start going to Chemical Dependency on

Adolescent," Bronwyn said. She was clearly angry about this, but I became secretly jubilant—it meant I wouldn't have to face the Adolescent Unit alone!

Bronwyn continued, "It's utter bullshit. I'm sure Ratched will just love the idea. She's being such a bitch lately, don't you guys think?"

Everyone nodded, but no one spoke. I guessed that would be cross talk.

"I hate this place. I'm thinking about writing my 72-hour letter and getting the hell out of here. That's all," Bronwyn said.

Whoa. Her 72-hour letter? Was she serious? It was the first time I'd heard someone talk about signing themselves out. It was unsettling. It suddenly shook the foundations of the program—trusting staff's opinions, working the program through its stages. It negated all of that.

"Thank you, Bronwyn," Monica said, like Dr. Wexler in group. Except, even though I'd only had three group sessions with Dr. Wexler, I knew he would have pushed back. He would have asked Bronwyn something like, *What are the feelings behind your anger?* Or, *What do you think signing out would do for your chances of recovery?* Or maybe ask her more about what happened with her family. But Monica wasn't Dr. Wexler. Actually, she seemed to look perkier and increasingly interested the more Bronwyn talked about being angry and miserable.

We continued around the circle. Heather and Thriller passed on their turns, but everyone else spoke. Even though we all admitted our diseases when we introduced ourselves— anorexic, bulimarexic, bulimic, or compulsive overeater—it became clear that this OA meeting wasn't really about over-eating or undereating, or food issues at all. It was a place to rag on staff and complain about the program.

When it was her turn, Eleanor said, "I'm Eleanor and I'm bulimic. And excuse the cross talk, but I think you all are letting your sicknesses be in charge. This is a whole bunch of 'stinking thinking'." She made air quotations. "You all need to just quit your bitchin' and work this program."

People rolled their eyes and looked irritated. But I was glad she said it. Because the longer the meeting went on, the more weird and unsafe and…sick it felt.

I was last. "I'm Jennifer and I'm bulimarexic."

It was strange to put it out there, just like that.

"Hello, Jennifer."

"I've been feeling like…I don't know if I can do this. Chuck says I can, and I want to work this program, I want recovery. But I just feel so overwhelmed and hopeless. I miss my family." A wave of homesickness hit me, and I started crying.

Bronwyn handed me tissues.

When she saw that I was finished sharing, Monica said, "Okay, so that's it."

Everyone stood and held hands with their neighbors.

"God…," Monica began.

Immediately, before Monica had even finished saying the word, everyone joined in: "God, grant me the serenity to accept the things I cannot change, the courage to change the things I can, and the wisdom to know the difference."

After the prayer, I let go of Amanda and Monica's hands, but they held on, squeezing harder. Everyone said, "Keep coming back. It works. If you work it," pumping their hands up and down to the words. Only then was it over.

I went straight to the pay phone. I couldn't wait to hear Mom's voice: normalcy, softness, comfort. As I punched in the long series of numbers—phone number, calling card number, PIN code—I thought about the meeting. In some ways, my first Twelve Step meeting had been reassuring, because I wasn't alone in my frustrations and misery.

But in other ways, it dragged me down.

It was as if we were all in the ocean because our boat sank, and every one of us was struggling not to drown. And while we were ostensibly trying to help each other, we were actually just pulling each other under.

♥ ♥ ♥

Time for lights-out. But instead of being in bed, Heather was huffing around our room, shoving dresser drawers, letting out heavy sighs. She did this every night. Every night.

"Heather? Is everything okay?" I asked, as I had every night.

She didn't answer, as usual.

"Not to be annoying, but we're both supposed to be in bed, with the lights off," I said. "I don't want you to get in trouble again."

She rolled her eyes. "I don't care, Jennifer."

"Okay. But if you're upset about something, you can talk to me. I'm a good listener."

She looked at me, heaved another sigh, and went back to slamming drawers.

Sharing a room with an angry person had been scary at first. I basically cowered, waiting for her to yell at me. Or hit me. Was it me she was angry at? Had I done something wrong? Heather wouldn't say. She never volunteered to talk. Dr. Wexler had cajoled her into talking in group on Friday, and even with all his efforts, she only coughed up a sentence or two: *Thanksgiving sucked. My dad was mean, what else is new?*

Monica was the only one Heather ever opened up to. Monica told me not to take Heather's gruffness personally; she said Heather had a lot of "unresolved issues." As to the specifics of those issues, Monica was vague—she would only say that Heather's dad was abusive, and that Heather used fat as a shield to protect herself. That's all Monica would tell me.

But Heather's slam-moping was going from scary to irritating to tiresome. Plus, it made a mess. Her half of the room was a pigsty, with dirty clothes and wet towels and messy bed and random, crumpled rolls of wrapping paper—even though it was forever until Christmas.

Maybe I could accept all of it better if I understood more of what she was going through. Maybe I should keep trying to be a good friend?

But Heather had never given me anything other than snorts of derision when I tried to be nice. Not once. Plus, she never reached out to me, any of the infinite number of times I cried underneath my blankets.

I was so tired. I just wanted to go to sleep.

How much more energy should I spend trying to relate to a person who obviously didn't want to be friends?

Wasn't the whole point of this place to open up and share your feelings? Without forcing people to drag it out of you?

Monday, November 28, 1988

"Could you please tell me about your family life?" Dr. Prakash asked in individual.

"Oh, my family is fine. That's not an issue."

She lit a cigarette. "Not an issue?"

"It's me that's the problem, not them. My parents love each other. They support me and my brother."

"So you are all happy and healthy? It does not seem like you have been happy and healthy."

"Well, exactly. I'm the one who hasn't been happy. Or healthy."

"Jennifer, a family is an ecosystem. Girls who contract eating disorders usually have a good reason for doing so."

"I guess..."

"Let us be more specific. How would you describe your relationship with your mother?" She pronounced it *muttah*, but I was getting more accustomed to her accent.

"We're really close. We get along great."

"Mm. And your father?"

"It's okay. We like to read and watch movies together. We argue sometimes. He can be hard to live with."

"How so?"

"He seems angry a lot. And he's totally socially awkward. My mom and I have a good time making fun of him."

"You make fun of your father together?"

I shrugged. "We both live with him, so we both know what a true dork he is."

"Is it fair to say your mother makes negative comments about your father in front of you?"

"Yeah, but we're just joking around."

"Often we say we are joking, but we are really being quite serious. Is that a possibility, Jennifer? Is it possible that this 'joking around' is something more serious?"

"I suppose it's possible."

"That doesn't sound like something a happy family does."

"But he deserves it. My dad is a total nerd."

"What is so terrible about being a nerd?"

"Ha. You're obviously not in high school."

She smiled. "No, I am not in high school. But neither is your father."

"No."

"Again, what is so terrible about being a nerd? Nerds, as you call them, tend to get called such because they work or study hard. They are often bright, successful people. Why would your mother pick on him for being smart and successful?"

"Sometimes he's mean to her."

"Mean? To your mother?"

I nodded; the tears came.

"Tell me. In what way is he mean to your mother?"

"He yells at her. Like, really loud and…cruel."

"What does he yell at her about, Jennifer?"

"Anything. How dinner is made, or how she handled something with me and Rich." I wiped my eyes. "It's like he's always angry on the inside. It's always there, and anything can set it off."

"That sounds very different than being a nerd. This anger, it is simmering? But unpredictable?"

"That's the perfect way to describe it."

"And tell me, Jennifer. Does your father drink alcohol?"

"Never. His dad was a really bad alcoholic, remember? He died from alcoholism. His sister, too."

"When you say they 'died from alcoholism,' what does that mean? Were they in a car accident?"

"No. They didn't die at the same time. It was something about their livers. Sertosis or—"

"Cirrhosis? Of the liver?"

"Yes."

Dr. Prakash uncrossed and recrossed her legs. When she shifted, her skirt moved, revealing her bare knees. Her stockings covered her feet and calves, but ended at the bottom of her kneecaps.

Knee-highs. The ultimate fashion faux pas.

Dr. Prakash opted for comfort in her hosiery yet she wore stiletto heels, which must have caused absolute foot torture.

It felt like being let in on a little secret.

Dr. Prakash was saying, "Cirrhosis in two generations would indicate a serious pattern of alcoholism. Let us return to that in a minute. For now, I would like to ask, does your father have other addictions?"

"No. Like what?"

"Other drugs? Marijuana? Cocaine? Prescription drugs?"

Dad snorting coke? "No," I said.

"Nicotine?"

"No."

"How about food?"

It hit me then. "Um. Yes. He eats too much, and he goes on crazy diets."

"Crazy diets? Can you be more specific?"

"He goes through fad diets. Like last month, he only had hot water with lemon for breakfast, because it's supposed to kick-start your metabolism. And he always makes Mom buy nonfat, sugar-free diet food."

"And does he lose weight on these diets?"

"No. He complains that they don't work. He's overweight."

"Does he talk to you about it?"

"About what?"

"Dieting?"

"Sure," I said. "We talk about it a lot. We compare notes."

She went quiet again. After a while, she said, "And?"

"And it feels like a competition. Which is totally messed up. Because he is overweight, and I'm not!"

"And he's an adult and you are not," she said. "You sound angry."

"I am!"

"What about your mother?"

"What about her?" The abrupt change of subject confused me. "What do you mean?"

"Does she show signs of addiction? Does she drink alcohol? Or use drugs? Prescriptions? Marijuana?"

Mom lighting up a big doobie? I giggled. "No way. She's too straightlaced for that."

"What about food?"

Another truth bomb. My throat got tight. Slowly I nodded. "Yeah."

"Can you say more about that? Does she diet, like your father does?"

"No."

"Does she eat compulsively, or binge?"

"I don't think so. Not that I know of."

"Jennifer, using what you have learned so far in the hospital, how would you characterize your mother's eating?"

"I...she...I think maybe she's an emotional eater."

"She uses food as medicine? To soothe herself?"

"Yes. No." I shook my head. It didn't sound quite right. "Not medicine. It's more like she uses food to stuff her feelings down. My dad can be so mean, but Mom doesn't fight back. She's always kind and loving."

"Except that she makes fun of your father," Dr. Prakash said. "Does she do that in front of him?"

"Sometimes, but mostly she does it with her friends."

"And with you."

"Yeah."

"Making fun of your father together is an indirect way that you help your mother fight back against him."

"It is? I guess. Maybe. But I'm also the only one who stands up to Dad when he's angry. Directly."

"When he yells at your mother?"

"And when he yells at Rich. Or me."

"How does he yell at you and your brother?"

"He doesn't just yell. He screams. Mostly at Rich."

"About what?"

"Usually about not putting tools away after he works on his motorcycle."

"Your father has a motorcycle?"

"No, my brother has dirt bikes. He uses Dad's tools. It makes Dad so angry. Like, furious. Rage."

"What does your brother do when your father unleashes his anger at him?"

"When we were little, Mom would tell us to go to our rooms."

"To get away from your father?"

"Yeah."

"She was trying to protect you?"

"Dad would get mad at her, but she wouldn't fight back. I would listen to them through the heating vent, and I would scream at him to leave her alone."

"And your brother? What did he do?"

"He just stayed in his room."

"You said that is what you did when you were little. What do you and your brother do now?"

"Rich is out with his friends most of the time."

"Meaning it is you and your mother at home," she said.

"Yeah."

"You are a team, against your father."

"Sort of."

"You stick up for your mother, the way you wish she would stick up for herself? It sounds almost as if you are acting as an extension of your mother."

"I guess."

"That is an example of what we talk about when we talk about enmeshment."

I shrugged.

"How does all this make you feel? What are you feeling right now?"

"Angry, I guess. Sad." *And overwhelmed by all these new insights.*

"Now, Jennifer. I know this is difficult. But I want you to think. Do you believe your father is good enough for your mother?"

My throat constricted. "No."

"You characterize your father as a nerd and as constantly angry. You characterize your mother as kind and loving, yes?"

I nodded.

"But that cannot be all they are. I wonder...I wonder if you have a habit of idealizing people."

"What do you mean? I don't idealize my dad. Obviously."

"No? When we idealize people, we place them on the head of a pin. If they are perfect—kind and loving, like your mother—there they will stay. But if they are less than perfect, they will topple off. One mistake, and down they go."

"Screaming at your family all the time is a lot different than one mistake."

"I agree." She lifted a finger, "But. If we idealize people, we also create a wide space between ideal and not ideal. I really want you to think about this, because I believe you do this to yourself, too."

"What? I definitely do not think I'm perfect!"

"When we are perfectionists, we idealize ourselves. You are making yourself stand on the head of a pin. It is a grueling balancing act. You do not allow yourself to make any false moves, any mistakes. You have no freedom. You must earn top grades, or you will fall off the pin. You must excel in extracurricular activities, or you fall off the pin. You must be liked by every single person, or you fall off the pin. You must do the socially correct thing at all times, or you fall off the pin. You must look a certain way, or you fall off the pin. You must maintain a dangerously low weight, or you fall off the pin. Jennifer, it sounds quite exhausting."

A sob shook loose from my chest. "It is. It is exhausting. I can't do it anymore."

"You do not have to do it anymore. What if I told you that you can set both your feet on solid ground and still be quite good at being you?"

"How?"

"By accepting that you are not perfect, nor should you be. You will be required to relax your standards a little bit. You will be required to give yourself a break. Do you understand what I am saying?"

"I don't know. I guess so."

"And do you think that all of this idealizing is exhausting not just for you, but for the other people in your life? Is it fair to your mother that she need always be kind and loving, or she will fall off her pin?"

I shook my head.

"Now. Think hard. Is it fair to your father that he has fallen from grace, as the saying goes?"

"He deserves his fall from grace."

"That may be, but I suspect he has many good qualities that make him worthy of another chance. He supports your family financially, does he not?"

"Yeah."

"He does not hit you or your brother, or hurt you physically?"

"No."

"He attends your school activities? Your dance recitals?"

"Yes."

"In many, many ways, he is a very loving and attentive father. He does not drink or abuse drugs, because he does not want you or your brother to be raised in a house with an alcoholic father, like he was."

"That's true."

"These are all things that speak to his integrity. Are you able to see these things? That your father is not terrible? That your mother has some faults, too?"

I made a face.

"Think, Jennifer. Think about a fault your mother has."

"I don't want to," I said. But I smiled, a small joke.

She smiled back. "Go on."

"She doesn't stick up for herself."

"Yes. What else? What about the position she puts you in, when she makes fun of your father with you?"

"I guess it's unfair?"

"Yes. How is it unfair?"

"Because it's kind of…using me? It makes me feel like she's sticking me in the middle of their marriage."

"Yes. It is inappropriate for her to complain to you about your father. If she has issues with him, what should she do?"

"She should talk to him. Not me."

She lifted her hands, palms up, like, *Yes, there you have it.* "So your mother is not perfect, either. Will you push her off her pin now?"

"I hope not. I don't want to."

"What about me, Jennifer? What will you do when I make a mistake?"

"You asked me that the other day."

"Yes, well, I am certain to make a mistake in our time together. Do you have me on the head of a pin right now? When I fall off, will we continue to be able to work together? Or will our time have been useless?"

"It's not like that. It's not all or nothing."

"Is it not? I hope you are right about that." She leaned forward. "Jennifer. You must learn that recognizing people's flaws is a fine thing to do, as long as you recognize their strengths, as well. This mix of flaws and strengths, this is what makes us who we are. We cannot live our lives on the heads of pins. It is an intolerable and untenable situation."

"I guess I'm learning that."

"I guess you are."

♥ ♥ ♥

I started 1800s at dinner. It was a smack in the face after my week of 1200s. 1800s was more food. It meant the start of gaining weight. Packing on the pounds until I reached a "healthy" maintenance range.

Staff was always saying, *Healthy recovery requires healthy bodies. You can't have a healthy mind in a sick body.*

But wasn't "healthy" just another word for "fat"?

How could I have a healthy mind if my body felt obese?

Fat is not a feeling. What's the real issue? That was another staff refrain. Meaning if you felt fat, it was because you were avoiding what was truly bothering you.

But what if my weight truly bothered me?

Fat sure felt like a feeling.

I poked a fork at my pasta. The food was gross, as usual. Spaghetti with meat sauce, wilted salad, a huge clump of cauliflower, an orange, two percent milk.

Bronwyn wrinkled her nose. "This spaghetti is so overcooked."

"Do you know how Italians test whether pasta's cooked right?" Monica picked up a noodle that wasn't covered with sauce, twirled it over her head like a lasso, and threw it at the wall. It hit and fell to the floor. "See?" she said. "It should stick. If it falls, it's overcooked."

"I'll show you what will stick." Bronwyn picked up her straw wrapper, rolled it, wet it with spit, and stuck it in her straw. Then she squeezed one eye shut and took aim. The wad shot out and stuck to the wall behind Monica.

"Dude! You almost shot me!"

"Ladies," I said. "It's all fun and games until someone loses an eye."

We laughed, until Bronwyn stopped and blinked, and we fell silent. It was like we had just remembered we were in the EDU. We looked over at the nurses. Thank goodness it was Chuck and Baldy. If it had been anyone else, Bronwyn and Monica would have already been written up. Or electro-shocked, if it was Ratched.

Chuck smiled. "Knock it off with the noodles. Those, you need to eat. But if you're going to shoot spit wads, you might as well have one of these." He rummaged in the cupboards and pulled out a paper plate. With a marker, he drew concentric circles.

We had a target.

"What should we put in the bull's-eye?" Bronwyn asked.

"Ratched?" I said. "Maintenance weight? Bathroom privileges? Weigh-ins? Group? The food?" So many frustrations and challenges here—whether staff would deem them "real issues" or not—the EDU blessed us with a real cornucopia of choices.

♥ ♥ ♥

Mom and Dad and Rich came after dinner. I gave them huge, long hugs. We went to my room for a modicum of privacy. Heather was writing in her journal.

"Hi, Heather. This is my family—" I started introductions, but she picked up her stuff and left without a word.

When she was gone, Dad said, "Gosh, she seems like a peach. Did you two have a fight or something?"

"She's always like that. But thanks for assuming it's my fault."

"I didn't assume anything of the sort—"

"Why don't we all sit down and get caught up," Mom interrupted.

I sat on my bed, Bearibubs in my lap. I tried to shake off my irritation at Dad's question. I didn't want to ruin the visit by fighting.

Mom sat next to me. Rich and Dad sat in the chairs. As they got situated, I realized I'd never had my whole family in my bedroom at once. It was weird. On top of the fact that we were in an EDU.

We sat there, looking at each other, gazing around the room. That was another thing: no distractions. We weren't sitting down to a meal, or playing a board game, or watching a movie, like we would normally do if we were all together.

Plus, all these new insights were boiling inside of me—alcoholic, less-than-perfect family dynamics, problems in my parents' marriage. Dr. Prakash had told me not to talk about that stuff until family therapy, because she wanted those conversations to happen in a safe environment, guided by a professional. But keeping them inside made me feel far away from my family. Now that they knew about my eating disorder, I had thought we would all be closer. But we were still a million miles apart.

"Would you like me to bring anything from home, to spruce up your room?" Mom asked. "Are you allowed to hang posters?"

I looked at the bare walls and nodded. "That would be good. Could you bring my Georgia O'Keeffe poster? The red poppy?"

"Of course."

"Thanks."

Awkward silence.

"How's the food?" Dad asked.

"Terrible," I said.

"Institutional..." Dad frowned. "Er, that is, hospital food... is often terrible."

Awkward silence.

"Are the other patients nicer than your roommate?" Mom asked, even though she knew from our phone calls that I'd made some friends.

214

"Yeah, most of them."

"That's good," Dad said.

More silence.

"How's school?" I asked Rich.

"It's school," Rich said.

And more silence.

"Do any of your friends know I'm here?" I asked.

"I don't know." He looked annoyed, like I shouldn't care whether his friends knew. Which was true, I shouldn't. But his friends were cool seniors, so I did care. A lot.

I poked at my quilt. "Have they said anything about me?"

"You're not a main topic of conversation, Jen."

"Oh." Harsh.

And silence again.

"Is Chuck working tonight? Could we meet him?" Mom asked. She turned to Dad and Rich. "Chuck is Jenny's favorite nurse."

I jumped up. "Yes! I'll go see if he can say hi." I'd waited all week to see them, and now I was rushing out of the room.

I returned with Chuck. He made small talk.

I needed someone to make small talk with my family.

It was excruciating, and sad.

Why did being with my family feel so…unfamiliar?

Tuesday, November 29, 1988

"Monica, want to peel my orange?" I asked.

"You bet I do." Monica plucked the orange off my tray. She loved peeling oranges. I hated it. I hated how the white part got stuck under your fingernails and the sides of your fingers got a funky roughness from the peels. Monica was my designated orange peeler.

So far, the nurses let her do it. I was surprised they didn't say it was "diseased behavior" to peel someone else's orange.

I took two packets of sugar from the condiment basket, tore them open, and made a sugar pile next to my eggs. I slid a piece of yellow washcloth into the sugar. This, too, was probably "diseased behavior."

Nurse Ratched held something in front of Bronwyn. It was a packet of butter wrapped in gold foil. "You need to eat this, Bronwyn."

"No, I don't," said Bronwyn. "It wasn't on my tray."

"Doesn't matter," Ratched said. "You need to eat it."

Bronwyn shook her head. "No. I'm back down to 1800s for maintenance. I have one butter. I don't need another fat exchange."

Ratched crossed her arms. Her eyes narrowed. "Yes, you do. Eat it."

Bronwyn stared straight ahead, not looking at Ratched. "No. It's not on my food plan."

"It's not. It's not on 1800s," Amanda chimed in. She was a human encyclopedia of the EDU meal plans. "There's only one fat exchange at breakfast on 1800s."

"This does not concern you, Amanda," Ratched said. "Bronwyn, you cannot leave this table until you eat it. If you don't, it will follow you. And you will lose privileges."

Bronwyn's face turned dark reddish-brown. She closed her eyes and spoke through gritted teeth. "I know it is not on my food plan. I will eat it. But I want this reported in my case notes. Write down that I strongly object. A nurse is forcing me to eat something that is not on my food plan."

Nurse Trendy, who had been monitoring a different table, came over. "Bronwyn," she said. "Why do you have a problem with staff telling you what to eat?"

"My problem is with that specific staff"—Bronwyn pointed her fork at Ratched—"telling me what to eat."

Trendy frowned. "We're just holding you accountable."

Ratched said, "Because we care about you."

"No. That's not it," Bronwyn said. She glared at Ratched. "You and I both know exactly what this is about."

Ratched's face went white. She threw the butter onto Bronwyn's tray and walked out. Which left Trendy as the only nurse in the room. This was a big no-no. There were always supposed to be at least two, if not three, nurses at meals. Trendy had to stand in the doorway and call for Bosom, who was in the nurses' station.

I looked around the table. Everyone's eyes were wide. A nurse storming out? Unprecedented.

You and I both know exactly what this is about. What did Bronwyn mean? What just happened here?

Wednesday, November 30, 1988

Treatment-planning Objectives for Jennifer

1. Patient will begin writing personal eating disorder history.
2. Patient is medically cleared.
3. Patient will attend Chemical Dependency group on Adolescent Unit.
4. Patient request for weekend passes—*approved.*

"Do you think I'm depressed?" I asked Monica in the lounge after group. "Will I get put on medication?"

"They haven't started you on anything yet?"

I shook my head. "I get my blood test tonight."

"Hm. Let me see you." She looked deep into my eyes, as though the color of my irises or the clarity of my pupils was a depression scale. But she'd also seen me weep every day for the past eight days.

"Yes." She nodded once, decisively. "Depressed. That means drugs."

"Does medicine really help?" I asked.

"It doesn't make you feel happy all of a sudden," she said slowly. "But it kind of pushes away that feeling of total despair and hopelessness."

"That would be nice," I said.

"Yeah," she said.

"What do you take?" I asked.

"Prozac."

I had heard of Prozac. There was a big article about it in *Time* magazine. Or *Newsweek*, maybe. My parents subscribed to both. Bathroom reading.

"All the psychiatrists love it," Monica said. "They act like it's a wonder drug."

"Wow. Do you worry because it's so new?"

Monica tilted her head. "What do you mean?"

"Sorry. That came out wrong. Never mind."

"You can't ask a question like that and then say 'never mind.' Tell me what you meant."

"I just meant, do you worry that maybe there are long-term effects that no one knows about yet?"

Monica raised her eyebrows.

"Sorry," I said. "I'm sure it's fine. They wouldn't prescribe it if it wasn't safe, right?"

Monica sighed. "Jennifer, I figure even if there are bad long-term effects, they can't be worse than anorexia and suicidal depression, you know?"

"True," I said. "Those are definitely worse."

"Yup."

"Did you...try to kill yourself?" I asked Monica.

"A couple times. But mostly I just wanted my disease to do it. Death by anorexia. I wanted to waste away."

"What if there were drugs that were reverse antidepressants! Prescriptions that *caused* anorexia and depression?"

"There are."

"No way."

"Yes way. Anorectics. Heather came in on Fenfluromine,"

Monica said. "Her parents made her take it, to try to control her appetite. Did you know her dad put a padlock on their refrigerator?"

"Are you serious?"

Monica nodded. "An actual padlock."

"Is she still on the appetite drug? Fen-whatever?"

"No, the doctors here took her off it. She's on Norpramin now, I think."

"What's that?"

"It's a tricyclic. Tricyclics are the old standby of antidepressants."

Monica knew a lot about this. It was almost like looking things up in a book. "Does everyone here take something?"

"Pretty much. Amanda's on Prozac. Bronwyn takes lithium."

"Lithium? Isn't that for bipolar disorder?"

"Yeah. She's manic-depressive." Monica looked around the lounge. "Let's see. Thriller's on Elavil, that's a mood stabilizer. Eleanor takes Anafranil. That's another tricyclic."

"How did you learn all this stuff?"

"I was studying nursing. I haven't told you that?"

I shook my head.

"At community college. I had to drop out last spring."

"Do you think you'll go back? You would be a good nurse."

She gave a sad smile. "Maybe. I don't know. I have to get better first."

"You will," I said.

"I'm not so sure," she said. Then it seemed like she wanted to change the subject back to medication. "So they're giving you your DEX test tonight?"

"Yup. Tonight's the night."

Dr. Prakash had told me I'd get blood drawn after snack, and then I'd have to take a pill at bedtime, dexametha-something. The pill didn't do anything; it was just a marker to go in my blood. Tomorrow morning, they'd take another blood sample, to see what happened to the dexametha-something.

They were also going to look at other chemicals in my blood. Dr. Prakash listed a bunch of them. Some I recognized from biology class, some I didn't: cortisol, adrenaline, norepinephrine, serotoni-something.

Chemical markers, blood draws, pharmacology. So much science to try to pinpoint what was wrong with me, and how to fix it.

Or was I unfixable?

Was I doomed to bulimarexia, and sadness, and monsters, for the rest of my life?

Could a little pill really bring hope?

Thursday, December 1, 1988

My family arrived while I was still doing my thirty minutes at the breakfast table. They peeked in at me from the hallway, and a middle-aged white lady came into the lounge.

"You must be Jennifer. I'm Dianne, a social worker here," the woman said. "I'll be leading your family therapy sessions."

I guess she met my family down in the waiting area.

"You may be excused, Jennifer," Trendy said.

Slowly I pushed back my chair.

"First one's always rough. Be strong," Monica said quietly.

"Good luck," Bronwyn whispered.

Mom put her arm around me as we walked to my room. We settled into chairs, some borrowed from the lounge.

My armpits prickled with sweat. For days I'd been thinking about how to break my new insights to my family. On top of all the costs and inconvenience I was already causing, how could I tell them I was an alcoholic? How could I confront them about their marriage dynamic?

And how would they react? Would Dad get angry? Would Mom cry? What would Rich say?

Dianne looked at her notes and my file. "Again, it's nice to meet all of you. We'll meet on a regular basis, so we'll get to know each other quite well by the end of Jennifer's time here. So. Let's begin. Why don't we start with you, Jennifer?"

Despite all my anticipation, I wasn't prepared. I drew a nervous blank. "Start with what?" I asked.

"How things have been going. Anything you want to share."

"Um. Okay," I said. "Well, I guess I've realized that I have a need to be the center of attention—"

Dad snorted. Which gave me a flash of anger. And hurt.

But Dianne didn't say anything. I soldiered on.

"I know in the past I've been a pain, so I'm sorry about that." My voice sounded like it was coming from far away.

Dianne still didn't say anything. I looked at her, waiting for some support. She nodded at me to continue.

"And I know I tend to be sarcastic with Dad," I said.

Mom and Dad both started talking at once.

"Your attitude makes it awful for all of us," Mom said.

"Your sarcasm is inappropriate and destructive," Dad said.

"Sarcasm is unladylike," Mom said.

"It's unbecoming," Dad said.

"You need to learn how to be nice to people," Mom said.

"Or you won't have any friends," Dad said.

"You don't understand," I said, trying to hold back tears. "I know I'm sarcastic with you, but that's because I'm nice to everyone else all the time. I only let myself be bitchy at home. Because I'm exhausted. I let myself be that way around you guys because you're my family, and you have to love me."

Mom sighed. "Yes, Jenny, we love you. But lately we don't like you very much."

My family doesn't like me.

The dam broke. Flood of tears. "I already feel bad. You don't have to make me feel worse."

"I'm sorry, honey," Mom said. "But you've been very hard to like."

"Fine, but I'm not the only one with a problem. A family is an ecosystem."

I looked at Dianne, waiting for her to back me up and explain that the whole family was involved in this. It wasn't just me. But she still didn't speak. Why wasn't she helping?

So I went on. "I've learned that maybe you guys don't have a perfect relationship? And Mom, sometimes you drag me into stuff that should be between you and Dad. Plus, I think Dad's anger is a big dynamic in our family."

Mom and Dad looked surprised. They bristled, like ducks whose feathers had been ruffled by a strong wind. Rich didn't react. It was like he was tucked inside himself.

"Admit it," I said. "Dad's always angry. And he can be so…cruel!"

Dad's face turned red. His body went into total defensive posture—arms crossed, legs crossed, furious face.

I looked from Dad to Dianne. She still didn't speak.

It felt like we were on a boat with no oars or captain, being pulled toward a waterfall.

"I mean, you're either completely sarcastic and harsh, or you're having tantrums and making Mom cry," I said. "You explode. Everyone's always afraid of you."

Well. That did it.

"You're the reason you're here!" Dad shouted. "Not me! Not my anger!"

"Dad—"

"No!" he yelled. "*You* are what we came here to talk about! And by God, that's what we're going to talk about!"

Mom looked scared. Rich looked scared. Dianne looked scared. She said, "Er, Mr. Johnson, it does seem that you may have an issue with your anger—"

Dad turned on her. "You don't know me! You don't know anything about me!"

She looked completely flustered. Mom and Rich were both starting to cry.

I yelled back, just as loud as Dad. "Obviously your anger *is* an issue! Look at you right now! You're screaming! You're even yelling at the social worker! And look at me! I've got an eating disorder and I'm going to die if we don't deal with it."

"Don't exaggerate, and don't tell me your problems are my fault!"

"It's not your fault that you terrorize your family?"

"Shut up!" he screamed. "Just shut up!"

And then Dr. Prakash came in. She must have heard us from all the way down the hall. In a quiet voice she said, "Dr. Johnson, Mrs. Johnson." She shook their hands.

Super smart of her to call Dad "Dr. Johnson." He must have listed his Ph.D. in mathematics somewhere on my admission forms. It worked like a magic soothing balm. It immediately calmed him down.

She turned to my brother. "And you must be Richard. I am Dr. Prakash." She shook his hand. "Now. I appreciate all of you coming here today. What about if we move down to my office? It will be more comfortable."

We looked at the social worker.

"I will take it from here, Dianne," Dr. Prakash said. "Thank you very much for your time."

Dianne handed Dr. Prakash the folder and practically fled out of the room. She still hadn't said anything. What a big help she had been.

We followed Dr. Prakash down the hall. As we passed the nurses' station, Ratched and Bosom looked at us curiously. Patients peeked out the lounge door. Monica's eyebrows were knit in sympathy; Bronwyn crossed her eyes and stuck out her tongue.

Everyone had heard us.

But the walk down the hall gave us some time to cool down. Clever Dr. Prakash.

We filed into her office. Rich and Dad sat in the two chairs by the window. Dr. Prakash sat in her big leather chair. I sat on the couch, next to Mom. Even though I was mad that she hadn't spoken up to defend me, I wanted to snuggle into her for comfort after that horrible scene.

Except she'd just said she didn't like me very much. That she hadn't liked me for a while. I started crying again.

Dr. Prakash didn't waste time. "Thank you all for coming. Jennifer has something to tell you."

"I do?" I said. I was so shaken up. Which something did Dr. Prakash mean?

"Yes, Jennifer," she said, gently but firmly. "About alcohol."

Holy crap.

I took a deep breath. "I told you how I'm starting a class downstairs?" I blurted. "The reason is…it's for chemical dependency." The words were sticking in my throat. "Er. On alcohol. It seems that…I guess…they think…and I think…maybe I'm an alcoholic."

Dad broke into loud laughter. It set me off into nervous giggling, even though it wasn't funny. It was so not funny that it was hilarious.

Wait. Dad wasn't laughing. He was sobbing.

The look of anguish on his face—I'd never seen anything like it.

"Oh, my God!" Dad wailed. "Oh no! No! This is my worst fear! This is the worst fear of my life! No, please, God, no!"

"Dad, it's okay," I said. I didn't know if he could hear me, he was crying so loud.

"Oh, God. You are so much like my sister," Dad cried. "Oh my God. Oh my God! I'm sorry. I am so sorry."

"It's not your fault, Dad," I said.

I was crying. Mom was crying. Rich was crying. It was impossible to see Dad like that and not cry. It was unbearable.

I truly felt like I had destroyed my family.

"Dr. Johnson, you are very upset," Dr. Prakash said. "It is, indeed, upsetting to think of your daughter as an alcoholic. But tell me, is this news more upsetting than learning that Jennifer has an eating disorder?"

"This is worse!" Dad wailed. "This is so much worse!"

"On the contrary, Dr. Johnson," Dr. Prakash said. "Think of it this way: one can abstain from alcohol. But food is ever present. One must face one's addiction, or disease, three or four times a day."

Dad kept crying.

Dr. Prakash said, "Jennifer, I believe you have more to share on this subject?"

Jesus. I took another deep breath. I had to just get it all out, get it over with, so we didn't ever have to go through this again.

"I get drunk every weekend. I come home drunk a lot," I said.

Dad buried his head in his hands. Mom and Rich's eyes, already red and wet, went round. Owl eyes.

"You look surprised, Mrs. Johnson," Dr. Prakash said. "Had you any idea about this?"

"No," Mom shook her head. "I had no idea. Jenny mentioned alcohol in the screening interview, but..." She trailed off.

"And what about you, Richard?"

"I didn't know." It was the first thing Rich had said all morning. And it was surprising. Hadn't he heard about my public drunken hijinks? Plus, I thought we'd shared a bunch of *Hey, it's cool, I know what you're up to, but we'll cover for each other* knowing glances in the kitchen late at night. Apparently these sibling bonding moments were completely one-sided. Self-delusion.

We sat for a while. It wasn't actual silence, because everyone was sniffling and cry-hiccupping. God, I was a piece of shit. For doing this to my family. For getting sick. For lying and sneaking around. For making them drive here and sit for hours and go through all this.

Dr. Prakash said, "This may be difficult to hear. But Jennifer's alcoholism and eating disorder are likely related to a bigger issue, an organic issue. An issue of brain chemistry, if you will. The latest research suggests that people such as Jennifer utilize extreme dieting or alcohol abuse as an attempt to self-medicate, or self-modulate—albeit problematically. We would like to see if we can do better for Jennifer. With psychiatric medication.

"We have run some tests on Jennifer's blood," she continued. "We will wait until all results are back before we decide on a course of treatment. But I would like to ask your permission to prescribe Jennifer medication, when the time comes."

"Will you let us know the specifics?" Dad asked.

"Of course," Dr. Prakash said. "Now, I need to be very clear. Many psychiatric medicines react negatively to alcohol. If Jennifer were to binge drink while on medication, it could be very dangerous. Perhaps even life threatening."

Yay. An extra incentive not to drink.

Mom and Dad seemed pretty numb. They just nodded.

When the session ended, we were the walking wounded. I was depleted, exhausted. My family looked like they felt the same.

I walked them to the end of the hall.

"Um. Thanks for coming," I said. "Sorry it was so…" Brutal? Scarring? Hellish? I couldn't find the right word.

"I'll see you tomorrow," Mom said, her eyes still red from crying. "Think about what you want to do on your pass."

I nodded. My first pass. Instead of excitement, all I felt was guilt. "Sorry it's so far for you to come. All this driving you have to do."

"It's okay," Dad said. It felt like a generous thing for him to say. He looked wrecked.

"See you, Jen," Rich said.

"Thanks for coming," I said again.

What would their ride home be like?

Poor Rich, being stuck with my brutalized parents for ninety more minutes. And then getting dropped off at school and having to go to class and concentrate like nothing had happened. At least I had support. He just had to try to resume normal life.

Ha. *Normal life*. After today, and more family therapy in the future, would our family ever be able to resume normal life? Or was our version of "normal" what put me here in the first place?

Were there actual answers to any of these questions?

Or did we all just have to muddle through, broken and breaking each other, over and over again?

Friday, December 2, 1988

Eleanor left today. It was the first discharge I'd witnessed, and it brought up a messy mix of feelings: sadness, envy, hope, inspiration. Seeing someone successfully leave, having "graduated" the program, felt momentous. It was a light at the end of the tunnel. I wanted it to be me.

I hadn't become super good friends with Eleanor, but I would miss her. All of us on the EDU lived so closely together, in such extreme circumstances, that we couldn't help but be connected. More importantly, Eleanor was the only patient totally dedicated to recovery. Everyone else complained or struggled or doubted. Eleanor was a rock. She seemed to have no doubts or fears whatsoever.

We gathered after lunch to say good-bye, even though Eleanor had officially "terminated" with each of us during group. Terminations were official, required, staff-facilitated good-byes. But there were two unofficial, patient-led good-bye traditions: journal-swapping and the song circle. No one knew when these traditions started. Monica said they pre-dated her admission.

Journal-swapping meant writing in the back of each other's journals. It was like school yearbooks, except instead of *Stay the same* or *Have a great summer!* you got deep and personal, because this was about disease and recovery and struggle.

I wrote to Eleanor: *Thank you for that talk in my room. You are an inspiration. You are the strongest, most dedicated to recovery person I know. Good luck and keep in touch if you ever need support!* And I gave her my home address, to write to me when (if) I ever got out of this place.

In my journal, Eleanor wrote her address and said: *Embrace recovery! You are doing this for YOU. I know you have what it takes!*

Was she right? Did I really?

God, I hoped so.

The song circle was even better than journal-swapping. We stood in a huddle—all of the patients on the EDU—with our arms around each other, and someone put on a tape with "That's What Friends are For" and "Lean on Me." We all swayed and sang along—loud—laughing and crying and smiling and hip-bumping.

It was the best thing, my favorite thing so far. Even though it was totally cheesy, even though it meant saying good-bye to someone, even though I was still stuck here. Everyone participated, everyone sang. No one was jaded or resistant. For five minutes, we were all on the same team. We all wanted recovery. For ourselves and each other.

If only it could always feel like that.

Saturday, December 3, 1988

Mom took me out on my first pass. I was 20 percent worried she'd still be upset from our family session, but I was 80 percent dying to get out of the hospital and do something normal.

She was escorted up to the EDU after lunch. She looked tired. Was it because of Thursday's family session? I didn't ask. I didn't want to bring it up.

She came bearing gifts. One was a new poster of a long poem, "I Am Me, I Am Okay: My Declaration of Self-Esteem." It was corny but inspiring, and a thoughtful gesture. She also brought my Georgia O'Keeffe painting, poster tape, another calling card, and quarters for laundry.

We went to T.J. Maxx to hunt for bargains, because it had always been my favorite activity when we went to Syracuse.

What had I been thinking?

I stood, frozen, amid the rows in the Juniors section while Mom browsed shoes. I stared at the racks of jeans.

Dread, panic.

What jeans size would I be at maintenance?

I already felt fat. How could I gain more weight?

How could I possibly maintain it when I got out?

It was impossible. All of it, this whole thing.

A tear rolled down my cheek.

What a loser, crying in the middle of discounted jeans.

I looked over at Mom. She was sitting on a bench, staring vaguely at shoes.

I was putting my family through so much pain.

Was it worth it?

At least when I was sick, it was just me who suffered.

Now I was dragging my family down with me.

Mom must have felt my gaze. She glanced up, and came quickly over.

"Oh, honey. You look like a deer in the headlights." She hugged me, which squeezed more tears out.

"I'm sorry, Mom. I'm so sorry."

"It's all right, sweet one. It's all right."

"But I'm breaking our family."

She rubbed my back. "Oh, honey. You're not breaking our family."

"Yes, I am."

She sighed. "Jenny, I thought about it all yesterday and all night."

"See? You didn't sleep because of me—"

"Listen to me. Listen. Yes, I had trouble sleeping. But it was worth it. Because I figured something out. You're the truth teller. You are the truth teller of our family. You were trying to tell us something with your eating disorder, and now you're figuring it out, and telling us in words. I can't pretend it isn't hard for us to hear. But it's worse for you."

"No, it's okay, Mom—"

"It's not okay. I'm the one who should be apologizing. I'm so sorry that this burden is on you. It shouldn't be. It should be on grown-ups."

It sounded like something Dr. Prakash would say.

"What about Dad?" I asked. "Does Dad think I'm a truth teller?"

She frowned. "Your dad is having a hard time with all of this. But he loves you."

233

"Does Rich hate me?"

"Rich doesn't hate you. Our family is not going to break because you are in the hospital."

I wasn't sure I believed her.

"Let's get out of here. How about a movie?"

I nodded. "A movie sounds good."

We went to see *The Naked Gun*. It was ridiculous. It must have been just what we needed, because we laughed and laughed.

Maybe it was because we were tired and needed a break from the heavy stuff.

Or maybe it was because when you went through something this painful, it cracked open a part of your heart and made some room for joy.

Sunday, December 4, 1988

Dad came this afternoon. I was more nervous than I had been with Mom yesterday, but I was still excited to get out of the EDU.

He looked okay: weary, but not completely torn apart. "So, what would you like to do, JJ?"

"Um, well, I thought, since it's nice out, we could go to the zoo?"

"Syracuse has a zoo?"

"A small one. I've been to it before, on a school field trip. Chuck said there's a new boardwalk that's really nice."

"You're allowed to go there?"

"Yup. It was Chuck's suggestion. He even drew a map for directions."

"Okay. The zoo it is. It's cold out, so bundle up."

I nodded. Usually I would have said something about being fifteen and knowing how to put a coat on. But I decided to see Dad's directive as a way of showing he cared about me. I got my coat, hat, mittens, and scarf.

He signed me out, and we drove to the zoo.

It *was* really cold outside. But I'd bundled up. And the sun felt fantastic.

Dad and I were careful with each other. Polite and courteous. We watched the animals and read the informational displays to each other.

It was the first time in ages that I didn't lie to him, or act fake and perfect, or cover everything up.

We didn't seem broken.

It seemed like progress.

♥ ♥ ♥

After dinner, I decided to have a Sprite as an optional liquid, above and beyond the required 1800 calories of my meal plan. It would be my first voluntary, full-size, nondiet can of soda in four years. (From a taste-bud standpoint, I would have preferred Coke, but patients weren't allowed anything with caffeine.)

I was super nervous.

But I needed to do this. Confront my irrational fear. Check it off the list. Just have a damned Sprite and live to tell about it.

Chuck offered to chaperone me to the soda machine. We went to my room—Heather was in the lounge—and I dug some quarters out of a roll.

"You're hiding those well, right?" Chuck asked.

"Yup." I held up my snow boot.

"Did you ever find out what happened to those other quarters?"

I shook my head.

He frowned but didn't say anything.

We walked to the vending/laundry room at the end of the hall.

As I put my quarters into the machine, my hands were shaking. I was incredibly nervous about drinking a full-size soda on top of all the calories I was already eating.

Would it immediately make me fat?

Would all the sugar go straight into the bubbles of cellulite on my thighs?

No. Of course it wouldn't. People drank soda all the time. One soda didn't make your body parts burst into freakishly large whale proportions. One soda didn't turn you into the Hulk.

I hit the Sprite button. As the can tumbled inside the machine, something hit me in the back of the leg. I looked down. A Ping-Pong ball was rolling away from my foot.

"GOOOOOOAAAAAL!" Chuck did a slow-motion lap around the tiny room.

"You're hitting me with stuff? Hello? I'm *trying* to embrace recovery over here."

"I'm trying to embrace victory over here."

"What?"

"Vending room soccer. Goals are the soda machine and the doorway."

"I hope you're ready to embrace defeat." I retrieved the ball from the corner and gave it a kick.

"Yo, you know how we were talking about your grades," he said, trapping the ball with his foot, "and you told me you get straight As, except for the—"

"Occasional threat of an F in my interim reports?" I blocked his attempt at a goal. "Ha. Denied." I dribbled with my toes and kicked it out the door. "Good day, sir!"

"Darn." He retrieved the ball and set it down for kickoff. "I've been thinking about it, and I realized: those are both ways of getting attention."

I looked up at him. "I never thought of it like that."

"Astute." He tapped a finger to his temple. "That's what I'm here for." He kicked the ball straight past me. "GOOOOAAAAAL!"

He beat me, three goals to two. Then we sat on the floor, our backs against the warm clothes dryers.

I popped the Sprite open and took a small sip. It was cold and fizzy and absurdly sweet on my tongue. I tried not to think of cellulite and calories. "My brother's coming to visit Friday."

"That's good." He was drinking a regular, full-caffeine Coke.

"It's the first time he's coming to see me without my parents bringing him."

"Cool beans."

"I bet my parents are paying him to come. They must have instituted some kind of incentive program. Or maybe it's just plain coercion."

"Carrot or stick?" Chuck made a face. "What makes you say that? He seemed nice when I met him."

"He doesn't like me." The words caught in my throat. I took a sip of Sprite, trying not to cry.

"He's your brother. He loves you."

"Nope. Doesn't want to be seen with me."

"He's older than you, right? That's standard older brother behavior."

"I guess. But if I ever show up at a party and he sees me, he leaves. He literally rounds up his posse and leaves."

"His posse?"

"His posse."

"Okay, not subtle. But still probably normal."

"I just wish we could hang out sometimes. We used to ski and ride bikes together. Then again, Mom made him take me along, so that's not a good example."

"You sound like you look up to him a lot."

"I do. He's the cool one in the family."

"You're not cool?" He looked aghast. "Then why am I hanging out with you? I'd better get out of here."

"Ha ha. My brother says I'm a geek."

"You're not a geek," Chuck said.

"But I'm not as cool as Rich. He gets along with everyone. He's an amazing skier, and he's good at sports and stuff like that."

"You're good at things, too."

"Good at being a bitch to my family," I said. "He hates me. This visit couldn't have been his own idea."

Chuck bumped his shoulder into mine. "Hey. Don't put words in people's mouths, or feelings in their hearts."

"Just make up imaginary problems for them, like the strangers in the window?"

"That was different. Now we're talking about the people who are in your life. You shouldn't assume you know what they're thinking and feeling. If you want to know how your brother feels, ask him. He'll probably tell you. But until then, don't assume. You know what happens when you assume."

I rolled my eyes at the old joke. "You make an ass out of *u* and *me*."

"Correct. Good student." He drained the last of his Coke and nodded toward my Sprite. "You going to finish that or what?"

"Yeah. Give me a second." I drank the rest, wiped my mouth with my sleeve, and let out an involuntarily burp. My cheeks burned. Uncontrolled bodily noises: so mortifying. "Excuse me," I muttered.

"Good one!" Chuck stood and put his hand out. I grabbed it and he hauled me up. "Whatever the reason, it's nice that your brother's coming," he said.

"I guess you're right," I sighed.

"Of course I'm right. You should listen to me more often."

"I listen to you all the time!"

"Good girl. Now go work on your personal eating disorder history thingymabob."

"Oh crud. My essay. Do you think treatment planning will give me an extension? Without limiting my passes?"

"Have you even started it?"

"Yeah. But there's so much to write about. And I want to do a good job."

"Well, get back to it. Just show the team you're working hard."

"Okey-dokey, artichokey," I said, heading into my room. I looked back at him. "See Jen. See Jen listening to Chuck. See Jen doing exactly what Chuck says."

"See Chuck saying 'Good job, Jen.'"

I went to my room, got out my notebook, and tried to concentrate, despite Heather tunelessly singing along to her new Whitesnake tape. And despite constantly rechecking my legs and thighs for evidence of Sprite fat.

Monday, December 5, 1988

"Jennifer, we need to have a check-in," Ratched said, like she was doing me a huge favor.

I plastered a big smile on my face. "Oh, okay. I'm happy to check in with you, but I checked in with Chuck last night, and not much has happened since then. It's all in the notes, I'm sure."

She sucked air through her teeth. "Well, I'm your primary."

I kept smiling. "Yes, but I know you're busy, because you're so many people's primary. Chuck only has one secondary. He has a lot more time. Plus, he needs the practice, so that's why sometimes I talk to him instead."

I hoped my explanation appealed to her need to feel superior to Chuck and everyone else in the universe, while omitting the significant facts that (1) Chuck was a pleasant, decent person and a good listener, and I vastly preferred his company, and (2) Ratched was a foul, power-hungry troll.

It seemed to work.

Later, I was about to knock on Bronwyn's door-frame, but I froze when I saw Ratched in there. Her head was bent toward Bronwyn's like they were having a serious heart-to-heart. Apparently they had made up since the Great Butter Incident.

They didn't even notice me or look up. My insides twisted with jealousy. Was Bronwyn telling Ratched stuff she didn't tell me? Was I less of a confidant to her?

Ugh. I could almost hear Dr. Prakash admonishing me: *Friendship is not a competition, Jennifer.* And a nurse-patient relationship wasn't the same as a friendship.

I knew I shouldn't make everything a competition, just like I shouldn't try to stand on the head of a pin. I knew I shouldn't. I just didn't know how not to.

But. The more time Ratched spent with Bronwyn, the less time Ratched had for me. And the unlikelier it was that Bronwyn would follow up on the 72-hour letter she had mentioned in OA. And both of those were good things, no matter what.

♥ ♥ ♥

Today was my last lunch tray on 1800s, and it was a doozy. A warm sandwich of corned beef, Swiss cheese, sauerkraut, and Russian dressing on rye bread. I'd never had corned beef or sauerkraut or rye bread before, and I hated them already.

"It's called a Reuben," Monica said.

"It's called revolting," I said.

Bronwyn and I finished around the same time, and Bosom took our trays, moving the napkins and straw wrappers around, shaking the milk cartons to be sure they were empty. The normal routine.

Bronwyn crossed her eyes and blew out her cheeks like a puffer fish. "I'm going to explode."

Amanda groaned and put her head on the table. There were some bread crusts on her tray she needed to finish. She was still on 3000s.

"Well. I'll get the mail from downstairs," Ratched said.

"Thank you so very much, Sheryl," Bosom said, sounding overtly, extremely courteous—as if she was one step away from eye-rolling.

Hm. Did Bosom find Ratched annoying? Was there dissension in the ranks? Interesting.

"How about we drown our sorrows with a game of clever deception?" Bronwyn asked.

"Bullshit," Monica said.

"You know it." Bronwyn smiled.

I didn't follow.

Bronwyn leaned her chair so far back I thought she'd tip over, but she deftly steadied herself with a foot under the table while she opened a drawer in the cabinet behind her. She rocked back to the table, a deck of cards in her hands. The cards were tattered, their edges frayed.

Bronwyn shuffled the cards and set them in front of Monica, who cut the deck. Bronwyn stacked it back together. "Amanda, you playing?"

"Sure." Amanda stabbed her last crust with her fork, chewing it slowly. She never ate with her fingers, and she was always the last one to finish. Always. Bosom checked her tray and carried it to the cart.

"Jennifer?" Bronwyn smiled. "A game of Bullshit?"

"I've never played."

"Never?"

I shook my head. "What's Bullshit?"

They looked at each other.

"Oh, girl," Bronwyn said. "Your life is about to change." She started dealing. "Okay. So I deal out the whole deck. The object is to get rid of your cards. You add them to the pile and say what they are."

"But you put them facedown." Monica gathered her cards. "And you can lie."

"You can lie about how many you're putting down, and you can lie about what they are," Amanda said in her quiet voice, stacking her pile neatly.

"If you think someone's lying, you call 'bullshit.'" Bronwyn finished dealing and started organizing her cards. "If you call bullshit and you're right, then the person who lied has to take all the cards on the table. If you're wrong, you have to take them. Got it?"

"I think so," I said.

"Monica, you start," Bronwyn said. "Oh wait, I forgot to say, you have to go in order. So Monica has to put down aces because she's starting, then Amanda does twos, I do threes, you do fours, like that. Okay?"

I fanned my cards out, putting them in order. "What if you don't have the card you're supposed to put—"

"Then you lie." Bronwyn wiggled her eyebrows. "Thus the name of the game."

Monica set a card facedown in the middle of the table. "One ace."

Was she lying? I had no aces, so I couldn't tell. I looked at Monica, and Bronwyn, and Amanda, and they looked at me. Monica didn't seem like she was lying.

But then again, look where we were.

If there was one thing everyone on the EDU was extremely skilled at, it was lying.

"Two twos." Amanda put down cards.

"Bullshit," Bronwyn said.

Amanda sheepishly took her cards back, along with the card Monica had put down. "You liar," she said to Monica. "That was no ace." She held up the card: a jack of clubs.

Monica laughed and wiggled her fingers. "I'm very very tricky."

"My turn," Bronwyn said. "One three."

"Two fours," I lied. It was a three and a four.

The other girls narrowed their eyes at me. I adopted the expression I always used after purging, or when I came home drunk, or when I told Mom I'd already had dinner at Kelly's. I didn't avoid eye contact, but I didn't hold anyone's gaze too long. I willed myself to exude neither innocence nor guilt.

Apparently they bought it, because Monica slapped down her cards. "Two fives."

"One six."

"Two sevens."

"Three eights," I said.

Bronwyn bugged one eye out at me.

"Uh-oh, she's giving you the stink eye," Monica said.

"Hm," Bronwyn said. "You look so innocent and sweet over there. But I'm going to have to call bullshit."

"Read 'em and weep." I flipped my cards over.

"Damn it!" Bronwyn scooped all the cards into her hand. "Fine." She picked through the cards. "Monica, your turn."

Monica put down her cards. "Five nines."

We looked at each other, then broke into hysterics.

"What's so funny?" Monica looked indignant. "It's five nines."

Was she kidding? I couldn't tell. How could she not know there were only four of each number in a deck of cards?

Bronwyn laughed so hard she farted. It was so long and loud, it vibrated to the rhythm of her laughter. Which made all of us double over.

Wiping tears from laughing, Monica grudgingly took the pile. "Fine. But it could have been five nines."

"No, it really, really couldn't," Brownwyn laughed.

We kept playing. I busted Amanda twice and Monica once.

Bronwyn set down her last card. "One king. And that, my friends, makes me the undefeated Bullshit champion of the EDU. But you guys can keep playing to vie for second place."

"No! I call bullshit," Monica said.

"Nope, not bullshit." Bronwyn bulldozed the huge card pile over to Monica. "They're all yours."

Monica picked them up slowly, one at a time. "You know, I quite enjoy having practically the entire deck," she said, affecting a British accent. "It makes it a *titch* easier to tell when you lasses are lying your little knickers off."

"Unless you think there are five of every number," I said.

Which set us all laughing again, even Monica.

It was the best after-meal half hour to date.

Until Ratched came back with the mail. She saw the cards, her eyes went wide, and she slammed down the envelopes, which scattered all over the table. "Girls! No games after meals! That is avoidance! You are distracting yourselves from your feelings! That is diseased behavior!"

"Seriously? Are you kidding?" I asked, not able to hide my irritation. But it was a stupid question. She was not kidding. She didn't even seem capable of kidding.

Monica threw down her cards in annoyance.

Why was it against the rules to have fun in this place? Why couldn't Ratched grant us one tiny sliver of silly happiness?

But if a nurse said no, it was no. Especially when it was the head nurse. No fun allowed.

Tuesday, December 6, 1988

I had been plugging away on my essay. My Life With My Eating Disorder. But it was adding up to a ton of pages and I still had a lot more to include. It was the most intimidating, most important assignment I'd ever been given. Somehow, I needed to cover:

When and how my bulimarexia started.

How it affected me—emotionally, physically, mentally.

How it affected my relationships.

Plus, significant things that had contributed to me getting sick—or, after I was already bulimarexic—sicker.

That meant writing about my drinking and all the bad stuff that had happened when I was drunk.

It meant talking about Dad's anger and Mom's issues, and what our family dynamics were actually like.

It meant talking about my depression and loneliness and cutting my wrists.

It meant going into my first love—or what I'd thought was love, but turned out to be a boyfriend who talked me into having sex before he dumped me.

And not only did I have to write down all the hard stuff, the worst stuff, but then I had to share it. Read it out loud, to staff and patients.

I had one chance to get it right. I knew it wouldn't be graded, but I wanted to do A+ work. I wanted to be honest with myself. Writing my entire story—the good, the bad, and the ugly—meant confronting my disease and my history. And maybe confronting it would bring me one step closer to accepting it. And maybe acceptance would bring me one step closer to recovery. Maybe.

Chuck and I confabbed about my treatment-planning requests. I asked for an extension on my essay deadline when I made my next requests for treatment planning. I also asked for one six-hour divided pass (two hours before lunch, four hours after) for Saturday, and one four-hour pass for Sunday. Both would be with Mom, because Dad was on a business trip.

Nurse Chuck initialed my requests with a big flourish, drew a big star, and wrote, "Patient is talking about her feelings and working hard!!!"

I didn't say anything. I was proud, but even with Chuck's three exclamation points, I felt depressed and mopey. I missed Spike. I missed home. I had the blues, like that old Carpenters song we sang in chorus, "Rainy Days and Mondays."

Thinking about the Carpenters in an EDU. How fitting.

I left the lounge and headed to my bedroom, trailing my finger along the wall, ruminating.

Back in fifth grade, we were discussing current events in social studies. Mrs. Clark mentioned a singer who had died from anorexia.

I leaned over to Kelly and whispered, "Anorectia? What's that?"

"Anorexia," she whispered back. "It's what Karen Carpenter died of. Because of the ten-pound rule."

"The ten-pound rule?"

Kelly rolled her eyes. "Haven't you heard the saying 'The camera adds ten pounds'?"

I shook my head.

Exasperated best friend look. "You at least know who Karen Carpenter is, right?"

I didn't, but I nodded. "Duh."

"Karen Carpenter wanted to look good on TV. So she went on a diet, but then she didn't stop, and she got way too skinny and died. That's anorexia."

"Oh." Inside my brain, wheels turned. I didn't wonder *why* someone would do it. I wondered *how* someone would do it. And what it would feel like, to starve on purpose.

I was thin, normal at the time. But I wondered—what would it be like to be super skinny?

A year later, Kelly and I were watching *Fame* (our favorite TV show), and I got some new information. The character Holly ate a big lunch and then went in the girls' room and threw it up. Interesting. Filed that tidbit away for later.

In seventh grade, Mom and I watched *Kate's Secret* together, eating Milk Duds and learning all about bulimia.

Not long after, I rented *The Best Little Girl in the World* at the video store. While I was watching it, alone, on the VCR in my parents' room, my brother's girlfriend came in. "Ew!" she said. "That girl looks disgusting. She's too skinny."

Too skinny? I thought she looked gloriously, powerfully, inspirationally thin. Plus! All the attention she got when she went in the hospital. And tried to escape from the hospital. And then went back into the hospital.

I started haunting the 616.85 section of the library. Memoirs about anorexia, information about bulimia. For me, they were instruction manuals: diet tips, weight loss ideas, how to protect your teeth from the acid in vomit.

Kelly got so sick of my eating. That's what she called it: *Your eating.* I didn't blame her. I was sick of it, too. For her birthday last summer, we took a bus to Darien Lake and I promised to eat whatever she ate and not talk about food the entire day.

But even for her birthday I couldn't do it.

♥ ♥ ♥

By the end of my first full day on 2500 calories, I felt AWFUL.

I hadn't kept this much food in my stomach in a long, long, long, long time. Maybe never.

I couldn't get comfortable, my stomach was so full.

When calories came from so-called "healthy" food—although it was debatable how healthy this food was—instead of junk food, it took up insane amounts of stomach volume. And it stayed there, in my stomach, moving around, pushing on my insides.

It was horrible.

And it meant I was gaining weight. Truly, undeniably gaining weight.

Wednesday, December 7, 1988

Treatment-planning Objectives for Jennifer

1. Patient is granted extension on personal history essay.
   Patient should plan to share it this week.
2. Patient request for weekend passes—*approved*.

Notes: Patient should work on feelings of individuation/separation from family.

Bronwyn and I went to our first Chemical Dependency meeting on Adolescent today.

"Which of the stages of alcoholism would you say you're in, Jennifer?" the social worker asked as she escorted us downstairs.

We'd only met CD Lady yesterday. She was straightforward and no-nonsense; brusque, but not mean. She had handed us thick packets of reading and worksheets to do on a weekly basis, in preparation for CD meetings. And she made it clear that she had read our case notes and met with our therapists. She told us she was "fully informed" about our chemical use.

"I think stage one," I said.

"I agree. Tell me why."

"Because I drink to escape. And I look forward to it all week. But I don't think I'm physically dependent. And I haven't developed much of a tolerance."

"Good. And you, Bronwyn?"

"Probably early stage two," Bronwyn said.

"Yes. Why?"

"Because I've started blacking out more."

"Very good. I think both of you girls are right on target. And you did your homework." She leafed through our worksheets, not really looking at them. She sounded pleased and surprised. Probably the kids on Adolescent were uncooperative. Adolescent was where parents sent kids who were defiant, suicidal, addicted, and alcoholic.

My heart was in my throat. I'd had visions of the Adolescent Unit as a prison, with inmates reaching through cell bars trying to grab me. Hard-core punkers with safety pins in their faces, and überweird goths. Also with safety pins in their faces.

We turned the corner from the elevator and walked down a non-prison-cell hall, into a big room filled with Adolescent patients.

It was totally silent. No tin cups banging on cell bars.

Everyone stared at us when we came in. The freaks from the EDU. They'd probably heard as many stories about us as we had about them. How messed up everyone on the EDU was, and how we had to eat everything on our trays, and our bathrooms were locked, and we couldn't flush our own toilets, and we had to measure our urine, and get our vital signs taken and be weighed every day. Maybe they were glad they were on Adolescent and not the EDU.

The kids all looked like they were between thirteen and eighteen. It was a mix of girls and boys. It hadn't occurred to

252

me that there would be boys. Boys had thus far been such a nonpart of my life in the hospital. I self-consciously ran my fingers through my hair, realizing that it had been good to have a break from worrying about how I looked to the male species. I was not ready for their return to my life, not yet.

Most of the kids were white. There was one African-American girl, along with Bronwyn. The patients didn't look goth or punk or have piercings. They looked normal, except none of their shoes had laces. And every one of them seemed angry or annoyed. They all sat with their arms crossed over their chests. Not one of them smiled at us or said hello.

The room was the size of our lounge, but without couches, or carpeting, or any soft surfaces whatsoever. In the corner, a TV was strapped to a three-shelved, wheeled cart; a VCR was cable-locked to the middle shelf, just like at school. The room had tile floors, like in our nurses' station, and lots of mismatched chairs arranged in a circle.

I sat next to Bronwyn and tried to look around without looking like I was looking around. Did these patients wonder about me and Bronwyn the way we wondered about them? Were we one zoo exhibit looking at another? Monkeys looking at bears?

"Slouching, two points," a male nurse said to a patient.

The kid sat up, but only a little.

There were three nurses in addition to CD Lady. Two were big African-American dudes who looked like bouncers, like they should be checking IDs outside a college bar. The other nurse was a young white woman. All three had clipboards.

"Slouching, two points," the same nurse said to another patient.

The kid rolled his eyes as he sat up.

"Eye roll, two points." The nurse made a note.

And when a kid whispered to another kid, the nurse said, "Talking, two points."

Holy cats. Talk about strict. How did this point system work? Did "two points" mean two points added or taken away? Did the most or least points earn something? Passes? Privileges?

And, significantly, selfishly, I wondered: were Bronwyn and I on their point system while we were in this group? I didn't want to ask, because I didn't want to know. And I didn't want to give the staff ideas.

CD Lady turned on the TV and struggled with the VCR controls. We watched a movie about PCP called *Desperate Lives*. It starred the blond actress from *Girls Just Want to Have Fun*. It was extremely hokey. I think it was an old Afterschool Special, because CD Lady fast-forwarded through commercials.

When it was over, we had to go around the room and share our responses to the movie.

One girl, young, with short hair, shook her head and refused to talk.

"Opting out, ten points," a nurse said.

Another kid, older, with a mullet, said he thought it was "bullshit propaganda."

"Swearing, five points," two nurses said in unison.

The girl next to him said, "I think it seemed unrealistic, because no one would ever jump out a window or drive off a cliff like that."

Goodness, did that set CD Lady off. "The dangers of drugs like PCP are very real. Very real." Her voice was low and quiet, but hard as nails. "How about every one of you writes an essay about the dangers of PCP?"

The room groaned, but no one said any actual words. We

kept going around the circle. When they got to us, Bronwyn said, "It was certainly food for thought."

I knew she was joking: *Food for thought! Hello, I'm from the EDU! I'll be here all week!* But I was too scared to giggle.

My hands were shaking when it was my turn. I said, "It makes me worry about my brother. I hear rumors about him and drugs."

It was true. There was always gossip about Rich smoking pot. And his eyes often looked bloodshot.

What if my brother had a chemical dependency? Did... did he need to be on the Adolescent Unit while I was on the EDU?

What if he was on something more dangerous than weed? Should I bring it up in family therapy?

No, no, no. My family didn't need more dramatic accusations and confrontations. Plus, my brother would disown me.

But how would I feel if he got hurt, or overdosed, and I hadn't said anything to my parents, just because I didn't want to cause a fuss?

♥ ♥ ♥

"What if my brother has a drug problem?" I asked Dr. Wexler toward the end of individual.

"Is that a concern for you?" He opened the paper lunch bag on his desk and pulled out a baggie of peanuts and raisins.

"Well, obviously." I said. "Or I wouldn't bring it up."

"Why is it a concern?" Dr. Wexler tossed a peanut into his mouth. He often munched on snacks during sessions. I couldn't decide whether he was truly hungry, or whether eating in front of EDU patients was some sort of therapeutic technique.

"Because I hear rumors about him using drugs," I said. "What if he jumps through a window or drives off a cliff, like in the movie we had to watch?"

"That seems unlikely. Are you focusing on your brother because you want to avoid your own issues?"

"I just spent forty minutes talking about my own issues. Dependency issues, individuation issues, perfectionism issues, anxiety issues…"

Dr. Wexler said, "If you're truly concerned about your brother's safety, that would be a good thing to bring up in family therapy. Which, by the way, I'll be leading from now on. I spoke to your parents."

"Why not Dr. Prakash? She handled it like a pro."

"Dr. Prakash doesn't do family therapy."

"She did the other day."

"That was…unprecedented. You're stuck with me."

I groaned and tipped myself over on the couch. Like I didn't get enough of Dr. Wexler in group every day? Plus individual?

And bringing up my concerns in family therapy? Sure. Look how great that went last time.

But what if he really had a problem?

What was the difference between telling and tattling?

Thursday, December 8, 1988

Tonight's dinner was liver. A huge, grayish-brown blob of organ meat.

It was the most disgusting thing I had ever seen. Just looking at it made me want to vomit.

"Nurse Chuck?" I said.

"Yes, Patient Jennifer?"

"I've found my third dislike."

"Okay. I'll write it down. Remind me, what are your others?"

"Broccoli and mushrooms."

Monica said, "Are you sure you want to put liver as a dislike? I know it's grody, but it doesn't get served very often."

I looked at the gelatinous mass on my tray. Prodded it with my plastic fork. "I have never been so sure of anything in my whole entire life."

"All right, Jennifer," Chuck said. "Just get it down, and it'll be the last time you have to eat it in your whole entire life."

Since I was on 2500s, it was a honking big portion. I cut the liver into tiny pieces and tried to tell myself it was steak. I started with my salad, taking bites of liver with every forkful to attempt to mask the taste. Then the zucchini and liver, then the roll and liver, then the banana and liver, with sips of whole milk in-between.

I looked around, trying to find something to distract me.

Trendy was standing next to Thriller, who was on 3500s.

She came over to our table. She checked her notes. "Jennifer, how many fat exchanges did you have?"

I choked down a bite of liver. "Um, just salad dressing. No, wait, also a butter with my roll."

"Just one butter?"

I nodded, trying to keep the liver from coming back up. "That's what was on my tray."

"How many calories are you on?"

"Twenty-five hundred."

She scrunched her nose. "I'm sorry, dear, but you were missing a butter. You should have had three fat exchanges."

I looked at Amanda. She tilted her head in pity. Which meant Trendy was right. Three fat exchanges.

"Can't she eat an extra butter at breakfast tomorrow?" Monica asked.

"It's not like she was trying to be sneaky," Bronwyn said.

I looked at my tray. I had two bites of liver left. My salad was gone, my roll was gone, my zucchini was gone. The only thing left was a quarter of a banana and a few sips of milk.

"I'm sorry," Trendy said again. She sounded like she meant it. She set a foil-wrapped rectangle of butter on my tray. "But it has to be with this meal."

I looked at Chuck. He nodded in what looked like reluctant agreement.

"All right butter. Come to Papa," I said. Sometimes you just had to buck up and do what had to be done, whether you wanted to or not. But dang, recovery was unpleasant work sometimes.

I choked down my last two bites of liver.

And then I ate banana slathered with butter.

It wasn't good. But it was better than the liver.

Friday, December 9, 1988

Ratched informed me that I would have no more extensions on my Personal Eating Disorder History. Sunday evening was the allotted time for me to bare my soul. She wrote it on the calendar in the nurses' station, in thick black ink.

I worked on my essay all afternoon, taking breaks only to call Mom and then Kelly. (Fridays at 4:00 had become my standing appointment for Kelly calls. She would fill in the details of whatever she'd hinted at in her notes and cards. Daily mail—most loyal friend, ever.) I checked the clock constantly—I couldn't wait for 7:00, when my brother would come visit. I decided I wasn't going to confront him about pot smoking or talk about anything heavy. I was just going to enjoy having him all to myself. Maybe I could teach him how to play Bullshit or something.

After dinner, I worked on my essay. And watched the clock. I watched 7:00 come and go.

I started to worry. What if Rich had hit a deer? Or gotten lost? Or driven off a cliff in a PCP-induced hallucination?

After 7:30, as soon as the phone was free, I called home. Mom answered. "I'm so glad you called again, Jenny! I'm sorry, but Rich isn't going to be able to visit you tonight."

My heart sank. "Earlier you said he was all set to go."

"I know, honey. But the roads are bad, and the news says it's worse in Syracuse."

I looked at the snow coming down. I sighed.

"Okay. Well, can I talk to him at least?"

"Oh, he's not here. He's at Laura's."

"So the roads were too bad to drive to Syracuse, but they were clear all the way to Laura's?"

"Well, Jenny, Syracuse is farther than Laura's. Be reasonable, hon."

I let out another long, heavy sigh. "You don't have to defend him, Mom. I'm just disappointed."

"I know you are," she said. "Maybe he could come next week."

"Maybe."

"I'm sure he's sorry."

I'm sure he's sorry meant Rich hadn't actually *said* he was sorry.

Rich knew how to drive through snow. He just didn't want to visit his loser sister in the psych ward.

Saturday, December 10, 1988

The roads were clear when Mom took me out on a pass. We went to the Penn-Can Mall, which was all done up in holiday decorations. We browsed B. Dalton; she gave me ideas for books Dad would like for Christmas. I tried my best not to dwell on whether I'd still be in the hospital for Christmas. That line of thought was treacherously gloomy. I wanted to try to be cheerful, and enjoy being out on pass.

We walked around for a while, looking at earrings and greeting cards, and the new music releases. But we stayed well away from clothes.

Then we sat at a table in the pizza place. I had a small Sprite. I was allowed to have an optional liquid on passes.

"There's something I need to tell you," Mom said.

Nothing good ever came after those words.

"What's going on?" I asked, trying not to panic.

"Your brother is thinking about going skiing with Pete. In Colorado."

"Oh!" Relief. "That's cool. I mean, I'm slightly jealous. And I wish he'd come last night, but that's fine—"

"For Christmas."

"Oh."

"Honey, we know Christmas means a lot to you."

I nodded.

"And no final decisions have been made." She sounded vague, as if she wasn't one of the two grown-ups responsible for making the final decisions.

I fidgeted with the straw in my Sprite. "Okay."

"We wanted to talk with you first. But your brother thinks Christmas is going to be sad, with you in the hospital—"

My throat got tight. "I was hoping I would be home by then. Or if not…that I could come home for the day. On pass. And we could all be together. Not in the hospital."

Her eyes filled with sympathy. "Do you really think that could happen?"

Slowly I shook my head. I had to be honest with myself. I would not be home for Christmas. Not even for a day pass.

I was still gaining weight. There was no way I would be discharged in two weeks. And there was also no way staff would even give me meal-out privileges, which I would need, to have enough time for the trip home and back.

Mom reached across the table and took my hand. "Honey. Your dad and I have been thinking about it. What we think we'll do is get a hotel room at the Genesee Inn, across from University Methodist. We can go to the Christmas Eve service, and then hang out at the hotel. Christmas morning, we'll pick you up right after breakfast and open presents."

I could feel my lower lip sticking out. Pity party. "*If* I keep getting all my passes."

She nodded. "I'm sure you will."

I told myself not to cry. Not here, not in the mall. Look at everything my parents were doing. Trying to make Christmas as nice as possible. I had to think about my family, not just myself. I had to be mature. "Okay. I understand."

"Thank you, honey." She squeezed my hand. "You're growing up, you know that?"

That made the tears tumble out.

Sunday, December 11, 1988

My notebook shook, I was trembling so much. Writing my essay, reliving every terrible thing that had brought me here, had been grueling. And now I had to read it out loud?

Forget butterflies. My stomach was hosting a plague of locusts.

These pages contained my deepest secrets, things I'd never admitted to anyone. Things so shameful, I'd never even written them in my diary, for fear someone might read it.

Everyone had gathered in the lounge—all the patients and nurses on evening shift. Bronwyn gave me her teddy bear to tuck under my arm, along with Bearibubs. Monica rubbed my back.

I took a deep breath and started reading.

♥ ♥ ♥

Seventeen hand-written pages later, I finished. I was relieved, and horrified: I'd gotten it over with, but now everyone knew everything, the whole sordid, ugly truth about me. Would Chuck think less of me? Would Monica and Bronwyn still like me?

I looked up from my notebook. Half the room was crying. Everyone looked stunned. All my fellow patients, plus Baldy and Chuck—even Ratched—looked affected.

Baldy's face was red, and he kept wiping his eyes. "I just…I thought you were this nice girl with an eating disorder," he said. "Not that you're not nice. But now I see all this crap you've been through. You hide it well."

I shrugged. "I've had a lot of practice pushing it down."

"Listening to you, I know exactly when your disease started," Baldy said. "It was in second grade."

I shook my head. "My eating disorder didn't start in—"

"Maybe not the eating part. But the instant you started receiving praise without learning to give it to yourself. It forced you to think you needed to be perfect." He rubbed his face.

Ratched said, "It reminds me of something, and I think this might help you." She drummed her fingers on her knee. "Think of yourself as a flower."

A flower? Really? No thanks.

She continued, "All of you girls. I want you all to picture yourselves as flowers, uncurling from your stems."

Gag.

"When you rely on other people's praise and opinions for your self-esteem, like you talked about in your essay, Jennifer, it is as though you, the flower, need someone to glue petals onto you. When what you really need is to take up nutrients from your roots, and bloom from within."

I had to admit, that kind of made sense.

"All of you girls, you need to internalize your self-worth. Grow your self-esteem from inside yourselves. Then you don't have to be insecure about your petals—worrying about them falling off, or fading, or needing someone else to come along and glue on new ones. You can just grow your own."

Wow. Lessons learned: (1) I was a flower and needed to bloom from within, and (2) sometimes wisdom could come from an unexpected source.

Chuck said, "That's a cool way of looking at it, Sheryl."

Baldy said, "You know what I wish, Jennifer? I wish I could take an eraser to your past. I want you to be able to start new."

"You have everything going for you, kid," Chuck said.

Did I have everything going for me? It didn't feel like it.

I picked at the fur of Bronwyn's teddy. My hands kept shaking. I didn't feel a major catharsis or awakening. I just wanted this to be over: my unveiling of secrets, and my whole EDU stay, and my entire eating disorder.

Like an eraser to my past.

Monday, December 12, 1988

Dr. Prakash had warned me, *Norpramin might make you a little drowsy the first few days.*

A little drowsy!

That was like saying the EDU lounge was a little smoky. The *Titanic* was a little leaky. Nurse Ratched was a little bitchy.

I took my new tricyclic antidepressant for the first time before bed last night, lining up with the other patients for meds. It was like the weigh-in line, minus the paper gown, plus the promise of drugs. So: much better.

This morning a nurse worked me up as usual for vitals and weigh-in, but instead of taking a shower afterward, I dropped back down and slept past Heather's alarm. Monica came and dragged me out of bed, throwing clothes at me from my dresser. We got to the lounge in the nick of time; trays were on the table and Ratched was coming to look for us.

We sat. Bronwyn told me I'd slept through the loudest Jesus Lady commotion in the history of Samuel Tuke. I stared, bleary eyed, at my tray.

♥ ♥ ♥

I fell dead asleep on the couch during group. Dead asleep.

I only woke up because Bronwyn was jabbing me. I was too groggy to be embarrassed.

"Jennifer," Dr. Wexler said. "What are you trying to avoid by sleeping through group?"

Apparently I answered, "I'm trying to avoid being awake," and went back to sleep.

I missed the ensuing laughter and Monica reminding him that I was going through my induction into the Norpramin club.

Tuesday, December 13, 1988

Dr. Prakash woke me up from an impromptu morning nap today. She sounded annoyed. "Jennifer, the medicine cannot possibly be making you this sleepy. You are on a minuscule dose."

"Sorry." I wiped drool off my face. "But I mean. Look at me. The evidence is pretty clear."

Dr. Prakash sighed and wrote something in my folder.

I sat on an aluminum folding chair to stay awake in group. It worked, just barely. I kept waking up when my head bobbed.

This was ridiculous. I'd wanted drugs, wanted relief from depression and sadness, but sleeping my life away wasn't what I'd had in mind.

To add insult to injury—or gluttony to sloth—it was my first full day on 3000s. (Not to mention the weekly joy of urine collection day.)

I could not believe how much food 3000 calories was.

It looked like a lot more when it was your own tray instead of your neighbor's.

It took me an hour and three sugar packets to get through my breakfast eggs.

Also I was afraid that I would fall asleep and dump my face onto what seemed like eighteen yellow washcloths.

Lunch was enormous.

Dinner was massive:

- a buttload of green beans cooked with red peppers
- two dinner rolls
- three packets of butter
- one pear
- salad with dressing
- a crap-ton of mystery meat
- a big square of chocolate cake (which I ate first, since I'd be too stuffed to enjoy it later)
- apple juice
- chocolate milk

That was the volume of food I had to eat three times a day. Oh, plus a mondo snack.

I just had to keep shoveling food in my mouth the entire hour.

I was a sleepy, fat, disgusting mess.

Correction:

I was a sleepy, healthy-ish, very human mess.

Wednesday, December 14, 1988

Treatment-planning Objectives for Jennifer

1. Patient will learn potential side effects of Norpramin.
2. Patient will explore ways in which she can be more spontaneous in everyday life.
3. Patient request for weekend passes—*approved*.

"What are you doing, kid?" Chuck asked.

"Waiting for the phone." I was lying on a couch, super dopey and half asleep. Norpramin life felt like short, choppy scenes between naps. Disjointed and strange.

He swatted my feet. "Shove a bum, chum."

I made room for him.

"So, what's up?"

I shrugged.

"Come on," he said. "You know you want to talk to your pal Chuck."

I sighed. "I still have so far to go." From nowhere, I started to cry. Typical. "It's so hard and I'm so tired and I still have so far. Why should I even bother?"

He passed the box of tissues. "Did you think this would be easy?"

"Everything else in my life has been."

"Huh. You think? It didn't sound that way in your essay."

"What do you mean?" I didn't follow. Slow brain.

"You're smart and get good grades, sure. But it sounded to me like you've been working really hard just to pass for normal and healthy. Let alone all the other burdens you put on yourself—be cool, be thin, be perfect."

"That's true."

"So you've already been working hard. You just have to shift from working hard at pretending to be healthy, to working hard at actually being healthy. Just...pivot. Like in basketball. Pivot." He mimed a jump shot.

"Okay. But..."

"But?"

"I'm scared," I said.

"Of what?" he asked gently.

"Of failing. What if I can't do it?"

"Hey. Take it easy. It's not all or nothing."

"Yes it is. You're either in recovery or you're not."

"Don't make it so hard for yourself."

"But it already is hard. Too hard. I don't know how to be, without my eating disorder."

"Just keep going," he said. "You'll make it."

"Ugh!" I pulled the hood of my sweatshirt over my face. "I'm tired of people saying that! What if you're wrong?"

"Just because you're tired of hearing it doesn't mean we're wrong. Unmask thyself."

He stayed with me a while, writing his shift notes. I must have fallen asleep, because I woke up when he touched my arm.

"Phone's free."

"Oh. Thanks."

He smiled. "You're very welcome, Snorey McSnorespants."

Thursday, December 15, 1988

"So. You are adjusting to the Norpramin?" Dr. Prakash asked.

I nodded. And yawned. "I'm going to bed earlier, and getting a little more used to it."

"Very good." She made a note. "And what is on your mind today, Jennifer?"

"I'm wondering whether I should quit dance. When I get out of here. Because I was looking at posters at the mall this weekend."

She took off her shoes and swiveled to light a cigarette. "I do not follow one to the other. Quitting dance because of posters?"

"Oh. Sorry. Norpramin non-sequitur. The train of thought was: there were ballerina posters at the mall. And in Wellness and Nutrition, we were talking about exercise, and how I need a regular exercise plan, but noncompulsive. And non-eating-disorder-competitive."

"Ah. And dance..."

"Is both compulsive and eating-disorder-competitive."

"I see. Do you enjoy it?"

"I used to. I liked my dance classes, and I liked teaching the little kids. But lately it's not fun. It's stressful. Plus, the leotards, the mirrors, the performances...it might trigger me to want to lose weight and be skinny. Not *might*. It definitely will."

"What does your intuition tell you to do?"

"Quit. At least for a while," I sighed. "Find different ways to exercise. But it makes me sad to give it up. It seems like it's been a big part of my life."

She nodded, paused. "Tell me, Jennifer. Do you know what narcissism is?"

"Don't think so."

"How about the myth of Narcissus? Are you familiar with it?"

"No."

She tapped her cigarette ash and leaned forward. "In the Greek myths, Narcissus was a hunter. He was proud. He believed himself to be beautiful. In order to defeat him, his enemy led Narcissus to a pool of water, where Narcissus saw his own reflection. That was all it took. Narcissus became so entranced with his reflection that he could not leave the water's edge. He was utterly self-absorbed. He ultimately died there, Jennifer. That is where the term narcissism comes from."

"Well, there are a lot of reflections in the dance studio. A whole wall of mirrors."

"Yes, I imagine it can be quite conducive to narcissism."

"But I'm not in love with myself. Most of the time I hate myself."

She lifted her hands, holding them like a balance scale. "Hating or loving ourselves can be much the same. Either way, the narcissist is the center of his own universe. He is fixated on himself."

"Oh. I never thought of it like that."

She nodded slowly, giving me time to think.

"I guess I see what you're saying," I said. "Even when I'm hating myself, I'm still just thinking about...myself."

"When we keep ourselves at the center of our own universe, we miss out on other things. Do you understand what I might mean?"

"I think so."

"Tell me."

"Like, if I'm just always looking down at my thighs, my eyes are glued on them, and I'm literally not able to look at anything else."

She smiled. "Yes. And?"

"And it's not just what I'm looking at. It's what I'm thinking about."

"Not only what you are thinking about, but also the way you are thinking about it. Eating disorders are terribly narcissistic, Jennifer, whether one is loving how thin one's thighs are, or loathing how 'fat'"—she made air quotes—"one looks. Either way, it distracts you from many of the much, much more interesting things life has to offer."

"Such as?"

"Such as ideas, art, travel. Reading, learning, exploring. You name it, Jennifer. What would you like to be thinking about instead of your thighs?"

"I don't know."

"Then you must find out. You will have renewed mental resources when you are in recovery. Some of your thoughts will need to focus on the recovery itself. Other thoughts, some of the perfectionistic, obsessive energy…let us just say, it will be helpful to find an outlet."

"I like reading. And drawing. And writing."

"Very good, Jennifer. Very good. Just remember not to stand on the head of a pin. Follow your interests, do your drawing and reading and writing, but keep your two feet on the ground, yes?"

"Yes."

"Aspire to be ordinary."

I rolled my eyes. "I know, I know. You want me to stop competing in everything I do."

"Yes. And how will you do that?" She stubbed out her cigarette.

I scrunched up my face. "I don't know. Maybe when I'm more comfortable with myself? I won't need to compete as much?"

She touched her nose. It meant: *Exactly.*

♥ ♥ ♥

I lay on Bronwyn's bed and watched her do her makeup, getting ready for our EDU outing. We were going to the two-dollar movie theater to see *Big*.

Most of us didn't wear any makeup on regular days. It wasn't a drastic change for me—cherry ChapStick was the extent of my makeup routine at home—but it did seem like a big change for Bronwyn, Monica, and Amanda, because whenever we left the hospital, they put on full foundation, blusher, everything.

We all did our hair every morning, though. Everyone except Heather. Mornings echoed with the sound of Conairs, checked out from our baskets, blow-drying coiffures in every room and bathroom.

"Hey, Bronwyn?"

"Yes, my Chiquita Banana?" We'd been keeping and trading the stickers from our bananas lately. I was still wearing the one from dinner on my forehead.

I peeled it off and stuck it on her teddy bear's chest. "Why do they make us keep dental floss in our baskets?" I'd pieced it together that hair dryers could be used for electrocutions, and the belt precaution was to prevent hangings (duh). But some

275

of the other stuff, like floss, was still a mystery to me.

"Ah. The floss question." She peered in the mirror, then closed one eye to dab mascara on her lashes. "Sheryl used to work at another hospital, about five years ago."

"Ratched?"

Bronwyn looked at me. "Yes, Ratched. She's not that bad, you know."

"Um. Yes she is."

"Anyway. A girl hung herself with dental floss."

"What? With dental floss?"

"Yes. Actually, no. Maybe the girl cut her own throat with it?" Bronwyn paused, looked at the ceiling. "No, she hung herself. Anyway, Sheryl was the one who found her."

"That's horrifying," I said. I had no great love for Ratched, but to go through that? How awful.

"Yeah. They were really close." She swept mascara across her lower lashes. "Sheryl doesn't like to talk about it."

"How did you find out?"

She shrugged.

"It's weird some of the things they do let us have, though," I said.

"Like what?"

"Like on Shop Walk this week, I got that new Neutrogena shampoo and conditioner. Why do they let us have shampoo and conditioner and soap in our bathrooms, but not mousse or hair spray?"

"Because of the aerosol cans, probably."

"No, they don't even let you have the pump kind."

"I guess it's more poisonous than shampoo?"

"Yeah, but you could sneak anything into a shampoo bottle."

"Good idea," she said. "Salon Selectives, whiskey edition."

"Now, now, Bronwyn," I said, wagging my finger at her.

She sucked in her cheeks and put on her blusher.

"Did you notice when Ratched and the other nurses checked our bags, when we got back from Shop Walk, what they wrote in our notes?" I asked.

Bronwyn shook her head.

" 'Patient denies contraband.' They used to write 'No contraband,' but now they say 'Patient denies contraband.' "

"I bet they changed the policy. Probably after Thriller snuck in laxatives."

"What!"

"You didn't know?"

I shook my head.

"She admitted it in group."

"When? Where was I?"

"Oh! It was probably that day you were completely conked out. Yeah. She said she wasn't trying to lose weight, but she was so constipated she couldn't stand it anymore."

"She said all that?"

"Yup. It was the most I've ever heard her talk. Her sentences were almost coherent. Almost."

"Maybe she's gaining enough weight that her brain is starting to work again."

"Could be."

"So what happened?"

"Um...they revoked her weekend passes and searched her room."

"Good Lord. What else did I sleep through?"

"Not much." She snapped her blusher case shut. "But now you know who to thank for the contraband policy change."

I propped my head on my elbow. "It just bugs me. 'Denies contraband.' Even when you don't do anything wrong, you still feel—"

"Untrusted."

"Yeah."

"Could be worse. I bet the nurses on Adolescent search everything like crazy."

"I know. When we go down there for CD, everyone looks so miserable."

"That's because everything on Adolescent is group process." She rifled through her cases of eye shadow.

"Group process?"

"It means the whole group is punished for what one person does. Like, say, if Thriller snuck in laxatives, and got her passes revoked—"

"Which she did."

She swept shimmery eye shadow on her lids. "Yes, but if *we* had group process, all of us would have gotten our passes revoked."

"Holy nightmare. Why do they do that?"

"It's reverse peer pressure, I guess. Knowing that the whole group will be held accountable for what you do is supposed to help you make good decisions. Plus, your friends want you to follow the rules, because if you get in trouble, so do they."

"And vice versa."

"Yup. You pressure everyone else to do the right thing so they don't get you in trouble."

"So it's still based on self-interest."

"Huh." She nodded. "Yeah."

"And why don't any of them have laces in their shoes? Is it…is it like dental floss?"

"No. Someone probably tried to run away. They take your laces so you can't run fast."

"You're kidding."

"Nope."

"That sounds hellish. It makes the EDU look like a picnic."

"Yes, it's totally a picnic here! Picnics with heaping trays full of disgusting, smelly old food!" Bronwyn said. "Except for you, my little Chiquita Banana snack. You are fresh from the vine. Tree. Bunch. Whatever." She ran her fingertips under her eyes to make sure there were no mascara flakes or unruly eyeliner marks.

She picked up her basket. "I'm going to sign this in. Be right back."

"Sure." I loved watching Bronwyn get ready to go out. It seemed like when she looked in the mirror, she liked what she saw. Bronwyn seemed comfortable in her body—relatively. For here.

Comfortable in your body. I literally could not imagine what that would feel like.

I hadn't bothered with makeup for our outing, but I was wearing nice big silver earrings and one of my standard going-out outfits: big black shirt, untucked of course, hanging loose over my favorite jeans—which were getting agonizingly tight, especially around the waist—and slouchy black boots. I was going for Edie Brickell's look in her "What I Am" video.

At home I used to wait and wait for that video. Late at night, after I'd binged and purged, I would sit and watch MTV, feeling alone and empty. And the video would come on, and usually I wouldn't cry, but sometimes I would. And I'd think that maybe if I was as pretty as Edie Brickell, and as laid-back as she looked in the video, maybe I could be okay. Maybe the inside could match the outside.

Friday, December 16, 1988

Heather voluntarily spoke in group today. She said, "I know I have a lot of work to do before I leave next week."

Everyone's eyes bugged out. We were all like, *SAY WHAT?*

"You're leaving?" our newest patient, Charlotte (bulimarexic, 18, took Eleanor's old bed in Bronwyn's room) asked. Emphasis on *you're*. Of all of us except Thriller, Heather talked the least, cried or emoted the least, worked the program the least.

"Heather's parents are signing her out," Dr. Wexler explained. "Tuesday will be her last day with us."

"They don't think this is working," Heather mumbled.

Tuesday. I quickly did the math. Four days.

Four days until I didn't have to room with her anymore!

Yes! Yes! Yes! Hallelujah! Yes!

I knew I should feel sorry for Heather; her family was obviously unsupportive. And I did pity her. But I was also so, so happy. No more moping, stomping, grunting, unfriendly, messy roommate!

Monica, who was basically a saint, and therefore always nice to Heather, asked, "How are you feeling about going home?"

"Not good." Heather was looking down, frowning at her arms folded over her belly. "My dad's making me get braces. To lock my mouth shut."

Um. She was kidding, right?

"Are you serious?" Monica asked. She looked from Heather to Dr. Wexler. "They can do that? They can force her to do that?"

"They can," Dr. Wexler said. "It's an orthodontic procedure, like braces, but the top and bottom braces are wired together so the individual cannot open her mouth." He did not sound happy.

"How…," I started. "How will you eat?"

"Liquid diet," Heather murmured.

Oh my God.

Uncomfortable silence.

Then Charlotte said, "I still don't see how you get to leave. All you do is pout and be passive-aggressive. You've never done one thing for recovery."

Monica said, "Lay off, Charlotte. It's not her choice to quit the program."

More uncomfortable silence.

Dr. Wexler said, "Why doesn't the group share ways we can support Heather until her discharge?" He turned abruptly to me. "Jennifer, what do you think?"

What did I think?

I thought Heather didn't stand a chance.

A father who would wire your mouth shut? And I thought my family had issues.

But how could it help her at this point, to tell her that?

So what I said was, "I'm here for you, Heather, if you ever want to talk."

Saturday, December 17, 1988

Bronwyn had signed out nail polish and superglue from her basket; she was attaching little pieces of coffee filter onto her fingernail where it had torn. It was fascinating. And the fumes were rather potent.

I was kind of morbidly waiting for the superglue fumes to mix with cigarette sparks so the whole place would blow up. Some excitement for our Saturday night.

Annie Lennox's video with Al Green, "Put a Little Love in Your Heart," came on. It was in heavy MTV rotation because of the new Bill Murray movie, *Scrooged*, which Mom and I had just seen, out on pass. I went to the TV to turn up the volume. Bronwyn and I sang along. But we didn't dance; we didn't dare.

"She's so gorgeous," Bronwyn said when the video ended. She blew on her nails, tickling the air with her fingers.

I nodded while I turned the volume back down.

"I think short hair is sexy on a woman," she said.

My cheeks went pink. I had short hair. Did that mean she thought I was sexy?

It shocked me whenever Bronwyn or anyone here talked about a woman being sexy. Never, never would a girl have said something like that in Norwich. You could describe Molly Ringwald as pretty, or Cindy Crawford as beautiful, but *sexy*? No way. It would have meant you were a lesbian. Which meant everyone would call you a dyke. Which meant the end of your social life. Possibly even the end of your actual life. Kids got the shit kicked out of them for being—or acting—gay.

But hearing Bronwyn talk about women as sexy was like hearing my own thoughts expressed out loud. Because I thought women were sexy.

Which terrified me. Because did that mean I was a lesbian?

Could you think a woman was sexy without being a lesbian? What if you got flustered and...turned on...thinking about women?

No, no. I liked boys. I had loved fooling around with Conrad, before things went bad. Hot guys made me horny and libido-y. But I also felt that way about girls.

Was there even a word for someone like that?

I was scared there was a word for it.

I was scared the word was *freak*.

Sunday, December 18, 1988

Laundry. I'd been handing off my essentials—socks and undies—for Mom to wash at home. But I really needed to do a big load of everything. My sweatshirt sleeves were practically crusty with dried snot and tears.

So Bronwyn, Monica, and I dug out quarters (mine were hidden in my snow boots) and got Trendy to escort us to the vending room. All three washers and dryers, shared between EDU and Adult, were, miraculously, available.

"Whites and darks separate," Monica reminded me.

"That's clothing apartheid," I joked. Then I froze. I felt my face go beet red. Bronwyn was African-American and I just made a joke about apartheid?

"I agree." Bronwyn didn't seem too bothered. "And I just don't believe in it. I shove whites and colors in together."

"Me, too," I said, relieved. "Free South Africa." I dumped the entire contents of my laundry hamper into the machine: sweatshirts, turtlenecks, jeans.

And then I pulled my favorite jeans back out. I'd had them since eighth grade, since the beginning of my eating disorder—the eating part of my eating disorder. I had measured every ounce lost and gained by their feel. They'd gotten baggier and baggier as I'd gotten sicker and sicker.

Now they were tight.

What if my maintenance weight made me too fat to fit in them? How big was I going to get?

"If I grow out of these jeans, I'm going to puke." I said.

I meant, *I won't be able to deal with it.* Not literally, *I will purge by vomiting.* But too late. It was out.

Trendy said, "That is some stinking thinking, my friend."

"I didn't mean it like that," I said. "I just meant..." But I let it drop. And I dropped my jeans into the washer.

Bronwyn and Monica gave me half smiles. They knew what I meant.

"Can we leave our stuff?" I asked. "Come back when it's done?"

"It's better not to," Monica said.

"People from Adult will toss your laundry on the floor to take over the machines for themselves," Bronwyn said.

"I guess it's a dog-eat-dog world in the laundry room of a mental hospital," I said.

"Ruff," Bronwyn said.

"Bow wow," Monica added.

We waited, sitting on the washers, shimmying with the spin cycles.

Monica's washer shuddered to a stop, then Bronwyn's, then mine.

I pulled out my sweatshirts and jeans and set them in my basket. The rest of my clothes I put in the dryer.

"You're not drying those?" Trendy asked.

"No way, José." I shook my head. "I'm hanging them to dry in my room. I don't want them to shrink."

Trendy rolled her eyes.

I'd been trying to shrink for so long. Now I was growing bigger.

I needed my clothes to stay big enough to hide in.

Monday, December 19, 1988

"Hey, Heather?"

"What."

"Have you seen my journal?"

"It's in Monica's room."

"What? Why?"

"I was writing in it. A good-bye note."

Um, it would have been nice if she had *asked first* before she took my journal. Monica's room? Jesus. But I didn't say anything. She was leaving tomorrow. It wasn't worth creating drama.

Monica had said Heather's parents were planning to take her straight to the orthodontist on their drive home. To get her jaw wired shut. Just in time for Christmas.

I felt so sorry for her. But I still couldn't wait for her to go. Selfish, but true.

I looked through my books on my dresser and nightstand, trying to find my *Calvin and Hobbes* collection. No Calvin, no Hobbes.

"Okay. Well, have you seen *Calvin and Hobbes*?" I scanned my dresser again. "Or, wait...or *Bloom County*?"

"I don't know. I didn't take them," she snapped.

That was a weird response.

"I didn't say you took them," I said slowly. "I asked if you've seen them."

"I haven't seen them."

So I left. Retrieved my journal from Monica's room. Went to the lounge. Sat on a couch, half watching MTV, half writing in my journal, half eavesdropping on Charlotte's phone call.

Which was actually thirds. Der.

"Jennifer?"

I turned around. It was Monica. "Hi," I said. "What's up?"

"Can you come into your room with me?"

"Why?"

"Heather asked me to come get you."

Bleh. Did I feel like dealing with Heather? No, I did not.

"Just, please?" Monica said.

I tucked my pen in my journal and followed Monica to my room. It was an even bigger mess than before—torn wrapping paper was crumpled all over the floor.

Heather's bed sagged under her weight. Monica sat down next to Heather and put her arm around her.

Would I ever be as nice as Monica? How did she manage to always be so kind to everyone, including Heather?

Monica said, "Heather has something to say to you."

Heather started snuffling. "Changed my mind."

"No, Heather. This is important. You can do this," Monica said. "Jennifer is a toughie. She's working hard for recovery. She understands the importance of forgiveness and making amends. She's the best person to start with."

Start with? Forgiveness? What was going on here?

"She'll understand," Monica told Heather.

Heather got up and lumbered over to her desk. "Here." She started shoving things at me.

Four cassettes—Sting, Prince, INXS, Crowded House.

And three books: *Calvin and Hobbes, Bloom County,* and *The Prophet.*

Then she put a bunch of postage stamps on top of the pile. It was my stuff. I was stunned.

"Um. Where were these?" I asked.

"I...wrapped them up."

Oh my God. All the wrapping paper! "So...you were going to give my stuff away as Christmas gifts?"

"Don't get mad! I can't help it. It's part of my disease!"

Holy hell. Stealing my stuff and wrapping it up. I couldn't believe it.

Was it part of her disease? How would I know? She never talked about anything.

I had a really bad feeling that there was more. "Is there anything else I should know?"

She made a sour face. "Yes, but I don't have them."

"Have...what?" But flashcubes started popping in my brain:

Dr. Prakash sticking up for me, believing I hadn't used my quarters as weights.

Dr. Prakash suggesting a calling card with a secret PIN.

Chuck telling me to hide my stuff well.

They had known.

They had known my roommate was a kleptomaniac.

And they hadn't told me!

Because they couldn't tell me; it would break Heather's confidentiality. They had to keep her secret, even if it meant causing harm to someone else—to me, in this case. They had to hope Heather would tell me herself.

"I took...I took your quarters." Heather said.

"My quarters," I said flatly. "You took my quarters. As soon as I got here."

And...my God. *Had Ratched known?*

"I spent them," Heather whined. "I spent all the money. I don't have—"

"You had them all along." I couldn't keep the anger out of my voice. "You were lying here that morning when they accused me!" I pointed at her. "You were *right there*. You heard the whole thing. You could have told them."

She sobbed miserably.

I blew out a big breath. I honestly did not know what to say. I was furious. I was baffled and incredulous. I also pitied her. What must it be like to be her? To have parents who padlocked the refrigerator? Who thought it was okay to wire their daughter's mouth shut? It was medieval.

"I promise I'll pay you back," Heather sniffed. As though making amends was just a matter of replacing my cash.

"That's..." I knew she wouldn't pay me back. And even if she did, it sure as hell wouldn't change the fact that I was humiliated and basically strip-searched because she'd stolen my stuff and then lied by omission.

"It's a disease," Heather said again. "There's nothing I can do about it."

"But there is," I said. "That's the whole point of this place."

"You've already taken the first step," Monica said to her.

"I have a lot more people to tell," Heather said.

Who else's stuff had she helped herself to? How would they react?

Monica suggested, "Why don't you tell Jennifer how you feel."

"I'm really scared." Heather wiped her nose. "That you and everyone else won't like me or trust me anymore."

Um...hello? What about *sorry*?

"I think people will be more willing to trust you if you try to talk about these things," I said.

"You see?" Monica patted Heather's shoulder, then looked at me. "That's what I told her. That people will trust her more, now that she's opening up."

"Yeah," I said.

I mean, God. She was leaving the next day. So maybe that little bit of hope was my good-bye gift to her. She needed it more than I needed to stay angry about something that was already done. I'd learned at least that much by now.

Tuesday, December 20, 1988

Heather's parents came to get her before lunch.

Her dad barged into our room, didn't say hello, or acknowledge me, or hug her. He just picked up her suitcase and grunted, "Let's go." Her mom came in after him. She was meek, small, quiet.

I ran to the lounge to tell everyone to gather for the song circle. But Heather's parents were already hurrying her out. All we had time to do was shout good-bye down the hall.

They were headed straight to an appointment to wire their daughter's jaw shut.

This place was opening my eyes to how truly horrible the world could be.

For example: Monica's older sister. She was (1) stabbed to death (2) by her own husband (3) on their honeymoon (4) when she was twenty-five. Monica was nineteen when it happened. She had been the maid of honor.

Another example: Charlotte's father (1) raped her, (2) got her pregnant, and (3) pushed her down the stairs, so (4) she would have a miscarriage. This was last year. When she was seventeen.

For some of these girls, an eating disorder was the least of their problems.

It made me realize how good I had it. My family had issues, but nothing, nothing like that.

Anyway, Heather. I closed my eyes and silently wished her good luck. She would need it.

I hope you steal stuff from your orthodontist's office. He must be a sadistic son of a bitch to do that to you.

I hope you find solace somewhere. Because it probably won't be from your parents. And it can't be from food anymore, either.

I wondered if any of us would ever hear from her again.

In the meantime, to be totally, completely, obnoxiously selfish:

No roommate! Private room!

Wednesday, December 21, 1988

Treatment-planning Objectives for Jennifer

1. Patient will work on feelings of dependency and separation from family. Patient will limit phone calls to family to one call every other day.
2. Patient will continue to explore ways in which she can be more spontaneous in everyday life.
3. Patient request for weekend passes—*approved.*

I sucked it up for my first 48 hours after arrival. That was the rule. After 48 hours, you got to use the phone. Everyone. That was the deal this whole time. And now, on my one-month anniversary, they were changing the rules on me. Not anyone else. Just me. *I* could only call every other day.

And why now? Was this about Wexler and Prakash talking so much about individuating and becoming my own person and all that crap?

Well, thanks a lot. What a great reward for working the program. How very nice of them.

I was so mad, I didn't even feel like talking to Chuck.

I was so mad, I snapped at Dr. Wexler during group.

I was so mad, I scribbled nasty doodles in my journal.

I was so mad, I didn't talk to anyone during lunch.

I was so mad, I fumed at Dr. Prakash during individual.

Okay, no, I didn't do that last thing. I respected Dr. Prakash too much to fully fume. I was…respectfully angry. But she knew I wasn't happy.

"Jennifer, I understand that you do not like this new treatment goal," she told me. "But can you try to understand the reasoning behind it?"

I sighed. Loudly.

"Can we talk about your need to tell your mother everything that is going on in your life?" She lit a cigarette.

"I don't have a need to tell my mother everything that's going on in my life."

"You do not call her every day?"

"Obviously not anymore."

"But up until now, you have called her every day, yes?"

"Yes."

"I wonder if talking to your mother so much helps you avoid becoming your own person."

"It's normal for daughters to talk to their mothers. Don't your kids talk to you?"

"My daughters do not have eating disorders."

"That you know of," I said.

She raised her eyebrows.

"Sorry," I said, and meant it. What an evil thing to say. I sighed again. "I thought I'm supposed to talk to people. We're supposed to reach out for support. Staff tells us that all the time."

"Of course," she said. "But the key difference is—and this is important, Jennifer. Are you with me?"

I nodded, though I was still sulking.

"The key difference is that I suspect you do not feel like something has really, truly happened unless you share it with your mother. Does that sound about right?"

Was that right? It didn't sound right. But I wasn't the expert. I shrugged.

"If this is true, it would indicate that you are enmeshed. That you are not your own person. And so your treatment team has given you this guideline in order for you to learn how to be your own person."

"I'm still not convinced."

"Jennifer, the hospital is the perfect place to practice the skills you will need to be healthy in the real world."

"The real world," I grumbled. "Are there no phones in the 'real world'? And how about—will I have to room with a kleptomaniac? Is that a 'real world' skill, too? Or is that just in the hospital?" I waited for her to say something. She didn't. I felt suddenly shy and nervous. But I needed to ask: "Did staff know? About Heather?"

"Oh, dear," she finally said. She tapped her cigarette on the ashtray. "I am sorry. That was an extremely unfortunate situation."

"So you did know. You could have warned me."

"No, I could not have warned you. For one thing, I—we—were still piecing that information together. For another, patient data is strictly confidential, except in the case of endangered life or limb. As I suspect you already know."

"But you just let her steal my stuff. And that whole quarters nightmare—"

"Jennifer. We could not tell you. But we can talk amongst ourselves. Tell me, did Nurse Sheryl pursue her accusations of you using weights?"

"No. But she's still a total—"

She held up a hand to stop me. "As soon as I put the pieces together, I spoke with staff, and we did the best for you that we could."

"Oh." *Use a calling card. Hide your quarters.* "Well. I mean. Okay. Thanks, I guess."

"I am sorry we could not do more to protect you. We are not perfect, Jennifer."

"So I hear."

She smiled and glanced at her watch. "It is time for you to scoot to Journaling. Will you think about our earlier conversation? About separating from your mother?"

"Sure, I'll think about it all the times when I *should* be able to call my mom," I said.

She smiled. "Fair enough."

"I still think it sucks," I added.

"Duly noted," she said.

♥ ♥ ♥

After journaling, I brooded in my (private!) room for a while. Then I meandered into the lounge. The energy there was tense. More tense than usual. Everyone, including staff, was crowded around the TV. There was no sound in the room, except for a special news report.

I sidled up to Bronwyn. "What's going on?" I asked.

Without taking her eyes from the screen, Bronwyn whispered, "A Pan Am flight crashed."

"Oh no. Where?"

"Over Scotland. It killed everyone on board. It hit some people in the town, too. It might have been a bomb."

♥ ♥ ♥

At dinnertime, everyone was still watching the news. Our dinner trays sat, ignored, on the cart. I felt like I'd stepped into a parallel universe. Usually our rigid meal schedule was the axis on which the EDU spun. But tonight, everyone was focused on something else, something outside of the EDU and meal plans and therapy and disease and recovery. It was freaky.

Trendy held a crumpled tissue. She was crying.

Monica waved me over. "It looks like there were a bunch of Syracuse University students on that flight."

"Oh no," I breathed.

"Thirty of them," Bronwyn said.

"Maybe more," Amanda added.

"They were coming back from semester abroad," Bronwyn whispered, "in London."

Monica tilted her head to indicate Trendy. "She did semester abroad in London a couple years ago. She took the same flight back."

"Oh God," I whispered. I looked at Trendy. Bosom sat next to her, patting her shoulder.

"They think it was terrorism."

"No!" I whispered. "Why? Who?"

Monica shrugged. "Nobody knows yet. Libya? The IRA? The PLO?"

"Oh my God," I whispered again. "I can't believe it."

"I know. Everyone here knows someone who goes to SU."

Trendy just cried and cried.

Thursday, December 22, 1988

The plane crash had cast a pall over the unit. It was so sad. My private room was the only good, happy thing in EDU life.

But after lunch, when I went back to my bedroom, the door was closed.

I stood in the hall, staring at it, gobsmacked.

Bedroom doors were never supposed to be shut. And that definitely wasn't how I'd left it.

I pushed the door open. And instead of my very own, very Heather-free sanctuary, there were people in my room. A bunch of them. Some were sitting on my bed, and some were clumped around a girl who was sitting in Heather's chair.

Dr. Wexler was there, too. He was the only one who noticed me come in. Dr. Kanduri, Monica's psychiatrist, stood next to him. Then there were three older adults, four teenagers or twenty-somethings, plus the girl in the chair. Was this a new admission? Why were there so many other people here?

The girl's long blond hair hid her face; her head was in her hands, her elbows on her knees. Her shoulders were shaking, a sure sign of crying.

"Er...sorry," I said.

They all looked at me, including the girl. She looked so distraught. Her eyes were pleading...for what? I didn't know. But I got a feeling it had to do with the commotion, like she actually wanted to be here, but she wanted peace and quiet.

Seemed like I was getting a new roomie.

My private room had lasted 24 whole hours.

Fingers crossed the new girl wasn't a surly kleptomaniac.

♥ ♥ ♥

Sophia. That was the name of my new roommate.

The basics: bulimic, wouldn't have to gain weight, twenty-two. She had just finished her first semester in Cornell Veterinary School. Which meant she loved animals, so she understood how much I missed Spike.

We sat together at dinner. I scooted up an extra chair for her at my table. Now it was my turn to talk a newbie through her first meal. Sophia was a trooper. She didn't cry or anything.

After dinner, we talked. After snack, we talked. Later, we got ready for bed and lights-out. It was strange to have someone in the room besides secretive, sullen Heather. Sophia was willing to share actual information about herself.

"So…you're bulimic?" I asked. She'd already told us she was. But in EDU language, *So, you're anorexic/bulimarexic/bulimic/a compulsive overeater?* translated to *Commence the rest of your life story in three, two, one. Go!*

"Yeah. But…" She hesitated.

I waited in the semidark. Her sheets and blankets rustled while she shifted.

"This is embarrassing," she said. "I've never told anyone."

This was going to be juicy. "You don't have to tell me, if you don't want to," I said, of course secretly hoping she would.

She was quiet a little longer. "I think I want to. That's why I'm here, right?"

"Right," I said.

"I never throw up," she said.

"But...you're bulimic," I said. Which was probably the absolute worst thing to say.

"I know!" she said.

"Thus your secret shame," I said. Oh great. What if she couldn't tell I was joking?

Fortunately, she laughed. "Yes! Thus my secret shame. I tried making myself throw up, but I just couldn't do it. How embarrassing is that? It makes me not even bulimic, right?"

Honestly, I'd never heard about a bulimic who didn't vomit. "Did you use laxatives?"

"No. Nothing like that. Just exercise."

"Huh."

"That makes me super weird, right?"

"Well," I said. "Since I'm completely normal, yes, I think you're weird."

She was quiet.

"Because I'm so completely normal that I'm a patient in a mental hospital?" I said.

"Oh," she said.

Then we both started giggling.

"Shh! Don't make Beverly come in here," I said.

We both took deep breaths, trying to stop laughing.

I turned onto my side to face her, even though I could only make out the rough shape of her silhouette. "When I came here, I was worried, too. I was worried I wasn't sick enough to be a proper bulimarexic."

"But you were so skinny." She'd seen my photos, taped to the wall.

"Not anymore," I said.

"Please," she said. "You're still tiny."

"Blurg." I puffed my cheeks out. "Anyway, I guess my point is, maybe we all question ourselves?"

"Yeah." She went quiet.

"I think it's bad enough," I said. "For you, I mean. Even if you didn't throw up."

"You do?" The hope, the relief in her voice; it was like I'd thrown her a life jacket.

"Definitely. I mean, it must have been bad, if you ended up here."

She laughed. "True."

"Besides, barfing is gross," I said.

A pause. "Could we really get in trouble for being up late?"

"Probably," I said. "But we've got our lights out, so we're technically following the rules. And Beverly—the night nurse—she's nice. She'd understand for one night. Plus, everything's still off-kilter, because of the plane crash."

"That's so sad," she said.

"It is," I said.

We went quiet for a while.

"I can't believe I'm here," she said.

"It feels weird, right? But it gets better."

"It does?"

"Not really."

We laughed again.

"It doesn't get better," I said. "It always sucks. But you make friends, and you get used to it."

"I can't believe Christmas is in a few days," she said.

Holy Napoleon. As sad as I was about being here for Christmas, it would be worse for Sophia. It was her first week. No passes, no visitors.

"Would they bend the rules, do you think?" I asked. "Let you have visitors?"

"They said maybe, depending on how my first few days go."

"I was here for Thanksgiving my first week."

"Did they let you have visitors?"

"Nope," I said. "Christmas would be harder, though."

"Well, my family's a mess, so it's probably better that I'm here than home. Especially during semester break."

"Was that your family in here, before? All those people?"

"Yeah. Mom, stepdad, Dad, two brothers, one sister, and my boyfriend, Rob."

"Wow," I said. "Big family."

"Yup. I'm the oldest. Do you have any siblings? Is that your brother in the picture?"

"Mm-hm. One brother, three years older. Mom and Dad, still together," I said. "Is it worse at home than when you're away at school? Your eating disorder?"

"Worse? I don't know. I think it's actually worse at school. But home can be crazy. My family is crazy."

"Like, psychiatric hospital crazy? Unlike us…"

She chuckled. "Seriously, they are certifiably crazy. All of them in different ways. Every one of them thinks they need to be involved in my life, all the time. Like, they *all* just *had* to be here to see me admitted?"

"It did seem a little crowded."

"My family means well. But Mom's an alcoholic. Full blown. And my dad is schizophrenic. Diagnosed."

"Oh," I said. "Wow. Does he take medicine?"

"He does until he feels better. Then he stops, because, you know, he's all better, right? And then he gets bad again. And then it's a huge fight to get him back on his meds."

"Is that why your parents got divorced?"

"Yup. And after my mom wasn't around to take care of him, I got the job."

"Because you're the oldest."

"Because I'm the oldest," she said.

We went quiet again.

"Sometimes I worry I'm schizophrenic," she said.

I didn't know what to say. What if she was? Wasn't mental illness sometimes genetic?

"You seem pretty normal to me," I offered lamely.

She didn't seem to hear me. "I feel like... Sometimes I feel like there is this thing inside me..." She trailed off again. "Now I really do sound crazy."

"No," I said. My heart was in my throat. Was she going to say what I thought she was going to say? "Go on," I said. "Sometimes you feel like there's...what inside you?"

"I don't know. I don't want you to think I'm psychotic. Or, more to the point, schizophrenic."

"You feel like there's a monster inside you," I said.

"Yes," she said.

"Oh my God," I said.

"I know. I'm crazy, aren't I?"

"No, no," I said. "I meant, *Oh my God. I know exactly what you mean.*"

"Really?"

"Yes. I feel that way, too. I feel like there's this ugly thing inside me that is completely separate from me—"

"Like it's just this *thing* living inside you—"

"Yeah, just squished in there somewhere, sometimes in my gut, sometimes in my—"

"Brain," she said.

"Yes!" I said. "And it tells me that I'm horrible—"

"And disgusting—"

"And totally messed up—"

"And nobody will ever understand—"

"So don't ever tell anyone."

"Yes," she said.

"Nope, no idea what you're talking about," I said.

She laughed.

I couldn't believe it. She had the exact same monster. "I basically came here to figure out how to kill it, the monster," I told her. "Or get rid of it somehow."

"Did it work?" She sounded hopeful and excited, but cautious.

I thought about it. "I don't know. I've never actually said it before. Out loud. To my doctors. Or anyone."

"Me neither," she said.

"Going into recovery, you know how they say it's a journey, not a destination?"

"I haven't heard that," she said. "But it makes sense."

"Oh, get ready. You'll hear it in groups all the time. People get all philosophical and spout these nuggets of wisdom. *Recovery is a journey, not a destination. Happiness is being able to enjoy yourself on the detours.*"

"Great," she said. I couldn't see it, but I knew she was rolling her eyes.

"Oh yeah, it's something to look forward to," I said. "When I'm really bored, I keep track. I count how many times someone mentions a saying. The record is nine in one hour."

"Impressive."

"It was me," I said. "I was trying to see if anyone would notice."

"Ha!"

"Anyway," I said. "I think it's true about the journey. And enjoying the detours—"

"JESUS! I AM JESUS!

"Water into wine!

"Water into wine!"

"What…," whispered Sophia, "is that?"

"Don't worry," I said. "It's a patient in the Adult Unit. She does this every once in a while. But it's not every night. And she's harmless."

"JESUS!

"I AM JESUS!"

"Um. Will she stop?" Sophia asked.

"Eventually," I said. "Either a nurse will calm her down, or they'll call a—"

The intercom clicked on. "Code Blue. Code Blue. Adult Unit. All available nursing staff to Adult Unit. Code Blue. Adult Unit."

"Okay, now there will be some commotion," I said. "But honestly, don't worry."

"What will they do to her?"

"Give her tranquilizers, I think? I don't know for sure. It's creepy, but like I said, it doesn't happen often. And she's totally harmless. She did this my first night, too, actually. Maybe it's a good omen."

"Okay…" but she didn't sound sure.

"Are you ready to go home now?" I said.

"Yup. I'm all better and ready to go home now."

We laughed so hard we cried. God, it felt great.

Friday, December 23, 1988

After breakfast, Dr. Prakash pulled me into the hall, away from the lounge door. "Jennifer," she said. "I want to let you know that you have reached your maintenance weight."

I felt a chill—how fat was I, exactly?—but mostly I was happy happy elation happy.

"I did?" I asked.

"Yes," she said. "You have reached stage three. You should start asking for walks."

Stage three! Walks! And soon—bathroom privileges!

"Do I have to wait for treatment planning to ask?"

"No," she said. "We like to get patients moving as soon as we can. Walks only. Not jog-walks or jogging."

"Got it." I nodded.

"You can request other privileges at treatment planning."

"Okey dokey."

"Now Jennifer," she said, "I need to tell you something. We have lowered your calories to 2500 per day."

"Great," I said. No more 3000s!

"Because the treatment team estimated the target adult weight range for your height."

I nodded.

She spoke slowly. "We made a mistake. We should have estimated your *adolescent* weight range."

"Oh. Did I go over my adolescent weight? Am I fatter than I have to be?"

"No, no. We caught it in time," she said. "And please, Jennifer, do not say 'fat.' You are just the right weight for your age and height."

Her forehead was crinkled, her eyebrows knit. She was looking at me with concern and trepidation.

Aha. She expected me to freak out about the mistake.

That's why she had told me herself, and why she pulled me into the hall.

But I didn't care!

I didn't have to gain any more weight! Ever again in my whole life!

And I could start getting really good privileges, like unsupervised bathrooms and meals downstairs.

Yay! Yay! A thousand times yay!

I went back into the lounge, beaming, and announced my news for all to hear. Amanda gave me a high five. Sophia and I did a little touchdown dance.

I couldn't wait to tell Monica and Bronwyn, but they were downstairs in the main hospital dining room. They had both earned their breakfast dining room privileges.

"How do I look?" I asked Amanda. "Be honest."

She looked me up and down. "Healthy."

The dreaded answer.

"How did I look when I came in here? Is there a difference?" Immediately I wanted to take my question back. What if Amanda said no, I didn't look any different? What if she thought I had already looked healthy, not skinny?

"Your legs were sticks when you got here," she said.

This, coming from an anorexic. I'd looked that thin to her. It felt like an angel choir of praise. Which was, I knew, insanely messed up.

— Stage Three —

Saturday, December 24, 1988

Bratwurst with sauerkraut and noodles for Christmas Eve dinner. And boiled spinach.

Thanks a lot, Samuel Tuke Center.

At least I was back on 2500s, so I had slightly smaller portions of bratwurst, sauerkraut, and spinach. But I wouldn't have minded my 3000s slice of cake—to celebrate Stage Three, not to mention Christmas.

Christmas Eve staff was the best combination possible: Chuck, Baldy, and Bosom. And luckily, our dinner conversation was a lot better than the food.

You'd think we would have been mopey because we were stuck here, and because people were still upset about the plane crash. But it was the opposite. Dinner was downright jovial. We ended up having an EDU talent show while seated at the table.

Amanda wiggled her ears. It was impressive. I didn't know human ears could move so much.

Charlotte balanced a plastic spoon on her nose.

Bronwyn put her forefinger and thumb in her mouth and whistled louder than I thought possible.

Monica held one eye steady and moved the other.

Sophia bent her thumb down to her forearm.

I flipped my tongue.

"Wow. I have never seen anything that cool before," Sophia deadpanned.

"Ah, but you have not witnessed the entirety of my skills. Behold!"

I flipped my tongue the other way.

"Uh huh, that's right." I nodded. "Now that you have beheld it, dare you to mock my talent?"

"That's nothing," Baldy said. "I can make my bald spot turn red. Want to see?"

"Of course!" we chorused.

He drew in a big breath and put his head down, like in prayer, so we could see the bald top. He stayed that way, perfectly still, holding his breath. We waited, in thrall, for his pink skin to darken.

Then he slapped his bald spot, over and over.

"See?" he said. "It turned red, didn't it?"

Bronwyn laughed so hard that milk came out her nose.

After dinner, we all moved to the couches. I read aloud a short page from *The Upper Room*, which I had picked up at an off-campus OA meeting, about being grateful for blessings—warm houses, food on the table, hope.

Bronwyn read '*Twas the Night Before Christmas* from an old picture book.

At 6:30, some families started trickling in, including Mom. We were planning to meet Dad at church.

"Let me see you, Maintenance Girl!"

I turned in a circle for her. I was such a mix of feelings: accomplished and happy, but shy and nervous that I looked different. And uncomfortable with my pants fitting so tight.

"You look wonderful! I am so proud of you!" She gave me the biggest, most proud mama hug ever.

Before anyone left, Mom told my favorite Christmas story, *The Polar Express*. When she had finished, she gave every

EDU patient a gold sleigh bell on a red ribbon so they could each have a little piece of Santa Claus magic. Almost everyone was teary eyed. It was a sweet, poignant moment, full of faith and hope and trust and the spirit of Christmas.

"You'll have to keep the bells in your baskets, ladies," Bosom said. "Sorry. But see here?" She pointed to the star-shaped openings. "That's sharp metal."

Poignant moment, over. Kaboom.

♥ ♥ ♥

University Methodist was big and beautiful. The service was nice, except that I didn't know anyone other than my parents. At home, we knew everyone at the Christmas Eve service. At home, even the minister was my friend.

When it was over, we bundled up and crossed the street to their room at the Genesee Inn. Mom and Dad had brought a small potted pine, decorated with tiny gold and red bulbs, so I'd have a Christmas tree to look at. It sat on a table in the hotel room, surrounded by presents.

I looked around the room, realizing that I'd been secretly hoping they would bring Spike.

But no Spike. Dogs were against the hotel rules.

We called the place in Colorado where Rich was staying with Pete and his family, but there was no answer. So we sat and talked for a little while. I caught them up on stuff that every-other-day phone calls didn't allow enough time for. I told them more about Sophia, and joining the "maintenance club." Now Thriller was the only one on the unit still gaining.

They shared some Norwich gossip.

I got to open one present: a flannel Christmas nightgown (one size fits all). Then it was time to go back to the hospital.

♥ ♥ ♥

Sophia was in the lounge with Chuck. Staff was allowing her to have visitors tomorrow, but she was on her own tonight. I had made Chuck promise me he would keep her company. They were watching *Santa Claus: The Movie*. Sophia seemed okay, maybe even better than I was. The evening had been as nice as my parents could have made it, but somehow I was feeling sad, and moony, and wistful, and tired.

Chuck nudged my chin with his fist, like a slow-motion, gentle punch. "Chin up, kiddo. Merry Christmas." He dropped a handmade card in my lap.

It was a picture of a disco Santa. It said:

> *We hope your Christmas be as groovy as you is.*
> *Love, your secondary and your roommate*

Sunday, December 25, 1988

"Merry Christmas, Jen." Sophia rubbed her eyes and reached for her glasses.

"Merry Christmas, Sophe," I said as I stretched. I'd slept funny and my neck was sore.

I had never been with anyone other than my family first thing on Christmas morning.

It was actually kind of nice to be with Sophia. And nice not to wake up to the snap of the reading light, and the cold fingers of a nurse taking pulse and blood pressure. One of the many benefits of both of us being at maintenance: vitals only twice a week.

Breakfast was French toast—the usual for Sundays. It wasn't a special Christmas meal, but French toast was still the best breakfast of the week by far. Lucky timing.

Mom came and got me after breakfast, around the same time Sophia's family showed up. I gave Sophia a look, trying to tell her, *Good luck, I hope your family doesn't drive you nuts.*

Dad was waiting for us at the hotel, drinking coffee and reading the newspaper.

We opened presents.

They gave me baggy shirts and socks and two large sweaters, Benetton and Esprit. No pants—I bet Mom didn't want to risk buying anything with a waistband. She was treading carefully since the T.J. Maxx debacle.

I also got the black-and-white checkered bedsheets I wanted, a cute book called *All I Really Need to Know I Learned in Kindergarten*, and another book of cool, inspirational quotes. Plus, a hugely oversized stuffed Snoopy and Woodstock. In my stocking was a Swatch watch and a rubber string ball thing called a Koosh.

I gave Mom and Dad the gifts I'd bought during mall trips on passes: I gave Dad a necktie and the new Tom Clancy book, *The Cardinal of the Kremlin*. He looked happy.

Mom seemed to like her turquoise clip-on earrings and a Love Coupon for ear piercing (if she ever dared), and the new Richard Bach book, *One*.

I confessed that I'd read some of the book before I wrapped it. It was about using quantum physics to travel to your past or future self—*exactly* like the promise I'd made to myself those first awful days in the hospital, for grown-up me to come back and help fifteen-year-old me. What kind of crazy coincidence was that? Richard Bach must have been my soul-friend, riding the same idea wavelength.

As I opened presents, I kept thanking my parents, over and over, like a tape on repeat. And even though I meant it, I knew I sounded hollow and robotic.

It wasn't that I didn't feel grateful. It was that I felt overwhelmingly guilty.

Every time I unwrapped a present, I felt more and more like I was ruining everything. Because we shouldn't have had to be in a hotel on Christmas, with Rich halfway across the country. I was causing everyone pain and trouble.

At 11:30, Mom drove me back down to the hospital for lunch (mushroom burgers on buns—so I got to scrape off the mushrooms).

♥ ♥ ♥

After lunch, Mom and Dad took me to see *Rainman*. When we got to the theater, Dad and I went to the concession stand while Mom used the restroom. He ordered a large popcorn, a pack of Twizzlers, a box of Junior Mints, a Coke for Mom, and a Diet Coke for himself. Yikes.

I didn't mind the drinks, but the snacks seemed inconsiderate. Hello? If your daughter was in an eating disorder hospital, wouldn't you maybe not binge in front of her? I didn't say anything, though. Perhaps this was his way—his unhealthy way—of dealing with a difficult Christmas.

"Anything else?" the teenager at the counter asked Dad.

"And a small Sprite, please," I said.

The guy reached for a cup.

"No. Cancel that Sprite," Dad said to the counter guy. Dad turned to me. "I don't think that's a good idea."

I looked over the counter at the vast spread he'd just ordered. "I'm allowed a small soda on passes," I said quietly.

The guy glanced from Dad to me.

"I don't know if that's true or not." Dad didn't bother to lower his voice.

"Mom knows it's true," I said through gritted teeth. "Ask her. I can have a small soda as long as it isn't diet and doesn't have caffeine."

"How does your mother know?"

"Because I've had Sprite when I've been out on pass with her."

"But did she hear it directly from your doctors at the hospital?"

Dad might as well have announced it on the loudspeaker. Everyone was staring at me. Who was this girl? Why did she have *doctors* at a *hospital*? Which hospital? Why was she at the movies? What was wrong with her?

"No." I looked at the carpet, trying to hold in my tears. Angry tears. Sad tears. Embarrassed tears.

"Well, I'm not going along with anything unless I hear it straight from Dr. Wexler."

"You don't trust me," I whispered.

"You're really asking me that?"

"I wouldn't lie, not about this."

"Right. Sure," he said. "Because you've never lied or tried to manipulate us before."

"This is different."

"Ring this up, please." Dad got out his wallet and paid the guy. He had trouble carrying all his stuff. Mom came scurrying over. She saw the food, looked at Dad, looked at me. She shifted uncomfortably.

"Hon," she said to Dad. "Can't you see Jenny's upset—"

"This is between her and me," Dad snapped. "Don't get in the middle of it, Juanita."

Mom looked startled. She closed her eyes as if she was thinking about what she should do. Then she looked at me and made an apologetic grimace, like she couldn't do anything when Dad got this way.

Merry Christmas, Johnsons.

♥ ♥ ♥

I was relieved when they brought me back to the hospital. I was still upset with Dad. I was upset with Mom, too, for not figuring out why I was upset, and for not sticking up for me.

But I also hated coming back to the hospital, because it meant…coming back to the hospital.

Christmas dinner was a special meal of roast beef, mashed potatoes, and peas. Each tray had an envelope taped to the lid.

315

Inside was a card from the head honcho of the Samuel Tuke Center wishing us *A happy, healthy holiday, with best wishes for good things in the New Year to come.*

It was a nice touch.

But still, the whole thing, all of Christmas, was a major downer.

Everyone, except maybe Sophia, had been so, so upset about being in the EDU for Christmas.

But Christmas turned out to be just another crappy day.

Monday, December 26, 1988

"Well. How was Christmas?" Dr. Wexler asked in group.

Monica was upset about her meal out with her family. "I ate way too much, I know I did," she said. "And everyone was hovering over me. It was awful. I wanted to restrict so bad."

"Did you restrict?" Dr. Wexler asked. He leaned forward into his favorite position, elbows on knees, index fingers propping up the middle of his nose. It made him look like he had a pig snout, with one cavernous nostril.

"No." Monica frowned.

"Are you sure?" Dr. Wexler asked.

"Yes!" Monica snapped. "God! I'm so sick of all your accusations. Why can't you ever just leave me alone!"

Youch. I'd never seen Monica lash out like that. She'd had a rough Christmas, sure, but this was a whole different Monica.

Bronwyn said quietly, "I have to say something."

Monica cut her eyes to Bronwyn, like she was simultaneously terrified of and furious about what she thought Bronwyn would say.

"I weighed myself when I was home," Bronwyn said.

Monica looked relieved. But I was stunned. Bronwyn had weighed herself? Unbelievable. You weren't supposed to know your weight until your final week. It was one of the last privileges you earned. If you weren't ready for the information, the numbers could totally mess with your mind while you were trying to get your body healthy again.

Was everyone falling apart or what?

"Is that all that you did, Bronwyn?" Dr. Wexler asked. "Did you also purge? Or drink?"

Bronwyn shook her head. "No. But I wanted to get smashed after I stepped on that scale, let me tell you."

"Your treatment team will need to discuss this."

"I know," she said.

What would her consequence be? It was a whopper of a rule to break.

♥ ♥ ♥

In individual, I told Dr. Wexler about my cruddy Christmas, even if it felt tame in comparison to Monica and Bronwyn's experiences. I talked about feeling guilty while unwrapping presents, about Dad being mean at the concession stand, about the chasm between me and Mom after that.

"Hm. You felt there was a wide space between you and your mother?"

"Yeah. A hugely wide space."

"Sounds like the normal distance between a fifteen-year-old and her mother to me."

"Right, like the 'normal distance' of only calling every other day?" I made a face. "How is it normal to have a mom who can't stand up to my dad?"

"It's normal to sometimes feel distant from your mother. It's important to be able to tolerate that distance."

"Why? Why is it important?"

"It is necessary for you to individuate."

"That's what you keep telling me. But you know, there are cultures where children are close to their families their whole lives."

He cocked an eyebrow.

"My mom's family had an exchange student from Denmark, Inge, back when Mom was a teenager? Well, Inge and her husband and kids came over from Denmark a few years ago. To see us and travel around. And their whole family was close. The teenagers were sweet to their parents. Inge and her daughter wore matching outfits."

"You sound like you've been thinking about this."

"At school, a guest speaker came in who had visited Papua New Guinea. And she said that there, whole families were close, even siblings. They were tight-knit, and they were nice to each other. They acted like best friends. Their culture was closeness and love, not fighting and chasms and distance."

Dr. Wexler said, "We don't live in Papua New Guinea or Denmark."

"That's not the point," I said.

"No," he said. "But I wonder about your point."

"What, you can never be wrong?" I asked.

"Seldom." He smiled. "But yes, I can be wrong. Can you?"

"I can be wrong. But I'm not wrong about this. I saw it with my own eyes. Inge's family was so close and did everything together and I don't see why this whole individuation thing is such a big obsession."

"The point is, perhaps there are cultures and families that are close. But do the children in those families have eating disorders? Do they find themselves hospitalized?"

"No," I admitted.

"No," he repeated. "That's the difference. And it's a pretty important one, wouldn't you say?"

"I guess."

He waited.

"But what if it's not?" I said.

"Not what?"

"What if it's a chicken and egg thing? You and Dr. Prakash say that enmeshment with my mom is the problem. But that doesn't feel like what started the problem."

"No?"

I shook my head. "I feel like what started the problem was being anxious and worried all the time. So then I turned to Mom for comfort."

He tapped his pen on my folder. "You think the anxiety came first."

"I think, maybe. Yeah."

"When did you first experience your anxiety?"

"At school."

"So…"

"I know what you're going to say. You're going to say my anxiety was caused by separation from Mom when I was at school. And that came from enmeshment. But what if it really did come first? The anxiety?"

"Well. Then what caused the anxiety? Where did it come from?"

I threw up my hands. "I don't know! That's the million-dollar question, isn't it?"

"Indeed."

"I don't have an answer." I sighed. "I was kind of hoping you could tell me."

Samuel Tuke Center
Adolescent Chemical Dependency (CD) Group Workbook

This exercise will help you get in touch with the emotional, mental, and physical parts of yourself in the here and now. These will probably change day to day, especially the emotional part.

Complete the sentences:

- Right now, today, I feel...*exhausted.*
- Right now, today, I am thinking about...*my upcoming therapy sessions, getting out of here.*
- Right now, today, what am I doing? *Feeling pain.*

Answer the questions in this exercise to help you understand who you really are.

1. What is more important to you than anything else in the world? *People liking me.*
2. How are you feeling about being here? *Sad, depressed, angry, anxious, relieved.*
3. Are you ever depressed? Describe? *Yes. It sucks.*
4. Have you ever been told you are hyperactive? *Yes.*
5. How do you feel about yourself? *Okay. Fat. My self-esteem could certainly improve.*
6. Have you ever thought you were crazy? *Yes.*
7. Do you lie when it would be easier to tell the truth? *Sometimes, yes.*
8. Do you have difficulty completing things? *Yes.*
9. Have you ever felt like hurting yourself? *Yes.*

10. Have you ever wanted to die? *Yes.*
11. Have you ever attempted suicide? If so, when and how? *Yes, last year—cutting wrists—never bad enough to be hospitalized.*
12. Is it hard for you to get close to someone? *No.*
13. Do you have trouble concentrating? *Yes.*
14. Do you feel you have a problem with drugs and/or alcohol? *Not sure, maybe. Yes.*
15. Do you think you are an addict or an alcoholic, or both? *Alcoholic.*
16. Of the following, which describes you best in relation to how your family sees you?

    A. The good guy/girl, taking care of everyone. *Mostly this one. The Good Girl.*
    B. Black sheep, always in trouble.
    C. Withdrawn, unnoticed, never missed.
    D. Clown, hyper, always on the go.
       A little bit. Hyper.

17. How are you feeling right now?
    Down, desperate, exhausted.

Reading assignment: continue reading *The Big Book of Alcoholic Anonymous*

Share written work with your primary.

December 27, 1988

To Whom It May Concern,

    I'm done. I'm not going to do these CD worksheets anymore. I've been doing them religiously, but no one is checking them or even asking about them. Unless I nag Chuck to look them over, these worksheets go completely unnoticed. I'm being honest with myself about my diseases—eating disorder, alcoholism. I'm reading the Big Book, because that seems like a legit endeavor. But meanwhile I have a ton of stuff to do for all my other groups, not to mention homework for my tutors who finally started showing up. Honestly, whoever is reading this (which will be no one, ever, thus the whole point of this note), I'm supposed to be individuating and figuring out who I am. Well, I've figured out that I'm someone who doesn't bother with pointless worksheets when there is real work to do for recovery.

                                      Sincerely,

                                    Jennifer J.

Wednesday, December 28, 1988

Treatment-planning Objectives for Jennifer

1. Patient will continue individuation by limiting phone calls to family to every other day.
2. Patient will continue to explore ways in which she can be more spontaneous in everyday life.
3. Patient may continue morning walks—*formal approval, walking only.*
4. Patient request for unsupervised bathrooms—*approved.*
5. Patient requests for weekend passes—*approved.*

Notes: Patient treatment-planning days are moved to Fridays. Next treatment-planning date will be Friday, January 6.

"You know, Jennifer," Dr. Prakash began, "you have talked about your father sometimes intellectualizing things." She lit a cigarette. "But I have been thinking. I have begun to wonder whether it is the case that, emotionally, your father is the most spontaneous person in the family."

"He's spontaneous with his temper tantrums, that's for sure."

"Let us lay the anger issue aside for now. I wonder if you

and your mother most often intellectualize and rationalize your feelings. And other people's feelings, as well. And whether you hold those intellectualized, rationalized feelings in."

"Wow." I was stunned. "Honestly, I hadn't thought about it. But…yeah. I think you're right."

"And tell me, Jennifer, where does your brother fit?"

"On the continuum of spontaneity versus holding things in?"

"Yes."

I rested my head on the back of the couch. Insights were tiring. As I stared at the ceiling, I said, "Not sure. He really just…melts away."

I could hear her recross her legs, her knee-highs brushing against each other. "By being spontaneous, you could avoid overanalyzing your feelings, Jennifer. You could express your feelings as they come. The way you report you are only able to do when you are—"

"Drunk?"

"Yes. But without the loss of responsibility. Or safety."

"So, being spontaneous," I said, looking at her, "is supposed to mean that my inhibitions are gone, that I don't worry so much about acting or sounding dumb?"

She smiled and spread her hands. "Yes."

"But what if I do?"

"Do what?"

"Act or sound dumb?"

"So what? Would the world end?"

I rolled my eyes.

"Jennifer, this may surprise you, but normal teenagers look and sound dumb sometimes."

"Sure. *Normal* teenagers."

"Let us discuss what you could do to start being a normal teenager."

"Go for it," I said. "Knock yourself out."

She ignored my snarky tone. "One thing you could do is start allowing your mother to be your mother. You do not need to protect her, Jennifer. Nor do you need to listen to her gripe about your father. Does this sound like something you could do?"

I nodded.

"You must also think about the things in your life that your parents *should* take more control over. Meals, curfew, whether you can stay home sick from school, and so on."

"I don't like the sound of that."

"You might not like the sound of that, but it is something that must be done. You need for your parents to be your parents. You cannot pick and choose the ways in which they take care of you."

"Why not?"

"You know why not. Picking and choosing is not letting them be your parents. It opens doors for you to begin manipulating, and lying, and hiding your feelings—"

"I know. I was kidding."

"Very well," she said. "Please, tell me some of your own ideas for being a normal teenager."

"Partying and drinking?" I suggested. "Isn't that normal for a teenager?"

"Allow me to revise my question. Tell me some of your own ideas for being a normal and *healthy* teenager."

I thought about it. "I guess I could stop telling everyone I'm doing okay all the time."

"Very good! You can start being honest and—"

"If you say 'spontaneous' I'm going to gag." Oops. "Not gag as in purge. Gag as in—"

She held up a hand to stop me. "Fine, fine. Continue. What will you begin being honest about?"

I shrugged. "I don't know. A lot of things. Like, if I'm mad, or upset, or feeling down. Or if I need help."

"That is a good start. But tell me, Jennifer, is a teenager's life always so serious?"

"Mine is."

"Perhaps that is something else to look at. For now, I want you to do this for me. Make a list, yes, of purely fun things that you like to do."

"Things I like to do for fun?"

"Yes, for fun. What do you enjoy? Write a list. This dovetails beautifully with our discussion of how to be yourself without all the competition and narcissism. Do you remember?"

"Bleh," I said.

"You must do this," she said. "It will be a wonderful resource for you in the weeks to come."

♥ ♥ ♥

Things I Like to Do, Just for Fun*
*That are also not unhealthy or dangerous

- Friday night dances at the Y.
  This is my very favorite thing ever.
- Go to the movies.
  Sometimes even by myself. Which makes me the lamest loser ever. But I don't care. Okay, actually, I do care, but I know I shouldn't.
- Go shopping for shoes, books, and tapes.
  Because it doesn't make me feel fat, like clothes shopping does. But, unfortunately, it does require transportation and money.
- Pet and cuddle with my dog.
  Spike! Give me Spike!

- Hang out with Kelly.
  *But not be gossipy and talk behind people's backs,
  because that makes me feel mondo guilty.*
- Hang out in nature, at Roger's
  Conservation Center.
  *This does not make me feel lame, but I need a ride to
  get there.*
- Go skiing.
  *Except I get ultracompetitive. If I go with my brother
  it's not as bad, because then I'm just trying to keep
  up and not break my legs. But this requires a ride and
  lots of money. And him being willing to be seen
  with me.*
- Browse the library for a good book. Bury my nose
  in it.
  Stay away from the 616.85 eating disorders section.
- Build tree houses with my next-door neighbor.
  Even though it sounds childish.
- Play Ditch or spies with my neighbors.
  Even though that sounds childish, too.
- Play with the little kids at my after-school job, or
  the little kids I babysit.
  Holy crap, I don't just sound childish—I am childish.
- Convince my brother to let me ride motorcycles
  with him.
  But this almost never happens.
- Go for walks in the rain.
  *But not if I think anyone can see me. Then I start
  thinking about how I look. And that is not fun
  or relaxing.*
- Art: drawing and painting.
  But thou shalt not compare thy art to other people's art.

- Listen to music.
  But not music I used to listened to when I was super depressed or drinking. No more Smiths.
- Decorate my room. Sketch decoration ideas.
  I heart decorating.
- Go mini golfing and alpine sliding at Song Mountain.
  But I would need a ride. And moolah.
- Hang out with the "nerds" in my class.
  Except I worry about becoming a nerd. But they are so nice, and really funny.
- Watch MTV.
  But not if I start comparing myself to skinny girls in videos. Which I usually do. So maybe instead:
- Watch *Star Trek: The Next Generation*
  Übernerd alert!

♥ ♥ ♥

"I miss Rob," Sophia said before lights-out.

"I miss Spike," I said.

Heavy sighs.

"This room is boring."

"Agreed. Let's redecorate." I put my journal aside.

"How?" she asked.

"Rearrange!" I said.

She grinned like the Cheshire Cat: slow, wide, toothy.

I popped out of bed. "What should we start with?"

"The beds."

"Let's put them in an L shape."

"This way." She motioned. "We'll put the foot of your bed up against the foot of mine."

I started scooting my bed, uncovering nasty carpet dust bunnies and who knows what else. "Gross!" I said. "I don't think these have ever been moved."

"Not in the history of the Samuel Tuke Center, and whatever hourly-rate motel this was before that. Disgusting."

We moved our dressers so they were back to back. We put our chairs in a little sitting area made from the space in the L of the bed.

Unfortunately, the headboards, nightstands, and reading lamps were permanently attached to the wall.

"It looks a little odd," she said.

"Not my best interior design scheme, that's for sure," I said.

Still, it was a change.

Thursday, December 29, 1988

A small crash. Something clattered onto the floor. "Ow!"

I sat up. A large, dark shape was hopping around.

1:02 a.m.

Shit! Had Jesus Lady come to get us?

No. It was Beverly doing night checks.

"Ow! Oof!" She tumbled onto Sophia's bed.

"What is it, Trombone Sam?" Sophia yelled, waking up from a deep sleep.

"Great gosh darn it!" Beverly said. "Gosh darn it."

Dark shapes wrestled in Sophie's bed until someone plopped unceremoniously onto the floor.

"Girls!" Beverly said. "What did you do?"

"Um. We rearranged?" I said.

"It is against the rules to rearrange your furniture."

"Shoot," Sophia said, her voice croaky with sleep. "We didn't know."

"I think I broke my toe," Beverly said, getting up.

"Are you okay?" Sophia asked.

"She thinks she broke her toe," I said unhelpfully. "Close your eyes. I'm turning the light on." I found my way to my formerly bedside reading lamp and turned it on.

Beverly, in pink scrubs, looked like an enormous flamingo, ruffled and discombobulated, standing on one leg.

"Sit." Sophia patted her bed and reached for her glasses. "Let me see your toe."

"It's fine," Beverly huffed.

"Sophia's in vet school," I said.

"I am not a dog," Beverly said.

"I didn't mean you were a dog," I said. "I just meant—"

"This is a fire hazard," Beverly said. "You two need to move things back the way they were. Right now." She hobbled out.

"Well, that didn't go as planned," Sophia whispered.

"Patients are not supposed to rearrange the rooms," I answered sternly.

"It's clearly a fire hazard."

"Have you no care for your safety?" I asked. "Or that of your nursing staff?"

"Nursing staff that elbowed me in the boob." Sophia rubbed her chest. "Jeezum. I thought the roof had collapsed."

We moved the furniture back into place, trying to do so quietly and trying really, really hard not to laugh.

When everything was back in place, I said, "Sophe?"

"Yeah?"

"Who's Trombone Sam?"

"What?"

"When you woke up, you said, 'What is it, Trombone Sam?'"

"You're making that up."

"I swear to God."

"I have never heard anything about a Trombone Sam."

"I swear I'm not making it up. You totally said it."

"So basically I said something that makes no sense, and that I don't remember saying."

"Yes."

"In other words, what you're telling me is that this place is making me truly crazy."

"Yes."

"I'm ready to go home now."

Friday, December 30, 1988

Sophia and I were on pins and needles all day. Was Beverly's toe broken? How much trouble were we in? Injuring staff…it couldn't be good.

Chuck didn't say anything about the room rearrangement, so Beverly must not have written us up in her notes. Yet.

When she hobbled in for night shift, my stomach sank. She had a removable Velcro cast/bootie-thing on her foot. Her toe was, indeed, broken.

Sophia and I looked at each other, then motioned Beverly to come with us into our room.

"We are so, so sorry," I said.

"We really are," Sophia added.

"We should have thought about you, how it would affect your night checks," Sophia said.

"We totally should have," I agreed.

"Well," Beverly said, "to tell you the truth, girls, if I were stuck in this place, I'd probably want to rearrange my room, too."

It was a bighearted thing for her to say.

"We're still really sorry," Sophia said.

"Are you going to tell how it happened?" I asked. "I mean, I'm sorry. I don't want to sound selfish. The main thing is that you got hurt, I know that. But I'm worried. Are we going to have consequences?" I felt like such an ass. "Sorry. Never mind. It was my idea. Give me the consequences."

"You know, I've thought about it," Beverly said. "I've had a lot of time to think—when I was getting X-rays, and then later, trying to sleep with this stupid thing on." She looked at her foot. "And I think no."

"No?" I asked, brightening.

"No," Beverly said. "It was an accident. You two are good girls, and you didn't mean any harm. If I report it, it'll get blown out of proportion. So, no."

"But...you shouldn't have to lie for us," Sophia said.

I wanted to scream, *Yes! Lie for us!*

"I told my supervisor I stubbed my toe and left it at that," Beverly said.

"Thanks, Beverly," Sophia said.

"We owe you one," I said.

"Don't mention it," she said. "Really, don't mention it ever again."

So we didn't.

But too bad I couldn't tell Dr. Prakash, because I realized later: the rearrangement was damned spontaneous. Maybe she would have been impressed.

Saturday, December 31, 1988

"He told me he won't refund our money from last summer," Mom said as soon as we sat down in Dr. Wexler's office for family therapy. "Partly because the camp would just lose that tuition and partly because, after interviewing other campers and counselors, they think your accident was preplanned."

"How does that make you feel, Jennifer?" Dr. Wexler asked. He passed me the tissues.

"Ashamed. Embarrassed."

"I was embarrassed, too," Mom said.

Which made me feel worse. I was the lowest slime on earth. What kind of person threw herself down stairs to get sent home from summer camp?

"And how about you?" Dr. Wexler asked Rich.

Rich shrugged and shook his head a little, like this wasn't any of his business and he wanted to stay out of it. I wished I could stay out of it, too.

"And you?" Dr. Wexler asked Dad.

"Extremely embarrassed," Dad said.

Which, for some reason, made me furious.

"You *should* be embarrassed!" I said. "Of your own self!"

Dr. Wexler looked surprised. "You seem very angry, Jennifer. What's going on?"

"I'm sick of talking about everything that's wrong with me. I'm not the only one who screws up and does embarrassing things. Why don't we talk about that?"

Dr. Wexler lifted his hands. "Go ahead."

"I just think my parents are being phony half the time they're here. Maybe subconsciously, maybe not. But ever since that first session, Dad acts all proper and doesn't let on about how vicious he can really be."

"Can you be more specific?" Dr. Wexler asked.

"I sure can. On Christmas, at the movies—"

"Oh, here we go," Dad said, rolling his eyes. "I'm the bad guy again."

"Can I finish?" I looked at Dr. Wexler. "Aren't I allowed to talk without being interrupted?"

"Will you give your father a chance to respond afterward?"

Dad snorted. Mom looked uncomfortable. Rich looked like he wanted to disappear.

"Yes," I said.

Dr. Wexler said, "Then yes, Jennifer, continue."

"On Christmas day, at the movie theater, I wanted to have a Sprite as one of my optionals, and Dad wouldn't trust me that I could. And he was totally mean about it, and loud, and embarrassed me for being in the hospital."

Dr. Wexler nodded. He turned to Dad. "And how do you respond?"

Dad sighed. "This is absurd. I explained to Jennifer that I had no basis for trusting her. And she blew it out of proportion, as usual."

"No. You're the one who brought my entire past into it! Like I can't make a fresh start here? Try to build up trust?"

"This is ridiculous," Dad said.

"Ridiculous? How about the fact that you were also basically bingeing in front of your daughter who has an eating disorder!"

Dad jabbed a finger at me. "You're jealous because you have problems and I don't. And that's just tough shit for you!"

336

"Jealous!" I said. "Of what! Of being someone who thinks he doesn't have issues when he's completely self-deluded?"

Dr. Wexler held his hands out like a referee. "Please. Slow down. There's clearly a nerve being touched here." He turned to Mom, then Rich. "I'd like to hear from Richard."

Rich shrugged. "Don't ask me. I wasn't there."

"He was in Colorado," I said. "It was just Mom and Dad and me."

"Okay, then." Dr. Wexler looked at Mom. "What is your perspective? You were present for this disagreement?"

Good. Maybe she would finally stick up for me.

"I came in at the end of it," Mom said.

I said, "Dad told her to butt out—"

"Jennifer, please. Let your mother talk," Dr. Wexler said.

Mom frowned. "Well...I...I could see they were disagreeing about something, and I was concerned, but..." She trailed off.

"You were concerned, but...," Dr. Wexler prompted.

"Earl asked me to stay out of it, so I did."

"Like always," I huffed.

Dr. Wexler ignored me. "And what was that like for you? Being told to stay out of it?"

"It was upsetting. Jenny looked distraught, and Earl looked angry. But I know I'm not supposed to get in the middle of things. Isn't that right?" She looked at Dr. Wexler plaintively, like she was a kid looking for guidance from her teacher.

Dr. Wexler leaned forward, fingers on nose.

"I—" Mom started crying softly. "I'm not supposed to team up with Jenny against Earl. That's been made clear. So I let it be."

Everyone was quiet.

"Can I say something?" I asked.

Dr. Wexler nodded.

"Well, okay. You and Dr. Prakash have been telling me not to gang up with Mom, against Dad. But that's so Mom doesn't use me as a confidante, not because she's not supposed to get in the middle of me and Dad. I don't know exactly how to say it. But isn't that a big difference?"

"Parse out that difference for me a bit more," Dr. Wexler said.

"It's the difference between Mom not teasing Dad with me, and Mom sticking up for me when Dad is mean. Sticking up for me and Rich."

"They're both ways your mother gets in the middle of things so you don't have to grow up and be mature," Dad snapped.

I grit my teeth. I was trying so hard to be reasonable. "I...I don't know. It feels different to me. Something about it is different. The power, or something."

"The power?" Dr. Wexler asked.

"I'm the daughter, right?"

Dad rolled his eyes. Again.

"I'm the daughter, Rich is the son, and you guys are the parents. So if one parent is being unfair to me, or Rich, shouldn't the other one stick up for us? Isn't that what parents do? Protect their children?" I started crying hard.

"Jennifer," Dr. Wexler said. "You're very upset. What's going on?"

"I feel like they haven't protected me at all. From any of the important things." I couldn't look at my parents. The sadness and hurt that had come over me was unexpected and intense.

"Say more about that, Jennifer," Dr. Wexler pushed.

"They think they protect me, but they don't. It's all the

wrong stuff. Dad gets radon testing for our basement. Mom makes me carry a whistle when I walk somewhere alone, to call for help if I get mugged. But they don't know the real stuff. They've been blind to how sad and sick I've been since like, the second grade. They haven't protected me from what I really needed help with!"

Mom started crying. "I'm sorry, Jenny. I'm so sorry."

"We do everything wrong, is that it?" Dad asked.

"No," I sniffed. "Well, yes."

We sat in silence until Mom and I stopped crying so hard.

Then Dr. Wexler said, "Richard. What is this like for you?"

Rich shifted uncomfortably. "I don't know. Jen has problems, and she's dealing with them, so that's good."

"And what about this conversation about protection? Does any of this ring true for you?"

Rich said, "I don't need protection. I'm fine."

"Hm." Dr. Wexler looked at me. "Jennifer, do you have anything to say about your brother's point of view?"

Oh, man. Dr. Wexler was prompting me to voice my concerns about Rich using drugs.

Dr. Prakash would tell me to be spontaneous, say what was on my mind.

But why was the onus on *me* to bring things up? What good did it do? It just pissed Dad off. Made Mom sad. Made Rich uncomfortable.

What was it Mom had said in T.J. Maxx? *You are the truth teller of our family.*

The truth teller of our family.

But she also said she knew it was a burden. And that I shouldn't have to carry all that responsibility myself.

Besides, I wasn't sure what the truth was. I didn't know

for certain whether Rich was smoking weed, or using other drugs, or putting himself at risk. So why upset everyone and alienate my brother?

"I think if Rich feels like things are okay for him, then that's good. I'm glad," I said.

"That's it?" Dr. Wexler said.

"That's it," I said.

My family had had enough truth for one day. And I was sure tired of being the only one telling it, killing myself trying to make them listen.

Sunday, January 1, 1989

1989. A new year. And my third major holiday in the hospital.

In honor of the beginning of the end of the decade, I made not just one, but two New Year's resolutions: (1) Recovery. (2) Never ever spend another holiday in a psychiatric institution, ever again ever.

After breakfast (French toast, yay), I solved the mystery of why my treatment-planning meetings changed from Wednesday to Friday, thereby unfairly delaying any new privileges for two extra days. It was because Dr. Prakash was leaving for a twenty-day vacation to Greece.

Happy New Year.

She pulled me in for individual, even though it was the weekend and a holiday. She was all business.

"First, Jennifer, I want to check in about how you are doing on your Norpramin."

"Okay, I guess." I shrugged. "It hasn't really been the miracle drug I was hoping for."

"You have been on it, what, two weeks now?"

"Three weeks, as of today."

She wrote a note in my file. "You have not noticed a shift in mood or attitude?"

I shook my head. "Not really. My dreams are more vivid, though. That's pretty cool."

"With luck, you should be feeling some benefit soon. Are you experiencing side effects? Not so sleepy, I hope?"

"Not so sleepy."

"Constipation? Dry mouth?"

"Uh, nope, I'm fine." I tried not to show my embarrassment. I truly did not want to discuss bowel movements with my therapist.

"Have you noticed, Jennifer, that over time, you have become a bit more animated? Cracking a few jokes? Smiling and laughing more?"

I scrunched my nose, thinking. I hadn't noticed. "Really?"

"Yes. It can be difficult to parse whether that is the Norpramin, or whether it is the process of becoming renourished. Either way, it is nice to see."

"Huh." Was it true? Could being fed actually change me that much?

She tapped her cigarette ash into the heavy glass ashtray. "Now, Jennifer. While I am away, you need to tell your mother that you need a mother, not a best friend, not someone who picks on her husband in front of you. Do that in your next family therapy session, yes?"

"I already tried," I said. "I brought it up yesterday and it went nowhere. My family acted like I dropped a dead fish in their punch bowl. I also talked about needing Mom to stick up for me when Dad gets mean. She should do that, right?"

Dr. Prakash nodded thoughtfully. "I want you to understand that the dynamics between your mother and father may require a longer process of change, one which you do not, and will not, have control over. So, you must focus on your direct relationships with your parents. That of you and your father. And you and your mother."

"Oh. Okay." That was disappointing, to say the least. I wanted an ally when Dad got angry. But it made sense. Why hadn't Dr. Wexler explained it to me like that?

"You have been working hard here. I hope you will continue to work hard, with Dr. Kanduri, while I am away. Will you do that?"

I nodded.

"Good. Now. I want you to request breakfast downstairs at your next treatment planning. Then next week, I want you to request lunch downstairs and snack out."

"Got it."

"The week after that, request meal out and regular trays and to learn your weight."

My weight. Yikes. "Do you think I'll be ready for that?"

"Dr. Kanduri will advise against it if she observes significant regression or backsliding. But barring that, yes. I am confident you will be ready."

"Okay," I said.

"You will not forget?"

"Are you kidding? I live for privileges. Besides, Chuck gives me advice about what to request."

"You have a nice relationship with Chuck, do you not? You have forgiven him for not being able to tell you about Heather's condition?"

"I never held that against him," I said. "He's the best nurse. You should give him a promotion."

She chuckled. "That is good. It makes me feel less guilty."

"Guilty! Why? You deserve a vacation." I would miss her, of course, but I didn't begrudge her a break from what had to be a fairly intense job.

"That is generous of you to say. But I find myself feeling quite guilty, leaving you, surrounded by all this…muck."

"Oh." I shrugged. "You mean everyone constantly complaining and threatening to sign themselves out." The mood of the EDU had gone downhill fast since Christmas.

343

Dr. Prakash exhaled, letting out a big trail of smoke. "Among other things. Yes."

"Yeah. It's pretty sucky."

She looked intently at me. "You have a nice friendship with your roommate?"

"Yup," I said. "Sophia's solid. But she's worried her insurance will run out."

"Oh dear. Would she qualify for Medicaid?"

"I think so? I'm not sure. I don't understand a lot of that stuff."

Dr. Prakash stubbed out her cigarette. "Well, hopefully it will work itself out. In the meantime, be careful about… just…" She trailed off. "Jennifer, have you heard the saying, *Not my circus, not my monkeys?*"

I shook my head.

"No? It is an old proverb. Polish, I think. Can you guess what it means?"

"Keep your nose out of other people's business?"

She smiled. "Partly. Also, it means to recognize when a problem is not your own. It means do not get swept up in all the"—she circled her hands around—"in all the hullabaloo."

"No hullabaloo. Yes ma'am." I saluted.

"Keep working hard, and I think you should be home in about four weeks."

My heart took flight. Home! "Really?"

"Indeed. I think you will most likely be in your last week when I return. Will you still be working hard toward your goals?"

"Of course."

"Please stay committed to your recovery, Jennifer. And remember: Not my circus—"

"Not my monkeys."

Monday, January 2, 1989

"I hate Mondays," Bronwyn groaned as Baldy set down her breakfast tray. "It always messes up my shit schedule."

"Thank God for unsupervised bathrooms," I said.

"Amen," Bronwyn said. "Praise Jesus they didn't take that away from me." Staff had revoked her meals downstairs privileges for weighing herself, but since she hadn't purged, they let her keep bathrooms.

Sophia lifted the lid off her Styrofoam cup, put it back down, and stared at it. "What is that?"

"Prune juice." I sighed in commiseration. "We have it every Monday. And then, every Monday, we all have to poop after breakfast. Like clockwork."

Sophia looked sick. "We did not have that last Monday."

"No?" I tried to remember.

"You didn't notice?" Amanda asked.

I shrugged. "I guess it was our Boxing Day miracle."

Sophia's face was nearly green. "I can't drink that."

"I know," I said. "It's awful."

"I can't drink it," Sophia repeated.

"It's gross," I said. "We all hate it. But you can do it. You just have to plug and chug. Observe." I pinched my nose, shut my eyes, and poured the whole thing down my throat.

Tears filled Sophia's eyes. "No, you don't understand. I can't. I can't drink this."

"What's wrong?" I asked. This wasn't like Sophia. It was starting to remind me of my showdown with the eggs, my first breakfast here.

"Can't I put it on my dislike list?" she asked Baldy. She sounded on verge of hysteria. "Can I put prune juice on my dislike list?"

"You have to drink it this time," he said. "Then it can go on your dislike list."

"But if I know it's going to be a dislike, why do I have to drink it?" Sophia was officially crying now.

"What's the issue?" Trendy asked.

Sophia rubbed her eyes with the back of her wrists. I handed her my napkin. "It smells like ipecac," she said. "I took ipecac once. To try to throw up and..."

Trendy huffed. "It's not fair to the other patients if you don't drink it. They all had to eat their dislikes first."

"It's fine with me," I said. "I don't mind."

"Fine by me, too," Charlotte interjected from another table. "Don't make her drink it because of us."

"If the reason she has to drink it is because it's not fair to us, and we all say it's fine, can you let Sophia not drink it?" I asked.

"I'm sorry," Trendy said. "Rules are rules."

"But you didn't say she has to drink it because it's the rule," I said. "You said she has to drink it because it would be unfair to us. And we all agree, don't we?" I looked around the room. "It's okay with us."

Everyone nodded, or shrugged, murmuring things like, "Yeah. Okay. It's fine."

I looked at Baldy, who was more likely to cave. "So it's okay then?"

I was walking a fine line. I felt like I needed to push staff

346

into a decision, but I couldn't seem like I was being insubordinate, because then they'd clamp down.

"Well..." Trendy hesitated. "If it's truly all right with you other girls."

"It is!" I said quickly.

Baldy took the dreaded Styrofoam cup from Sophia's tray. He replaced it with a plastic container of apple juice.

"Thank you," Sophia said to Baldy. "Thank you," she said to everyone. Then she turned to me and whispered, "Thank you."

I smiled and wiggled my eyebrows.

Victories were so rare here. It was fricking awesome to be able to help a friend.

Tuesday, January 3, 1989

"This is Patty," Charlotte said. We always started our weekly Community Meetings with introductions if there had been a new admission. "She was admitted last Friday."

Yes, Patty had already been here for four days. And if, after four days of living, eating, and therapizing with someone, you still needed an introduction, you were either catatonic or dumber than a box of rocks (or both). These introductions were as silly as having to state your name during in-house OA meetings.

Things I already knew about Patty: She was twenty-four. She was a demi soloist in the Houston Ballet. She just broke up with her long-term boyfriend. She was in Syracuse to visit her parents, who were rich. She came here straight from University Medical, because of acute dehydration and potassium deficiency from laxative abuse. She was bulimarexic, relatively physically messed up, and quite underweight. So she was about as far up the eating disorder hierarchy as a bulimarexic could get.

"Her likes include Baskin-Robbins mint chocolate chip ice cream, the Talking Heads, and foreign movies," Charlotte continued. "Her dislikes include racism, cilantro, and socks." Charlotte had a strong upstate New York accent, speaking in short, sharp vowels, so when she said "socks," it sounded like "sex." We were all used to it, but in this case, it was too good to ignore: *Her dislikes include racism, cilantro, and sex.*

Boy howdy, did that get staff's attention. Trendy, Baldy, and Ratched had all been looking bored, but they snapped to attention. They scribbled this down. *Patient lists sex as a dislike!* I could just imagine the field day Dr. Wexler would have with Patty's "issue."

I raised my hand. "Charlotte? Sorry to interrupt. But does Patty dislike all socks? Or just certain socks, like the itchy wool ones?"

"All socks," Patty answered for herself. She looked relieved to be able to put the kibosh on sex-dislike misunderstandings.

Then it was time to brainstorm possible "recreation outings." Staff loved to shoot down our ideas for anything good as too expensive, too dangerous, too far to travel. We invariably ended up seeing a movie at the two-dollar theater, because it was cheap, safe, boring, and easy for staff to chaperone.

"How about sledding?" Amanda suggested quietly.

"Yes!" I said. "Great idea."

"Fresh air," sighed Sophia.

"That sounds great," Monica said, and everyone agreed.

"Ah, hold on a minute, girls. I think you are in serious denial about the state of your health," Trendy said, right on schedule.

"Oh, come on, please let us? It would only be the medically cleared girls," I said. Sorry, Patty. Sorry, Thriller—who would possibly never get medically cleared, in this decade or the next.

Ratched stood and put her hands on her hips. "I don't think so. Trudging up a hill, over and over, in the cold? You girls think just because you're medically cleared that you're healthy?"

"Exactly, exactly," Trendy agreed. "You are not healthy individuals. We know it, and so should you. You've got a long way to go."

Ratched said, "And one of the first steps is acceptance. You need to accept the fact that you have brought ruin upon your bodies."

Brought ruin upon our bodies?

"Sledding would be freezing, anyway," Monica grumped.

"About as freezing as showers have been lately," I commiserated.

"Wait. Have your showers been cold, too?" Sophia asked. "I thought maybe you were using up all of our room's hot water or something."

"Mine's cold," Amanda said.

"Mine, too," Bronwyn added.

"My showers have been ice-cold for days," Monica said.

Even Thriller nodded.

"Why didn't you girls say anything?" Ratched asked.

"Maybe we didn't want to be seen as whining," I said, treading carefully. I didn't want to piss her off. Though I was annoyed that she didn't seem to understand that anything you said in here could and would be used against you.

Baldy asked, "Don't you see the difference between whining and being assertive?"

Bronwyn made a tooth-sucking sound. "That distinction has more to do with which staff is on shift than with the situation."

Ratched crossed her arms. "What do you mean?"

Bronwyn looked at Ratched, then down at her hands. She seemed to be backing down a little. "I just mean...staff can be inconsistent. Sometimes."

The air between Ratched and Bronwyn felt heavy. Ratched looked meaningfully at Bronwyn. "Inconsistent. How?"

Bronwyn didn't answer.

Sophia took up the slack. "I agree with what Bronwyn's saying. One nurse might say that breaking a dinner roll apart is diseased behavior, but another nurse will acknowledge that yes, that's how most civilized people eat a roll. Or you might say we can't have two juice cups in a row, but someone else will think it's fine."

Bronwyn added, "Two juices in row is not bingeing behavior."

"You are eating disordered," Ratched declared. "All of you. You have a disease. You're not the judge of what is or isn't diseased behavior."

"You need to be careful about the way you consume things," Trendy agreed.

"When you complain about food, you might could be avoiding something else," Baldy said. "You could be substituting food for whatever the real issue is."

"Do you ever eat the food here?" I asked. "It's disgusting."

Some of the girls giggled.

"Food isn't the real issue," Ratched said, unamused. "What is the real issue, Jennifer?"

"Sometimes food *is* the real issue," I said.

"Didn't you guys study Freud in nursing school?" Sophia asked. "'Sometimes a cigar is just a cigar.' Sometimes food is just food."

Ratched cocked her head. "You're changing the subject. You accused staff of being inconsistent."

We all nodded.

"Well. What am I supposed to do about that?" Ratched asked.

"You're the head of nursing staff," Sophia said. "You're supposed to do...everything...about that."

Ratched lifted her hands, palms up. "What can I do? People are inconsistent. Should I just fire everyone?"

"No, you shouldn't just fire everyone. That's flippant," Sophia said. "Patients aren't supposed to be flippant; you shouldn't be flippant either. We're trying to have a *conversation*."

"Well, I don't think there's anything that can be done."

"The showers," I said, rescuing Sophe from what might turn into a major showdown with Ratched. "Can anything be done about the hot water?"

Ratched nodded. "Yes. We will talk to custodial and see what can be done about that."

"But you girls aren't the judge of whether nursing staff is doing our jobs," Trendy said. "You need to learn how to be assertive without being passive-aggressive."

Opening your mouth to speak in here: still a lose-lose proposition.

But Sophia was my new hero.

Wednesday, January 4, 1989

Lately, I'd been having major trouble with maintenance weight.

To clarify: I was having trouble *thinking* about my maintenance weight.

I was not going to stop maintaining it. No no no. Privileges, privileges, give me more privileges.

But lately, I had been feeling enormous. Obese. Disgusting. Huge.

Chuck was off today, so I forced myself to talk to Ratched about it. I had to appease the beast once in a while.

"I'm having a hard time with the fact that I'm bigger," I said.

"Well," she said, picking at her sweater, "that's par for the course. If you want recovery, you'll learn to accept your healthy weight."

"Yeah. I guess."

"What's the real issue, Jennifer?"

The woman was like a broken record with her *real issues*.

"Um…I'm not sure. I mean, sometimes, can't it just be that I liked being skinny? And that it's hard not being skinny?"

"That's your disease talking. You need to get to the real issue. I bet it's because of your separation issues, and individuating, and finding out who you really are."

"But—"

"Gaining weight is not the issue, growing up is."

"Fine. But I still feel fat."

"Fat is not a feeling. Sad, happy, angry, frustrated, those are feelings. Fat is not a feeling."

I was pretty sure anger was a feeling.

Because I was feeling a lot of it right then. Toward Ratched.

She was the most unhelpful person to talk to in the history of the world. That flower metaphor she came up with was the one exception to prove the rule.

Yes! Fine! There were underlying reasons for my eating disorder! I knew I had to deal with them. It was a disease. I needed to individuate. I had to learn to express my feelings. Blah blah blah. But I couldn't help it: I still worried—what if being skinny was part of what had made me special, what made me *me*? Who was I, at my new weight? Sometimes it just sucked, how much I had to suck in my sucky stomach to fit into my favorite jeans anymore.

Samuel Tuke Center
Wellness and Nutrition—Homework

Write a letter to yourself, from the point of view of your body.

Be prepared to share your letter with the group at our next class meeting.

January 5, 1989

Dear Jen,

Thank you so much for finally listening to me! I feel so good since you've been feeding me nutritious and nourishing meals (even if the food can be kind of gross), and since you've put me at a healthy weight. Now I can defend us against feeling so sick!

You don't need to be tiny to be taken care of. Your mother or friends or future boyfriend or whoever will nurture you that much more now that you are getting healthy, because you are learning how to reach out and ask for what you need.

I know that sometimes you feel very fat, and you wish you could be stick thin. But I also know that you _know_ I am feeling better. More healthy. And when I feel more healthy physically, you can focus on feeling healthy emotionally. You can't work on your feelings and thoughts and beginning _recovery_ with a sick, weak body. Now you can begin learning who the real _Jen_ is!

I love you,
Your body

P.S. We have nice feet, don't you think?

Friday, January 6, 1989

Treatment-planning Objectives for Jennifer

1. Patient request for breakfast downstairs—*approved.*
2. Patient request for jog-walks—*denied. Continue walks on mornings when resting heart rate is less than 120 BPM. No walks if resting heart rate is greater than 120 BPM*
3. Patient will continue to individuate by limiting phone calls to family to every other day.
4. Patient requests for weekend passes—*approved.*

"So. Did you guys figure out the rules for me when I go home?" I asked during family therapy, just like Dr. Wexler and Dr. Prakash had instructed me to do. This session was just me, Mom, and Dad. Rich was at school.

Mom pulled out their list. It looked long. Way too long. I got a bad feeling about it.

Mom read out loud:

Rules for Jennifer When She Returns Home

1. *Jennifer must attend individual therapy as prescribed by Dr. Wexler or Dr. Prakash.*

2. *Jennifer must attend the outpatient support group at Samuel Tuke (led by Dr. Wexler, Thursday evenings) and Overeaters Anonymous in Norwich (Monday evenings).*

3. *Jennifer must attend family therapy as prescribed by Dr. Wexler.*

4. *Jennifer may not miss school unless she is sick with a fever greater than 100 degrees. No exceptions.*

5. *If Jennifer is absent from school without her parents' approval, she will be restricted from all activities (e.g., the YMCA dance, seeing friends, babysitting, etc.) for one month.*

6. *Jennifer will have a minimum of one hour of "quiet time" each night, during which there will be no television, phone calls, or music.*

7. *Jennifer will be limited to one hour of watching TV each school day. She may watch unlimited television on the week-end.*

8. *Jennifer will clean her room and both house bathrooms on a weekly basis.*

9. *Jennifer will participate in family "work projects" (e.g., mowing the lawn, washing the car, raking leaves, etc.) if she is asked to do so.*

10. *Jennifer will attend "family time" each Sunday from 5:00 p.m. until 7:00 p.m.*

11. *Jennifer will attend one church activity per month.*

12. *Jennifer will engage in no outside activities (e.g., dance class, babysitting, school clubs, etc.) during the first month after she returns home from the hospital.*

13. *Jennifer will use <u>no</u> alcohol, drugs, diet pills, laxatives, diuretics, or other substances that her parents deem harmful.*

14. *Jennifer will not use sarcasm with her father.*

Mom set the paper down.

"Oh, is that all?" I asked.

"That's sarcasm," Dad said. "And it's against the rules."

"That rule is preposterous," I said. "What happened to freedom of expression? I believe it's in the Bill of Rights."

"I just love how you know everything at the age of fifteen," Dad said.

"He can be sarcastic, but I can't?" I said to Dr. Wexler. "That is so unfair."

"Unfair! You don't know what's unfair," Dad said.

"Yes, I do!"

Dad laughed.

"Nice, Dad. Laugh at your daughter." I looked at Dr. Wexler. "How am I supposed to deal with this? 'Jennifer can't use sarcasm with her father.' But he can be as nasty as he wants? What a hypocrite!"

"Jenny," Mom said. "We are your parents. We are supposed to act like your parents. We are supposed to set clear boundaries. You wanted us to protect you, right?"

I couldn't believe she was using my own words against me.

"Listen to your parents, Jennifer," Dr. Wexler said.

I started crying. "I feel like you're all ganging up on me. Yes, I need you to be my parents, but *nice* parents! This is way too many rules! It will be like prison."

Or the hospital, all over again.

I had wanted to go home more than anything. Cripes. Be careful what you wish for.

Saturday, January 7, 1989

Breakfast downstairs was awesome. Awesome awesome awesome. It was a buffet!

The main dining room was about the size of my high school cafeteria, but carpeted, and with smaller tables and nicer chairs. All the patients from the Adult and Addictions units (I didn't know anything about the Addictions Unit, except that it was the biggest one at Samuel Tuke) ate in the dining room, as did their nurses, and any other staff who were foolish enough not to have brought food from home.

We weren't supposed to mingle with patients from other units, which was fine by me. I wasn't looking to strike up a friendship with a middle-aged heroine addict. Or Jesus Lady. It was weird to think I was in the same room as Jesus Lady—which one of these women was she? Everyone looked pretty normal and subdued. If anything, it felt like the EDU patients were considered the weird ones, based on the strangely wide berth other patients gave us when we went up to the buffet.

Buffet. I had to meet all my exchanges, of course, but I got to choose what to eat! Without any EDU staff making notes or staring over my shoulder!

The food in the buffet looked like the same food as on our trays, but there was more of the good stuff, and I could avoid any disgusting things. And there was dessert, even at breakfast—a big basket of pastries and doughnuts.

No doughnuts for me, though. It wasn't even tempting. I was determined to do everything right.

I chose Cheerios, because of the name. Maybe they would cheer me up.

And I got pineapple juice for my fruit exchange, because: yum.

And peanut butter instead of eggs! Peanut butter instead of eggs! Peanut butter instead of eggs! Peanut butter instead of eggs!

The tables reserved for EDU patients only fit two people each, but they were close enough together that we could chat between tables if we wanted.

I sat with Monica. She seemed a bit distant—not quite her usual self—but being there was still great. Amanda sat at the next table with Bronwyn, who had gotten her breakfast privileges back.

I sat there like a regular person—in a mental institution, granted, but still, a regular person! Adding a dash of milk and sugar to my coffee—grody, decaf, instant Sanka, granted, but still, coffee! I sipped it happily, acting like I was in a restaurant or something.

It was divine.

It was fabulous.

No more eggs, ever again!

Suck eggs, eggs.

Sunday, January 8, 1989

"Code Blue. Code Blue. EDU. All available nursing staff to EDU. Code Blue. EDU."

It was 1:48 a.m. And this time, the Code Blue was on our unit.

I hurried to the bedroom door. Sophia put her glasses on and followed. We looked up and down the hall. Nothing.

Bronwyn was at her door across the hall. "What's going on?" she asked, rubbing her eyes.

"I don't know," I said.

The door at the end of the hall banged open. Two male nurses rushed past us—straight toward Monica's room. Nurse Beverly appeared and waved them in.

Monica didn't have a roommate at the moment, so it had to be something to do with her.

"Come on," Bronwyn said. We ran down the hall to check on Monica.

A nurse blocked the door. "Get back to your rooms. Now."

We didn't move.

"Now!" he yelled.

We walked back slowly. Amanda, Patty, and some other patients were standing at the doors to their rooms.

"What do you think is going on? Did she hurt herself?" I said.

Bronwyn shook her head. "I don't know. Monica seemed pretty down earlier."

"Seems like she's been having a hard time ever since Christmas."

"I wish she would talk about it."

"Me, too. She puts on such a brave face to everyone all the time." I knew what it was like to put on a brave face. I had done it all the time at home. I hated to think of Monica pretending to be happy when she wasn't.

"What do you think is going on with her?" I asked again.

"The only thing I can think of is stuff about her sister."

"Maybe going home triggered her?"

"Yeah. I have a…I don't know…a feeling she's starting to remember some things she repressed. Really hard stuff gets repressed sometimes."

"God." People talked about repressed memories in group, but it was beyond anything I'd had to deal with. "Poor Monica."

"*Get into your rooms and stay there!*" the nurse shouted.

"Keep your pants on, we're going," Bronwyn told him. She gave me a sad little wave as we separated.

Sophe was waiting in our room. "Is it Monica? Is she okay?"

"I don't know."

"I hope whatever it is, it's not too bad," she said as we climbed back into our beds.

"Me too."

We lay there, listening, until we heard footsteps in the hall and the voice announced, "All clear."

♥ ♥ ♥

Beverly hobbled in for room checks at 2:45.

"Is Monica okay?" I whispered. Sophia had been quiet a long time; I figured she'd gone back to sleep.

Beverly sighed, "Oh, hon. I probably shouldn't talk about it with you."

"Please, Beverly," I whispered. "I can't sleep, I'm so worried. Please?"

"All right. But I don't want you to get upset."

"I won't."

I heard Sophia's sheets rustle. She sat up to listen.

"Monica cut her wrists," Beverly said.

"No!" My stomach twisted. "Is she okay?"

"Yes. I found her before she did too much damage."

"Did she need to go to the hospital?" The medical hospital, I meant.

"No, she was conscious and responsive, and she didn't need stitches."

"What did she use?" Sophia asked. "To cut herself?"

Beverly hesitated. "A staple."

A staple. My stomach felt oily, rancid.

"You found her?" Sophia asked.

"Yes," Beverly said.

"Are you okay?" Sophia and I asked at the same time.

Beverly took a deep breath and let it out slowly. It was quiet. Our room lights were off, but the hall light was on, as always. I could see her wipe her eyes.

"Yes, girls. I'm all right. It's upsetting, but don't you dare worry about me, you understand?"

We nodded in the semidark.

"You girls, you just don't realize that your problems are temporary. You have to remember that. 'This too shall pass.' You need to take care of yourselves. You are each a gift from God. Understand?"

"Yeah," Sophia said quietly.

"Is Monica...did she have to go to the ICU?" I asked.

"No, hon. She's in her room. She's resting. And I want you to do the same. Try to get some sleep."

Sophia and I lay back down.

"We'll get everything sorted in the morning," Beverly said.

We listened to her leave, shuffling on her bootie.

When she was gone, Sophia said, "Get everything sorted? What does that mean?"

"Maybe they'll have to put Monica on one-to-ones again? Extra staff watching her all the time?"

Sophia sighed, "That girl is troubled."

"I guess…," I said. But Monica wasn't any more troubled than the rest of us. Was she?

"I know you guys are close…" It sounded like Sophia was trying to be careful.

"She saved me when I first came here," I said. "I mean, *saved* me. I thought I would die, literally die of sadness and homesickness. She was so kind to me. It was a lifeline."

"Mm," Sophia said.

"My first week, she tied a string around my finger so I wouldn't forget that she loved me, and that I could talk to her anytime."

Sophia was quiet for so long I thought she'd fallen asleep. But then she said, "I don't want to dis your friendship. I'm just not sure she's the best person to depend on."

"She's been having a hard time lately. You haven't seen how she usually is."

"I'm sorry, Jen. I'm really not trying to be mean. But a lot of these girls—most of them, actually—I just don't want you to get hurt. I think you should be careful."

"Okay. Thanks." I didn't know what else to say.

I lay there, wondering.

Did Sophe see things in Monica, in my other friends, that I didn't? Or couldn't? Or wouldn't?

Were her eyes better trained to see illness, coming as she did from a truly crazy family?

Was I as blind to my friend's pain as my parents had been to mine?

♥ ♥ ♥

In the morning, Monica looked tired and pale. Her wrists were wrapped in gauze bandages, secured with white tape. She sat quietly in the lounge; she didn't want to talk.

Chuck didn't let her out of his sight.

She would probably have to eat breakfast in the lounge now; no more dining room for her. Was she back to stage one? One-to-ones? No longer medically cleared?

As Bronwyn, Amanda, and I headed downstairs for breakfast, Ratched stopped us in the doorway. "Hold up a second." She addressed the whole room. "I want you all to know, we're doing a unit-wide room search."

A ripple of alarm spread through the lounge. Trays had just arrived; everyone was here for breakfast, so people were trapped. No one could run off to hide anything.

"We'll be collecting any stapled papers. We're looking for sharps, contraband, you name it," Ratched said. "We'll be collecting earrings, too. They'll need to stay in your baskets from now on. After breakfast, we'll have you sign in your jewelry and double-check that we've accounted for everything."

Sophia widened her eyes at me. *Shit.* She had a bottle of hair spray on her dresser. I had reminded her to check it back in, but she'd said she didn't see why hair spray had to stay in baskets. The nurses hadn't noticed. Yet.

I tried not to look at Monica, but I couldn't help it. She was sitting at the table next to Chuck, staring at her hands in her lap, crying silently. She had created this situation. Now she was going to get Sophia in trouble. And probably other people as well.

But, I shouldn't be mad. It was her disease. Obviously she was going through something painful.

♥ ♥ ♥

I sat alone at breakfast. Amanda and Bronwyn were at the table next to me. All of us were pretty quiet. My thoughts kept drifting up to the unit. Would Monica be okay? How much trouble would Sophia be in? Would they take away her privileges—passes and unsupervised bathrooms? Who else was in trouble?

After breakfast, Ratched had us sign in our earrings and jewelry and watched us take staples out of handouts and homework. As soon as we were done, I found Sophia in the lounge.

"Did you get busted?" I asked.

"Yeah," she said. "But so many other people had mousse and hair spray in their rooms that staff let us off with a warning and a week of early bedtimes. Big wow. I need the sleep anyway."

"Phew," I said. "So you're on teenager bedtime, like me."

"Anyway, Rob should be here any minute now."

"What are you guys going to do on pass?"

"Oh, you know..." She wiggled her eyebrows.

"Make good choices," I teased. "Don't do anything I wouldn't do."

"Never and always."

♥ ♥ ♥

Monica was curled up in the corner of a couch, smoking. Bronwyn sat next to her.

"Hey," I said. "You okay, Monica?"

She didn't say anything. She took a drag of her cigarette.

Bronwyn looked at me and shook her head, like she hadn't had any luck, either.

Chuck sat in a recliner next to Monica, writing notes in a file. He gave me a sad little smile.

Bronwyn and Amanda both tried to hug Monica before they left on their morning passes. Nothing.

My pass wasn't until after lunch, so I stayed in the lounge. Chuck and I tried to get Monica to play cards with us—Bullshit or poker or anything she wanted—but she shook her head in tiny, almost imperceptible movements. So Chuck and I sat on the floor next to her and played Spit on the coffee table.

A short time later, Monica said, "I need to get something from my room." Her voice was raspy, maybe from disuse, maybe cigarette smoke.

Chuck got up.

I followed them down the hall, an uninvited tagalong. Monica didn't seem to want me around, but I couldn't bring myself to leave her. She had been everything to me when I got here. I couldn't let her go through this alone.

"I should probably get my homework," I said. "You're lucky you don't have tutors, Monica. I honestly don't know how they expect me to concentrate on schoolwork in a place like this." I knew I sounded artificially happy.

"Would you rather get even more behind in school?" Chuck asked.

"Oh, stop talking sense," I told him. "I'm trying to complain here. Right, Monica?"

Suddenly Monica collapsed.

Chuck caught her on the way down.

She was as white as a ghost. Her head bobbled as Chuck laid her down on the hall floor. She was out cold.

"Code blue!" Chuck yelled. "Jennifer, go to your room, please."

I didn't go to my room. I ran to the nurses' station. Ratched was already out of her chair.

"I-i-it's Monica," I stammered. "Code blue."

"Get to your room." She picked up the phone and jabbed buttons.

The loudspeaker clicked on. Calm male voice: "Code blue. Code blue. EDU. All available nursing staff to EDU. Code Blue. EDU."

"Get to your room," Ratched repeated, pushing past me.

The door at the end of the hall opened, and nurses swarmed past.

A horrible smell burned my nostrils. It was so powerful, it felt like breathing caustic poison. It took me a moment to register: ammonia. What Mom used to clean the oven. What smelling salts were made of. They were using smelling salts to wake up Monica. Through the crowd of nurses, I saw Monica's head wobble.

Chuck and another male nurse helped her stand, supporting her with their arms, half-carrying her to her room.

First her wrists. Now this.

What had she been doing, to faint like that out of nowhere?

♥ ♥ ♥

Mom took me to the movies after lunch. On the drive to the theater, I told her what had happened. How worried I was.

How hollow Monica seemed.

Mom just listened. Which was exactly what I needed.

We saw *Twins*, with Danny DeVito and Arnold Schwarzenegger. It, too, was exactly what I needed. It made me laugh, and helped me get my mind off things. Thank Hollywood for silly movies.

By the time I got back for dinner, Monica had started talking again. Soon I started to wish she hadn't.

"I'm done with this place," she said. "I'm signing myself out of here."

"God, me too," Bronwyn said.

Sophia and I exchanged a look across the table. We were both so tired of people threatening to write their 72-hour letters for self-discharge.

I wanted to shake Monica. I wanted to take her by the shoulders and scream, *Hello! Earth to Monica! What do you think would happen if you were outside these walls on your own right now? You could die! You've had two code blues in less than 24 hours!*

It had to be a record. Even Jesus Lady hadn't managed two code blues in less than a day.

I ate my dinner—dry chicken, stringy squash, wilted salad, and bruised orange (peeled by me, not Monica)—in silence. My ears were hot. My neck was sweating. I was literally hot under the collar.

When people talked about signing themselves out, as though they could just decide this "journey" was over and they were capable of being in charge of their health and not *dying*, they were shitting on what this place stood for. The potential for recovery. The safety it provided while we were confused and in danger—even if it felt like a hellish prison sometimes. The benefit of having a place to belong while we figured out how to be well.

They were rejecting this program and the whole healing process. Which I took personally, because it was everything I was working hard at.

As soon as I could leave the lounge, I went to my room. Chuck's shift was over. Sophia was on the phone. I was alone, and lonely.

I lay on my bed, squeezed Bearibubs, and covered my ears to block out everyone else.

Not my circus, I told myself. *Not my monkeys.*

I repeated it like a mantra:

Not my circus.

Not my monkeys.

Except it *was* my circus. Because, as I lay there, I noticed all my things out of place from the room search.

This was my circus. I was stuck with these monkeys.

Monday, January 9, 1989

Dr. Kanduri told me my tentative discharge date: February first! A light at the end of the tunnel!

Three weeks and two days left in this hellhole.

23 days.

Equals 552 hours.

Equals 33,120 minutes.

Equals 1,987,200 seconds.

"It's right around the corner," Dr. Kanduri told me.

She was nice; she wasn't trying to take Dr. Prakash's place. We weren't delving deep into my past and my issues, which I appreciated, because I really didn't feel like starting over. Our sessions were five minutes long. She seemed to just want to make sure I was staying on the right track.

Dr. Kanduri said, "The last three weeks will fly by."

"I don't think you've ever been a patient in a mental hospital," I said.

She laughed.

Home. I would walk into my house and give Spike the biggest hug and never let him go. And choose my own snacks, and eat Mom's noninstitutional cooking, and use the bathroom without having to collect my pee for 24 hours every Tuesday, and use the phone for longer than ten minutes at a time, and laugh at my brother's stupid jokes, and watch *Star Trek: The Next Generation* with Dad, hang out with Kelly, and take Spike on long slow walks around town.

Except, would people stare at me on those walks? Would they drive by and think, *There's the girl who was in the eating disorder hospital?*

Would I join the ranks of the shell-shocked man? Would I become one of the town weirdos?

♥ ♥ ♥

"I got my tentative discharge date!" I told Sophia.

"I got breakfast downstairs," she said.

"Yay! We can sit together!"

"Yeah." She was sitting cross-legged on her bed, which was covered with envelopes and papers.

"What's wrong?" I asked. "Aren't you happy?"

She held up one of the papers. "My insurance is definitely running out."

"No way," I said.

"I think I have about a week left."

"What are you going to do?" I asked. "Have you figured out about your Medicare?"

"Medicaid," she corrected. "Medicare is for old people."

"You're old people."

"Very funny."

"Well? Medicaid, then?"

She slumped, resting her back against the wall. "It looks like I'll have to go home for about a week, and then Medicaid will kick in and I can come back."

"Will you go to your mom's or your dad's? Or Ithaca?"

"I don't even know."

"I'm so sorry," I said.

"Yeah," she said.

"If I had my own house, you could come live with me."

"Thanks."

"Spike would love you."

"We could have a zoo."

"'Lions and tigers and bears.'"

"'Oh my.'"

Sophia moved to the edge of her bed carefully, so she didn't disrupt all her papers, then stood. "I'm going to go see if the phone is free."

"Call my mom for me," I said.

"Sure. After I call the insurance company. And Rob."

As she walked out, Ratched came in.

"Jennifer, don't you have any treatment-planning requests?" she asked.

"Nooo..." I was confused. Why was she asking? "My treatment-planning day is Friday."

"No, it isn't. Your treatment planning is today."

"What? No. My treatment planning moved to Friday."

"No, it's today. You need to turn in your requests. They're already late."

"But..." I started crying. Treatment planning was everything here. Everything. Passes, privileges, progress. "It's supposed to be Friday! I don't know what to ask for!"

"Jennifer, calm down," Ratched said. "Your response does not equal the situation. This is not the way someone in stage three should be acting. Pull yourself together."

Pull myself together? I was frantic. "I don't know what passes to request! I haven't talked to my parents! I can't call them until tomorrow! How will I know when they can come?"

"Why are you so unprepared? You need to take responsibility for your own recovery."

"I am! I do! But my treatment planning is Friday!"

Ratched shook her head slowly, like she was absolutely disgusted. She turned on her heel and walked out.

Sophia came back. I was still bawling. "Jen! What's wrong?"

I told her what happened. She disappeared. I tried to think what to do, but I couldn't make my brain work.

Sophia reappeared, with Dr. Kanduri.

"Oh, Jennifer," Dr. Kanduri said calmly. "Please tell me what's going on."

I told her what happened. Dr. Kanduri's lip curled; she looked intensely annoyed. But I could tell her irritation was with staff, not me. She marched off to the nurses' station looking like she was going to kick Ratched's ass.

Sophia and I looked at each other. We ran over and pressed our ears on the wall, but we couldn't hear anything.

Then we heard the nurses' station door, followed by footsteps heading our way, so we dove onto our beds. Sophia's papers scattered all over.

Dr. Kanduri came back in. "Not to worry, Jennifer. It is all straightened out. You were right, of course. Hopefully they will not make that mistake again."

"Thank you," I said.

"You are most welcome. And thank you, Sophia, for bringing this to my attention."

"Yeah, thanks, Sophe," I said.

"No problem."

Dr. Kanduri left.

I rolled out of bed and started picking up Sophia's papers and envelopes. "You know what I love?" I asked, sniffing. I was a mess, still taking shuddery breaths from crying.

"Do tell." Sophia leaned over her bed, stacking the papers as I handed them to her.

"I love how staff keeps telling me I need to be more independent. But look at this place! Everything is set up for dependency. I try to be assertive and say when my treatment planning is, and staff doesn't believe me, so we have to depend on other staff to straighten things out with the first staff. No matter what, I'm completely dependent."

Sophia laughed. "Irony."

"I probably did overreact, though…," I said meekly.

"I don't actually think so. Maybe in the outside world. But in here? One false move—as defined by staff, of course—and any and all privileges can be yanked. It's high stakes."

"Everything we've worked for can just go poof."

"Yup. Anything that gives us a shred of dignity or control—"

"Or happiness…," I mused, thinking of how Ratched had shut down dancing with Bronwyn, and our after-meal game of Bullshit, and our sledding idea.

"So you *should* freak out if staff tries to change the rules on you." She started a new pile of papers. "I'd like to see what Ratched would do if she was a patient, and staff tried to change the rules on her."

"I would pay to see that," I said.

"Can you just imagine? She'd go batshit crazy. It would be hilarious."

"It would be funnier if it wasn't so infuriating."

"Ah, but it's funny because it's true," she said.

"PS," I said. "Thanks again. You're an awfully good friend."

"You too, you big dumb stinker."

"Big dumb stinker! You're going to give me a complex. And an eating disorder."

She grinned. "How about a complex eating disorder?"

"God. I try to have a serious, heartfelt friendship moment, and look what it gets me."

"Sorry," she said. "I guess I'm not as mature as you are."

"Old people–Medicare notwithstanding," I said.

"Shut up," she said in an old lady voice. "You kids, get off my lawn."

Tuesday, January 10, 1989

"So, how have you been doing lately?" Dr. Wexler asked.

"Crappy. Dizzy."

He flipped to the vitals page in that stupid folder dedicated to the life of Jennifer H. Johnson. Whoever that was.

"My pulse this morning was one hundred forty. It's been super high for ages. I never get to go on morning walks."

"We're monitoring the situation. Your pulse and dizziness are likely a somaticized response to stress." He sighed. "It certainly seems that you're attuned to what's going on physically."

I groaned. "You asked me how I was doing."

"And you answered by listing physical symptoms."

"So my body doesn't matter? I thought the whole point of getting healthy is there's a mind-body connection. It's all supposed to be integrated."

"We've gone over this before, Jennifer. You tend to somaticize things. You feel your emotions in your body, when you should be talking about them and dealing with them in sessions."

"You asked me how I was doing, and I answered the question, and then you got all sarcastic and snippy."

We just went around and around like that, like two dogs chasing each other's tails, until time was up.

In therapy, sometimes there wasn't a big insight, or emotion, or even much of a conclusion.

Sometimes you just had to show up, put your time in, and stop when your fifty minutes was over.

Wednesday, January 11, 1989

"Travel to all four corners of the room," Therapy Liz instructed. "There's no order, no right or wrong."

I was the sole fan of Movement Therapy. God bless Therapy Liz, who led all the most loathed EDU classes: Movement, Wellness and Nutrition, Aerobics, Body Image. She had to do the impossible: convince EDU patients that butter and olive oil were healthy, or that we could exercise—"noncompulsively!"—in a mirrored studio. She withstood a constant barrage of resistance. Her leotards must have been armor-plated.

But Movement was as close to dancing as we could get in this place. Plus, unlike walks and aerobics, staff was still letting me do this, even with my high pulse.

We were in the movement studio, in the newer wing of Samuel Tuke. The room had a high ceiling, a huge bank of windows covered in purple curtains, and unfortunately, one wall of mirrors. Which was triggering for everyone.

Hello, body image issues! Hello, dance class memories!

They should have hung curtains over the mirrors instead of the windows. I would rather have natural light and zero reflection.

I wore baggy pants and my biggest sweatshirt in the studio. The opposite of a leotard and tights.

"The first time we travel, we'll move indirectly," Therapy Liz said. "I want you to wander. Just do what feels good, don't think about it too much. Then we'll go through a second time, with direct movement." She ignored everyone's grumbles and put on slow, new age music with wind chimes and pan flutes. "Okay, indirect movement. And. Allow yourselves to begin."

I wanted to dance around like a silly Muppet. But I was still a little dizzy. And all the other girls were moping around, zombie shuffling from place to place. It reminded me of a school dance, before anyone starts actually dancing, and everyone just stands around, waiting for someone else to get things rolling. I did sway a bit, but felt too inhibited by every-one's gloom to do any major interpretive dancing.

I saunter-swayed to the windows and pulled the curtains aside. Big, fluffy snowflakes were floating down from the sky, doing their own little dances on small updrafts, decorating the benches in the courtyard like frosting on a cake. It was beautiful. Therapy Liz smiled and came over to look.

After a few more minutes, Liz paused the music. "Okay. Very good. And now, show me some direct movement!"

I marched from corner to diagonal corner. Some of the girls power walked. There was a lot of giggling.

"Great job!" Liz turned the music low. "Let's gather in the middle and talk."

It was funny how Movement Therapy and Art Therapy and Journaling were all supposed to be stream of conscious-ness, uninhibited, and...duh duh duh...spontaneous. *Just let the feelings flow. Don't analyze or judge.*

But what did we always, always do after the spontaneous movement, or art, or writing?

Analyze the crap out of everything.

I guess the point was: do first, think later.

And it was cool, how you could get crazy insights from stuff you thought was totally subconscious. But where was

Wednesday, January 11, 1989

the line between appreciation and overanalysis?

Wasn't there a way to not ruin the beauty of what you created with too much jibber jabber?

We all circled up on the floor and processed. Using non-judgmental language, of course.

When Liz got to me, she asked, "Which movement felt more comfortable for you, Jennifer? Direct or indirect?"

"Indirect, definitely."

"Ah." Liz nodded. "You know how you stopped and opened the curtains? It was wonderful, because it prompted me to go over and look. I wouldn't have seen the beautiful snow if you hadn't stopped to look at it along the way."

"That's pretty cool," I said.

"It is pretty cool. Have you heard the saying *Recovery is a journey, not a destination?*"

I looked at Sophia and raised my eyebrows.

Liz continued, "It can be easy to overlook the beauty in our journeys." She leaned back, quiet for a moment, like she was thinking. "I noticed something else. Jennifer, you said indirect movement felt more comfortable for you. Yet you always looked like you knew right where you wanted to go. Does that ring true?"

I considered. "I guess I'm always concentrating on where I'm going, rather than where I am. But that's ironic? Because I like moving indirectly better than directly. It's a contradiction," I sighed. "It's confusing. I'm a bundle of contradictions."

Liz smiled. "It's okay to be a bundle of contradictions. The point is that you are gaining insight into who you are. What your contradictions are."

I scrunched my nose. "I should try to be more in the moment, though." I knew Dr. Prakash was right: I did need to be more spontaneous.

"Maybe." Liz shrugged. "Don't be too hard on yourself. It's good to know where you're headed. It's good to have goals. As long as you also remember to stop and smell the roses."

I actually hated the smell of roses. But I got her point.

Thursday, January 12, 1989

Today in group, Patty, the socks/sex-hating former ballerina announced, "I just think I have to leave this place, in order to be true to myself."

"That's exactly how I feel," Monica said.

This again. Right.

I wanted to shout, *Patty, you just signed yourself in directly from the medical hospital! What are you thinking! And Monica, you cut your wrists and passed out!*

Stop complaining and focus on what you can do here!

Or, you know what? Forget it.

Just shit or get off the pot. Everybody who's not committed to recovery, just go. Pack your bags and leave. Don't let that heavy glass door hit you in the ass on your way out.

Or do let it. I don't care.

But who would be left?

Me and Sophia.

Not Charlotte, Patty, or Monica.

Thriller? That girl was still an enigma. She never complained, but she also barely talked. I had a feeling she was working the program as hard as she could—laxatives notwithstanding. Her brain and body just weren't re-fed enough to be capable of good decisions, or much other thought, insight, or energy yet.

As for Amanda, she had her discharge date: January 25.

I still couldn't believe it. When Amanda had told me, I tried to smile and be happy for her, but she was still fighting the program as much as she was working it. I bet staff wanted to keep her longer, but Amanda's obnoxious dad was pushing for her release.

Bronwyn had her date, too: January 20. Eight more days.

Even though it was only eleven days earlier than my tentative date, I was so far beyond jealous, I couldn't even see jealous from where I was standing. Eleven days felt like a lifetime. Dr. Kanduri had said my last three weeks would fly. Wrong. Time was dragging slower than ever.

Patty nodded, emboldened by Monica's encouragement. "I don't have any issues. I just want to be skinny."

I almost snorted. What a load of crap.

I liked being skinny, too. But that wasn't the same as not having issues.

"Jennifer, what do you think about all this?" Dr. Wexler asked.

I looked around the group. I didn't want to sound mean or bitchy. I didn't want to make anyone mad. I wouldn't have survived my first week without Monica or Bronwyn. But I was sick of Monica talking about signing out, when she clearly wasn't healthy enough for outside life. And I was fed up with everyone being so cynical. "Um, well, I guess I just...I feel like I'm going to stay and you know...work the program."

"Patty, how do you respond?" he asked.

Patty frowned. "I think the only reason Jennifer is working the program is to get other people's approval. She wants a Certificate of Completion or something."

My whole body went hot with anger. Just pure fury. *Fuck you, Patty. Fuck you and the horse you rode in on.*

But I didn't need to create more drama in this place. I needed less drama. Less drama.

"Well, okay, sure," I said, willing myself to be calm. "Approval is nice. But…I believe in this program. I believe it's saving my life. And also I'm fifteen, so I can't really sign myself out, can I?"

"I'm old enough to sign myself out, and to know what's best for me," Patty said. "I don't need a stamp of approval."

I wanted to punch her in the throat.

Friday, January 13, 1989

Treatment-planning Objectives for Jennifer

1. Patient request for lunch downstairs—*approved*.
2. Patient will continue phone use every other day for family phone calls.
3. Patient requests for weekend passes—*approved*.

Today, Charlotte confessed that she'd been faking a stomach flu to cover up the fact that she had been PURGING FOR THE LAST TWO WEEKS. I couldn't believe it.

Back to stage one for her.

I did not ever, ever want to go back to stage one.

So even though I was coming down with a cold—sore throat and stuffy nose—I didn't say anything to staff about it, didn't ask for any Tylenol or Chloraseptic. Not after the fake-flu brouhaha. They'd probably overreact and somehow I'd be punished horribly for actually being sick.

Even if I was dying of Spanish flu, I would just suck it up.

If this place was teaching me anything, it was to lie low. Not to seek attention unless I truly needed help. Hup-two. Buck up. Suffer in silence.

Saturday, January 14, 1989

"Your mother and I have discussed it, and we do not want you to think about Samuel Tuke as a second home," Dad said in family session. "So if you ever need to go back into a hospital, it will be somewhere new."

"Fine by me," I said.

Dr. Wexler's eyebrows flew up. "Jennifer, you're comfortable with this?"

"Sure. I don't ever plan on coming back here, or any other hospital. This is it. I'm done."

Dr. Wexler looked at my parents. "May I ask what prompted this decision?"

I had an inkling. Sure enough, Mom said, "We have close friends whose daughter was admitted to a psychiatric hospital—a different one, not here—for depression. Shortly after she was released, she went back in. My friend, the girl's mother, told me that she thought her daughter was trying to avoid real life. That she was using the hospital as an escape."

"Ah." Dr. Wexler turned to me. "Jennifer? What do you think?"

"Dude. It's totally fine," I said.

"But I would suspect you would want to come here. Since it's familiar—"

"Seriously," I interrupted. "It's fine. It's not an issue. Let's move on."

He looked incredulous. "All right, then…"

"Anyway, I thought you said there's no doubt I would make it."

He shifted in his seat, but he had to concede a small smile.

♥ ♥ ♥

"You know what?" I said to Sophia. "I need a lunch box. For going back to school."

Mom had taken Sophia and me out. I wanted them to meet, so Mom drove up separately from Rich and Dad, and after family therapy, the boys went home and Mom took us to the Penn-Can Mall.

While Mom went to the department store to get boxers for Dad and Rich, Sophia and I poked around the drugstore, looking at lotions and mousses, magazines and greeting cards.

"Do you really want a lunch box?" She tilted her head thoughtfully. "Not paper bags? A lunch box is so conspicuous. And kind of…young. Although I like the thought of you packing your lunch. That's good. Meet those exchanges. Be a recovery hero."

"Do you remember what a high school cafeteria is like?"

She shuddered. "I've blocked it out."

"Let me remind you, then. The cafeteria is nothing less than a torturous agony of torment. Maybe they're over this way? School supplies." We walked to the next aisle. "I'm already going to feel conspicuous. So I might as well embrace my conspicuousness."

"It's going to be hard, huh?" she asked, getting serious.

"Yeah."

We found the lunch boxes. "Okay," Sophia said. "Wait. Let me pick one out for you. Close your eyes."

I closed them. "Just don't give me Smurfs. I hate the Smurfs."

"Good Lord. Who hates the Smurfs? You need therapy."

"Clearly."

I could hear her moving around, shifting things on the shelf. "Hm...G.I. Joe? No. Ninja Turtles? No. Looney Tunes—"

"From the loony bin."

"Appropriate, but no. Barbie? No way. What the heck are Dino Riders?"

"No idea."

"Star Trek: The Next Generation..."

"I do like Captain Picard."

"No."

"Too geektastic?"

"It's just not the right fit," she said. "I'm looking for some-thing more...yes. Yes. This is the one. Hold out your hands. But keep your eyes closed."

She set the smooth, hard plastic box in my hands.

"Okay, you can look."

I opened my eyes. "Transformers."

"For your transformation," she said. "From eating disorder Jen to recovery Jen. Do you like it?"

"Oh my gosh, Sophia."

"You can pick something else if you don't like it."

"Sophe. I love it. It's perfect."

Sunday, January 15, 1989

Reverend Stanley from home: the world's coolest minister. Never the *You must accept Jesus and confess your sins* sort of minister. Always the *Let's paddle a canoe and hang out and feel peaceful in nature* sort of minister. Except, were there enough canoe-paddling ministers to warrant an entire category?

He arrived just before snack. He was my first nonfamily visitor to enter my EDU bubble. When people had started requesting to visit me in the hospital, I realized it would be too hard to mix my Norwich life with my EDU life. So Mom had run interference. She deflected visiting requests by suggesting folks send mail instead. Kelly understood that I needed to keep my two worlds separate. But Reverend Stanley was different. He was relaxed and easy, and full of that warm, unconditional kind of love.

It was so nice to see his smile and get a solid Reverend Stanley hug. We sat in my room, me on the foot of my bed, him in the chair. Sophia was in the lounge.

"I'm so sorry I haven't been to visit sooner, Jenny."

"That's all right," I said, and I meant it. "The holidays are probably a busy season for a man of God."

He laughed. "Yes, they can be. So. How are you? How has it been here?"

I shrugged. "I'm doing okay."

He cocked an eyebrow.

"Really," I assured him. "It was hard at first, really hard, but it was the right thing, for me to come here."

"You think so?"

"Definitely."

"Well, I'm proud of you, then." He looked around my room. I could see his eyes take in the big Print Shop banner my bio class had sent, and my posters, and all the cards from friends I'd taped on the wall, including several from him. "How's the roommate situation?"

"My first roommate was terrible. But my new roomie is the best. Except her insurance is going to kick her out."

He shook his head. "Insurance companies can be so harmful to the very people they're supposed to protect."

"My insurance only covers half of the hospital costs," I said. "My parents are using my college savings for the rest. So Dad says I'll have to go to a state university. But it's a good investment, I figure. This place, I mean."

"Do you know when you're getting out?" he asked.

"Not sure. My tentative discharge date is February first. But they could change it."

"You're looking healthier."

"Er, thanks." I tried not to cringe. Translation: *Wow, they've really fattened you up.*

"How's the food here?"

"Nightmarish!"

He laughed. "Oh, Jenny. I do always love your choice of words. Hey! How about I go out and get you a milkshake?"

"Thanks, but we're not allowed outside food."

He slumped in disappointment. Then he brightened. "Wait, I almost forgot. I brought you a present."

He reached into his satchel. "It's not a milkshake, I promise." He handed me a package wrapped in smiley face paper. It was the size of a hardcover book.

"Thanks," I said.

"Open it."

I knew I should be grateful and excited, but my stomach lurched with apprehension. Had he told the staff about this gift, like visitors were supposed to? Not likely. If he thought he could bring me a milkshake, it wouldn't have occurred to him to get staff's approval for bringing a present.

I told myself to relax. How bad could it be? I slid my finger under the tape and unfolded the paper. Pulled the box out. My heart sank. "Oh, um, thanks."

He scooted forward in his chair. "I know you like to put things together, and you love art. It's a mobile to hang from your ceiling. Peace doves, see?" He pointed to the picture on the box. "I thought it would cheer you up, make your room more...Jenny."

"It's really beautiful. Thanks."

The box pictured a cluster of silver birds, hung with invisible fishing line. They looked metal, and sharp. I opened the box. Yup. Thin, pointy metal strips.

The man had given me a box of sharps.

"You don't like it." Reverend Stanley tried to smile, but he looked crestfallen. "Shoot. I'm sorry, Jenny. I thought it would brighten things up for you. I've been thinking about you a lot, and—"

"No, no, I love it," I said.

"You do?"

"I do, I love it. I'll put it together as soon as I can. Thank you."

"Good. Oh good. I'm so glad." He laughed. "And relieved. You had me worried. I thought I'd really messed up."

"No, it's so thoughtful, thank you."

He stayed a little longer, asking about my nurses and

tutors. I tried to hold up my end of the conversation, but I couldn't concentrate.

A box of sharp metal and strong fishing line. Could he have given me anything worse? A bottle of whiskey, maybe? A bag of cocaine?

He was just totally clueless about this kind of hospital. No, not clueless; innocent. It was nicer than clueless, more well-intentioned.

When Reverend Stanley got up to leave, he gave me another hug. Then he patted my shoulders. "You be tough, Jenny. Keep up the good work. We'll see you at home soon. We'll go for a paddle. Or a hike to the quarry."

"I can't wait," I said.

The minute he walked out of my room, I shoved the gift in my dresser.

Holy cat turd.

What should I do?

Turn it in?

Declare my contraband. That was what I *should* do.

But who was on shift?

Bosom, Trendy, and Ratched.

Any single one of them would freak.

If they found out that a visitor had brought in contraband, they would definitely start searching all visitors. Which would be a huge pain in the ass for everyone. Monica had made staff wary of sharps. Thriller had snuck in laxatives. Charlotte had been purging. Staff was already on red alert. I didn't want to be the one who instigated massive visitor shakedowns.

If only Chuck were here. I could tell him. He would believe me. But he wasn't coming back for a week. He was taking time off because he had worked all the big holidays.

Why didn't I just tell Reverend Stanley that I couldn't have metal? Or mobiles? And have him take his gift back?

Because I didn't want to hurt his feelings, that's why.

People pleasing, that's what Dr. Prakash would call it.

Getting me into trouble again.

I would just...I'd wait until Mom came. When would that be? Family therapy on Friday. She'd smuggle it out for me. Friday. Five days.

I could hide it for five days, couldn't I?

Oh my God. I felt so guilty.

It was like "The Tell-Tale Heart" by Edgar Allen Poe. The box of sharps was pulsating from deep within my dresser.

I was breaking the rules. Did that mean I wasn't working the program?

But I *was* working the program! I was completely dedicated to recovery.

Following the rules just to follow the rules wasn't the point. Was it?

♥ ♥ ♥

"What should I do?" I asked Sophia in our room after snack.

"I think you're right," she said. "Your best bet is to give it to your mom."

"You don't think Mom will freak out about me sneaking around and lying to the nurses?" This was a new worry I'd had during snack.

"I don't think so. You've been doing so well. And she knows your minister?"

"Yeah, of course," I said.

"So she probably knows he was just oblivious to the rules."

"Okay." I nodded, trying to calm down. "Okay."

"You hid it well?"

I glanced at the door to be sure no one was around. "In my dresser. Where else is there?"

"Here, give it to me."

"Why?"

"Put it up high in our closet. Most people don't think to look up, above their sight line."

"What are you, a Soviet spy?" I dug through my drawer and gave her the box.

"Give me a couple of sweaters, too," she said. "And keep a lookout."

I handed her my Christmas sweaters and went to the door.

"Okay, I'm wrapping it up in this sweater, and I'll make a little stack up here." She slid things to the back of the overhead shelf in our closet. "That should do for the time being. Have you told anyone else about it?"

"No."

"Good," she said. "Don't."

I nodded.

"I'm serious, Jen. Not Monica or Bronwyn or anyone."

"They wouldn't say anything," I said.

"Just please, Jen. Promise, as a favor to me, that you won't tell them."

"They wouldn't—"

"Promise me."

"I promise," I said reluctantly.

"Pinkie swear." She held out her pinkie.

I took it in mine. "I pinkie swear."

"I know you're friends, but I don't trust those girls any farther than I can throw them."

"You could have thrown them farther, before they hit maintenance."

"Jennifer Hope Johnson," she warned.

"All right, okay. I promise."

Monday, January 16, 1989

Well, she did it.

Monica wrote her 72-hour letter.

Despite the fact that she had tried to kill herself, or at least given two major cries for help. Despite the fact that she was backsliding, and unhealthy, and wasn't ready to live outside the EDU, she did it.

She would be gone Thursday.

Tuesday, January 17, 1989

Monica wouldn't talk to me. I tried, but she was determined to leave.

At first I cried.

Now I was mad.

How could she sign herself out? She had helped me, urged me to work the program, told me she believed in recovery. She had helped me be strong—or fake being strong until I started to actually feel that way. *Fake it 'til you make it.*

Now Monica needed to be strong. She needed to work the program. Her life was at stake.

But she wouldn't. She was unreachable.

What was she going through, that she could change so much from my first days here? It was like she wasn't even the same person.

Or...was it me who had changed?

Was I seeing her in a different way?

Had I ever really known her? The real her?

So many questions. So much anger. And so, so worried about my friend.

♥ ♥ ♥

Great, I had a private room again. Only this time, I didn't want it.

Sophia got the boot. Her insurance company cut her off. It was so unfair—Monica could stay but was choosing to leave, while Sophia wanted to stay but couldn't.

Sophe refused to sign my journal, because she said she'd be back. Hopefully in less than a week. Dr. Kanduri promised to put her back in our room.

"I'll call you tons," she said.

"But what if the pay phone's busy? Which it is, all the time. My mom has never once gotten through."

"I'll write down all my numbers: my dad's, my mom's, Rob's, my apartment in Ithaca. I'm sorry, Jen. I'm just not sure where I'll be."

"Don't go to your apartment. I don't think you should be alone."

"You're right. It will be my last resort. I promise."

"At least you're not family."

She frowned. "What you talkin' 'bout, Willis?"

"I'm allowed to call you every day because you're not a blood relative."

"It's a good thing soul sisters doesn't count."

"Maybe not to treatment planning. But it counts to me."

"Aw, shucks." She gave a sad smile.

When I came upstairs from CD with Bronwyn, Sophia was gone.

Wednesday, January 18, 1989

"Special Community Meeting," Baldy said as he walked from room to room, rounding us up. Everyone settled onto couches and chairs in the lounge. Staff sat together in a clump.

Heart pounding all the way up in my throat, I found a seat.

Oh God oh God oh God.

What was this about?

Had they found my box of sharps?

Ratched cleared her throat. "Staff has some concerns. That's why we've called this meeting."

"It's come to our attention," Baldy said, "that some of you are doing diseased behavior."

"Enabling others," Trendy added.

"Specifically, we are talking about what's going on down-stairs, in the dining hall, during breakfast and lunch," Ratched said.

My heart leapt: not sharps.

But: meals downstairs.

That meant me, Sophia (who was gone), Bronwyn, Amanda, and Monica, who had gotten breakfast downstairs back.

No one said anything. Staff waited, trying to smoke us out.

"Do any of you have anything to say for yourselves?" Ratched asked.

Still nothing.

"Fine," Ratched said. "I'll do the talking, if you girls won't. Amanda, Bronwyn, and Monica. You have been seen pouring most of your milk into your Sanka and leaving it on your tray."

Say what?

"Coffee is an optional," Bronwyn said.

"Yes. But milk is not an optional," Ratched said. "And you've been hiding food under your napkins. All three of you."

Unreal. This had been happening right under my nose?

Monica, Bronwyn, and Amanda all looked down at their hands.

Monica took a deep breath and said, "It was just me. I was doing the milk trick, and it was my food."

"Nice try, Monica. I don't believe you, first of all," said Ratched. "Bronwyn and Amanda were seen doing it, too. But even so, even if it was only you, we need to figure out who was aware of it. Because if you're aware of diseased behavior, harmful behavior, and you don't confront it or tell staff, that is enabling."

More silence.

"Jennifer, did you know about this?" Ratched asked.

"No."

"Are you sure?" Ratched asked. "Are you telling us the truth?"

"I swear I didn't know."

"Okay," Baldy said.

Ratched leaned forward. "Wait. I want to know—"

"We believe you, Jennifer," Baldy said, like he was trying to thwart Ratched from coming after me.

Trendy said, "Bronwyn, Amanda, and Monica. We're pulling you back upstairs for all meals."

"Are you changing my discharge date?" Bronwyn cried.

Amanda was crying, too. Monica was stoic.

"We'll certainly need to discuss it, Bronwyn," Ratched said. "Amanda, we'll need to discuss your discharge, as well. And Monica...again, we strenuously, strenuously object to you signing yourself out."

"Don't do it, Monica," Baldy said.

Monica looked at the nurses. You could see her jaw muscles working. She looked at Amanda and Bronwyn. Amanda was sobbing, Bronwyn was swiping at her tears.

Someone passed a box of tissues down the line.

I stared at Monica. *Enabling. Diseased behavior.* And suddenly I was picturing Heather's final night on the EDU: Monica with her arm around Heather in our room. She had encouraged Heather to come clean. But how long before that had Monica known Heather was stealing from me? Had she ever bothered to tell staff?

Trendy looked at the rest of us. "Do any of you have anything to say about this?"

"I don't think it's that big of a deal," Charlotte said.

"It's scary," someone blurted out.

It took me a minute to realize: I was the one who'd said it.

"Scary? Why?" Baldy asked.

I didn't even bother to take a deep breath or gather my thoughts. "It's scary because you all talk about loving and helping each other, but then you do something like this? Enable each other? And you tell each other it's fine to sign out even though you're still sick? That's not love. That's not help. You say you're friends, but you're helping each other stay sick. And what about all the recovery advice you've given me? I'm following it. So is it all bullshit? Do any of you believe anything you've ever told me?"

All eyes were on me.

Oh my God. What had I done? They would be so mad. They would hate me.

But what was the point? What exactly was the point of all this, if I didn't speak up now?

"And what does it say about how you'll do when you get out of here? I'm so worried about you guys." My tears started to fall. "And what does it say about the integrity—the actual meaning—of this program? Of achieving stage three?

"This is bad, you guys. This is so terrifying. And I'm already scared. I'm so scared of falling back into my eating disorder, and I'm scared of you guys falling back into yours, because…because what if it's really that hard? What if it's basically impossible? Or what if it's contagious, this enabling, sick behavior?"

Amanda, Bronwyn, Monica, Patty, Charlotte. Narrowed eyes. Flared nostrils. Like bulls about to charge.

I wished Sophia was here. But I held the line. "This stuff, this hiding food, and the milk trick, as you call it? It's bad. This is you gaming the program that's my life. It's all of our lives! We're supposed to be here to get better, to help each other fight our diseases. I just…I just…I can't believe you would do this together." I was running out of steam. "So yeah, it's scary. I mean, I'm sorry. But it's scary."

Dead silence.

"Excellent, Jennifer!" Trendy clapped her hands sharply, once, twice. "Well said. Anyone else have anything to add?"

Silence. They looked so angry.

"I'm sorry, you guys," I said. "I care about you. I just said what I was feeling. We're supposed to do that, right?"

"I'm sorry, too," Monica said.

I had been holding my breath, but now I exhaled in relief. We could get through this.

But Monica's voice was snide. "I'm sorry we're not all as perfect as you, Jennifer."

My cheeks burned. "I'm not perfect! I'm not perfect. But at least…I mean, I'm trying. And I'm just expressing my feelings. I love you so much. All of you. I want you to get better. I want us all to get better."

"So we should all just try to be more like you," Monica said.

"I'm not saying—"

"Be like you?" Monica spat. "And hide a box of sharps in our rooms?"

Oh my God.

How did she know?

"Excuse me?" Ratched asked.

Trendy looked from Ratched to Monica to me. "What is this about?"

Monica crossed her arms. "Little Miss Perfect is hiding a box of sharps in her room. A visitor gave it to her. So why didn't she just declare it? What's she hiding it for? To hurt herself? Or to enable others?"

Ratched cocked her head. "Jennifer. Is this true?"

"I...I..."

"Just look in her journal if you don't believe me," Monica said.

So. Monica had read my journal.

Sophia had been right. Monica was dangerous.

Who else had betrayed my trust? Who had read my journal, my most private thoughts? Bronwyn? Amanda? Others?

"We need to search your room." Ratched stood and motioned for me to follow.

"Wait." Baldy put up his hand to stop her.

"What!" Monica said. "You're not going to search her room?"

"Relax, Monica," Baldy said, "Let staff handle this." He turned back toward Ratched and said, quietly, "I'll do the room search."

Ratched looked none too happy. But she acquiesced.

"Jennifer, come with me," Baldy said.

♥ ♥ ♥

"Please sit right here." Baldy moved my chair to the center of the room, between the two beds.

I sat. Snorting, hiccupping, crying. Betrayed and terrified.

He started with my dresser. One drawer at a time, emptying everything.

I watched.

Should I just tell him? Show him the box? Confess, and get it over with?

Or was there still hope he wouldn't find it?

I kept my mouth shut. It had gotten me in enough trouble.

He looked under my bed. Lifted my mattress, checking between it and the box springs.

Next, my nightstand.

Then, the closet.

Sophia's side was empty. Baldy pawed through my shoes: snow boots, slouchy suede boots, button shoes, sneakers. He lifted each pair, looked inside, shook them upside down. Took the quarters out of my boots and set them on my bed. He searched through my puffy down coat. My Navy surplus peacoat. Patting them, turning out the pockets.

He reached up and lifted my sweaters off the top shelf.

I held my breath.

He took them down.

He shook them over my bed.

Nothing.

He emptied the whole closet.

Nothing.

Nothing?

Nothing!

Where was the box?

402

It was just…gone. Disappeared. Like magic.

Baldy kept searching—the bathroom, Sophia's empty dresser and nightstand.

Ratched came in to "help." She looked everywhere Baldy had searched. He watched her; he looked irked.

At long, long last, they stopped searching. They looked at each other. Baldy raised his eyebrows and lifted his shoulders in a mild shrug.

"Jennifer," Ratched said. "You need to tell us right now. Are you hiding sharps?"

I kept quiet.

"We need to see your journal," Ratched said.

"Um," I said, looking from her to Baldy. "Do you really need to?"

Ratched tapped her foot impatiently. "Monica said she saw something in your journal about sharps. Should we have her show us what she meant? Or do you want to show us, right now?"

"It's better if we just resolve this, okay?" Baldy said. "Can you work with me on this, Jennifer?"

I picked up my journal and flipped through pages.

When had I written about Reverend Stanley and his fateful box of sharps? Sunday.

I flipped to Saturday, January 14.

Monday, January 16.

There was no Sunday. It had been neatly—so neatly you'd never notice—ripped out.

I snapped my journal shut and offered it to Baldy. "You can look through it if you want."

Ratched intercepted the journal.

Baldy sighed heavily. "No, Jennifer. That's okay." He took my journal from Ratched, which didn't look easy. He handed it to me. "I think we owe you an apology, Jennifer."

Ratched didn't say anything. She looked mad. Possibly disappointed.

Trendy tapped on the door frame. "How goes it in here?"

"I think we might have been given the runaround," Baldy said.

"You think Monica sent us on a wild-goose chase?" Trendy asked.

"Let's put it this way," Baldy said. "If we had to choose someone's word to put faith in at this point—"

"It wouldn't be Monica," Trendy finished. "Well, Jennifer, I apologize. I'm very sorry we doubted you. And I'm proud of you for speaking up. You did good." She left.

"Do you think Monica made this whole thing up? Just to spite you?" Baldy asked me.

I wiped my eyes and shrugged. Maybe a better person would have said, "No, Monica wasn't lying." Maybe that would have been the right thing to do. But if getting my privileges taken away because my minister had given me a gift—when I was truly trying to get healthy, doing my best to work this program—if that was the right thing, well…then I wasn't someone who did the right thing. Not in this case, at least.

Baldy motioned to Ratched, who mercifully took his hint. She followed him out of the room. I watched the door close partway. Baldy knew I would want privacy.

Monica. I thought she was my friend. My good, bighearted, close friend.

I looked at Sophia's bare mattress.

I felt so lonely.

I went to the doorway to make sure no one was lurking outside my bedroom. Then I slid a chair over to the closet and looked up high.

Nothing.

I took a deep breath.

I set to work putting all my stuff back.

♥ ♥ ♥

I lay on my bed with Bearibubs until Trendy called snack time. Then I walked slowly back into the lounge.

Everyone glared at me. Mean, evil looks.

I ate my Fig Newtons and drank my milk alone at a table.

I didn't even try to talk to Bronwyn or Amanda. They were huddled with Monica and Charlotte and Patty. Maybe if I could get one of them alone, I could apologize. I'd meant what I'd said, but I hadn't meant to be so harsh. I wanted to smooth things over. But I couldn't do it with them banded together like an army platoon.

As for Monica? She could go to hell.

Charlotte turned on the TV the moment that Amanda, still and always the last one to finish eating, handed her empty milk carton and wrapper to Trendy.

I ran to the phone. Punched in my calling card number.

"Jennifer," Ratched said from across the room. "Who are you calling? It isn't your day to call your family—"

"Sophia," I answered, wedging the handset between shoulder and ear. I held my journal in one hand, open to the list of phone numbers Sophia had given me.

I dialed her father's house. No answer.

I called her mother's house. The answering machine clicked on. I left a message, trying to sound cheerful, trying not to sound desperate.

I hung up the phone. Patty was waiting. I had to give her a turn.

Growing Pains was on. I sat. I tried not to cry. I wanted to go back to my room to escape the glares. But I wanted to talk to Sophia even more. If she called, if she managed to squeeze through the busy signal, no one would make the effort to find me. I needed to stay put.

The phone rang during *Head of the Class*. Patty, who had just hung up, answered. "Jennifer," she said. "It's for you."

I took the black handset. "Hello?"

"Hi, stranger!" Sophia said.

"Oh my God," I whispered. It was so good to hear her voice. "How are you?"

"I'm okay. It's weird, being free."

"Where are you?"

"At my dad's."

"I tried to call you there. Fifteen, twenty minutes ago. No one answered."

"Dang it. I'm going to kill my sister. She doesn't believe in call waiting. She probably ignored your beep."

"Oh," I said. "Okay. Kill her for me, too."

"You got it."

"Did you meet your exchanges?" I asked. As bad as my day had been, hers had been worse.

"Yes, *Mommie Dearest*!" She laughed. "I did. Although I felt like I was eating way too much. I feel like a blimp."

"You weren't eating too much," I said. "Just stick to your meal plan, okay? Hang in there until you come back."

"Ergh, enough about me," she said. "How's life in the loony bin?"

Quietly, hand cupped around mouth and phone, I told her about the meeting, the milk trick, Monica. "They searched our room," I whispered. "But they didn't find anything."

"Well, of course they didn't," Sophia said.

"How do you know—"

"When I was packing up, the nurses left me alone for a minute. So I grabbed your little gifty and took it with me. Ha, that rhymed."

"Sophe!" It was all I could say. I breathed, "Oh, Sophia. Thank you."

"No problem."

"You saved my ass," I said.

"Don't mention it."

"And, oh, wait. Does that mean—"

"Yes, I took your journal page, too. Sorry about that. I didn't want to invade your privacy, but I had a feeling you'd write it down." She said the last bit in a teacherly tone.

"How did you know they would look?"

"I told you, I don't trust those girls. Not one bit."

"Oh my God, Sophe," I said. "You saved my life. You truly saved me."

She laughed. "Don't mention it," she repeated.

"But Sophe, you took a big risk—"

"Jen," she said. "Stop. That's what friends are for."

Thursday, January 19, 1989

Monica left. Deep down, I partly forgave her for ratting me out.

Most of my anger and hurt was overtaken by massive concern. I was so afraid Monica would crash and burn.

We never talked before she left. We didn't sign each others' journals. But I cried during the song circle.

I cried because I didn't know if we'd ever be friends again.

I cried for the end of my first, lifesaving, complicated friendship in this place.

I cried because it was good-bye.

♥ ♥ ♥

I talked to Bronwyn. It took all my courage.

"Are you okay?" I asked after snack.

I knew she must have been missing Monica.

She sighed, lifted her shoulders to her ears.

"Can we talk?"

She shrugged again.

"I just wanted to tell you, I'm so sorry," I said. "I really didn't mean to say anything hurtful. I was just...I was just trying to share my feelings."

"Well, you did that."

"I know, but I could have been nicer about it. I just...I was surprised. And scared. But I value our friendship so much. I'm really sorry if I hurt your feelings."

Something changed in her eyes, something in her shoulders loosened. "Okay," she said.

"Okay?"

"Yeah. I'm sorry, too. I didn't mean to let you down."

"You didn't let me down," I said.

But this was a lie. She had let me down.

"And I don't agree with what Monica did," Bronwyn said. "Trying to drag you down. Reading your journal. That was a low blow."

"Yeah," I said.

"So, we're good?" Bronwyn asked.

"We're good." But the air between us still felt chilly. And awkward.

"You'll always be my Chiquita Banana."

"You'll always be my healthy lunchtime snack."

It made it better. Not all the way better. But enough.

Friday, January 20, 1989

Treatment-planning Objectives for Jennifer

1. Patient request for snack out with staff—*approved.*
2. Patient request for dinner out with staff—*approved.*
3. Patient request to weigh self and learn maintenance range—*approved.*
4. Patient request for regular trays—*approved for January 25–28.*
5. Patient request for menu planning—*approved.*
6. Patient request for weekend passes—*approved.*
7. Patient should maintain family phone calls every other day.
8. Patient should begin terminating with staff.
9. Patient's discharge date is set for Saturday, January 28.

Notes:
Patient has been very competitive with other patients regarding discharge date.
Patient has been "homesick" with ongoing difficulty with separation/individuation.

"I have something to address before Jenny comes home," Mom said, once we had settled down for family therapy.

Friday, January 20, 1989

"And what is that?" Dr. Wexler asked.

She hesitated, then said, "I think Jenny manipulates me before I go on business trips."

"Do you go on business trips often?" Dr. Wexler asked.

I sighed, "Yeah. She travels all over the country to teach people how to teach *Caring Parenting* courses."

Mom looked at the floor. The irony of teaching parenting skills while her daughter was in a psychiatric hospital was not lost on her, on me, on anyone. "I do think you try to manipulate me," she said quietly.

"To what end?" Dr. Wexler asked.

"To try to keep me home," she said.

"Can you say more about that?"

"It seems like Jenny comes to me the night before most of my trips. While I'm packing, and preparing, she comes and tells me something upsetting."

"For instance?" Dr. Wexler prompted.

"Well, one time, when she was in eighth grade I think, she told me that she didn't understand English."

Dr. Wexler looked at me. "You didn't understand English?"

"I said more than that! I told Mom that I'd be sitting in class, or with my friends, and they'd be talking, and it felt like everything was going on around me, and none of it made sense. Like words were just swirling in the air, but I couldn't make them mean anything. I said all that, Mom!"

"You sound defensive, Jennifer," Dr. Wexler said.

"Yeah, because she makes it sound like I'm purposely trying to manipulate her. Like I'm just a manipulative little bitch. But it was real! Dr. Prakash called it a..." I tried to think. What had she called it again? "She called it a disassociation experience."

411

"Dissociative experience," Dr. Wexler corrected. He opened my folder and leafed through papers. Without lifting his eyes from the page, he explained to my parents, "A dissociative experience is when a person feels that she is outside herself. Or when things seem unreal."

Mom looked concerned. Dad looked annoyed. Rich looked sleepy, but somewhat interested for a change.

"It's real!" I said. "I mean, it's real that it feels unreal. I don't know how to explain it. But Dr. Prakash knew exactly what I was talking about, right away. It's a horrible experience. It's freaky. That's why I was trying to tell you."

Dr. Wexler seemed to find what he was looking for in my notes. He was quiet for a moment, reading. Then he looked up. "These experiences can be quite unsettling. But they aren't terribly unusual."

"It felt terribly unusual to me." I turned to Mom. "What am I am supposed to do? Not tell you? I thought I was supposed to talk about my feelings."

"It sounds like your mother didn't appreciate the *timing* of your disclosures," Dr. Wexler said. "Can you see it from her perspective?"

"I'm glad if you talk to me," Mom said. "But why is it always right before a business trip? When I have so much preparation to do? It feels like sabotage."

I slumped. "I see your point."

"Do you think you were sabotaging your mother?" Dr. Wexler asked.

"I don't know," I said. The adults in the room seemed to think I was. "If I was sabotaging or manipulating, it was subconscious. Honestly."

Dad snorted.

Dr. Wexler ignored him. "How so?"

"I just think…it feels like a deadline. You know when an essay is due, and you rush to get it done? It's like that. I know that Mom is going away, so I rush to get it out before she leaves." I sighed. "I see how that looks like I'm manipulating her. But I really didn't mean to."

Dr. Wexler raised his eyebrows.

"I'm sorry, Mom," I said. "In the future, I won't talk to you about my feelings—"

"Jennifer," Dr. Wexler warned.

"I wasn't finished!" I said. "I was going to say, in the future, I won't talk to you about my feelings right before you leave for a trip."

Sheesh. Give me some credit. I was trying to grow here, people.

Saturday, January 21, 1989

Somehow, despite the milk trick, staff let Bronwyn keep her original discharge date. She left today.

I followed her out. I was leaving with Dad for a pass; she was leaving with her parents for good.

I stared at her suitcases wistfully. One more week. Just one more week.

We wrote the time in the Patient Out/In Log at the front desk, then waited for our parents to initial under "staff or chaperone" next to our names.

Things were better between Bronwyn and me. We hugged in the cold, snowy parking lot. Our breaths were clouds in the cold air.

"I'll miss you," I said.

"I'll miss you," she said. "But I won't miss this place."

I laughed. "Be good."

"You, too." She looked at her family, waiting in their BMW. "I'm scared, Jennifer," she whispered.

"I know. But be brave. You can do this. Remember from OA: Courage doesn't mean you're not afraid. It means being afraid, but doing things anyway."

She nodded solemnly.

"Write," I said. "Or call. Tell me how you're doing, okay?"

She nodded. We hugged again.

And that was it.

She got in the car and her dad drove away. She waved at me out the back window.

I got in the Delta 88.

"Movie?" Dad asked.

"Sure," I said. "Sounds good."

He pulled out of the parking space. "There's one with Harrison Ford that's supposed to be pretty good. You still like him?"

"Harrison Ford? Yeah." I stared out the window. Would Bronwyn be okay? Would I be okay when I left?

"You all right, JJ?" Dad asked.

"Yeah," I said. "I'm okay." Then I added, "Thanks for asking."

"Was she your friend? That girl back there?"

I nodded.

Past tense: "*Was* she your friend?" Not "*Is* she your friend?"

Were hospital friendships destined to become past tense?

How many of these girls would remain in my life?

How transient would our friendships turn out to be?

Sophia and I would stay friends, close friends, for sure. The end, period, full stop.

But the others? How many would disappear without another word, like Heather had? How many would fade quickly after one phone call or letter, like Eleanor?

How many would get better? Get into recovery?

How many would stumble, relapse, but pick themselves up again?

How many would give up completely, resigning themselves to a life of disease?

These, the sick girls, would I need to cut them loose?

To protect my recovery, how ruthless would I need to be?

♥ ♥ ♥

When we got back to Samuel Tuke, Dad walked me into the lobby, signed me in, and gave me a big hug. He kissed the top of my head. "I'm proud of you, JJ."

"Thanks, Dad."

"Mom will be here tomorrow. I'll see you in a week."

One week.

The next time I'd see him, I'd be going home.

"Okay. Thanks again for the movie."

"You bet."

The lady at the front desk smiled. She called the EDU to tell them I was coming up. They trusted me to escort myself these days.

Chuck was waiting at the door at the top of the stairs.

"You're back!" I said. "I missed you!"

"I heard you got your discharge date." He held the door for me.

"I did indeed. Will you be here this week?" I asked. "A lot?"

"Would I miss your last week?" he said. "I'm on shift Monday, Wednesday, Thursday, and Friday."

"Days or eves?"

"Eves."

"So you can take me on meal and snack out! Because Ratched has days this week!"

"Kid, for the love of monkeys. Her name is not Ratched. It's Sheryl. But yes, that's the plan." He punched me gently on the shoulder as we moseyed leisurely down the hall. "Where do you want to go? What are you in the mood for?"

"Piiiizzaaaa." I held out my arms like Frankenstein's monster. "Jen want piiiizzaaaa. Jen miss piiiizzaaaa."

"That can be arranged. Thin or thick?"

"Thick and goooeeeyyy." I dropped the act. We stood in the hallway. "Wait. You're not going to be here Saturday?"

"You'll be gone in the morning, kiddo. Figured I'd stay home and cry into my pillow."

"Very funny."

"Are you ready?" he asked.

"For what?"

"Duh," he said. "To leave."

"Oh. Duh." Was I ready? Would I ever be ready? "I think I'm as ready as I'll ever be?"

"Hm. Good. I like it. Thoughtful, but not overconfident."

"Over-confidence is not my weakness," I said.

"What is your weakness, then?" he asked. "Besides quoting *Star Wars*. You are quoting *Star Wars*, right?"

"But of course. *Return of the Jedi*. Luke tells the Emperor, 'Your over-confidence is your weakness.' And then the Emperor goes, 'Your faith in your friends'"—suddenly my throat got tight, my voice faltered—"'is yours.'"

"Whoa. You okay?"

"Not really. I mean, holy cow. That is my weakness. My faith in my..." I leaned against the wall and asked quietly, "Did you hear what happened? With the milk trick, and Monica, and my room search?"

"Unfortunately. I read about it in your case notes." He sighed. "That's a stinker, kiddo, no doubt about it. But listen. Maybe your faith in your friends isn't your weakness. Maybe you just need to be a better judge of who your real friends are."

"You're right." Tears came. "But how am I supposed to know?" I used my coat sleeve to wipe my face. "What's the secret? How do you figure out who your real friends are?"

"How do you think?"

I shrugged. "I don't know. Obviously."

"You have to trust your gut."

"Ha. Sure. Except my gut isn't trustworthy. I have an eating disorder, remember?"

"Good point," he said. "Well, here's what I think. Just take small steps as you get to know someone. And give it time. You have to take a risk on people at first, when you don't know them well, but make it a small risk. Small things, like little favors or secrets, nothing big."

"Ooh, like a spy."

"Excuse me? How do you get 'spy' from—"

I wiggled my fingers at him. "You plant a little tidbit of information, something untrue, a different thing for each person, and whatever gets out, you know who leaked it!"

"Okaaay," he said. "Or maybe something a little less…"

"James Bond? Brilliant and debonair?"

"Uh, sure. James Bond. Let's go with that. *Anyway,* as I was saying. The bottom line is, friends are people you can trust. They have your back. It's as simple as that."

"I know Sophia has my back."

"She sure does."

"I thought Monica did, too," I said. "I thought I could trust her."

"Did you really?"

"Of course I did. What do you mean?"

"I mean, were there any signs? That maybe she wasn't as trustworthy as you thought?"

I mulled it over. "Well, Sophia told me not to trust her."

"Interesting." He nodded. "And?"

"And…Monica wasn't committed to her recovery, because she signed herself out. And did the milk trick."

"Yes. And?"

"And she was hurting herself, and not being honest about it. And…she was always so nice to everyone, it was like…I wonder if maybe she focused on helping everyone else, instead of dealing with her own issues."

418

"So, what you're telling me is, there were actually quite a few red flags."

"I guess," I admitted. "Yeah. There were red flags."

"You just didn't heed them."

I shook my head. "No, it's not that I didn't heed them. It's that I didn't even see them. That's worse. It's scarier."

"You just need some practice. Learn how to see those flags, be sure you listen to them."

I sighed. "You make it sound easy."

"It's not easy. But you can do it, kid."

"Sure," I said.

"You listen to me. You've got this. You can do this. It's in the bag."

Sunday, January 22, 1989

I walked into my room and found Ratched behind my bed. She was peeling my cards and notes off the wall.

MY NOTES AND CARDS.

THAT PEOPLE SENT.

TO ME.

They hadn't announced a room search. Why was she in my room, pawing through my things? I tried to remain cool and collected, like the about-to-be-discharged, advanced-level-stage-three patient I was.

"Um, what are you doing?" I asked.

She whirled around. "This is not masking tape!" Her tone was demented and hysterical, like she was the victim in a horror movie. "You need to take all these down," she said. "Immediately!"

"It's poster tape," I said. "I used it specifically because it comes off without damaging the wall."

"Oh. Well. It's still not masking tape."

No shit, Sherlock.

"What about this?" Ratched gestured toward the window, where one of my sweatshirts was hanging from the curtain rod.

"I washed it. It is still drying. There was nowhere else to hang it."

"And your books! They are everywhere."

"No they aren't," I said.

"Yes! They are! You have things everywhere! You are the only one who ever has a room this messy!"

"What are you talking about? Remember Heather? She was a slob. Not to mention the fact that she was a kleptomaniac! How long did you know that!" I studied her face to try to gauge her response, but she was unreadable.

"No, no. You're the messiest patient in this hospital!" She sounded completely unhinged.

"Look, everyone hangs up their clothes after they do laundry. And maybe I have more books, but that's not the issue. Face it. You have some sort of bizarre obsession with me."

"Bizarre obsession!"

"That's right," I said. "You have a bizarre obsession with me. Something about me triggers you. You obviously have some kind of major issue with me." I took a deep breath. "You know, I'm leaving at the end of this week—"

"I know that, and I think—"

"Excuse me." I held up my hand. "I wasn't finished. Please don't interrupt."

She narrowed her eyes, like she could not believe how impertinent I was being.

"As I was saying, I'm leaving at the end of this week. And I don't think we have to love each other, but I would appreciate it if you would just leave me alone."

"I can't leave you alone. I'm your primary."

"Well, then, I think you should take a look at your own issues."

"Jennifer! That's not appropriate! My issues? That's not for you to say!"

"No? These cards on my wall? They have been up there for two months now. Two months. Why today? Why, less than a week before I leave, do you decide to come snooping around my room?"

She crossed her arms. "I am staff. If I come into a room, it isn't snooping."

"Sure, you are staff. So I guess that makes it okay for you to hate me?"

"I don't…I don't hate you," she said.

"Could have fooled me!" I said. "From day one you've had it out for me. Every day it was another smack in the face. Accusing me of tanking. Accusing me of sticking things up my you-know-what. Accusing me of enabling. Of hiding sharps."

"I was just…I was trying to keep you safe."

"Safe? I have done nothing, NOTHING, but work the program since the minute I got here."

She blinked. Didn't say anything. Was I getting through to her?

"And you know what? None of the other staff have accused me of any of those things. Not one. Have you ever noticed that? They don't seem to think I'm a horrible person."

Oh my God. I felt like fifty pounds had dropped from my shoulders. Not cellulite pounds; the myth of Atlas pounds. Unnecessary burden pounds—the weight of having to tiptoe around this landmine of a nurse.

"Well," she said. "I still—I think it's unfair to housekeeping to have to clean such a messy room."

"Sorry you feel that way," I said.

"That's all you have to say?" she asked.

"Hm. *Is* that all I have to say? I think so," I said. "No, wait. It isn't. I want to say that I think you're the one with the issue here. Except maybe I said that already. Goodness. I just can't keep track. Good-bye."

I dove onto my bed and hugged Bearibubs. I was giddy, relaxed.

"I think…you should consider the housekeepers and come up with a better response."

"I think I'm not supposed to think about it. I think I'm supposed to be spontaneous and express my thoughts and emotions. Which I just did. Quite admirably, if I do say so myself. An A plus for me."

"So you're not going to pick up your room? It's going to stay like this?"

"Yes. Yes, it is."

"Well, I think there should be consequences for that." She turned and walked out.

I looked at Bearibubs and repeated, "I think there should be consequences for that."

Usually I fell apart after a confrontation. But this time, I was content and happy.

I'd finally said what I'd needed to say.

I had told her where she could put my quarters.

Monday, January 23, 1989

They let me weigh myself this morning. I stood in the nurses' station, in my worn-out paper gown and bare feet, just like a million times before, except this time I was facing the scale.

"Go ahead," Bosom said.

My heart was beating fast. I stepped on the platform, taking a moment to balance and breathe. Slowly I slid the clanking weights. Higher, higher, higher.

I stepped off.

I weighed more than I'd ever weighed in my life.

I was in the exact middle of the five-pound adolescent weight range. My adult weight range was ten to fifteen pounds more. Which I seriously could not fathom ever weighing.

"You okay, hon?" Bosom asked.

I nodded.

"You look great," she said. "Now get ready for breakfast."

I ate breakfast in a daze, alone at the abandoned EDU tables. Thinking about my weight.

How could I have forgotten what those numbers could do?

I spread peanut butter on my toast. Chewed with dry mouth. Got through the cereal, juice, milk, everything.

♥ ♥ ♥

Dr. Prakash found me in my room. She gathered me into a big, cigarette-smelling hug. "Jennifer! It is good to see you!"

"How was your vacation?" I asked.

"Oh, wonderful. Greece is lovely. You really must go sometime."

She led me to her office. We sat.

My jeans felt five times tighter than yesterday, which meant they felt twenty-five times too tight.

"So, Jennifer. How have you been?"

"Okay."

She lit a cigarette. "I see you weighed yourself this morning. How was that? Are you comfortable in your body?"

Comfortable! In my body? At this weight? "Uh, no."

"Jennifer, I need you to listen to me," she said. "Whether or not you are comfortable with your weight, there is to be absolutely no going below the lowest number of your weight range. Do you know what that is? The exact number?"

"Yes," I said.

"Tell me."

I told her.

"Now promise."

"I promise."

"Good. And have you gone over your discharge plan with your primary? Remind me, who is your primary again?"

"Ratch—Sheryl." I did not try to hide my disdain.

She squinted as she took a drag of her cigarette. "And, Jennifer, your secondary is—"

"Chuck," I said. "Oh! Can I do my discharge planning with him instead? Please please please?"

"I think in this case, and at this time…yes. I will make a note of that."

"Please write it big, all over the front of my folder, so everyone will see it, and no one can accuse me of lying."

She chuckled, then opened my folder and wrote. "You will review this with Chuck when you fill out your discharge planner. But I trust you have already discussed follow-up care in family therapy?"

"Yup. I'm going to Dr. Wexler's outpatient group. Plus, we'll have family therapy once a month with him. And, let's see. There's an OA group in Norwich, so I'll go to that. And..." I hesitated. I always felt embarrassed, talking directly about my therapeutic relationship with Dr. Prakash or Dr. Wexler. I wasn't sure why. But, onward. "And I'll have individual with you. I'll see you on Thursdays before group?"

"Yes," she said. "In the out-patient building. Weekly at first, and then every other week, if things are going well."

"Sounds good," I said.

"And what about weigh-ins?"

"Once a week."

"With your family doctor?"

"No, a nurse practitioner. Mom heard she's nice."

"Jennifer, I want you to weigh yourself once every ten days. No more and no less. Can you do that for me?"

"In addition to the weigh-ins?"

She nodded. "It is a good habit to get into, since we will taper the clinical weigh-ins if you continue to do well. This way, you can be responsible to yourself and to me. You can be sure you are staying within your healthy weight range."

"Okay."

"But you must not weigh yourself obsessively or frequently. Can you do that?"

I nodded.

"I need a yes," she said.

"Yes," I said.

"Very well." She sat back. "Tell me, Jennifer, how are you feeling about your chances of recovery?"

I let out a deep, apprehensive breath. "I'm really nervous."

"Good."

"Good?"

"Nervous means you will be on your toes. You will have a better chance of recovery," she said.

"Do you ever fully recover from an eating disorder?"

"What do you think?"

What do you think? The classic therapy turnaround.

"I think…I don't know. That's why I asked. Because staff says an eating disorder is a disease that we'll always have. We can be in recovery, but it never goes away."

"And what do *you* think?"

"I'd like to think you can recover. I mean fully recover. Not just manage it and work around it, but leave it in the dust. But staff says that's denial, because I'll always have my disease." I choked on the last word, started crying.

Dr. Prakash waited.

I breathed, trying to rein in my tears. "I guess I thought I'd have to wait until the skies were clear, all my issues were resolved, and then I'd be in recovery. But now I'm realizing that there will always be issues. Life is never smooth sailing. So the trick is to figure out how to be in recovery while stuff happens. And that's what's scary."

"Yes. Well put. Jennifer, do you remember a long time ago, when you talked about your depression as a bouquet of balloons?"

"I'm surprised you remember that."

"It was a memorable analogy. I was wondering, how would you characterize your balloons now?"

"Do you mean, is the Norpramin helping?"

She shrugged, "The Norpramin, but also, everything else. Your balloons. The entire picture."

"I'm not sure."

"Take your time."

I picked at a thread on my sweatshirt and thought. "I don't feel a whole lot different on the Norpramin. So I don't know if that's really helping or not. But I guess I feel like I know how to get helium now. And balloons and string. So if my balloons are deflated, or float away, or my strings are cut, I know it's not forever. That's the difference. Now I know it can be fixed. I can get more."

"And where would you get more helium, or strings, or balloons, as you put it?"

"Hallmark."

"Very funny." She raised her eyebrows, waiting.

"Reaching out for support."

"Yes. From whom?"

"My family. My friends. Outpatient group. Therapy. OA."

"You have a big safety net, Jennifer. It bodes well for your recovery. You must be sure to utilize it."

"Okay."

"Can you do it? Reach out? Utilize your safety net?"

"I can do it."

"You do not want to stay in the hospital longer?"

"Good God no! I can't wait to get out of here," I said. "Oh, sorry. No offense."

She chuckled. "No offense taken, Jennifer. I am very, very proud of you. I am proud of the work you have done here."

It felt good to hear.

But what felt even better is that I didn't need to hear it.

I didn't need her to be proud, because I was already proud of myself.

Tuesday, January 24, 1989

Sophia came back! Her Medicaid or Medicare or whatever kicked in.

That was the good news.

The bad news: she was back on stage one.

It was incredibly unfair. But Baldy said it was policy that all admissions had to start on stage one.

My room felt complete again. And it was so good to sit with her at dinner.

Dinner was fried clams. Or possibly it was rubber bands dipped in breading and thrown in hot oil. There couldn't have been much of a difference.

I was on 2100 calories for maintenance. It wasn't too much food, but it was too many fried rubber bands/clams. There was also an orange, which made me think of Monica—the old, pretreachery Monica—and scalloped potatoes, and, as always, a carton of milk and a small, sad salad.

I looked at Sophia's tray. Since she was on stage one, and technically a new admission, they had her back on 1200s. A handful of fried rubber bands, a salad, skim milk.

"No," she said.

"It's okay," I said. "You can do it. One bite at a time." I was scared, though; how bad had her time on the outside been, if she was refusing to eat this piddly amount of food?

"I don't mean no, I don't want it." She turned to Baldy. "I mean, can I go up to 1800s? I practically starved last time on 1200s."

Baldy looked taken aback. "Yeah," he said. "I imagine that would be fine. I'll have to double-check. But...yeah, I think that's okay."

No patient had ever asked to increase her calories before.

I might have been hungry on 1200s, too. Yet I never would have asked to go up to 1800s. For one thing, I hadn't known a patient could ask for something like that, advocate for herself like that. But most importantly, I would have been afraid it was a sign of weakness, of a not-bad-enough eating disorder.

Good for Sophia. Good ol' Sophia.

Wednesday, January 25, 1989

It was snowing so hard that all travel was cancelled, but Chuck still took me for snack out. Instead of driving up to the frozen yogurt place by SU like we'd planned, we put on coats and boots and tromped around the fence to the Mobil station convenience store.

I got Peanut M&M's and a can of noncaffeinated root beer. The root beer I stuck in my coat pocket. But the M&Ms I opened right away. I didn't want to wait. My first candy in ten weeks. Chocolate and peanuts. At last. I popped a green one into my mouth. "Want some?" I offered Chuck the packet. "Oh wait, sorry. I'm probably not supposed to share."

He smiled. "How are they? Are they triggering you?"

"Nope."

"Are they as good as you remember?"

"Yup. The milk chocolate melts in your mouth, not in your hands."

"Catchy. You should write advertising jingles."

"I know." I ate a tan one. "Mmmm. So good. Here, have some." I tapped a few out of the package onto my hand. "I'll never get used to the red ones."

"I remember before they took red away." He took a red one. "And now they're back. Thanks."

"Because you're older than dirt," I said.

"Yup, I'm a dinosaur. A friendly brontosaurus." He helped himself to another M&M. "You have the rest. I know you've missed them."

"I've missed these, and Ben & Jerry's ice cream, and gum. I miss blowing bubbles."

He looked around the store. It was tiny, dirty, rundown. The man behind the counter was reading a magazine. We were the only customers.

"What's your favorite kind?" Chuck asked.

"Of gum?" I asked. "Bazooka. Grape. Because of the comic."

"Would you swear never to tell anyone if I bought you a piece?"

My eyes went wide. Gum wasn't allowed on the EDU because of its common, diseased use as a meal replacement. "I would double pinkie swear!"

"You have to wait until you're discharged to chew it. I could get fired."

"Yes! I swear I won't tell."

He selected a piece of Bazooka and set it on the counter. "My gift to you," he said. "You can blow bubbles on your car ride home."

Samuel Tuke Center
Eating Disorder Unit

EDU Discharge Plan for: *Jennifer Johnson*

The following is my plan for discharge:

1. Residence: *My house—with my parents and brother (Norwich, New York)*
2. Income from: *Mom and Dad. Spending money from after-school job at the Gathering Place*
3. Employment/School: *Norwich High School*
4. Follow-Up Care:
   - Name of Physician or Treatment Center: *Dr. Wexler—family sessions and group; Dr. Prakash—individual sessions*
   - Date and Time of First Appointment: *February 2 (Thursday) Dr. Prakash at 5:00 p.m., group at 7:00 p.m. (Group and outpatient therapy meets in the Samuel Tuke outpatient building.)*
   - Method of Transportation: *Mom (or possibly Dad) will drive me*
   - Medications: *Norpramin 75 mg per day*
   - Dietary: *2100 calories per day*
     - Lunch on day of discharge (if applicable): *Restaurant with family*
     - Dinner:
       - *2 oz. protein (hamburger)*
       - *2 breads (hamburger bun)*
       - *2 veggies (green beans, salad)*
       - *1 fruit (apple)*
       - *2 fats (butter, salad dressing)*
       - *2% milk*

- o Snack: *frozen yogurt or yogurt*
- o Next day breakfast: *2 thin slices French toast; an orange; 2% milk; Raisin Bran*

5. Additional Follow-Up Care:

- Spiritual: *OA meetings—Mondays in Norwich (can walk or ride bike there), AA meetings if necessary, church, meditation*
- Physical (weight and safety): *Once a week with nurse practitioner—for weigh-in and vital signs*
- Physical (well-being and exercise): *Aerobics classes at the YMCA three times a week (probably Tues., Wed., and Sat.), walks, bike rides, Friday night dances!*

Date: 1/26/89

Patient Signature: *Jennifer Johnson*

Staff Member Signature: *Charles Gordon, III*

Thursday, January 26, 1989

The snowplows had cleared the roads enough for us to drive up the hill to Chuck's favorite pizza place for my first meal out. It was fantastic. But scary. But fantastic.

I was scared in the same way I'd been scared about meals downstairs: there was no nutritionist determining your exchanges, measuring your portions. You had to figure everything out for yourself.

But I was ecstatic because this would be my first non-hospital meal in more than two months, Peanut M&M's notwithstanding.

Chuck found a parking space close to the restaurant. Snow was piled high, blocking the curb. We picked our way over the snowbank, treading carefully in the footsteps already punched in and hardened from the afternoon sun. Chuck fed the meter, which was almost buried by snow. Only the top of its little meter head could be seen.

The pizza place blasted us with warm air when we went in. It smelled of freshly baked bread and tomato sauce. I closed my eyes, breathed deeply. It felt so good. The place served thick rectangular slices. It was packed with SU students—noisy, but not rowdy. They probably all knew someone who died in the Lockerbie crash.

We got in line. When it was our turn, we ordered at the counter; Chuck paid for both of our meals with petty cash from the nurses' station.

We filled our waxed paper cups at the soda machine. I got club soda. Chuck got Coke.

We found a booth and waited for our slices to warm in the huge oven.

Chuck chewed ice from his Coke.

"That's bad for your teeth," I told him.

"I like to live dangerously." He set his cup down. "You nervous, kid? You seem nervous."

"I'm nervous."

"Just eat. *Mangia, mangia,*" he said in a broad Italian accent. "Food is one of the essential pleasures in life. Try not to stress. 'Don't worry—'"

"'Be happy'?" I cocked an eyebrow. "You're quoting Bobby McFerrin? At a time like this?"

"Wrong Bob. I was quoting Bob Marley. Or trying to, before I was so rudely interrupted."

"Sorry." My knee was bouncing under the table. Nerves. "Continue."

"You know the song. Sing it with me. 'Don't worry…'bout a thing…'cause every little thing…'"

I shook my head.

"Hell's bells, kid. You don't know 'Three Little Birds'? Bob Marley?"

I kept shaking my head.

"Greatest reggae singer of all time?" His eyes were wide, his mouth open. His face showed disbelief mixed with horror. He tried again, like I would recognize it if he just sang more: "'Rise up this morning…smiled with the rising sun…three little birds…'"

"Nope. Sorry."

"Unacceptable. I've been your secondary all this time, and this hasn't come up? I'm not doing my job."

"You're a great secondary. The best secondary."

"I'm failing in your music education, though."

"Music education? That's not a real part of being a PNA."

"It is to me." He was looking around the restaurant. "Shoot. I wish this place had a jukebox."

"Okay, Fonzie," I laughed. "You think a jukebox would have reggae?"

"Not just any reggae. Bob Marley!"

"Because white college kids listen to reggae," I said.

"Yes. They do." He put his head in his hands and groaned. "It's like talking to a wall. I can't believe this."

The guy at the counter called our order numbers; we went to get our food. The trays were smallish, light, flat red plastic; they weren't the huge, heavy, sectioned, orangey beige trays of Samuel Tuke.

I had ordered a slice of pepperoni pizza and a side salad of shredded lettuce with chopped apples and Italian dressing. Chuck had ordered two slices of pepperoni.

We set down our trays and slid back into our seats.

I scooped some napkins out of the dispenser on the table. "I forgot a fork."

"A fork for pizza? Blasphemy."

"A fork for salad," I said.

"Oh. Right. I'll get it," Chuck said. "They're over by the drinks. You want a refill?"

"No, thanks."

I stared at the food, hoping the numbers for my food plan exchanges would magically appear in the air above my tray. No luck.

Was a slice of pizza one fat exchange, or two? Or three—grease was pooling on the cheese.

Was it one bread exchange, or two, because the crust was so thick?

One protein, or two, all this cheese?

437

Another protein for the pepperoni. Another fat, too?

Did the cheese count as one dairy or two?

One fruit and veg for the tomato sauce? Another for the salad?

An additional fat exchange for the dressing?

Now I understood what Sophia meant. When you applied your meal plan to real food in the real world, it looked like a lot more. Or a lot less. I couldn't even tell.

Chuck slid back into the booth, setting a fork on one of my napkins.

"Thanks," I said.

"You okay?"

"How do you know how much to eat?" I asked.

"In general, you mean?"

"Yeah."

He shrugged. "I eat what I feel like eating, and I stop when I'm full."

Chuck was a little chubby, though. He had a small pot-belly. So could I truly trust what he said? Was that really what you could do? Eat what you felt like eating? Stop when you were full? How would I even know if I was full? My satiation meter was broken from bingeing. How would I not get fat?

Meal out was a big, cold dose of reality.

But it was a delicious reality. Chuck was right: it was the best pizza I'd ever had. So, so good. So thick. So gooey. Delectable.

Plus, it was lovely, just me and Chuck—and a bunch of college kids. But no annoying patients, no nurses. And we were in an actual restaurant. In the wild.

So, even though it was difficult, I felt like a real person again. And that felt good.

On the way back, I claimed control of the car radio. As

Chuck maneuvered through the hilly streets, narrowed by snowbanks, we rocked out to "Cherry Bomb," "Don't Worry, Be Happy" (speak of the devil), and "Got My Mind Set on You."

Then "Never Gonna Give You Up" came on. I turned up the volume.

"No! Noooo! Change it!" Chuck shrieked, not taking his eyes from the road.

"I will never change it. This is a good song!" I crooned, "'Never gonna give you up...never gonna let you down...'"

"Change it! Change it! My ears are melting! Change it!"

"Heh heh, never!" I sang, "Never gonna change the ray-ay-ay-dee-oh-oh."

♥ ♥ ♥

As soon as Chuck unlocked the door at the top of the stairs, we heard Baldy calling out, "Special Community Meeting, ladies. Right now. In the lounge, please."

Now what?

My mind flashed to the piece of Bazooka hidden in the lining of my coat. Please, don't let this be a room search.

Chuck and I went directly into the lounge.

"How was meal out?" Sophia asked.

"Good, but scary," I said.

"I know what you mean." She raised her eyebrows. "So. The legendary Special Community Meeting."

"Exciting, isn't it?" I said. "Aren't you glad to be back for this one?"

"Overjoyed," she said. "What's it about, do you think?"

"No idea. Enabling, accusations, room searches?"

"Oh my."

Baldy said, "Let's get started. Staff has an announcement."

Trendy and Bosom were there, as well as Baldy and Chuck.

Trendy said, "We need you to know, this is something that will very much affect our community."

They were so solemn and serious that I shivered. Had someone died? Monica! Or Amanda, who had left yesterday? Someone else? Bronwyn?

Bosom said, "I'm afraid this is going to bring up a lot of issues for all of you. So remember, staff is here to support you. Reach out to us and let us help. Okay?"

Curious, concerned heads nodded all around.

Baldy cleared his throat. "You may have noticed that Sheryl has not been on shift the past few days."

I breathed my relief. It wasn't about a discharged patient. Or Bazooka gum.

This was about Ratched. Hm.

Bosom said, "Girls, today Sheryl checked herself into a treatment center. In Pennsylvania. For anorexia."

I burst out laughing.

I slapped my hand over my mouth.

I shouldn't have laughed. This wasn't funny.

But oh my God!

"Ow!" Sophia had pinched me, hard, to try to get me to stop. She knew that if I didn't settle down immediately, staff would make it an "issue."

Too late.

"Jennifer," Trendy said. "You think this is funny? You think someone's disease is funny?"

"No." I pressed my lips together. I squirmed and wiggled. I tried to keep it in. But giggles bubbled out. I started shaking with laughter.

I could tell Sophia was about to join me.

"Sorry, I'm sorry." I took deep breaths. "Whew, sorry."

"I think it's brave, what she's doing," Thriller said. She was talking more and more lately, coming back to life.

"Uh-huh." I nodded, then crumpled into giggles again.

"Jennifer, this is incredibly inappropriate," Trendy said. "What do you think is so funny?"

"You guys don't think this is funny?" I wiped my cheeks; I was laughing so hard I was crying. "Seriously? Not funny ha-ha, but ironic funny?"

Sophia put her hand on my shoulder. "Jen and I can't possibly be the only ones who find this ironic. And not a little problematic. The head nurse of the Eating Disorder Unit has been sick with her own eating disorder? I mean, look what she's put Jen through."

Holy shit. Things were clicking into place:

Ratched always looking so pale, tired, thin.

Ratched being such a stick-up-the-ass control freak.

Bronwyn going apeshit that time Ratched told her to eat an extra fat exchange. Hadn't Bronwyn said something like, "I have a problem with you, in particular, telling me to eat this"? Had Bronwyn known?

And Eleanor! Way back when, Eleanor had said Ratched was a sick puppy.

Ratched accusing me of things other staff didn't back her up on.

Dr. Prakash's willingness to believe I hadn't tanked or used weights my first week. I'd taken it as a sign of Dr. Prakash's faith in me. But she had barely known me. It was more likely that Dr. Prakash knew Ratched was sick and out of control.

Dr. Prakash feeling guilty before vacation, talking about leaving me surrounded by "all this…muck." I'd thought it was about patients signing themselves out. She'd said, "That, and other things."

Dr. Prakash letting me do my discharge planning with Chuck instead of Ratched "at this time."

How much had Dr. Prakash known? How much had all staff known? Another secret kept, like Heather's, even when it was to the detriment of others.

"Did you guys know about this?" I asked, scanning from Bosom to Trendy to Baldy to Chuck. "Did all of you know?"

Chuck shook his head slowly but emphatically. I believed him. Either he wasn't in Ratched's inner circle, or he was a little clueless in a good way. But he hadn't known.

"Some of us were aware of it," Trendy said. "Sheryl asked us to keep it confidential. She didn't want this to get out."

I said, "Because she knew we wouldn't have listened to a thing she said. And we would have been right not to! What a hypocrite."

"No, because it was private," Trendy said.

"We wanted to respect her confidentiality," Bosom added.

Baldy, like Chuck, wasn't talking a lot. I bet he hadn't known, either. When had he found out? Today? Were Baldy and Chuck just as shocked as we were? Were they just better at hiding their surprise?

"Sheryl trusted us to keep it confidential, so we did," Bosom continued. "We have integrity." She sounded defensive.

"Trust? Integrity?" Sophia said. "What about the integrity of this program? What about our trust in this program?"

"Yeah," I said. "What does it say when the head nurse is anorexic? It's like having an alcoholic in charge of a Chemical Dependency Unit. Not a recovering alcoholic. A drinking, drunk alcoholic. A three sheets to the wind, wasted alcoholic."

"That's true," Charlotte said. A couple of other heads nodded.

"We get your point. We didn't all know," said Chuck gently. "And even if we had, would that make us any less effective as staff?"

"I don't know," I said. "Maybe?" I hadn't wanted to offend Chuck. I really hadn't.

"I think it's good she's getting the help she needs," Thriller said, repeating her earlier sentiment.

"It's also a structural issue," Sophia said, somewhat ignoring Thriller. "We're talking about the supervisor of nursing staff. She set the tone, the culture of this unit."

I said, "She established a culture of accusing patients of things we didn't do. Of making us eat things we didn't have to eat. I think that was her disease."

"Also." Sophia looked pointedly at Trendy and Bosom, "What about letting her be sick?"

"*Letting* her be sick?" Trendy asked.

"Yes!" I saw where Sophia was going. "What does it say about the people who knew? You just went ahead and let her be sick?"

"You girls, of all people, should know that you can't force someone to get better," Trendy huffed.

"No, but if you keep their secrets, isn't that enabling?" I asked. "Did we not just have a special meeting, exactly like this one, where you guys talked about how terrible it was for patients to enable each other? How is this any different than the milk trick?"

"You don't know what you're talking about," Trendy said.

"Why? Did you guys stage an intervention?" Sophia asked. "How long has this been going on?"

Bosom crossed her arms. Trendy's cheeks were flushed.

It was a standoff. Me and Sophia versus Trendy and Bosom. It was the Old West.

I waited for a buzzard to screech.

I waited for tumbleweed to roll through the lounge.

Baldy cleared his throat. "There are a lot of feelings in this room right now. And it's all completely valid. Maybe you should talk about this in group tomorrow."

"Jennifer is terminating in group tomorrow," Sophia said.

"Oh, that's okay." I met Sophia's eyes, but I was talking to the whole group. "We can make time to squeeze this little nugget in."

Baldy said, "Regardless of our feelings about this, there's some practical stuff we need to take care of."

"Yes." Trendy sat up a little straighter. "Those of you who had Sheryl as your primary, your secondary will now be your primary. We will assign you new secondaries later this week."

I looked at Chuck. A slow smile was spreading across his face. His mouth, cheeks, eyes—everything was smiling.

He was now a primary.

Friday, January 27, 1989

I terminated in group today. It wasn't very sad, because there were a bunch of new people I barely knew. I really only had to say good-bye to Charlotte, Thriller, Patty, and Sophia.

I didn't have a lot to say to Charlotte or Thriller or Patty.

As for Sophia, I wasn't going to say everything I wanted to say to her in group; we had already set aside our own time to say good-bye.

No, scratch that. Not goodbye. See you later, alligator.

Or something a little less dorky.

Still, Sophia was so sad. She kept crying, which was not her usual modus operandi.

Last night she said, "I can't believe you're leaving. You're my only ally."

"I know. I'm sorry. But there are so many new girls. I bet some of them will turn out to be cool."

"Maybe. But they won't be as awesome as you."

"Well. Obviously."

♥ ♥ ♥

I terminated with Chuck after dinner. That was far and away the hardest termination. The rest of staff—some were fine, some were annoying, I honestly didn't really care that much. And Dr. Wexler and Dr. Prakash I'd see next week. But Chuck...

He had been more than my secondary; he'd been a big brother and a good friend.

"Will I ever see you again?" I asked, tears streaming.

"You can visit the EDU after six months," he said. "But kid, I have to tell you. I'm not sure if I'll be here."

"Where—" I hiccuped. "—where will you be?"

"I think I'm going back to school."

"For what?" I asked.

"I've decided to complete my degree so I can apply to grad school."

"Oh," I said. I knew I should be happy for him. But I couldn't imagine my new, recovery life without him in it. "Um, for what?"

"Social work, maybe. Or a Ph.D. So I can run my own programs."

"That would be really good," I sniffed. "You would be so good."

"Thanks." His eyes were glassy, like he was about to cry, too. "I want to figure out a way to use music. Music therapy. Rock band therapy. I don't know how it would work yet."

"You'll figure it out." I got up and went to my dresser.

"Where are you going?"

I grabbed a tape from my box of cassettes. "Something to remember me by. You can use it in your programs." I handed it over.

He looked at it. "No matter how much I love you, kid, I will never, ever use Rick Astley in my programs."

♥ ♥ ♥

I thought packing would cheer me up, but it didn't.

Sophia kept giggling.

"What's with the total one-eighty?" I pouted. "Now you're happy I'm leaving?"

"Oh, nothing." She was trying not to smile. "While you're packing, don't you need your things from the closet?"

I narrowed my eyes at her. "Sophe. What did you do?"

"I didn't do anything."

"It's something to do with the closet?"

"I didn't do anything," she repeated, emphasizing the *I*.

Tentatively, I touched the sliding door. "You're freaking me out. What did you do?"

"Just open it."

I slid the door open. A long thread snagged. And suddenly a urine hat tumbled off the high shelf, spilling onto my head. I was soaked.

Sophia double over with laughter. "He worked on that for like, an hour!"

Chuck jumped into our room. "Did it get you? Yes! Victory! Sophia helped."

"You guys," I said. "You got me."

Chuck's key ring jangled as he unlocked our bathroom. "Why don't you go ahead and change," he said. I caught him looking slyly at Sophia.

"Yeah," Sophia said. "You should get changed. You're all wet. Um...why don't you change into something special?"

"Something special. Why on earth would I change into something special? Have you lost your mind?"

"It's your last night here. Let's make it a celebration or something."

Chuck was nodding his head like a maniac. "I'll get your basket so you can do your hair."

"Why would I—"

"Just humor me, okay?" Sophia said. "I've never seen you all dressed up."

"Fine. But you have to do it, too."

"I totally will!"

Chuck came back with my basket and a big towel, which he laid on the floor, stepping on it to sop up the puddle.

"Thanks," I said. "I certainly hope that was water and not urine."

"Gross." He giggled—a grown man giggling. He was super pleased with himself. He picked up the towel and left.

I sighed, sad again. I rooted through my suitcase to find something decent. What special outfit could I possibly cobble together out of these clothes? My pants had gone from hip-dangling to almost unbuttonable.

"All my tops are oversized sweatshirts or extralarge sweaters," I told Sophia. "Here. Does this count as something special?" I held up my Edie Brickell-esque big black shirt.

"Good grief. Definitely not." She opened her side of the closet and slid plastic hangers around. "Here. This." She handed me a sequined tank top.

"You must be high," I said.

"Please? For me? You'll look adorable in it."

I groaned. "Fine. For you."

I took the shirt and my jeans and my basket into the bathroom. Moussed my hair again and blew it dry. Changed into the top and jeans. My tummy pouffed over my waistband. But the top hung loose and sparkly and didn't look too bad.

I emerged from the bathroom. Sophia had changed into jeans and a shiny red top. She looked great.

"Shoes, too," she said.

I pulled on my button loafers. I twirled around for her to inspect. "Happy?" I asked.

"And earrings."

"Sophia—"

448

"No arguing."

I grabbed big gold hoops from my basket and put them on.

"Perfect. Now. Check your basket back in and come with me."

The nurses' station was empty. I set my basket on the shelf.

Sophia beckoned me, waving her hand, walking backward toward the lounge.

The lounge door was closed.

I had never seen it closed.

"Sophe, what's going on? You're being weird. And this is weird."

"Weirder than usual, you mean?"

"Definitely," I said.

"Ready?"

"For what?"

She swung the door open. "She's here!"

The lounge was dark. A focused stream of light popped on, shooting circles of white light onto the dark walls.

A disco ball. In the lounge. Hanging from the ceiling.

"Surprise!" a chorus of voices called out.

"Sophia, hit it," Chuck said. Sophia flipped a switch.

Colored flashing lights came on.

And music. Synthesizer, drums. "'We can dance if we want to, we can leave your friends behind…'"

"'Safety Dance'!" I yelled over the music. "I love this song!"

"We know you do!" Sophia said.

"You—you threw me a dance party?" I shouted.

"We threw you a dance party!" Sophia repeated.

"Because I seem to remember you saying something about being happiest when you're dancing," Chuck said as he boogied over. "Well, what are you waiting for? Take the dance floor, kid!"

449

All the furniture had been moved to clear a space.

"How did you...why did..."

But I knew how. And I knew why.

How: Nurse Ratched was gone.

Why: because Chuck and Sophia—and maybe even some of the other nurses and patients—loved me.

"Anyone below maintenance weight can only dance to the slow songs," Baldy shouted. "So don't ruin it for Jennifer by getting compulsive!"

"But...you're not supposed to hang things from the ceiling," I told Chuck. As if he didn't know.

"Let me worry about that, would you?" he said. "Go! Dance!"

The next song was Prince, "Let's Go Crazy."

"I love this song!" I squealed.

"We know!" Sophia laughed.

We all intoned the beginning along with Prince, "'Dearly beloved, we are gathered here today...'"

And then we went crazy.

In a good way.

— Discharge —

Saturday, January 28, 1989

And now I'm in the car, and I'm on the way home.

Mom and Dad are in the front seat.

I've got my Walkman with me in the back.

In it is a mixtape Chuck made for me. A Maxell 120, loaded with songs. The first side is the playlist from last night.

The side I'm listening to now is "For Jennifer, when you need a friend."

He put Bob Marley on there first. "Three Little Birds." Now I get it. Best song ever. Then it's James Taylor.

Mom turns and looks back at me. "What are you listening to?"

I press the Stop button, slide my headphones off. "Mixtape. From Chuck."

Dad's eyes flick from the road to the rearview mirror where he can see me. "Which one was Chuck?" he asks. His tone is a little too bright, like he's trying too hard to sound cheerful.

"My primary," I say.

"Her favorite nurse," Mom says. "You remember him."

"Huh," Dad says.

I figure that's it, but as I'm putting my headphones back on, Dad says, "Hey, JJ. Can we all listen to it?"

"Why?" I ask. Does he not trust Chuck? Is he going to criticize the songs?

Dad sighs. "I just thought it would be nice to listen to some music instead of NPR all the time."

"That sounds good," Mom chirps.

"Okay." I try to hide my reluctance. Do I want to share this with them? It's such a gift, this tape Chuck made me. Then again, it's nice of Dad to ask. He's really trying.

I press Eject and hand the tape to Mom.

She runs her thumb along the label. "Which side?"

"B," I say. No way are my parents ready for a dance party.

Mom pops it in. James Taylor fades out. The Traveling Wilburys song starts, with a guitar riff and a tambourine.

Well, it's all right...

Dad taps his thumbs on the steering wheel. Mom starts bobbing her head, just a few microinches.

Well, it's all right, doing the best you can...

Farms roll past. Bent, broken cornstalks poking through snow. Hills. Gray skies.

Well, it's all right, sometimes you gotta be strong...

"Wait. Is that—that's Roy Orbison!" Dad says. "Roy Orbison's in this?"

I laugh. "Yes, Roy Orbison. And Bob Dylan, and George Harrison, and Tom Petty, and some other guys."

"They're from our generation," Dad says.

"Your father loves Roy Orbison," Mom tells me.

"Everything old is new again," Dad says.

By the end of the song, we're all singing.

Then a weird boy choir starts.

"You must be joking," Dad says.

My heart sinks. What does he mean?

But Dad reaches over to the radio knob and turns up the volume. A horn and guitar.

I saw her today at the reception...

"The Stones, Juanita!" Dad says to Mom. "You remember when we first heard this song?"

"Oh, I remember." I can hear the smile in Mom's voice.

You can't always get what you want...

And we're all singing.

"These songs are great." Dad sounds surprised, and delighted, and happy.

We keep on like that. Singing the songs we know, listening to the ones we don't.

Out the window, I watch houses pass. Drooping front-porch roofs, swing sets draped with snow.

Had I known it before? That every person in every house has their own story? Had I thought about it at all, until that day I stood with Chuck by the window?

Through every window, every doorway: stories.

Maybe happy, maybe painful. Maybe both.

Before Reverend Stanley left the legendary box of sharps, he told me that Buddha said, "Life is suffering."

Life is suffering.

It makes me strangely happy to think this.

Because if the only guarantee in life is suffering, it means that any moment of happiness or joy is a total bonus. Because joy and happiness aren't guaranteed.

This moment, riding in the backseat, singing with my parents to the songs Chuck recorded for me, this is happiness.

This is not guaranteed.

This is a bonus.

♥ ♥ ♥

Am I different than I was ten weeks ago?

Did I kill the monster?

Here's what I wrote in the back of Sophia's journal. I left it on her bed, along with a Muppets lunch box.

> *Remember your first night in the hospital, when you said you felt like there was a monster inside you?*
> *I knew just what you meant.*
> *And now, I think maybe it's not about killing the monster.*
> *Maybe it's about making peace with it. Turning it into a fuzzy warm friend, maybe even like your favorite Muppet. (Long live Super Grover!)*
> *But most importantly, I think, is that you find people who love you—*
> *who understand you—*
> *monsters and all.*
> *I love you.*

This isn't the end of my story. In some ways, it's the beginning. It's the start of actual recovery, out in the world. I'll see Dr. Prakash and Dr. Wexler on Thursday. Sophia will be discharged in a month or two, and I'll see her then. I'll talk to her even sooner. Tonight, probably.

Chuck?

God, I'll miss him.

I'll listen to this tape and close my eyes and send him thanks, and tell him I'm okay.

♥ ♥ ♥

We're on the outskirts of Norwich now, passing the ice-skating rink.

I dig in my coat for the piece of Bazooka.

I unwrap it, save the cartoon for later. I work the hard gum in my teeth until it finally softens.

Mom turns around and smiles at me.

I smile.

I am different, but I am the same.

We drive past the Kurt Beyer Pool, then along Canasawacta Creek, left onto West Main, right onto our street.

I know every house. Do I know every story? Not even close.

We slow down and Dad pulls into our driveway.

We're here.

Mom ejects the tape and hands it to me. "Thanks for letting us listen," she says.

"Yeah, that was good," Dad says.

I wrap my headphone cord around my Walkman, put them in my backpack. I pull my backpack onto my shoulder.

My heart is pounding.

I take a deep breath.

I open the car door.

The hard-packed snow squeaks under my boots.

Dad is at the open trunk. He lifts out my suitcase. "Gracious," he says, closing the trunk and lugging my suitcase onto the back porch. "What have you got in here?"

"Bricks," I joke. And I remember to say, "Thanks, Dad."

"Welcome home, JJ," he says.

Mom squeezes my shoulders.

Spike is at the back door, tail wagging so hard his entire body is in spasms.

Rich appears and smiles. "Hey, nerd." He opens the door and takes my backpack.

Spike jumps into my arms.

I'm home.

Answers to Questions You Might Have—
And Some Words from the Author

You call *Believarexic* an "autobiographical novel." Isn't that like saying something is "true make-believe"?

Yes. I think of it this way: imagine a sine wave (a squiggly, sideways, repeating S curve) drawn over a straight horizontal line. Still with me? Okay. The straight line is what really happened. The squiggly line is *Believarexic*. The story follows the direction of the truth, and intersects with it often, but also...veers away.

I did go into inpatient treatment for bulimarexia in the winter of 1988–1989, when I was fifteen. My admission and discharge dates are real. The therapy sessions, rules, groups, and policies are real. The inner struggles are real.

But I exaggerated some elements, simplified or consolidated a few characters, and slid their timelines around a bit. My intention in doing so was to craft a better story, not to be deceptive or dishonest. In the interest of transparency, I've posted my actual journal from my actual hospitalization on *www.believarexic.com*. You can compare, if you want, *history* to *story*. The only editing I've made is taking out specific references to my pre-hospitalization and maintenance weights—I don't disclose those numbers because I don't want to trigger readers' own issues.

Your family is pretty...um...exposed in *Believarexic*. Have they read it?

They have read every draft. I'm humbled by their response. They've been unwaveringly supportive and generous, and we've laughed ourselves silly. We've all come a long way—individually *and* together.

Did you really make that promise to yourself in the hospital, that when you were grown-up and happy, you would travel back in time and help yourself through?

Yup. I really did. Writing *Believarexic* is one aspect of keeping that promise. I encourage everyone to engage in similar time travel. You don't need a flux capacitor.

Did you get into recovery? Are you recovered?

Yes, and yes. With a few stumbles and temporary relapses. If you want details, you can find them at *www.believarexic. com*.

What should I do if I think I have an eating disorder?

GET. HELP.

I'm not kidding.

If you have even just a glimmer of a spark of a thought that you maybe *might* have an eating disorder, then your eating is disordered enough to need help. The end. Full stop. No arguments.

You may think you're not "bad enough" for treatment. Or, you know you have an eating disorder, but you're convinced you *need* it. Or you may think there's no hope. Or you think "ana" or "mia" are your friends. (They are not your friends. They are conniving, backstabbing bitches.)

No, no, no no no.

There is SUCH A BETTER LIFE FOR YOU.

Recovery is possible. It's not easy, but it's worth it.

I promise.

Say something to someone. Write a note. Send an e-mail. Try a guidance counselor, minister or rabbi, trusted teacher, parent, guardian, mentor, older friend, Twelve-Step meeting, or eating disorder hotline. AND DON'T YOU DARE STOP REACHING OUT UNTIL YOU GET THE HELP YOU NEED.

- The National Eating Disorders Association (NEDA) has a free online chat Helpline at *www.nationaleatingdisorders.org/find-help-support* and a free, confidential phone Helpline at 800-931-2237. They can connect you to local help, as well.

- Eating Disorders Anonymous (EDA) is a Twelve-Step program with meetings online, over the phone, and/or in your town. The *only* requirement for EDA membership is a desire to recover from an eating disorder. Please go to *www.eatingdisordersanonymous.org/meetings.html* for information. Meetings are always free. (Those meetings were invaluable to me in the early days of my recovery—although back then it was called Overeaters Anonymous.)

- *HelpGuide.org* has excellent advice about HOW to ask for help, and how to start helping yourself in the meantime: *www.helpguide.org/articles/eating-disorders/eating-disorder-treatment-and-recovery.htm*

I know you think you can't or shouldn't ask for help. But you can. And you should.

I believe in you. I think you're smart and awesome.

I want to see you shine again. I want you to be able to think about something other than food and weight. I want your life to expand in good directions.

What are you waiting for? Go on.

Take that leap of faith. Trust that you'll grow wings.

I'll be right here cheering for you.

Photo by Jessica Arden

J. J. Johnson is the author of the acclaimed YA novels *This Girl is Different* and *The Theory of Everything*. Her books have received numerous honors and have been translated into six languages.

J. J. graduated from Binghamton University and earned a Master of Education from Harvard University, with a concentration in Adolescent Risk and Prevention.

Before writing novels, J. J. counseled at-risk teens and coordinated youth programs such as The Learning Web, Justice Summer, and Youth Advocacy.

J. J. still loves *Star Wars* and dance parties. She lives in Durham, North Carolina.

www.jjjohnsonauthor.com
www.believarexic.com